THE RO... ...ND

BOOK TWO: BORDER

J N WOOD

Copyright © 2019 J N Wood

All Rights Reserved

Again, thank you to my wife and my parents.

I should have been going home today.

The last two weeks should have been a road trip with my friend Jack, taking us through Colorado, Wyoming, South Dakota and Nebraska.

Only our holiday was ruined, when almost everybody died from an apocalyptic virus.

Then, to make matters worse, the dead rose up and tried to kill the few survivors.

Quite understandably, Jack wanted to get back home to his pregnant wife in California. Due to the fact I had no immediate way to get back to England and my wife, I decided to join him.

I'll be honest, it's been a bit of a struggle, and we've almost died more times than I care to remember. At one point, I was forced to continue on to California without Jack, with no idea of his fate.

When I finally arrived in Mountain View, California, I found it had succumbed to one of the many fires that had ravaged America after its fall.

Good news though, Jack was there, still very much alive.

Prologue: Friends Reunited

I looked around Jack to the charred remains of the house behind. 'Shit Jack, I'm so sorry. I was too late. It took me too long to get here.'

Jack did something I wasn't expecting. He smiled.

'Don't worry Chris. Beth left me a message, just like you did. They set off for Canada six days ago.'

'What? Really?' I blurted out.

'Yes, she left me a message outside our apartment.'

'Thank fuck for that,' I said. The relief made me almost forget about the amount of pain I'd been feeling. 'Although...' I began, but managed to stop myself.

'What?' Jack asked.

'Well...'

'What?' he asked again, sounding annoyed.

I'm gonna have to say it.

'I said she might set off for Canada before we got here. Didn't I?'

Shaking his head, Jack spun around and walked towards his three companions. 'Come on Chris. We need to get underground before the sun comes up.'

DAY FOURTEEN

Chapter 1: Slowly

'I will not carry you,' a gruff, heavily accented voice said.

Was the accent Russian maybe? Shit, did the Russians cause all of this? It must have been them that attacked America. What the fuck? Why have they captured me?

The Russian invader's hand painfully gripped my shoulder. I desperately tried to squirm away from my captor.

'Help! The Russians have got me!' I shouted.

'Chris, shut the fuck up,' a familiar voice called out.

I followed the voice in the darkness, to see Jack approaching me through the smoke.

Fuck, this is embarrassing.

I twisted my head around to find the huge Lithuanian guy called Gee looking down at me. Jack had of course introduced me to him earlier.

'Shit, sorry Gee,' I said. My cheeks suddenly felt very hot, like they were beginning to flush red. Luckily my embarrassment was hidden by the t-shirt wrapped around my face. 'I think I must have nodded off,' I told him, trying to explain.

'Were you sleepwalking just then?' Jack asked. The bottom half of his face was covered, but I noticed a slight smile creeping up to the corner of his one visible eye.

'Yeah must have been,' I responded.

'We cannot carry him,' Gee said. 'He is slowing us down.'

Above his mask, Gee's cold eyes stared straight at me, not showing an ounce of emotion.

'Gee, stop being an asshole.' This time it was the guy called Michael speaking. 'Now come on, we have to get to the parking lot.'

Gee pointed his finger at me, just a few inches from my face. 'I am not fucking Russian,' he said. 'Never call me Russian.'

'Yeah I know,' I said, leaning away from him. 'Sorry mate.'

The big Lithuanian stared directly into my eyes. It was beginning to get very uncomfortable, when he suddenly spun around and walked away. The others followed him, leaving me to try and keep up.

I should maybe avoid calling Gee a Russian again.

The woman, Jack had introduced her to me as Shannon, dropped back to walk alongside me. 'Don't worry about Gee,' she said. 'It takes him a bit of time to warm up. Give it a couple of weeks and you'll be the best of friends.'

I couldn't see the smile through her mask, but I could hear it in her voice.

'Brilliant,' I said, tripping up on a curb but managing to quickly regain my balance. 'Sorry, I'm not normally this pathetic.' I was exhausted.

'That's okay,' she said, chuckling. 'Not far to go now, five minutes maybe.'

After the Crossbow Crew found me outside the charred remains of Beth's friend's house, Jack told me we needed to get back to an underground car park. They'd been using it as their base for a couple of days. I had a million questions for him, but I barely had the energy to say hello when Jack introduced me to everyone.

It had been a long night.

The person who shot the first zombie turned out to be Michael, and Shannon was his wife. Gee was just a huge miserable bloke, who seemed to hate me already. He definitely wanted to leave me behind.

Jack grabbed me around my arm, dragging me from my thoughts. 'We're here Chris, it's just through there,' he said, pointing with his other hand to an arched entrance in a concrete building.

Burnt tree stumps lined the pavement. The building itself looked a bit singed from the fires, but as far as I could tell in the darkness, it looked structurally sound.

'I thought you said it was underground?' I asked, as we walked under the arches.

'There is another level down,' he said. 'We've been staying in the security office down there.'

Michael and Shannon were in front, leading us down a sloping ramp. Jack and I followed, with Gee at the rear. Ground level was full of burnt out vehicles.

At first I thought Jack was holding my arm to help me, but I soon realised he was using me as a crutch.

'Are you okay?' I asked him.

'Yeah, I'm fine,' he said. 'My ribs start to hurt if I walk any distance. I'll take some painkillers when we stop.'

Once we were all in the security office on the basement level, Gee closed the heavy door behind us.

'Does it lock?' I asked Jack, pointing at the door.

Jack was rummaging through his bag. 'Yes!' he hissed triumphantly, pulling his hand out of the bag and shaking a plastic bottle of pills. 'What did you say? Oh, the door. You can't open it from the outside,' he said.

'Then how–?' I started.

'It was open when we found it,' he quickly answered.

Jack passed me a bottle of water and then opened his own. I thirstily gulped the whole bottle down, while watching Jack's new friends removing their weapons and head gear.

'I needed that Jack.' I wiped my mouth with the back of my hand. 'Cheers.'

'Hey, time for proper introductions I think,' Michael said. He was stepping towards me, his hand outstretched. I took his hand in mine.

'Hi Chris, I'm Michael Presley.' He stopped shaking my hand and gestured towards Shannon. 'This is my wife, Shannon.'

She smiled and waved. 'Hi, again,' she said, before giving her husband a quizzical look.

'Hi everyone. You do know I wasn't actually asleep when Jack introduced us half an hour ago?'

'Just doing it properly, that's all,' Michael answered.

'Yeah sorry, good to meet you all,' I said. 'And thanks for helping me back there. I was pretty fucking knackered at the end. Don't think I'd have been able to finish off the last few zombies.'

'No problem at all,' Shannon said, laying her crossbow and bag on the desk in the windowless room.

'I do not understand single fucking word he say,' Gee said, in his stilted English. He was leaning against the door and pointing at me.

'*You* don't understand *me*?' I asked him, dumbfounded.

'What you say?' Gee asked, his face still deadpan.

'Come on kids,' Jack said. 'We all need to sleep. Chris, you look like you're about to collapse.'

Pulling my tired eyes away from the huge Lithuanian, I said, 'Yeah okay. Could someone make sure Lurch doesn't kill me in my sleep please?'

'What he say?' Gee asked, looking at Shannon. 'I do not understand single fucking word.'

Shannon shook her head, before stepping towards me. 'I need to clean the wound on your face before you collapse,' she said, briefly glancing at me before picking up her bag.

I touched the left side of my face. It was tender, and a bit sticky around my eye and cheek bone. In my exhaustion I'd almost forgotten about my altercation with the tarmac.

Shannon leaned in closer to me, inspecting my face. I awkwardly looked over her shoulder at a wall of blank monitors.

'It looks like there is still some of the road in there,' she said. 'Sit yourself down and I'll take care of it.'

'Okay, thanks.' I'd been really looking forward to sitting down all night.

When I opened my eyes, Jack was sat in the only chair in the room, his unobstructed eye staring at the plain white wall behind me. It took me a couple of seconds to realise I'd been asleep.

'Alright?' I said. 'What time is it?'

Jack seemed to blink back to life. He looked down at me, then eased himself out of the black leather chair and crept over to sit by my side.

Michael and Shannon were lying about four or five feet to my left, still fast asleep by the looks of it. The Lithuanian was slumped against the door, almost sat up straight. Every couple of seconds, an incredibly loud and angry sounding snore erupted from his wide open mouth.

'It's half three in the afternoon,' Jack told me, after he'd made himself comfortable. 'Shannon said she couldn't believe you slept through your face getting messed around with.'

'Oh shit yeah,' I muttered, lifting my hand up to feel a bandage on my face. 'I was pretty tired.'

'It's just some gauze to try and keep it clean. She keeps going on about things getting infected. She must say it to me twenty times a day.'

'Is she a doctor?' I asked.

'Yes, but not medical. Something to do with bioengineering, or biochemistry, or bio something. She seems to know what she's talking about though.'

'So?' I asked

Jack shook his head. 'So what?'

'So what the fuck happened to you? I couldn't find you, I thought you were dead.'

'Quiet Chris, they're still asleep,' he said, pointing at the other three.

'Okay,' I whispered. 'Where were you? And who the fuck are Michael, Shannon and Lurch? How are you all together?'

'Well, to be honest, I don't know what really happened. I remember being in the truck, and us getting slowly turned over by a load of zombies. Then I woke up in what I thought was a hospital, but it turned out to be a school.'

'What school?' I asked him.

'Austin School.'

'Where the fuck was that? I covered every inch of Austin looking for you.'

'It's on the outskirts, just after the graveyard.'

'I didn't see a fucking school on the outskirts,' I said.

'It wasn't a *fucking school* Chris. It was just an ordinary school, for kids,' Jack replied, a smirk on his face.

'Yeah, very fucking funny. Honestly though, I thought I searched everywhere around there.'

'Well, I don't know. It was well signposted. I saw the signs for it when we headed back into Austin, which was also when we saw your messages.'

'Fuck's sake,' I muttered.

'What happened to you then? And us I suppose?' Jack asked.

I took a deep breath and slowly let it out. 'So, the truck rolled down a hill and we finished upside down at the bottom. I dragged you out through the broken windscreen, which I had to kick out by the way, and carried you to some buildings in Austin, but then I lost you.'

'What do you mean? You lost me?' Jack asked. 'You just misplaced me?'

'Well, after very carefully placing you in...' I trailed off and gave him a sideways glance, before continuing. 'And don't forget the very carefully part. I very carefully placed you in a bin.' I stopped and waited for a reply. He looked fairly nonplussed, so I carried on. 'Then I climbed on top of a building to wait for the swarm to pass by.'

'Yep, kind of knew about the bin,' Jack said. 'Michael and Shannon said they found me in a dumpster. I had no idea what they were talking about. I kept asking them if they meant a truck. They got very annoyed.'

'I thought you'd be safe in there. I pushed it into a corner, but there were too many zombies. They smashed down a fence, and you and the bin just rolled away. I really am sorry.'

'Don't worry about it,' Jack said. 'It can't have been easy getting me out of the truck. I'll forgive you for dumping me in a bin.'

'It wasn't fucking easy. It was really fucking hard in fact.'

'Seriously, it's fine,' he said. 'Shannon took care of me. I was out of it for a few days. By the time I'd regained consciousness and gone back into Austin, you'd left.'

'What's actually going on with your eye?' I asked.

'Shannon thinks I've fractured my eye socket. She told me I'll be fine, but I think she's just trying to keep my hopes up. It's alright, I've got another eye.'

'You were almost blind anyway,' I said. 'Losing your sight in one eye probably won't make much difference to you.'

Jack looked at me with a confused look on his face. 'Surely it would be worse if I lost an eye? Rather than if someone with perfect sight went blind in one eye.'

'Actually, yeah, you're probably right. You'll be fine though. I'll get you a stick if not. Also, it means you won't run out of contact lenses as quickly.'

'That's true,' he said, with a grin. 'What happened to you after Austin?'

'Well, a few hours after leaving Austin, I bumped into a huge fucking swarm.'

'Why were you out during the day?' he asked.

'I wasn't. It was the middle of the night.'

'Are you sure it wasn't during the day?'

'What?' I answered, giving him an incredulous look. 'What the fuck? Of course I'm sure it wasn't during the day. There was a big silver thing in the sky. Not a big yellow thing. Oh yeah, and also, it was fucking dark.'

'Were you asleep and dreaming maybe?' he asked.

'Are you taking the piss? I wasn't dreaming.'

'Just a few hours ago, you were sleepwalking and talking about Russians attacking you.'

'I didn't fucking dream the swarm. It was real. Zombie parts were still on my car the next day. Unless I dreamt that as well?'

'Did you?'

'Fuck off,' I replied.

'Shit,' Jack slowly said. 'We'll have to tell everyone when they wake up. That's really going to mess everything up.'

'That's the only one I've seen, I haven't seen another one at night since then. I think that one just had too many zombies, so they couldn't stop to sleep. Maybe.'

'Yeah maybe,' he said. 'So what happened after that? How did you get here?'

I told Jack everything, the night in the mechanics workshop after escaping the tsunami swarm, and my failed plan to find a snow plough. I described my meeting with Gurbinder and the racist duck hunters, culminating in them chasing me into the hills. Then the trek through the snow and witnessing the zombie clean-up crew on the other side. All the while Jack nodded and made agreeable noises. He said they'd also seen, and travelled through, the burnt remains of California.

'And that was it,' I said. 'Piece of piss really.'

'Yeah, sounds it,' Jack replied. 'You killed some people then? Actual people, not zombies.'

I shrugged. 'Maybe. I mean, I didn't actually see them die, but maybe.'

'Okay,' Jack said, turning slightly to look directly at me.

'What?' I asked, leaning away from him.

'No long term psychological effects? Even if they were racist rapists.'

'I don't know. It's not been long term yet. And the world is better off without those arseholes, if they are actually dead. And I never mentioned anything about them being rapists.'

'The story sounded like it was heading in that direction, it was beginning to sound a bit like Deliverance,' Jack said.

'Anyway,' I said. 'Your new chums, what's going on with them?'

'There were about forty new chums in the school.'

'Forty?' I asked, in disbelief.

'A lot of them were from their local archery club in Austin.'

'That explains the crossbows then?'

'Yep. They turned that school into some kind of fortress. Michael, Shannon and Big Gee all said they wanted to go north, and agreed to help me. So here we are.'

'Did Gee live in Austin?' I asked.

'No, I'm not sure where he came from, obviously Lithuania originally, but I don't know where he was when all this started. I'm not sure if Michael and Shannon know either. Apparently he just turned up a few days after the virus.'

'That's a bit suspicious, don't you think?'

'Chris, what are you talking about?'

'Nothing, just thinking out loud. How the fuck did you get here before me?'

'I think we set off the day after you by the sounds of it,' Jack replied. 'Although we took the I-80, and until we made it to Sacramento, it was relatively easy. Relative to your journey anyway. You should have left me a more detailed message.'

'The knock on your head hasn't improved your sense of humour. I did wonder if I should go that way. Fucking hell.'

'We had to dig our way out of the snow a few times, but there weren't any burning airplanes, or racist rapists chasing us.'

'Lucky you,' I said. 'And I'm almost certain they weren't planning on raping me.'

'Ask Michael about crashed airplanes, he'll have something interesting to tell you.'

'What is it?' I asked.

'No, ask him. He'll want to tell you it.'

'Why can't you just tell me now?'

'Because it's his fucking story,' Jack said.

'Go on, just tell me now.'

Jack shook his head, saying, 'No.'

'Just fucking tell me,' I said, drawing out the words.

'For fuck's sake. He saw a fucking passenger plane get shot down by American fighter jets,' he hurriedly blurted out.

'Hey, that's my story,' Michael sleepily said from the corner of the room.

'Sorry Michael, he forced it out of me,' Jack said, almost sheepishly.

'That's okay, you tell it so well,' Michael replied. 'Keep the volume down though, I'm going to try and get a few more hours sleep.'

'Sorry,' Jack and I whispered in unison.

I looked over to the still snoring Lithuanian. 'Why did Gee come with you?' I asked, keeping my voice down low.

'Not sure, he mumbled something about Canada, and hunting. We were glad for the help though. He mostly keeps himself to himself. You'll like him. I think the first English words he learnt were fuck, fucking and shit. Because that's pretty much all he says.'

'He certainly doesn't like me,' I said.

'Nobody likes you. You're a twat.'

'Fair enough.'

'I think we should try and get more sleep,' Jack said. 'Big Gee's snoring woke me up earlier, but I'm going to try again.'

'Okay, I'll try as well.'

Jack crawled over to his makeshift bed and laid down.

They'd done well to find this little hiding spot. And Jack had done well to find these people, well, two thirds of them at least. Talking of achievements, Michael was punching above his weight with Shannon. She was obviously very intelligent by the sounds, but also very attractive. I didn't expect Michael's clean shaven and round face after witnessing the crossbow guy easily taking down that zombie.

'Are you sure you weren't asleep?' Michael asked me a few hours later.

I lowered my head in frustration. 'No, I wasn't asleep, and ignore my sleepwalking earlier, that isn't a regular occurrence. Unless I'm drunk.'

'Were you drunk?' Shannon asked.

'Oh for fuck's sake. Ignore my last comment as well. I wasn't asleep, or drunk. A huge swarm was wandering about at night. But like I said to Jack, it's the only one I've seen.'

After Jack had suggested trying to sleep again, I stared at the ceiling and listened to Gee's snoring. A couple of hours later everyone began to stir.

Gee was now stood in the corner, just staring at me. Jack, Shannon, Michael and I were stood around the desk. We were all eating energy bars that Michael had retrieved from his bag.

'If this is true,' Shannon said, giving me the briefest of glances. 'Then it could cause us huge problems.'

I let out an exasperated sigh, rolling my eyes.

If this is true. What the fuck?

'We can't let it change things now,' Michael said. 'Let's stick to our nocturnal travel plans.'

Why don't these arseholes believe me? Why would I make this shit up?

'What is the plan?' I reluctantly asked.

Let them believe what they want. They'll soon find out.

Shannon produced a road map from her bag, unfolded it and placed it on the desk. Gee continued to stand in front of the door, while the rest of us leaned in.

'To start with, we cycle back to the bus–,' Shannon said.

'A bus? Like a big tour bus?' I asked, imagining the huge things with beds, and lots of space.

'We found a school bus,' Jack replied, smiling. 'With a big snow plough on the front.'

'Like in Road Trip?' I asked.

'Yep, but much better than that,' Jack answered.

Michael and Shannon looked at us with blank expressions.

'It's a film, Road Trip,' I said, looking at them in turn. 'Not seen it?'

'We don't have a television,' Michael said.

Shannon turned her attention back to the map. 'So, after we get to the bus–,' she started.

'You don't have a TV?' I interrupted. 'How do you watch stuff?'

'We don't,' Shannon replied. 'We mostly read.'

'We're not gonna have much in common,' I told her.

Shannon shrugged her shoulders, saying, 'Okay.' She flapped out a baseball cap and placed it on her head, tucking loose strands of her curly hair behind her ears. 'We cycle to the bus, and then the best route is probably this.' She traced a route along the map with her finger. 'Staying on the US-97 means we avoid Portland completely, and can go around Seattle. Everything takes a bit longer now, so three days tops, two if we get lucky.'

'Erm...' I raised my hand into the air. 'I don't have a bike.'

Gee started to laugh scornfully from the corner.

'What?' I asked him, with an accusing glare. 'I'm literally just finding out what the plan is.'

'It's okay,' Michael said. 'Jack was adamant you'd be here, so we got you something. I'll apologise now, it was the best we could find.'

That doesn't sound promising.

It turned out Gee's laugh wasn't because I said I didn't have a bike. I think he'd been laughing at the prospect of seeing me ride the thing in front of me.

'Yer joking aren't ya?' I asked, looking down at a blackened mess of a bicycle. At one time, it had probably been a very nice mountain bike.

'We changed the seat, the chain, the wheels, and obviously the tyres,' Michael informed me.

I could almost hear the pity in his voice.

'Couldn't find any new grips,' he continued. 'So I gaffer taped them. Don't try changing gear though, it'll just lock up.'

'Erm...yeah. Thanks very much. I think.'

Everybody else's bikes looked brand new, and in pristine condition. I picked up mine by the handle bars, bits of metal flaked off in my hands.

'What gear is it in?' I asked. 'I'm not gonna have to ride it in top gear the whole way am I?'

'Third, I think,' Michael replied.

'How far away is the bus?' I asked.

'Twenty five miles,' Shannon answered.

'Fuck's sake,' I said, under my breath.

The five of us rode along the freeway, me obviously at the back. I couldn't even keep up with the injured Jack. It reminded me of the kids on their bikes in E.T. Michael even had a basket on the front of his. His crossbow was positioned in it so he could easily grab it.

I had an idea so I pedalled a bit harder to catch up with Jack.

'Hey Jack,' I said, once I was alongside him. 'If we pass my car, why don't we just drive the rest of the way to the bus?'

'Yep, best thing you've ever said. My ribs are killing me.'

'What was that?' Shannon asked, slowing down to let us catch her up.

'I'm not entirely sure to be honest, but I think I left my car a bit further up here. In Miltas, or Mapitus, Multipass, Millipedes? Something like that.'

'Milpitas?' Jack offered. 'That's about fifteen miles away.'

'Yep, that's it,' I said.

'Quiet guys,' Michael hissed. 'Zombies on the right.'

A group, maybe in the hundreds, were congregated in a car park off to our right. They were tightly packed in together and unnaturally still. They certainly looked like they were in their dormant state.

Gee looked over his shoulder towards me. 'Sleeping,' he simply said.

'Fuck off Gee, you twat,' I whispered. 'There's not many of them. You couldn't even call that a swarm.'

Before he turned to face forward again, I noticed a slight glint in his eye.

'Yeah, the car is a good idea Chris. Change of plan guys,' Shannon said, trying to get the attention of Michael and Gee. 'Aim for Chris's car, he says it's up this road. We can drive the rest of the way to the bus.'

Gee and Michael both nodded in agreement.

It was just over an hour later when I recognised the junction where I'd left the car. Hate was not too strong a word for how I felt about the burnt piece of shit I was sat on. Jack was also really struggling, looking like he was in a lot of pain.

I pointed to the freeway above us. 'It's just up there.' I turned my attention to Jack. 'How did you cycle all the way into Mountain View?'

'Slowly, really slowly,' he replied.

We climbed off our bikes and walked them up to the freeway.

'Have you got a thing for Toyota Corollas?' Jack asked, as he laid his bike down on the side of the road.

'Yes, it's my favourite car,' I replied, while quickly checking in my bag. Relief flowed through me as my fingers touched the car keys. I'd completely forgotten what I'd done with them.

'Really?' Jack asked.

'No, not really. It's alright though. Does the job.'

'Open her up Chris,' Shannon said. 'We'll throw our stuff in the trunk.'

We were soon driving up the I-680. The five foot three and very svelte Shannon was in the passenger seat alongside me. She'd insisted on sitting in the front after explaining she gets car sick. I looked in the rear view mirror, laughing when I saw the annoyed expression on Jack's face. He noticed me looking and gave me an ironic smile.

Big Gee must have been at least six foot five, and was sat behind Shannon. Jack was squashed in the middle, and I know that he's six foot one, while Michael was sat behind me. He was probably about five foot nine or ten, but I wouldn't have said he was exactly svelte. They'd all asked to drive, but there was no way I was handing the keys over to anyone.

'How much further Shannon?' Jack begged.

'Not far,' she replied. 'I can't look at the map for too long without feeling sick though.'

'Pass it back,' Michael said.

A couple of minutes later, after Michael had finally managed to fold the map into a manageable size in the cramped space, he said, 'About six miles to go.'

Gee and Jack both groaned in frustration.

Chapter 2: World's Strongest

The car's headlights illuminated a big yellow school bus, only this one had massive tyres, and a very battered snow plough attached to the front.

With more groans, the three guys spilled out of the back doors.

'They look like monster truck wheels,' I said. 'And what happened to the snow plough?'

Shannon paused as she was climbing out of the car. 'We picked it up on the other side of Reno. It's just what they use to move the kids about in the snow. And we didn't just use it to plough the snow. We used it to move anything that was in our way. It's a bit of a gas guzzler, but Gee is a very good gas scavenger.'

We retrieved our stuff from the boot, and climbed aboard the bus. It might not have had the comfort of a big tour bus, but there was more than enough space to fit five people. I counted thirteen rows of seats behind the driver.

'I take first driving shift,' Gee said, climbing into the driver's seat.

Nobody objected. I certainly wasn't going to.

'I'll navigate,' Michael quickly said, the map still in his hand.

Jack, Shannon and I took up the second and third rows of seats.

'Never been on an American school bus before,' I said. 'It's like we're in a movie.'

'I know,' Jack agreed. 'That's exactly what I said when I first got in.'

'Is it good, this Road Trip movie?' Shannon asked. Her back was up against the window, with her legs stretched out in front of her.

'Meh, it's alright,' I replied. 'I was thinking of Forest Gump just then though.'

'Yes, me too,' Jack declared.

'Not seen it,' Michael and Shannon said in unison.

'Fuck off,' I said. 'How have you not seen Forest Gump?'

'Just haven't,' Shannon replied.

Gee turned on the engine, saying, 'I watch Forest Gump.'

'I wonder if Tom Hanks is still alive,' Jack pondered.

'Who is Tom Hanks?' Shannon asked.

'Fucking hell,' I exclaimed. 'Right, I'm not talking to you. That's just fucking ridiculous.'

Gee turned the wheel and guided us back onto the main road. I could see an actual smile on his face.

As we were leaving the rest area, Michael told Gee we should avoid going anywhere near Sacramento again.

'Was Sacramento bad then?' I asked Shannon and Jack.

'Yep, pretty awful,' Jack replied. 'We drove around it, trying to keep to the outskirts, but there were still a lot of dead bodies. The streets were filled with them. Hundreds of thousands maybe.'

'And a lot of zombies,' Shannon added. 'They were unavoidable. We had to drive through a lot of the sleeping ones, which obviously woke the others up. You can drive for hours without seeing any at all, and then the next minute, they're everywhere.'

'It's scary driving through that many, all of them banging against the side of the bus, trying to get to us,' Jack said. He looked to Shannon before continuing. 'It was after Sacramento that we had a little issue.'

Michael had swivelled around in his seat to look back at us.

Shannon let out an exasperated sigh. 'Yeah okay. I got bitten by a zombie.'

There was an uncomfortable silence for a few seconds, my eyes darting between Jack and Shannon.

'Oh, right,' I eventually said, not really sure what to say. 'How's that been then?'

'Fantastic,' she replied. 'Absolutely fantastic.'

'She's fine,' Michael said, turning back around to look at the road.

'When we stopped after Sacramento,' Shannon continued. 'I got out to use the bathroom. There was a zombie stuck between the plough and the bus, and it fell out as I was passing. It caught me by surprise and clamped its teeth into the back of my leg. I just froze. Luckily Gee killed it before it did any serious damage.'

Shannon stood up and faced the front of the bus. She started to fiddle with something in front of her.

'You seem alright,' I said to her. 'No cravings for human flesh then?'

'No not yet,' she said, and pulled her trousers down to her knees, catching me by surprise.

'Whoa!' I said, looking away. 'You didn't need to prove it, I believed you.'

'You can look,' Shannon said. 'I've got my big underwear on.'

I turned my head back around to see if she was telling the truth. She was. They were huge. 'Did you steal them off your granny?' I asked, laughing.

Jack let out a little chuckle.

'Thanks Chris,' she replied. 'We are in the middle of the apocalypse. Now look at my bite so I can pull my pants back up.'

The lights in the bus were down quite low, but I could still see nasty looking puncture marks in her skin, forming the shape of a bite mark. They were just below her big granny pants.

'Yep, seen it,' I said.

Shannon pulled up her trousers and sat back down.

'I hope you're taking care of that? You don't want an infection,' I said, and smiled at Jack. He looked back at me with a straight face, shaking his head.

She spun around to face me. 'That is not a laughing matter Christopher. We can't just go and see a doctor now. We need to be taking care of ourselves. An infection could easily kill you.'

'Okay, alright, I get it,' I acknowledged, raising my hands. 'What does that mean then? The zombies haven't got the original killer virus? And they also can't pass on the zombie turning virus thing. Or does it just take a while to turn into one? Or what? I don't know.'

'Your girlfriend said the virus had gone,' Jack said to me.

Shannon shot me an accusing look. 'Jack said you were married.'

I looked at Jack and shook my head. 'Yes, I am married. Jack is just taking the piss. She was a friend, but also a girl. Well, a woman. She was of age, fucking hell, it doesn't matter. She did say she thought the virus had gone though. I'm not entirely sure she had any scientific data to back the theory up.'

'Neither do I,' Shannon said. 'But I think it's all been some kind of biological attack. The virus was stage one, wiping out millions of lives. The zombies are stage two, wiping out whoever is left. The virus was designed to only last a few days, and the zombies were designed to only kill, not make more zombies. So hopefully that means they'll waste away and die soon. Well, die again.'

'I'm not saying you're not right. But did you come up with this theory after you got bitten?' I asked.

'Some of it I did, yeah,' she replied. 'It's still a big if, but, if it is another country wanting to wipe us off the planet–.'

'It'll be Trump's fault,' Michael called out, still facing forwards. 'He'll have gone too far and annoyed the wrong world leader.'

'Anyway,' Shannon continued. 'They're not going to want a killer virus and zombies roaming the country afterwards.'

'Unless they have an antidote,' Jack suggested.

'What about the internet and phones all going down?' I asked. 'Any theories on that?'

'The Chinese, the North Koreans, the Russians maybe?' Shannon replied. 'They're always hacking into things over here, and in your country.'

I shrugged my shoulders. 'Yep, could all be true. Just let me know if you're considering eating me. Is this your speciality, bioweapons and the like?'

'No, not at all. I develop smart novel bio-electronic nano-systems for studying cellular processes on a molecular scale.'

'What the fuck?' I said.

'Sorry,' Shannon said. 'It's really all about the fundamental study of charge transfer from prokaryotic and eukaryotic cells, in addition to break through methodologies of surface functionalization and control of the nano-scale.'

All I could say was, 'Okay.' I caught Jack's eye, all he could do was smile and shrug his shoulders. 'Anyway,' I added. 'Don't suppose you've got any food?'

Jack got up and walked towards the back of the bus, he stopped a couple of rows back, returning with a plastic bag. He held it in front of me. 'Take your pick,' he said. 'It's a lucky dip.'

I pulled out an energy bar and a packet of crisps. 'Ta very much.'

'There should be some cans of Diet Pepsi under your seat Chris,' Jack said, before offering the bag to Shannon.

'How are you really feeling?' I asked Shannon.

'Honestly? No different.' Her hand came out of the bag holding a Mars bar. She pulled a face, and dropped it back in to look for something else. 'The bite still hurts a bit, but there is no sensation of the zombie infection rushing through my veins. Or anything like that.'

'She's fine,' Michael repeated.

It only took an hour for us to get out of the built up areas. The road was soon surrounded by tree covered hills, a world away from the devastated towns I'd spent the last few days and nights. It was a weird feeling not driving or navigating, but not entirely unwelcome. It was a relief to take a bit of the pressure off.

'Sorry guys, I need to take fucking shit,' Gee said, as the bus started to slow.

'Gee, I've told you about too much information,' Shannon said. 'Just say you need to use the bathroom.'

'I do not need bathroom,' he replied. 'I just need fucking shit.'

I laughed as Shannon leaned back and rolled her eyes to the ceiling.

Gee parked the bus at the side of the road. After grabbing some toilet roll and a torch, he left through the front doors. Michael and Shannon followed, presumably not to watch him take a shit.

'Where's your baseball bat?' Jack asked me.

'Lost it in the snow a few days ago, I think.'

'You're in luck,' he said, reaching under the seat in front of him. 'Because I've graduated to this.'

He sat back up straight, an axe in both hands. The wooden handle was about two foot long, and the axe's head was about the size of his face.

'Are you okay to swing that around?' I asked.

'Not at the moment, but I will be.'

'Why does it mean I'm in luck?'

He reached back down and picked up a baseball bat, it looked just like my Brooklyn Smasher. 'Because I don't need this anymore. They had it in the Austin School and said I could take it.' He passed it to me across the bus. 'It's yours. If you want it.'

'Yeah, cheers mate. I was thinking I'd have to do a bit of shopping for one. Thanks very much.'

'No problem,' he said.

It was almost identical to the one I'd lost, just with less blood stains.

'My turn to drive,' Michael said as he climbed back aboard, slipping into the driver's seat.

'Okay, I'll map read,' Shannon said, following her husband up the stairs.

A few seconds later Gee's head appeared through the doorway, he looked irritated when he spotted Michael in his seat. 'I am fucking tired, I go to sleep,' he said, and marched down to the back of the bus, stretching out on the back seats.

'Aren't you gonna need a sick bucket?' I asked Shannon.

'No, don't seem to get travel sick on the bus. It only happens in cars and boats.'

'How far are you expecting to get tonight?' Jack asked.

'You should never expect anything my British friend,' Michael replied.

Jack rolled his eyes and waited.

A few seconds passed by before Michael said, 'I'm hoping we can get to a place by the name of Bend. It's about seven hours away, give or take.'

'Do you do the same thing as your wife Michael?' I asked. 'Whatever that may be.'

'No, my new British friend. I am a high school math teacher. Or I was one.'

'They'll still have teachers in Canada,' Shannon said.

'Teachers in Canada? What a peculiar notion my dear wife.'

'Stop showing off Michael,' Shannon said. 'Right now you're a bus driver, so drive the bus.'

'Why yes, of course,' he replied.

I decided to take a leaf out of Big Gee's book, so I sat back and closed my eyes.

'Chris! Gee! Wakey wakey,' someone was shouting, it sounded like Michael's voice. I opened my eyes and sat up, just as Gee walked by the end of my seat.

'Sorry fellas,' Michael said. 'The road is blocked. It'll be quieter if you two move the vehicles, rather than us just driving through them.'

I looked out of the window. Buildings loomed out of the darkness.

'Where are we?' I asked.

'Redding,' Shannon said.

'Reading?'

'Wake up Chris,' Jack said. 'Redding, California. Not Reading, England. It's the zombie apocalypse. There are no Russians attacking you. Just a Lithuanian that needs your help.'

I raised my fist towards Jack and very slowly extended my middle finger. 'Can we not drive around?' I asked, trying to stifle a yawn.

'No, sorry,' Michael said. 'There are trees on the left and...' He trailed off, peering through the windscreen. 'And something on the right, maybe a church. There's no way around. It's only about six or seven cars deep, and then it's clear, as far as I can tell. Twelve cars to move, that should do it.'

As I passed Jack, I spoke in a baby voice, 'Ooh, I've got broken ribs and one eye, so I can't help the big boys.'

Jack shrugged. 'All very true.'

I got to the door before I remembered I'd need a weapon. I took the little axe out of the side of my bag. My new Smasher would be a bit too cumbersome to carry while pushing vehicles.

Michael pressed the button to open the doors, and I followed the big Lithuanian out into the surprisingly cold night.

We made quick work of pushing the cars out of the way, the drop in temperature probably speeding us up. Gee and I made a good team, barely speaking to each other, but otherwise getting the job done.

Most of the cars had been locked. Unsurprisingly, that included the last car that needed to be moved. After borrowing my axe and having a quick glance around, Gee smashed the driver's side window. He leaned in and placed the gear lever into drive.

Gee's head quickly popped back up at the sound of hissing. I heard it at exactly the same time, spinning around to find the source.

'Gee, can you see it?' I quickly spluttered.

'No,' he replied, passing me back my axe and unslinging his crossbow.

I couldn't pinpoint the source of the hissing, because it was coming from all around us.

The headlights from the bus picked up a figure, heading straight for Gee. Rather than warn him, it was quicker for me to step into its path. I slammed the blunt end of the axe into the thing's face. Its head erupted, splattering the back of Gee with thick, almost black blood. The headless body slumped to the ground and skidded across the tarmac, straight into the side of the car next to us.

I looked at the axe in my hand. That was easy. Its head just disintegrated.

'Move Chris! Back to bus!' Gee shouted.

We both set off at a sprint. Four or five, maybe six zombies were definitely going to intercept us before we made it back.

Two of them went down in quick succession, with arrows sticking out of the back of their heads. Michael and Shannon were stood in the doorway, illuminated by the internal light of the bus. Gee stopped and took aim with his crossbow, taking another down, before starting to run again.

Two zombies were sprinting for me, so I aimed for the closest one. At the last second, I went to go one way but changed direction. The zombie missed me, losing what little balance it had, and tumbling to the ground.

I slowed down to an almost complete stop as the second neared. I timed my swing perfectly, like a cricket swing, upper cutting and connecting with its chin. Again, the head exploded, this time the contents shot upwards, before falling to splatter onto me. The decapitated body instantly slammed into the ground.

Either I'm suddenly much better at this zombie killing lark, or these ones are much slower and weaker than usual.

I looked over to see Gee firing another arrow. It was a perfect shot, skewering a zombie through its wide open mouth, instantly ending its hissing.

'Run!' Jack, Shannon and Michael all shouted.

We both set off running. Even with Gee slowing to retrieve his arrows, we were back inside the bus within seconds. Michael was repeatedly jamming his fist into the button to close the door.

I was struggling to catch my breath. 'Maybe just use the bus to move the last car,' I gasped.

Michael put his foot down, aiming for the final car blocking our path. More shapes were appearing from the gloom.

'We must have woken them up,' Shannon said, as she gripped onto the back of Michael's seat.

'Everyone hold on!' Michael shouted.

I braced myself against the seat in front. When we collided with the car I was forced forward, almost smashing my mouth into the back of the seat. The car was catapulted into the air after being scooped up by the plough, loudly crashing back down to earth after clipping the side of the bus.

Michael had a quick glance behind him. 'That could have been bad,' he muttered.

I obviously wanted everyone to believe me about the night time swarms, but I was actually hoping we wouldn't see another one. This was definitely looking like one of the big ones.

More and more of them were coming out of the shadows, spilling onto the road in front of us. I looked at Jack. His eyes were fixed on the zombies.

Michael was trying to steer around them, but there was only a slither of clear road left to use.

'Just drive through them,' I shouted.

'Okay, but it's going to get messy again,' Michael said, flicking the windscreen wipers on.

Zombies started to make contact with us. The snow plough decimated their bodies, splattering them onto the front of the bus.

'Maybe you're asleep Jack?' I said. 'Maybe this is just a dream? Would you like me to repeatedly punch you in the face? Just to make sure you're awake.'

'No thanks,' Jack said flatly, still staring straight ahead.

The sound of zombies thudding into the plough and splattering across the windscreen blocked out everything else. For what seemed like an eternity, but probably only thirty seconds, we crowded around Michael in the driver's seat and stared out. Thankfully the swarm did start to thin, eventually down to nothing.

'I think it's fair to say Chris was telling the truth,' Shannon said, once we were clear.

'Yeah, obviously. Thanks very much,' I said.

'I always know he tell truth,' Gee said.

I shot him a confused look.

Gee clapped me on the shoulder, saying, 'You did good.' He walked to the back of the bus and started to rummage through his bag.

I turned back to the others and shrugged, gesturing towards Gee with my thumb. 'What the fuck happened then?'

'I did tell you,' Shannon said, handing me a packet of tissues. 'Takes him a while to warm up. I thought it would take longer than a day though.'

I started using the tissues to wipe the blood from my face. Looking to Shannon, and pointing at the gauze taped to my face, I asked, 'Do I need this changing?'

'Yeah, we better change it,' she said, already reaching for her bag.

'How much longer to Bend?' Jack asked. 'Will we get there before the sun comes up?'

'About four or five hours, so we should be,' Shannon replied.

'What difference does it make now?' Michael asked.

'There's still fewer of them at night than during the day,' I said.

'How do we know that?' Shannon asked, as she pulled out her first aid kit. 'We kept someone on watch during the day back in Austin, but they would never see anything. I never saw zombies roaming about when it was my turn. When was the last time you went out during the day Chris?'

'It will have been when Jack and I first got to Austin. There were definitely a lot of them around then. Enough to roll us down a hill. Tens of thousands of them.'

'We've been doing nights for a while now,' Jack said. 'Hopefully we're only a few days away from Canada. Why not just stay as we are for a bit longer?'

'Oh, actually,' I remembered. 'I was out during the day when I was up in the snowy hills. I barely saw anything then. But I was in the middle of nowhere.'

'Okay,' Shannon said. 'Nobody likes change, so let's stay as we are.'

'I don't mind driving,' Michael said. 'But could people stay awake? Just to keep an eye out.'

A loud snore erupted from the back of the bus.

'At least everyone apart from Gee,' Michael added.

We agreed and sat ourselves down. Shannon swapped my gauze for a clean one, making sure the wound underneath was healing okay. I stared out of the clean section of the windscreen. The parts the wipers couldn't reach were a very dark, almost black colour.

We sat in silence for a long time. Everyone must have been considering what the night time swarms meant for us.

'Michael,' I said.

'Yes Christopher,' he replied.

'Would you rather be completely bald and have a massive nipple on your head? It'd take up the whole of your hairless scalp. Or would you rather only be able to say one word for the rest of your life? And that one word would be penis.'

'So I'd look normal, but only be able to say penis?' Michael asked.

'Michael,' Shannon exclaimed. 'Don't indulge him please.'

'What?' I asked. 'It's a perfectly reasonable question.'

'And incredibly tame for a Chris Would You Rather, could be a lot worse' Jack said.

'Don't worry, the bad ones will come out eventually,' I said.

'Can I wear a hat?' Michael asked.

'Nope, no hat,' I replied. 'You have to proudly show off your great big nipple head.'

'I'd go for the penis one, and just learn sign language,' Michael said. 'Now give Shannon a bad one.'

'No thank you,' Shannon said. 'I'm perfectly fine with silence.'

'Okay,' I said. 'But I'm not allowing the sign language get out clause.' I turned to Shannon and said, 'Would you rather have sex with one half of conjoined twins, where the other half is a zombie, or the other half is your dad?'

'How would that be possible?' Shannon asked. 'My dad isn't one half of conjoined twins.'

'I don't think you're getting the point of the game darling,' Michael said.

'Oh, and also, your dad would be furiously masturbating,' I added.

'No!' Shannon declared. 'I'm not playing this disgusting game.'

'You don't watch movies, and you refuse to discuss your father masturbating,' I said. 'I don't know what else to talk about then.'

Michael, Jack and I quietly chuckled as we drove further into the darkness.

A few hours later, Michael announced we were crossing into Oregon, and a new road map was produced by Shannon. The roads had been clear, but the snow had started to fall.

Hopefully the snow plough would be able to do its job.

Not long after crossing the border, Shannon took over the driving, and Michael took the navigator job. Gee had also joined us at the front of the bus.

'So Gee, what's Gee short for?' I asked.

'Short for. What does this mean?' he responded.

I tried again. 'What is your real name?'

'You cannot say it properly, so I use Gee,' he said.

'I haven't even tried it. You never know, I might be able to say it.'

'Yeah Gee,' Michael said. 'What is your real name?'

'When I first come to America, people say it wrong, so I use Gee.'

'Tell us your name Gee,' Shannon said.

Gee just sat there, ignoring us.

'Tell us,' Jack said.

'First name!' I shouted.

'Just tell us your name,' Jack said.

'Come on Gee,' Michael said, laughing.

Jack and I started to chant, 'Name, name, name, name, name…'

'Okay, okay. Fucking shut up. I tell you,' Gee shouted. 'You are like my…' he started, before trailing off.

Shannon turned to give Michael a knowing look.

'It is Gintaras,' he said.

'Gintaras?' I said, before everyone else also repeated it.

'People always say it like alcohol, gin. But it is not said that way.'

'But…if you just tell people your name,' I told him. 'Like you just did. Then people will say it correctly, like we just did. No?'

After a few moments, Gee responded by shrugging his shoulders.

'Which do you prefer?' Jack asked. 'Gee or Gintaras?'

He seemed to ponder the question, before answering with, 'Gee, I prefer Gee.'

'In that case,' I said. 'Surely we're pronouncing Gee incorrectly? If Gintaras has got a hard G, then so should Gee.' I looked around at everyone. 'No?'

Gee stared out the window.

'Let's just leave it like it is,' Shannon said.

The time was approaching six in the morning. We hadn't quite made it to Bend as the snow had slowed us down after entering Oregon. The sun was just starting to rise so we all agreed to stop somewhere for the day.

'We can't stay in the bus,' I said, after Michael had suggested it. 'Remember what happened to Jack and me in our truck?'

'There isn't much around here Chris,' Michael said. 'And the bus is a whole lot heavier than your truck.'

'Where are we going to go anyway?' Jack asked. 'If the world's strongest men have all been turned into zombies, and they all just happen to show up here, all they'll do is push us into some trees.'

I looked around us. We were surrounded by woods. 'Okay, okay,' I said.

I thanked Shannon after she handed me a sleeping bag, and walked halfway up the bus to find some space. I decided on the floor so I could stretch out.

DAY FIFTEEN

Chapter 3: Shrapnel

My sleep had been fitful. Gee's incessant snoring hadn't helped, and people shouting at him to stop snoring had disrupted my sleep even more so.

It was silent now, so the Lithuanian must have been awake.

There was a slight breeze blowing into the bus, carrying with it the distinctive scent of coffee, along with the smell of food cooking.

I climbed up to sit on the seat and looked around. The bus was empty, so I unzipped my sleeping bag and headed towards the front doors.

'Good afternoon Chris,' Shannon said, after I'd appeared in the open doorway.

Gee was crouching over a little camping stove, a pan of what looked like baked beans was cooking over the flame.

'Coffee?' Michael asked me.

'Yes please.'

'No milk I'm afraid,' he added. 'The local stores were all closed.'

'That's absolutely fine,' I said, before joining everyone to sit on the road. 'No zombie swarms knocking about then?'

'Not seen anything. Maybe they've turned nocturnal as well,' Jack said. 'Can hear the birds though, can't remember the last time I heard them.'

'That's a good sign actually,' I recalled. 'I heard them singing when I was up in the hills, and there weren't any zombies there, well, only a couple. And a huge swarm had recently passed through, so it might not actually mean anything.'

Michael leaned over to pass me a cup of coffee. 'Very useful information. Thanks Chris.'

'Sausage and bean for breakfast. Okay?' Gee almost barked at me.

'Yeah brilliant,' I replied. 'What time is it? I really need to get a proper watch. The battery dies too quickly on my fitness watch.'

'Half two,' Jack said. 'We were just talking about setting off when everyone was ready. Not waiting for it to get dark.'

'That way we'll get to Seattle when it does get dark, at ten or eleven,' Michael said. 'Meaning we'll have plenty of time to sort out getting over the border once we get up there.'

'I don't think the border crossing will be all that easy,' Shannon said.

'I expect you're right darling,' Michael acknowledged. 'But you know me, ever the optimist.'

'Okay. If that's what you want to do,' I said. 'I'm happy to go with the general consensus.'

'It's decided then,' Michael said. 'Set off in an hour?'

We all agreed. I nipped off for a quick piss behind the bus, returning to find a plate of three sausages and a huge pile of beans waiting for me.

'Thanks Gee. This could be the best plate of food anyone has ever given me.'

'Sausage out of tin,' Gee said. 'Not real sausage.'

'You could have pulled them out of your pocket,' I said. 'It wouldn't have made any difference to me.'

'I honestly thought you were going to say arse, rather than pocket,' Jack said.

'Jack,' Shannon scolded him. 'I'm eating a sausage. I don't want to think about it coming out of Gee's ass.'

Jack apologised, but with a huge smile on his face.

The first plate of hot food I'd eaten for nearly two weeks was beyond delicious. I tried to remember the last time I'd eaten anything cooked. It must have been when I met the Rodriguez's, and Ali had made me some eggs.

An hour later and we were underway. I was driving and Jack had taken over the map reading duties.

'Why do I have to drive right now?' I asked. 'When we decide to set off in the day time.'

'Because it's your turn,' Jack said. 'And I've only got one eye at the moment.'

'Yes I realise that,' I said. 'But if I'd known we were gonna up the risk factor, I'd have volunteered to drive earlier.'

'You've just gotta suck it up Christopher,' Michael said.

'Thanks for the helpful advice Michael. I hope you're not expecting me to do Jack's shift as well? We're barely friends, I hardly know him really.'

'How do you know each other?' Shannon asked.

I looked to Jack, but he'd just started eating a Snickers. He nodded to me.

'I went to university with a friend of Jack's, then afterwards a few of us moved to Leeds, in Yorkshire. Jack moved to Leeds shortly after. Or had you already moved there?'

He swallowed his mouthful of Snickers, before saying, 'I was already there, moved over a bit before you all turned up.'

'Been friends since, Jack moved in with my wife and I for a few years as well, when he was homeless.'

'I wasn't homeless,' Jack said. 'I couldn't be bothered to look for somewhere else to live. It was just easier.'

'Fuck!' I shouted.

We had just reached the brow of a hill when they came into view. It might not have quite been a swarm, but a large number of zombies were already sprinting towards us. The road was full of them. They must have heard us driving up the other side of the hill.

'I'm going through them,' I said.

'Well, we'd prefer it if you didn't stop and offer them a lift,' Jack said.

'Turn your wipers on now,' Michael instructed me.

I did as I was told.

The zombies were all running for us, so the shape of the group had turned into kind of an arrowhead. The point of it was only twenty or so feet from us.

Seconds later, we hit them. I hardly felt the impact but the windscreen was hit by a wave of blood and gore. The wipers were hardly doing anything, just moving the blood from side to side.

'Just drive straight,' Shannon yelled.

Wave after wave of dark zombie innards slammed into the windscreen.

'Turn little right!' Gee screamed at me, his voice only just audible, like he was outside of the bus.

I turned the steering wheel to the right.

'More!' he shouted. 'Little more!'

'Little more!' he repeated.

'Now straight!' he screamed. 'Okay, no more dead.'

Once the barrage had ended the wipers began to work, allowing me to see where we were going again.

'There are no more. Road is clear,' Gee said, his voice now coming from close behind me.

I swivelled my head around to look at him. His head and shoulders were a deep maroon colour.

'What the fuck happened to you?' I asked, turning back to the road.

'I need to see,' he replied.

'He stuck his head out of a window,' Jack said.

'I only have one clean cloth left,' Gee said, before stomping down to the back of the bus.

'I think he means he only has one set of clean clothes left,' Shannon explained.

'I've only got what I'm wearing,' I said. 'I could do with getting some new clothes actually.'

Over the next few hours we hit three more similarly sized groups on the road. I only had two curved slithers of clear windscreen to see where I was going, and they were getting smaller and smaller each time we hit a group of zombies. It was also getting quite dark, which was hopefully good for zombie activity, but terrible for visibility.

Especially when your windscreen is covered in dried blood and shit.

As we approached the outskirts of a place called Yakima, I spotted a sign for Costco, and suggested stopping to clean the front of the bus. Everyone agreed. I also thought I could get some clothes.

Shannon suggested parking at the edge of the car park, and walking the rest of the way to the shop's large building.

'Why?' I asked. 'The car park is huge.'

'It's safer,' she replied.

'Surely it's safer to park up in front of the building and not have to walk far?' Jack suggested.

'Trust me. It's safer this way,' she replied. 'Our vehicle could be very desirable.'

'Come on guys,' Michael said. 'The boss has spoken.'

Jack and I exchanged looks. He puffed out his cheeks and shrugged his shoulders.

'Fine,' I said.

'Okay,' Shannon said. 'Clean the bus first, and then go shopping.'

We parked up between a petrol station and a peculiarly placed little park. Gee offered up his old and dirty clothes to wipe down the front of the bus.

Michael and I very carefully climbed up onto the front of the bus, making sure not to slip on the various zombie parts splattered on, and hanging from it. Gee had given Shannon a lift up to the roof of the bus. She was stood above us, pouring bottles of soda water, because none of us liked soda water, onto the windscreen, while we tried our best to wipe it clean.

I turned to see Jack stood watching us. He was very dramatically holding his ribs and bandaged head.

'If you're gonna do fuck all Jack, at least keep a look out,' I said.

Michael suddenly vomited all over the windscreen next to me.

'Fuck's sake Michael,' I said. 'We're trying to clean it, not make it worse.'

'Sorry. I'm alright now–,' he started, before very loudly vomiting again.

Half an hour of incredibly disgusting work later, the windscreen was almost clear. Clear enough at least.

Gee had been on fuel salvaging duties, and told us the bus was almost full. What he actually said was, 'Bus fucking full, almost.'

We managed to scrape the gore from our arms, before using what was left of the soda water to clean our hands.

Shannon pulled us into a huddle. Organised as ever, she passed us all torches. 'Michael and I are going to the pharmacy,' she said. 'You three grab yourselves some clothes, and then get food. And be careful. Any problems and make some noise. Don't worry about attracting more zombies. If you don't make noise, nobody will hear you, so nobody will come and help you. Okay?'

'Okay,' Jack said. 'Do we all put our hands into the middle now, and do some kind team chant? Like go...something something? Shit, I couldn't think of a name for our team.'

'No we don't,' Shannon replied. 'Now come on, let's go.'

We all kept low as we headed towards the shop, using the abandoned cars as cover.

On the corner of the building there were two entrances side by side. Neither of them had doors, so the pitch black shop inside was open to the elements.

As soon as we entered we all froze. The faint sound of talking was coming from inside the shop. It sounded aggressive, like an argument. Over in the far corner, beams of light briefly shot up to ceiling, before lowering again.

Michael turned to us all with his finger to his lips, before beckoning us to go back outside.

Just as I turned to leave, I could have sworn I heard someone say the name Alison, followed by a woman saying Gilberto.

There's no way they would be over here in Washington State. It's hundreds of miles out of their way.

The others had left but I waited inside the shop.

From outside, Jack whispered, 'Chris, come on.'

I quickly shushed him, trying to listen.

'Don't do it Richard,' a woman's voice said.

That couldn't have been Ali. Could it? It definitely sounded like her.

'We need to go and see who it is. What if it's Beth?' I heard Jack say.

I crept outside to join the others.

'Jack, do you remember the family that helped us?' I asked him. 'When we first got separated, the Rodriguez's?'

'Yeah of course,' he replied. 'I remember Ali, your girlfriend.'

I forced a quick smile and pointed back into the shop. 'Ha ha Jacqueline. I'm pretty sure that's them in there.'

'This is a long way from Utah,' Jack said.

'We're here, and we went through Utah,' I pointed out.

'There would be no reason for them to–,' Jack started.

'It doesn't matter who it is,' Michael interrupted. 'Like you said Jack, Beth might be with them. We have to check.'

'Thanks Michael,' Jack said.

Shannon and Gee both nodded their agreement.

These are really fucking nice people Jack has found, or that found him.

'Stay quiet. Flashlight off. Keep low,' Gee whispered, before heading back into the darkness of the shop.

We followed the sounds of the argument, weaving our way down the many aisles, using our outstretched hands to stop us from walking into anything.

'Please Richard,' someone was saying. 'Just take a moment to think about this.' I didn't recognise the woman's voice.

Gee stopped at the end of an aisle, torch lights were flickering across the floor in front of us. He turned and held his hand out to us, signalling us to stop.

'She might be okay. Why not wait, just a little bit longer.'

That was definitely Ali speaking. I turned and looked for Jack, eventually finding his eyes in the darkness. He just held his hands out and shrugged.

'Shut the fuck up Alison,' a man's voice said. 'Richard is right. We can't just wait for it to happen.'

I looked back to Jack, mouthing the word, 'See?'

I can't wait. If I do, something bad might happen.

'Hello,' I called out.

A couple of very audible gasps made their way to us from around the corner, followed by a strained silence. A hand rested on my shoulder, but I stood up straight and walked to the end of the aisle, stopping before I was visible to the other people.

'Pete?' Ali called out. 'Stay back.'

It's definitely them.

'It's Chris, we met...' I paused because I couldn't remember how long it had been. 'We met in Utah about a week ago. Ali found me in a basement.'

'Chris?' Ali said.

'Yep, it's me. I'm coming out,' I replied, and stepped around the corner.

In front of me was a kind of stand-off. In the centre stood a woman I didn't recognise. Her right hand was pressed against her blood soaked left arm, and tears were streaming down her face. There was a pistol very close to the side of her head, being held by a nervous looking man. His eyes were darting between the crying woman, me, and Ali, who stood only a few feet away from him. She was pointing a pistol at his head.

I quickly raised my hands above my head, and started walking towards them. I made it two paces before another man further to my right came into view. He was pointing a rifle at me. That was also when I saw Sandra, Ali's sister, pointing a pistol at the rifle man.

Fuck's sake. It wasn't like a stand-off, it was one.

'Hi,' I said, trying to sound casual. 'What's up?'

Ali rolled her eyes.

'Who the fuck are you?' the nervous looking man screamed.

'This is Chris,' Ali said, very slowly and calmly. 'We met him nine days ago. Chris, this is Richard,' she said, nodding to the guy she was threatening to shoot in the head.

'Hi Richard,' I said, waving with my hand holding the torch.

Fuck. Why didn't I wave with my free hand? Now he'll wonder why I was waving my torch at him. Why did I even wave at all?

Richard just stared at me. With his free hand, he wiped at the sweat pouring down his face.

'Richard, just look at Maya,' Ali said, in a soothing tone. 'She's frightened, and she's your friend. You don't want to do anything to hurt her.'

'She's been bitten,' Richard said, his voice cracking. He looked like he was trying to hold back his own tears. 'We have to kill her, before she turns and kills us.'

'Richard,' Maya cried. 'Just let me go. I'll walk away and you'll never see me again.'

'You said you didn't want to be like them,' Richard cried. 'I don't want you to be like that.' He wiped at his eyes.

Without thinking, I stepped forward two paces. The guy aiming the rifle at me shouted, 'Stop! Don't move!'

'It's okay,' I said, immediately regretting my decision to get so close. I was probably only a couple of feet from this Maya woman, and Richard's gun. 'I have a friend who was bitten, only a few days ago, and she's fine. The zombie thing can't be passed on.'

'Bullshit!' Richard spat.

'Please Richard,' Maya loudly sobbed.

'I'm being serious,' I said. 'Honestly, I'm telling the truth.'

Richard sniffed, and said, 'Sorry Maya.'

A loud explosion of noise filled the aisles. Almost immediately, something incredibly hot seemed to splatter across my face, like someone had thrown acid at me. I turned away, holding my face. The sudden sharp pain was unbelievable. For a very brief moment, I caught sight of Maya, lying face down on the floor. A pool of dark liquid quickly spreading out on the tiles under her head.

I could hear people screaming and shouting at each other. I turned back around, fully expecting the rifle guy to finish me off.

Had I been shot in the face? Why is it my fucking face all the time? Fuck. It can't be good to get shot in the face.

I could at least see. I still had my sight.

Richard was now aiming his gun at me, shouting something unintelligible and crying. Ali was closer to him now, screaming for him to put the gun down.

'He has it now!' Richard shouted, after regaining his composure slightly. 'The bullet went through Maya and into him. He has it now!' The gun in his hand looked like it was shaking uncontrollably.

What? Have I been shot in the face?

One moment, Richard was shouting and pointing his gun at me. Then, in a blink of an eye, he'd released his grip on the gun, and his arm hung limply by his side. At the same time, the gun seemed to fall to the floor in slow motion, loudly clattering when it hit the tiles. Richard however, was completely silent. Once the gun was still, everything became eerily quiet. Richard's mouth became slack and gaped open. Blood started to drip from his chin. I followed the trail of blood back up his face, to see an arrowhead protruding out of his now empty right eye socket.

Where the fuck had his eye ball gone?

He collapsed forward onto Maya's prone body.

A crunching noise drew my attention to the right. Big Gee was holding a rifle in his left hand, and seemed to be lifting the former owner of the rifle into the air. He was stood behind him, with his closed fist under the squirming man's chin. I was very confused as to how he was managing this bizarre balancing act. The man was now twitching uncontrollably, his eyes almost popping out of his head.

Behind them, Sandra's mouth was covered with her hands. Her uncle Gilberto was now stood behind her, looking shocked, his hands on her shoulders.

With another clattering noise, Gee dropped the rifle to the floor and gripped the man's throat with his left hand. With a sickening squelch, he wrenched his right hand away from under the man's chin. In Gee's hand was a huge knife, dripping with blood. He let go of the man's neck, and the now lifeless body collapsed to the floor in a heap.

Ah right, okay then, that explains the balancing act.

Gee was walking towards me. Ali didn't know what to do. Her gun was wavering between Richard, who was now lying motionless on the floor, and Gee.

'Chris,' Gee said, with obvious concern in his voice. 'Are you okay?'

'Dunno mate,' I replied. 'I think something hit me in the face.'

'Is anybody else hurt?' Shannon asked from behind me.

'Chris, who are these people?' Ali asked, sounding panicked, now pointing her gun at something behind me.

'Friends, they're all friends, they're alright,' I quickly replied.

Gee moved my hands away from my face and pointed his torch at me. The blinding light made me clamp my eyes shut. I could feel people closing in around me.

Gilberto was asking Ali to come to him.

'Was he shot?' Jack asked.

'No,' Gee said. 'I think it just shrapnel.'

'Shrapnel?' I asked. 'Like bullet shrapnel?'

The blinding white light from Gee's torch left my face, so I opened my eyes and tried to blink away the yellow spots in my vision. Jack, Michael, Gee and Shannon were stood in front of me, all with concerned expressions. Ali, Sandra and Gilberto stood by the guy Gee had killed with his knife, eyeing us suspiciously.

'No, not bullet,' Gee said. 'Shrapnel from woman's head.'

'You fucking what?' I asked.

Did I hear that right?

'Bits of bone. They leave woman's head,' Gee said, pointing down to Maya on the floor. 'And hit Chris in face.'

Yep, turns out I did.

Everyone looked disgusted, but nowhere near as much as I felt.

'Jesus fucking Christ,' I said. 'I need to get it out of my face.'

Shannon quickly took charge of the situation. 'Gee, you get Chris back to the bus,' she instructed. 'Michael and I will go to the pharmacy. Jack, you get clothes for Gee and Chris.' She leaned in closer to me, before whispering, 'What about those three? We did just kill two of them.'

'I've never seen the three dead people before. The ones left alive are friends, or were friends,' I whispered. 'Shall we tell them to meet us at the bus?'

Shannon and Michael shared a glance. I had no idea what the look was meant to convey.

'Up to you,' Shannon said to me. 'You know them.'

I nodded, before looking over to Ali. 'Our bus is over by the petrol station, the gas station, you know what I mean. Meet us over there?'

'Okay,' Ali replied, her voice sounding calmer than she looked. 'Ten minutes?'

The sound of running footsteps echoed through the building, making everyone take cover behind the aisles.

'Dad...Sandra...Alison,' a voice hissed out.

Ali quickly turned towards us, gesturing with her hands for everyone to calm down. 'It's just Pete,' she said. 'Pete,' she called out to him. 'We're okay, stay there, we'll come to you.'

Ali grabbed a hold of Gilberto and Sandra and walked them down one of the aisles closest to them.

'Right okay,' Shannon said. 'Everyone get going. Gee, let us know if anything heard the gunshot and is heading our way.'

Gee nodded.

'No sweat pants Jack,' I said. 'For me that is. You wear whatever you want.'

'Thanks Dad,' he replied, before spinning around to look for the clothing department.

'But make sure you get me proper pants, English pants. I need some underwear,' I called out. 'That makes it sound like I just shit myself,' I quickly added. 'I haven't shit myself.'

'Yes I know what you mean,' he called back. 'Now shut up.'

Outside, it all looked clear. Gee walked alongside me as we headed back to the bus. Blood dripped from my chin, so I needlessly leaned forward to stop it falling onto my already dirty clothes.

I lifted my face up slightly. 'How bad does my face look Gee?'

He shrugged his shoulders. 'It look okay,' he answered. His voice had become very high pitched.

'I thought you'd be a better liar than that,' I said.

'No,' he almost squeaked. 'It look okay.'

Chapter 4: Good Shit

It did not look okay. I looked in the rear view mirror on the bus, and counted nine puncture wounds on my face. I was lucky they'd all missed my eyes.

Just to even things up, somehow it was only the right side of my face this time.

Jack, Shannon and Michael piled onto the bus almost at the same time, all carrying full bags. Shannon lifted one of her bags into the air. The sound of glass clinking together came from the bag.

'Whiskey or vodka?' she asked me.

'Erm...whiskey,' I replied.

Shannon smiled. 'Good choice.'

Michael started laying out plastic sheets on one of the seats, while Shannon emptied her bags. I sat on the other side of the bus. She took out two bottles. One was vodka and one whiskey. I expected her to hand me one, but she placed them both on the floor. Next out was a little plastic container with a red label. She twisted the cap off and shook a couple of tablets into her hand.

'Here, take two of these,' she said, handing them to me. 'Actually, make it three.'

'Do I get any whiskey?' I asked.

'No, that's for me when I've finished,' she replied. 'Now lie down here.' She was pointing at the plastic covered seat. 'We can clean up the blood on your face while the painkillers take effect.'

I laid down on my back.

'Jack, you hold the flashlight,' Shannon said. 'Keep it on Chris's face at all times.'

Jack immediately shone his torch into my eyes, almost blinding me.

'Fuck's sake Jack. Just give me a couple of seconds warning.'

'Michael, you disinfect these with the vodka,' she said. 'Just soak them in a clean cup and leave it down here.'

I tried to open my eyes but the light was too bright.

'What are you disinfecting?' I asked. 'Tweezers?'

'Yes,' Shannon replied. 'And the razor blades.'

I lifted my hand to block the torch light, and looked at Shannon. 'What?' I asked her.

Jack moved the torch so the light was back in my eyes, making me quickly close them again.

'Jack,' I yelled. 'For fuck's sake.'

'Shannon told me,' Jack said.

'Twat,' I replied.

'Quiet Chris,' Shannon softly said, gently laying a hand on my shoulder. 'I thought I might have to shave some of your beard, but it looks like it's just around your eye.'

'Oh right, that's okay then,' I said.

'Also, I might have to make the holes in your face a bit bigger, so I can get the bones, I mean shrapnel, out.'

'Fuck's sake,' I said. 'By the way, you can say bones. There are human fucking bones in my face.'

We all heard two vehicles pulling up outside the bus.

'Hey, your friends are here Chris,' Michael called out, before I heard him exit the bus.

'Okay Chris,' Shannon said. 'I'm just going to get rid of the blood to start with. No cutting just yet.'

Shannon very gently started to wipe my face. It felt like she was using damp cotton pads. Sharp stinging pains shot through me every time she rubbed it over one of the wounds.

At some point during the painful cleaning process, the bus moved slightly as someone climbed the steps.

'I told them to wait for us outside,' Michael said. 'They seem okay.'

'How many of them are there?' I asked. 'Do they all look Hispanic?'

'Yeah I think so,' Michael replied. 'Six adults. The two women and the old guy from Costco were there, and three other guys, they looked like brothers. I think there were some kids but I couldn't really see them in the back of the second car.'

'Three young boys, one blond?' I asked.

'Sorry, couldn't tell,' Michael said. 'I can go and have another look.'

'No it's okay. Looks like they never found Sandra's husband and daughter.'

'Hey Michael,' Shannon said. 'Make sure Gee is–.'

'It's okay. Gee is already keeping an eye on them. You know he doesn't trust anybody.'

'Good,' she answered.

I could barely open my eyes, so I squinted through the bright light to see what was happening.

Shannon twisted her baseball cap around so it was on backwards. 'So Chris, I'm going to try it with the tweezers first. Hopefully I won't have to do any cutting.'

'Yeah, go for it,' I said, sighing and closing my eyes. 'Although I don't think those painkillers have done anything.'

'I don't think they'll do a great deal,' Shannon said. 'They might take the edge off slightly.'

'Great,' I said flatly.

She started prodding my face with her fingers, slowly moving around all the wounds.

'Okay,' she said. 'I'm going in.'

I'm not going to lie, it was fucking painful.

After rummaging around for what felt like an absolute fucking age, she pulled the tweezers out, triumphantly stating, 'Got it. One down, eight to go.'

'Fucking hell,' I softly muttered.

She quickly moved onto the next one. It only took a few seconds of stabbing with the tweezers, before she told me she was going to have to cut.

'On three. One...two...three,' Shannon said.

I felt the blade slice through my skin. It wasn't as painful as the tweezer rummaging.

I realised once she'd stopped cutting, Shannon had been talking to me. 'Sorry, you're gonna have to repeat all of that,' I said, through gritted teeth. 'Didn't get a single word.'

'I said...' She paused to pick up the tweezers to continue with the rummaging. 'You know these people. What should we do? I'm assuming they're heading north. Do you want to ask them to join us? Yes! Two down.'

I'd been holding my breath, releasing it when I felt part of another person being plucked from my face. 'Ow!' I exclaimed, and then tried to compose myself. 'I think they're nice people. Most of them hated me and Jack–.'

'They hated you,' Jack interrupted.

'They hated *us* because they were just trying to protect their family,' I said. 'I think you should definitely ask, but they'll probably say no.'

'Not in the bus though?' Jack asked. 'Do you mean in a convoy.'

'Yes of course,' Shannon replied. 'We'd all fit in here but it'd be safer to have a few vehicles.'

Shannon continued with her attempt at school bus surgery. I was desperate for it to end, and beginning to wish she would do more slicing, just to speed the process up.

There was only one bit of the dead woman left to remove when Gee started talking to somebody outside. I could only hear Gee's side of the conversation.

'No,' he said.

Silence.

'Have weapon?'

Silence.

'Okay,' he said.

A few seconds later, Ali called out, 'Hello, coming aboard.'

It doesn't take much to get past Gee then.

'Hello,' Jack said. 'Come in and see Chris's face getting cut open. It's delightful viewing.'

'Hi Jack,' Ali said. 'You look...different.'

'Oh yeah, Chris threw me into a dumpster.'

'He'd already fucked his eye up before I threw him into the dumpster,' I quickly said.

'Oh fuck,' Ali exclaimed.

I'm guessing she just saw me.

'Hi Chris,' Ali said. 'Are you two competing for the most fucked up face awards?'

'So much cursing,' Shannon said.

'Yep,' I replied. 'And I think I just took the lead. Ali, this is Shannon. Shannon, this is Ali.'

They greeted each other before Shannon introduced Ali to Michael. 'The guy with his head between his legs over there is my husband, Michael. He's just feeling a bit queasy.'

'Hello,' Michael wearily said. 'Sorry, I shouldn't have watched.'

'You've been in here for a long time, and the big guy outside was staring at us,' Ali said. 'You know the one. He just killed two people in Costco. He's really freaking the kids out.'

'I killed one of them, sorry,' Michael said. It sounded like his head was still between his legs.

'That's Gee,' Jack said. 'And don't worry about him. He's just looking after us.'

'We barely knew those people really,' Ali said. 'But that doesn't mean any of us wanted to witness what just happened.'

'Last one is out,' Shannon said, probably in an effort to diffuse the awkward moment. 'Well done Chris. Just need to get you cleaned up.'

'Thank fuck for that,' I whispered. 'How big are these holes? You're not planning on stitching me up are you?'

'No, they're only small.'

'Really?' I asked. 'It felt like you were cutting half my face off.'

I lifted my hand to feel my face. Shannon slapped my hand away.

'No!' she scolded me. 'No touching with your dirty hands. Infections Chris, we don't want infections.'

'What you said back there, about not catching the virus from bites. Is that true?' Ali asked.

'Yes, it was me that was bitten,' Shannon said, very openly. 'I'm fine. It was a few days ago.'

Ali initial response was very similar to mine, silence.

While Shannon was applying the final touches to my messed up face, we discussed both of our group's future plans. We turned out to share exactly the same plans. Ali said they'd be happy to follow us in their vehicles. While waiting for us outside, her family had apparently been talking about the advantages of following a bus with a snow plough all the way up to Canada.

Along with the gauze taped to my face, I also had nine circular plasters, or band aids as Shannon called them, dotted around the right side of my face.

'Yep, you're winning,' Jack said, pointing at me, and then at his bandaged eye. 'I thought I was ahead still, but you look fucking ridiculous.'

Gee was back in the driver's seat. Ali had gone back to her family, who were following us in two identical looking black Dodge Caravans.

The Intersate-90 took us around the few towns and cities north of Yakima, so the roads were soon surrounded by trees. It was a shame it was dark, because we might have been able to see Mount Rainier during the day.

'The black expanse of nothingness on our left is Keechelus Lake,' Michael said, after looking up from the map.

We all looked out through the windows, and saw darkness.

'Thanks Tour Guide Michael,' I said. 'Gee, I think it might be poo o'clock.'

'What the fuck is this?' Gee replied.

'Poo o'clock,' I said. 'You know? Time for a Poo.'

'You need shit?' he asked.

'Yeah, I need a shit.'

'Why not just say this?'

'Because that annoys Shannon, and she's already shouted at me enough today,' I replied.

'Please don't make me the mother figure in this group,' Shannon exclaimed.

'Anyway Gee, yeah, I need a shit,' I said. 'Could you pull over please?'

After we'd stopped, I stood in the open doorway, pointing my torch into the edge of the dark and very foreboding tree line. The torch light bouncing off the leaves made everything look like it was moving.

'What is going on?' a voice hissed from behind the bus.

I poked my head out and looked to my right. My torch lit up a squinting Steve, one of Ali's cousins.

'Hi Steve,' I said, in a hushed tone. I was genuinely happy to see him again. 'How are you doing? I'm just going for a shit.'

He spun around, mumbling something inaudible. I just about heard him telling the rest of his family we'd stopped for a bathroom break.

He still hates me then.

'Do you want me to come?' Gee asked.

'No, obviously not, I'm going for a shit,' I quickly responded.

'Hey, there will probably be bears coming out of hibernation around about now,' Jack said. 'So you better keep an eye out for them.'

'Not this close to the road though,' I replied.

'It's the apocalypse Chris,' Jack said. 'All the humans have died.'

'Very true. But there won't be any bears around. Not while I'm here.' I stepped off the bus, and into the woods.

Armed with a torch, a roll of toilet tissues, and some hand sanitiser, I looked for a suitable place to have a much needed shit.

Fuck, I'm breaking the promise to myself to only shit somewhere with walls and a ceiling. Forgot about that. Probably a very good rule.

After I felt I'd gone far enough, I pulled my jeans down and squatted. Before I could relax and let go, I heard voices and saw torch lights, much too close to me. It sounded like the Rodriguez brothers.

Fuck's sake.

I pulled my jeans back up and walked further into the woods.

It turned out to be a textbook turd, very little wiping was required. Ideal in this particular situation. I took the little plastic bottle of sanitiser out of my pocket, and squeezed some into my hand. The smell was strong, like pure alcohol.

I could just about see the headlights of the bus through the thick underbrush, directly in front of me. A low rumbling noise made me point my torch to the left, but all I could see were more trees.

It sounded like Gee's fucking snoring.

After finally convincing myself that nothing was going to jump out and attack me, I started walking back to the road. I only got two paces when the low rumbling noise started again. It soon turned into loud heavy grunts, the sound of snapping branches joined them, filling the woods and terrifying me. I tracked my torch upwards across a large dark mass, about nine or ten feet in front of me. I stopped when the beam of light reached a bear's open snout. It towered over me. The torch light illuminated the bear's hot and misty breath.

Panicking, I lifted my arms up and frantically waved them, trying to make myself look as big as possible. The bear dropped down onto all four legs and turned away from me.

Yes! The making yourself look big thing actually works.

The bear must have decided that technique didn't work, because it suddenly directed its attention back to me.

Fuck.

I very briefly considered pulling the axe out from my belt. Instead, I threw the toilet roll at the bear's head, spun around and ran in the opposite direction, as quickly as I could.

Why didn't I bring my gun?

Branches and twigs thwacked into my aching face and body. The fear coursing through me meant only running directly into a tree trunk was gonna slow me down. I could hear the big animal bounding through the trees behind me.

The whipping branches abruptly ended and I was out in the open.

Shite. Bears are supposed to be really fast runners, definitely faster than me.

There was some kind farm of building not far from me in the field, just visible in the moonlight. I quickly changed direction and headed for it. I didn't want to look, but I assumed the bear was still chasing me.

A group of about twenty zombies were sleeping by the building.

Zombies or bear?

Definitely zombies.

I started screaming as loudly as I could. 'Wake up zombies! Wake the fuck up!'

They certainly did wake up. Within a couple of seconds they were all sprinting towards me. I decided to risk a quick glance behind.

My heart rate jumped to a ridiculous speed, almost taking what little breath I had left away from me. The bear was really fucking close. I somehow found an extra gear within me, and started running directly for the zombies.

Please let this work.

The sound of the bear's breathing was so close I thought I could almost smell its breath. I started shouting, not for any practical reason, just through utter terror.

I took a sharp right turn when I was about six feet from the zombies. I could almost feel the air being moved by the huge animal as it passed close behind me. The sound of undead bodies slamming into the meaty body of the bear reverberated around the enclosed field. Then followed a loud roar, and the sound of flesh being torn apart.

The black wall of the tree line was ahead of me. I ran towards it, desperately hoping the bear wouldn't change its mind, and go for some fresher meat. I had a very quick glance behind me. The bear looked like it was tearing the zombies to pieces. They didn't seem to be concerned with me at all, and just clambered over the hungry animal.

I couldn't hold back the laughter. It almost erupted out of me. It really didn't help, because I was struggling to breathe from the exertion.

I had no idea where the bus would be, but I figured I'd hit the road at some point. I slowed slightly before entering the woods. Now the panic had eased a bit, I realised I didn't want to impale myself on a sharp and pointy branch. My face was really beginning to hurt and I wasn't looking forward to running through the underbrush again.

Twenty seconds later, with a stinging face, I snagged my foot on something, lost my balance, and fell down onto tarmac. I heard my name being shouted and looked in the direction of the voices. Multiple beams of light were being pointed into the trees.

After getting back to my feet, I called to them and started running. The beams of light turned to point at me, making me cover my eyes with my hand.

When I was almost there, I shouted to everyone to get back into the vehicles. I was surprised to see everyone immediately turn, either to climb back aboard the bus or run back to the two Dodge's behind.

I jumped up the stairs, and Gee pressed the button to close the doors. My breathing was really laboured and sweat poured down my face.

'Good shit?' Jack asked.

Between deep breaths I managed to say, 'Bear, and zombies.'

The bus started to move forwards.

'Bollocks,' Jack said, seemingly not believing me. Although I noted a slight uncertainty in his voice.

The state I was in made it obvious something had happened.

'What happened?' Shannon asked.

I sat on one of the seats and tried to calm down. I was just about to answer, when I noticed Gilberto, Ali, Sandra and two of the kids sat at the back of the bus.

Shannon noticed me looking. 'One of their vehicles was running low on gas, so we decided it was safer to leave it behind.'

'What happened in the woods?' Jack asked impatiently.

It was still hard to breathe, but I managed to say, 'Honestly. Chased by bear. Zombies saved me. They distracted the bear. I legged it.'

'I did warn you there might be bears around here,' Jack said.

'I'm still alive, and I finally saw a bear,' I jubilantly said, adrenaline still pounding through me. 'I'm well happy with that.'

Jack handed me a can of Diet Pepsi, saying, 'You need to be more careful. We all need to be more careful. Even if it's to go for a shit, we need to stay in pairs.'

'Pervert,' I said.

'Jack is right,' Shannon said. 'Until we're safely in Canada, we need to be ultra-vigilant. We should always pair up, no matter what we're doing.'

'Even if I'm having a–,' I started.

'No,' Jack interrupted. 'You can do that on your own. Unless Gee would like to join you.'

'What you talking about?' Gee asked from the driver's seat.

'They're not talking about anything Gee,' Shannon answered. 'Don't worry about it.'

Gee shrugged his shoulders. 'I not worry.'

'Good,' Shannon said.

Ali left her family members and walked down the bus towards us, sitting down on the row opposite me.

'Hi,' she said brightly. 'Apart from getting chased by bears, what have you been up to since you left us?' She looked to me, and then at Jack.

I hadn't quite got my breath back, so I let Jack tell his story. Once he'd finished, I filled her in on what I'd done after losing Jack in Austin.

'How about you?' I asked. 'Why are you all the way over here in Washington State?'

'After you left, the swarms continued getting bigger,' she replied. 'One afternoon, we looked out and the entire fence on one side of the warehouse was lying flat on the floor. The concrete posts had been ripped out of the ground. It wasn't hard to convince the rest of them we should leave.' She glanced over to the back row of the bus, before lowering her voice slightly. 'We drove towards Salt Lake City, to see if we could find Dale and Sophia.'

I leaned in towards Michael and Shannon, who were sat on the row in front of Ali. 'Sandra's husband and daughter,' I whispered.

'We couldn't find them,' Ali said, her eyes glistening, but her voice steady. 'We left a letter for them in the warehouse, detailing our plans. We're so far off that plan now, they'll never find us. We just have to hope they went north a long time ago. Sandra is devastated. We all are, but she's staying strong for the kids.'

She leaned back and let out a long sigh, only taking a few seconds to compose herself. 'Salt Lake City was bad,' she continued. 'The east side of Great Salt Lake looked like an atomic bomb had been dropped on it. And the zombies seemed to be endless. So we decided to go west, with the intention of getting back on track later. We'd written in the letter that we were going to try and get into Canada via

Sweet Grass, Montana. Every time we tried to go back east something would block us. The roads would be gone, or huge swarms would stop us.' Ali's head suddenly perked up. 'Hey, you guys seen the swarms moving around at night?'

'Yes,' we all answered in unison.

Ali actually leaned away away from us, literally taken aback.

'Okay,' she said. 'Well, we met up with Richard, Chris and Maya just after crossing into Oregon. It was Richard that suggested we shouldn't worry about where we cross the border, just as long as we did actually cross it. Then we could drive through Canada to the other side of Sweet Grass.'

'When did Maya get bitten?' Michael asked her.

'Just before going into the Costco. She woke up a sleeping zombie by accident, then killed it and ran into the shop.'

'Probably best Gee killed that Chris guy,' I said. 'There isn't room for two people called Chris in this story.'

'Chris,' Shannon exclaimed, her brow furrowed. 'You should never wish anybody dead, even if they were planning on killing you.'

'That doesn't make any sense,' I replied. 'And I thought you said you didn't want to be the mother figure in the group?'

Shannon shook her head, giving her husband a frustrated glance. Michael pretended not to see the look, making Shannon even more infuriated.

'And then we met you lot,' Ali said, probably trying to change the subject. 'Obviously not the best introduction, but it is the end of the world, so these things seem to happen quite often now.'

'Michael,' Gee called out. 'I think we leave 90 road now.'

'Sorry Gee,' Michael replied, spinning around in his seat to face forwards. 'Yes next right. Once we're around Seattle we'll stop for the day just south of Snohomish. I'm guessing there'll be a lot of swarms, as we now seem to be calling them, around Seattle. So we're probably best not attempting our day time driving again.'

'You drove in the day light?' Ali asked, wide eyed.

'Yes, a definite error on our part,' Shannon replied. 'We were cleaning all the blood off the front of the bus just before we met you and your family.'

Ali stood up, saying, 'Talking of family. I better keep an eye on my cousins behind us.'

'Ramrod isn't driving is he?' I asked her.

'No, Pete will be doing the driving. And Steve seems to have given up on wanting to be called Ramrod.'

'Good,' I said.

'Yes, very good,' Shannon agreed. 'Ramrod? It sounds too…sexual.'

'Sexual?' Jack asked. 'Maybe to you Shannon.'

Smiling, Ali walked to the back of the bus. Shannon let out an exasperated sigh and swivelled on her seat to face forward. I grinned at Jack before turning to look out of the window next to me. The pitch black night meant all I could see was my own battered reflection, and the reflection of a very disgruntled looking Shannon on the other side of the bus.

There was a very deep and distracting ache in the right side of my head.

Chapter 5: River Of Blood

There was a good chance I may have nodded off. Screams from the back of the bus dragged me back to consciousness. My head quickly shot upright. I could hear metal crunching and tyres screeching from behind us. The Rodriguez's were all shouting to stop. The bus started to slow down.

Jack looked as startled as me, so I guessed he may have also been asleep. We both climbed to our feet and headed towards the back of the bus.

'What is it?' Shannon asked from close behind me.

'The headlights behind us,' Gilberto said in a panic. 'They disappeared. Then we heard a loud crashing noise.'

'Gee,' Michael called out. 'Back us up. Let's see where they've gone.'

Incredibly loud beeps sounded out as the bus started reversing. I tried to look out of the crowded back window. Our reverse lights illuminated a small patch of road behind us.

A few people gasped as shapes appeared from out of the darkness. For a split second I thought it would be the Rodriguez brothers with the young orphan boy.

I have no idea what that kid is called.

It wasn't the brothers, or the boy with no name. The shapes were zombies. They started to sprint towards us, soon slamming into the back of the bus.

Sandra was repeating the word, 'No.'

Gee must have heard the banging, because he shouted over his shoulder, 'What happening?'

'Keep going,' Shannon instructed. 'There are zombies here. We'll tell you when to stop.'

Gee obediently carried on driving.

More and more of the sprinting dead were in the road. We were dragging them away from whatever they'd been interested in.

I hope they haven't made it into their vehicle. These night time swarms are really pissing me off.

A few seconds later and the bottom of a Dodge Caravan came into view. It was lying on its side, looking battered and bruised, like it had rolled a few times. The road between us and the Dodge was filled with a huge mass of dead creatures, all trying to gain access to the humans inside.

'Gee!' Shannon shouted. 'I need you to go straight back. I'll tell you when to stop. Go faster.'

What is she thinking? If we drive straight back we'll smash into the crashed vehicle.

Ali, Sandra and Gilberto all turned and gave Shannon very concerned looks. It was too late for Shannon to explain her plan, as the bus was already hurtling towards the Dodge.

Bodies were bouncing off the back of the bus, clearing a path through the dead.

'Stop!' Shannon shouted.

The bus screeched to a halt, stopping incredibly close to the Dodge. We must have crushed a lot of the zombies between the two vehicles.

'Can you see their van?' Shannon asked Gee. He shouted back that he could, so Shannon continued. 'Move us so we're side by side. I want our front doors as close to the van as possible.'

'Okay,' Gee said.

Shannon turned to look at us while Gee manoeuvred the bus into position. 'We clear a path to the van,' she said. 'Michael, Gee, Chris, Ali and I create a perimeter, using the bus and the van to shield two sides of us. Then Jack, Sandra and Gilberto get everyone out of the van. Okay?'

The bus suddenly stopped. We were in place. If anyone had any questions, or didn't agree with Shannon, they didn't say anything.

Everyone quickly made their way down to the front. I could hear Sandra trying to console her two kids behind me.

'Everyone, collect your weapons,' Shannon ordered. 'Slight change of plan. Gee, make sure nothing gets on the bus, protect the children.'

Gee's considerable frame seemed to look bigger than ever. I couldn't stop myself from smirking as I passed him. His shoulders were pulled back and his chest was puffed out.

I was stood at the doors, with nobody in front of me.

How the fuck am I right at the front?

I quickly checked my gun. I'd reloaded it in the security office of the car park, so it was ready to go. The lights from the bus barely reached outside, but I could see the zombies hadn't filled the space yet. There were a lot of squashed ones squirming around on the ground, but none on their feet.

'Chris and Ali go left,' Shannon said, with authority in her voice. 'Michael and I go right.'

I gripped my axe in my hand. My heart felt like it was going to burst out of my chest.

The doors opened, and fuck knows why, I rushed out into the night.

I'm blaming peer pressure.

My feet squelched into the mushy dead bodies beneath us.

I'm gonna need some new walking boots.

An arm stretched out for me, so I brought the blunt end of my axe down onto the head that the arm belonged to. The thing's forehead caved in, and the arm fell limply down. I quickly stamped my heel onto another's head, as it was trying to rise up.

Ali stood by my side, carrying some kind of assault rifle in her hands. It much more aggressive looking than the rifle she had when I first met her.

'Where the fuck did that come from?' I asked, nodding to the gun.

She slammed the butt of the rifle into the top of a zombie's head, as it slowly crawled towards us. 'Took it from a dead soldier in Sacramento.'

I glanced behind me and saw Gilberto on his hands and knees. Sandra was standing on his back, while Jack, who was already up on the side of the Dodge, was reaching towards Sandra to pull her up. Michael and Shannon stood with their backs to us, guarding a thin strip of darkness between the bus and the overturned van.

Why is their gap so much smaller than ours?

Gunfire suddenly erupted, right next my head. It was so loud I was sure it would deafen me. I swivelled my head around to see the dead coming for us. They were all I could see in the fucking huge gap we had been given to defend. Ali was firing her rifle into the masses of dead faces. I pulled out my Sig and very quickly emptied it, aiming for heads. I placed it back into its holster and positioned myself to start swinging my little axe.

Ali's rifle was empty a few seconds later. She fumbled at her pocket, pulling out a new magazine. Whilst the space in front of us was much bigger than Shannon and Michael's, you could still only fit six people, or zombies, side by side.

The lack of gunfire meant they were soon upon us. I aimed for the closest, bringing the axe down on the top of its head. I didn't wait to see if the blow had been sufficient to stop it. Whilst pushing them away with my left hand, I swung, and swung, and swung with the axe in my right, crushing heads with the blunt end.

Ali shouted for me to back away, before starting to fire her rifle again. I just had to bash in the heads of the ones that Ali's bullets missed. Only a few made it through.

The bodies were beginning to pile up. At first, the zombies struggled to clamber over the row of their fallen kind, but they soon started stumbling right over them, almost using them like a ramp. Ali was soon out of bullets again. We took two steps back as the creatures tripped over the collapsed bodies and fell to the ground. I stepped in and viciously swiped at the momentarily prone zombies. Ali grabbed my arm, pulling me backwards and out of the way when a new wave of them almost fell upon me.

Ali started to use the rifle like a bat, swinging it up and over her head, the butt of the gun connecting with the zombies.

'In the bus!' Shannon shouted. 'Back in the bus!'

I turned to see Jack climbing the stairs, carrying the kid. Steve was close behind him. Gilberto was still by the overturned Dodge, struggling to get to his feet. His face was twisted with pain. I spun back around to Ali.

'Ali, try and hold them back!' I shouted, before kicking a crawling zombie squarely in the face.

I tried to lift Gilberto up but he was incredibly heavy, much heavier than I thought he should have been. I looked down to see a half destroyed face emerging from the decaying mess on the ground. Its mouth was clamped onto Gilberto's wrist. Three arms were stretched out from the ground, clawing at his thigh. I couldn't tell who those arms belonged to. Blood soaked the right leg of Gilberto's trousers.

I slammed my heel down onto the head biting into his wrist, the skull disintegrating under my foot. I loosened my grip on the axe and spun it around. I swung the axe, aiming the sharp end at the clawing arms. My first swipe took out two of them, slicing half way down their forearms. My next strike chopped off the third at the wrist.

After ripping the still clawing hands away from Gilberto's leg, and hauling him to his feet, I started dragging him to the bus. It was only four or five paces away but he was like a dead weight. Gee was now outside the bus, single-handedly fighting off the swarm with a baseball bat. It looked like my Brooklyn Smasher. Ali appeared at the other side of Gilberto, halving the amount of effort it was taking me to carry him back to the bus. She went up the stairs first, dragging her uncle, while I was behind, pushing him.

'Gee!' I shouted. 'Time to go.'

I was only half way up the stairs when the bus suddenly lurched forward, knocking me off my feet. I glanced back towards Gee as the bus continued to move. The pile of dead bodies wedged between the front of the bus and the bottom of the Dodge started to topple.

I leaned out of the bus and grabbed a part of Gee's jacket, dragging him backwards onto the steps. He was sprawled on top of me, scrambling to keep his feet from dragging across the ground. I desperately clung on to him as zombies reached out for him. The bus slowly started to gain more speed, pulling away from the chasing dead.

'Somebody fucking pull us up!' I pleaded.

Two blood splattered arms suddenly reached over me and grabbed a hold of Gee at his shoulders. He was dragged upwards and over me so his legs were within the bus. The doors closed so I relaxed my hold on him. We both sat on the steps trying to get our breath back.

The calm after the storm was soon disrupted.

'Help me,' Ali shouted. 'I need some help. He's bleeding a lot.'

Gee sat upright, allowing me to get to my feet. Ali was sat on the floor in the aisle, her back leaning against a seat. Gilberto was stretched out in front of her, the back of his head resting on her lap. His normally tanned skin looked a very pale grey colour. There was a lot of blood under his right leg.

'Shannon!' I shouted. Within seconds Shannon was crouched down by Gilberto's prone body.

'Where is he injured?' Shannon asked, while scanning his blood soaked clothes.

'I...I don't know,' Ali stuttered. 'There is blood everywhere.'

'Left wrist and right thigh,' I quickly said. 'Bitten on the wrist, and kind of clawed on the thigh.'

Shannon pulled out a small knife from somewhere on her body. It came out so quickly I couldn't see where it had come from. She lifted Gilberto's right trouser leg up so it was away from his skin, finding the holes that had already been made by the zombie hands. She used the knife to make the holes bigger, before tearing it with her hands.

Clawed had been the right word. His thigh was a mess, like a tiger had viciously swiped at his leg. Blood literally pumped and oozed out of the foot long wounds. Ali's eyes were huge as she gripped tightly onto her uncle's shoulders.

Shannon looked at a complete loss. Her stupor only lasted a couple of seconds. She whipped off her belt. 'Chris, elevate his legs,' she shouted, giving me the briefest of glances.

I crouched down, grabbed both of his ankles and lifted them up to my thigh height. Shannon wrapped her belt around his leg, just above the wounds, and pulled it tight.

'Should I stop,' Michael called out, now sat behind the wheel.

'No, carry on until we're further away,' Shannon replied. 'Somebody get me some–.'

Gee stepped around me in the cramped space, dropped to his knees and jammed a handful of clothes onto the leg wounds. He continued to hold them in place.

'Thanks Gee,' Shannon said. 'How is his wrist?' she asked, looking at Ali.

Ali picked up her uncle's arm at his forearm. 'It's not bleeding that much actually,' she replied, a bit of hope creeping into her voice.

'He is dead,' Gee muttered.

'What?' a bloody Pete asked from behind Ali.

'Yeah, what?' Ali echoed.

'He stop bleeding much because his heart stop,' Gee explained.

There was a stunned silence. I looked up from Gilberto's face. Everyone stared in shock at the horrific scene playing out on the floor of the bus.

'No, he can't be,' Steve muttered.

'I'm really sorry,' Shannon said, now holding Gilberto's uninjured wrist, checking for a pulse. 'Gee is right. They must have sliced through the femoral artery in his leg.'

'Can't you fix it?' Theo called out. I could just see his bruised face poking through between Steve and Pete.

'I'm sorry,' Shannon said.

Gee stopped applying pressure to Gilberto's leg, and rose to his feet.

'I'm not a medical doctor,' Shannon added. 'I wouldn't...I didn't...I didn't know.' She slowly and gently removed her belt, and then got to her feet. She slumped backwards onto an empty seat.

I carefully placed his legs back onto the floor. A river of blood flowed down the aisle, running under my boots and down the steps to the doors.

'Why did you leave him?' Theo sobbed, now staring at Steve.

'I didn't,' Steve said defensively. 'He told me to go. He said he was right behind me.'

'You should have taken care of him,' Theo cried.

'I'm...I'm sorry,' Steve managed to splutter out.

'It's not Steve's fault,' Pete said, taking charge as the eldest of the three brothers. 'I was driving. I crashed. It's my responsibility.'

'The dead appeared from nowhere,' Theo said, slowly backing away, tears streaming down his face. He stopped when Sandra took him by the shoulders. She turned him around and hugged him.

I turned slightly to face forwards, and said, 'Stop when you get the chance please Michael.'

'No problem,' he quietly replied.

A few minutes later, Michael brought the bus to a complete stop. Nobody had moved. We were all in the same positions.

After what felt like a long time in silence, Michael spoke up. 'Right everyone, we've stopped.'

Nobody responded. I looked down at Michael and shrugged. He looked at a loss for what to say.

Pete eventually broke the silence, saying, 'I need a spade.'

I turned to see him step forward and lay a hand on Ali's shoulder. She was still cradling Gilberto's head on her lap.

Shannon's questioning eyes met with Michael's. He slowly shook his head. On seeing her husband's response, she closed her eyes.

'No spade Pete,' I said. 'But we'll help you. Jack, get me your big axe.'

I leaned under the front row of seats, and came back out with two of the torches. I flicked one of them on and asked Michael to open the doors. I had a good look around to make sure there were no dead humans wandering about, or big live bears.

At first it was just me, with Jack's big axe, and Jack with my little axe, doing all the digging, but soon enough, everyone was out and helping. People used whatever they could get a hold of, rifles, my baseball bat, and even using their bare hands.

I wasn't too happy when I noticed Steve using the Brooklyn Smasher to scrape the earth out of the grave. I would have looked like a complete arsehole if I'd asked him not to use it though.

The hole was about three feet deep, and I was pretty sure everyone wanted to stop, but nobody wanted to be the person to say it.

Luckily for us, Pete rose to his feet and told us we'd done enough. 'Steve, Theo, let's get our father,' he said stoically.

'Do you need a hand?' Michael asked, as the three brothers started up the steps.

'No, thank you,' Pete replied.

They soon emerged, carrying Gilberto's ravaged body out of the bus, and gently placing him in the shallow grave.

Pete slowly looked at us all stood around his father's body, before saying, 'Could you please help us cover him? Then, if you don't mind, our family would like some time alone. Don't worry, we won't be long.'

'Take as long as you need,' Shannon told him.

Everyone got down on their knees and scooped, or pushed the broken up soil onto Gilberto, eventually covering him entirely. There were a lot of loud sniffs and sobs.

'Thanks guys,' Sandra said, wiping her face and rising to stand up.

We took that as our cue to leave, and climbed back aboard the bus. Sandra followed us in, before heading back outside with all three of the kids in tow. Thankfully, the blond kid that had been in the crash looked relatively uninjured. The Rodriguez brothers on the other hand, all looked bruised and battered.

Jack sat down on the row behind me, wearily saying, 'Fuck.'

'Yep,' I replied.

'You didn't like it when that Steve guy was using your bat did you?'

My head snapped around to face him. 'Why, what do you mean?'

'You were staring at him, and you looked really pissed off.'

'Shite, nobody else noticed did they?'

'Nah, don't think so. Everyone else is normal, so they were worried about Gilberto being dead.'

'Good.'

A few minutes later, Ali entered the bus, and started walking up the aisle. Sandra and the kids were next, followed by Theo, Steve and Pete bringing up the rear. They were all silent as they passed, and seemed to avoid making eye contact with us. Nobody tried speaking to them as they made their way to the back of the bus.

Michael closed the door and turned the engine back on.

'Right, let's get going then,' he said quietly.

'We're not going to make it to Snohomish before it gets light,' Shannon told her husband. 'We'll need to find somewhere soon. We still have a lot of built up areas to pass through before we get to the border.'

'Once we get a bit further away from that last swarm, I'll find somewhere suitable to pull over,' Michael replied.

'Okay,' Shannon said, leaning forward and squeezing Michael's shoulder. He placed his hand on top of hers.

It wasn't long before the bus was parked up in a rest area on the side of the road. Bedtime was a bit more chaotic with eight more people on board. After we had taken shifts going for bathroom breaks, as Shannon likes to call them, and made sure people were protected during those breaks, everyone was more than ready for sleep.

I'd given up my sleeping bag for the kids, so I wasn't been expecting to sleep much.

Also, my face hurt. I could feel the skin around the puncture wounds tightening.

DAY SIXTEEN

Chapter 6: Barbie

I was wrong. I'd slept like a dead man.

Maybe that's a phrase I shouldn't be using at the moment.

I'd been pretty exhausted after yesterday's events, so my excellent sleep shouldn't have been that much of a surprise.

Everyone had been deathly quiet when I woke up.

Fuck's sake Chris. Stop thinking in death terms.

The Rodriguez's were still occupying the back of the bus. Gee also seemed to be just waking up, only two rows away from me. I had no idea how I wasn't kept awake all night by his snoring.

At least my face wasn't aching as much.

'Afternoon,' Jack said.

I looked over to see him sat on the row opposite me. 'Fucking hell,' I blurted.

The bandage around his head had been removed, so his injured eye was visible. The bruising around the eye looked awful. Every different shade of purple must have been on his skin, and the white of his eye was a very vivid red.

'It might look bad, but I can see,' Jack said, a huge smile on his face.

I sat upright and leaned against the window. 'That's good, but can you not cover it back up? It looks fucking disgusting.'

'No I can't. Shannon said to leave it uncovered.'

'I think you're back in the lead in the most fucked up face awards.'

'Don't worry,' Jack said. 'Your face will soon be back to normal, so you'll leap back into first place.'

I forced a smile and stuck two fingers up at him. 'Food?' I asked.

'Nothing cooked I'm afraid. Michael and Shannon don't want to risk it when we're so close to freedom. They're worried about the dead smelling our beans.'

'Can zombies smell?' I asked.

Jack just shrugged.

'They do smell. They fucking stink,' Gee said, sitting down behind me, his face showing no emotion whatsoever.

'Was that a joke Gee? I asked, with a smile.

'Maybe,' he muttered, still keeping a straight face.

But then, just for the briefest of moments, a smile touched his lips. It was just a little bit, but I definitely saw it.

'I think it was a joke,' Jack said. 'Hey Shannon, Michael. Gee just told a joke.'

'That's brilliant,' Shannon said, packing clothes into a bag. 'But maybe today isn't the day to turn into a comedian.' She nodded towards the back of the bus, and the grieving Rodriguez family.

Breakfast turned out to be another energy bar and a can of Diet Pepsi. I couldn't wait to get across the border and eat some proper food. I'd been having cravings for sausages, mash potato and gravy since Gee had served me his tinned sausages.

'We have a long wait until it gets dark,' Shannon said, after we had moved to the front rows of the bus, just to give Ali and her family a bit more space. 'The sun set at around eight o'clock last night,' she continued. 'So that's about five hours we have to wait.'

I raised both my thumbs, saying, 'Great.'

'Hey guys,' Ali said, startling us after managing to sneak up on us all.

'Hi Ali,' Shannon replied, in a hushed and sympathetic tone. 'How are you all doing back there?'

She shrugged. 'Not great. Theo's not doing well at all. He's blaming Steve. And we're all squashed into a bus together, so it's all a bit shit to be honest.'

'We're all really sorry about what happened,' Michael said.

'Thanks. We'll get through it, no choice is there?' She looked towards me. 'Hey Chris, just wanted to say thank you for getting my uncle onto the bus.' She forced a small smile.

I shifted uncomfortably on my seat. 'That's okay. Just wish it'd turned out better, obviously.'

'Thanks for trying.' She sat down next to Jack, briefly glanced at him, and then did a double take. 'Whoa Jack, your eye looks terrible.'

'Thanks very much,' Jack replied flatly.

Ali let out a little chuckle. 'Sorry, but it does.'

Apart from Jack, everyone at the front of the bus joined in with her laugh, even Gee.

'Chris, I think you could probably do with taking your gauze off,' Shannon stated. 'Let it breathe a while.'

'Ha,' Jack sneered. 'You can look fucking terrible too.'

After Shannon had peeled the gauze off my face, she handed me a little make-up mirror. The scrape didn't look that bad actually. It was healing really well. I just had a very red stretch of skin from just below my hairline, down to my cheek bone. It still looked disgusting, but it had shrunk a lot in size. I still had the stupid little circular plasters dotted all over the other side of my face though.

The afternoon passed by slowly. The Rodriguez family understandably kept to themselves at the back of bus. Occasionally two of them would pass us to use the exit. I think we all tried speaking to them, maybe not Gee actually, but we'd only receive the odd word here and there.

I was more than relieved when it had finally been time to set off. I'd sat myself in the driver's seat at seven o'clock, staring out through the windscreen, willing the sun to go down quicker.

We were soon heading north on the WA-9. The excitement amongst the people sat at the front of the bus was definitely noticeable. I could almost feel it in the air.

'It's only about an hour and a half, maybe two hours from here,' Michael said, shining a torch onto the road map.

'What do you think the border is gonna be like?' I asked him.

Michael took a long breath before answering. 'I honestly don't know. I just want there to be a border. If it was overrun at the beginning, and all this has spread further north...' He paused for a few seconds, before continuing. 'Well, let's just say it's a long way back down to Mexico.'

'The last time I heard anything from my wife, she emailed saying Canada and Mexico were building walls.'

'It would be very impressive if they got a wall up this quickly,' Michael said.

'I think you'd be surprised what people can do to survive,' I said.

'I'm not sure if there will be an actual wall, but I'm feeling confident Chris. The border will still be there.'

The roads north of Seattle had been quiet. We drove by Arlington, and decided to take the WA-534 so we could get onto the I-5. We hoped that would take us all the way to Blaine, the small town just before the Canadian border. Michael said that route would avoid most of the bigger places. Unfortunately though, it would take us right through the middle of Bellingham. After a brief discussion, we put it to a vote. We unanimously agreed to stick with the route Michael had decided on.

Bellingham had been empty, eerily quiet in fact. The city had been well and truly abandoned. It wasn't long after leaving the city limits that we started seeing the signs.

Every road sign near the Bellingham airport had either been spray painted over, or messages had been painted onto white sheets and then draped over them.

15 MILES TO BORDER
STAY QUIET
NO NOISE
NO VEHICLES
SILENCE PLEASE

As soon as we'd passed the no vehicles sign, I started to slow us down, stopping in front of another sign that read, *14 MILES TO BORDER.*

'What the fuck do we do now?' I asked.

'We can't walk fourteen miles with the kids,' Shannon said. 'It's too risky.'

'There must be a reason for the sign though,' Jack said.

'Hey guys,' Pete said, after joining us at the front. 'We saw the signs. What are you thinking?'

'I think we try and get a bit further in the bus,' Shannon said. 'Just a bit. Take it slowly and see what happens. There doesn't seem to be anything around here.'

Sandra had made her way up to stand behind Pete. 'I don't want to take the kids outside if I don't have to,' she said. 'But we'll do whatever everyone else wants to do.'

'It's okay Sandra,' Michael said. 'I agree with Shannon. Let's just drive a bit further.'

'Yep, it's decided then,' I said, and slowly started accelerating. I kept the bus below fifteen miles an hour. Everyone stared out of the windows, looking for any danger.

The 'no vehicles' and 'keep quiet' signs continued to appear in the darkness, and the miles signs slowly counted down. There were no people, no zombies, no anything of note. When we reached the three miles sign, I stopped the bus again.

'Well?' I asked.

'There isn't anything here,' Jack said.

'I don't think we are three miles away from Canada,' Michael said, looking up from the road map. 'I'd say it's more like four or five, maybe even six miles.'

We all sat, or stood, peering out through the windscreen.

Shannon broke the silence, saying, 'How about we get to the outskirts of Blaine and then walk the rest of the way.'

Everyone agreed, so we carried on driving. We passed the two miles sign, still there was nothing. Then we rolled by the one mile sign, and still there was nothing happening.

'The border can't be one mile away guys,' Michael said. 'We're further away than that.'

A few minutes later, not long after crossing Dakota Creek, I stopped the bus in front of a very confusing sign. A banner was stretched across the entire width of the road, held up by metal poles on either side. In huge red letters, it simply said *BORDER*, with a big red arrow pointing to our right.

'Does that mean we can't cross the border up ahead?' Jack asked.

'Maybe we just have to drive east,' Shannon suggested. 'The border might be closed here.'

'Fuck knows,' I sighed, and turned the engine off.

'Can you here that?' Ali asked. 'Sounds like crickets or cicadas.'

I leaned forward in my seat and tried to listen.

She's right, it does sound a bit like crickets, but it also sounds like a shitload of zombies.

A shockingly loud and high pitched screech came from our right. We all swivelled around to find the source.

'What the fuck was that?' I asked.

Before anyone could answer, a loud boom echoed around us, followed by the crackling and popping of fireworks. The sky was suddenly lit up in green and red. An engine in the field next to us roared to life. It seemed to be coming from a blue shipping container in the middle of the field, now illuminated by the fireworks.

A squeaky voice called out something over loud speakers, something about being a cheerleader, and being ugly.

I looked to Jack and we made eye contact. His face was screwed up in disgust.

'Is that Daphne and Celeste?' he asked me.

'Yeah I think so.'

The song continued, very loudly.

All of a sudden, while the lights of the fireworks slowly drifted to the ground, we heard popping noises, followed by the fizzing and whistling of more fireworks squealing into the air. The explosions when they reached their desired height were incredible. The sky was filled with a kaleidoscope of different colours.

'What is happening?' Shannon muttered.

The top half of a person suddenly popped out of the top of the shipping container, maybe to watch the fireworks.

I pointed the person out to everybody, and we all just watched the bizarre spectacle. After a few moments, the person seemed to notice our bus, and started to wave, before banging on the top of the container. Some of us actually waved back.

That was when the zombies appeared. They were running from the direction Canada was supposed to be, obviously drawn to the fireworks and horrific music.

I looked back at the container, where the person was vigorously gesturing for us to come to him. I realised we didn't have time to debate this, so I turned the engine back on and spun the steering wheel fully to the right.

When we drove over the first bump, I called out for everyone to hold onto something. It was a very bumpy ride. The field was full of peaks and troughs.

The occasional zombie started to thud into the side of the bus. The person on top of the container was still waving, but it was more like a side to side motion rather than a come to me gesture.

Is he saying here I am? Or telling us to stop?

Fuck knows.

My stomach lurched as the front of the bus suddenly dropped, coming to an uncomfortable and abrupt stop. My forehead very painfully slammed into the steering wheel. Panicked screams cried out from behind me.

I slowly lifted my all too damaged face, and put the bus into reverse. I very gently pressed on the accelerator, trying to bump us out of the ditch I'd fucking stupidly driven us into. We rocked backwards and forwards, but the bus wasn't budging.

'We're stuck Chris,' Shannon shouted over the cacophony of noise. The revving bus engine, the fireworks, and fucking Daphne and Celeste were overwhelming. 'Everybody,' she called out. 'We're getting off the bus and running to that container.' She pointed over to the pale blue and battered shipping container, looking very much out of place in the field.

It was probably about forty or fifty feet away from us. Dark shapes sprinted across the grass, each one casting multiple shadows from the lights of the fireworks.

'We have to go now,' Shannon ordered. 'No bags, only weapons. Let's go.' She looked at me, and then nodded towards the button to open the front doors.

I picked up the Brooklyn Smasher, and felt for my axe tucked into my belt. I had one last look at everyone, then out at the very strange shadows moving around in front us, and slammed my fist into the button.

Gee was out first, firing his crossbow before he'd even left the bus. Everyone else was following him out.

I was trapped in the driver's seat, and letting everyone pass me, meaning I'd be getting off last.

Fuck's sake.

Pete was the last person to pass by me, we gave each other a little nod and I followed him out, into absolute fucking chaos. I immediately swung my bat into the head of a charging zombie, before starting to run. Sandra was carrying one of the kids. I think Ali had another. I couldn't see who was carrying the blond boy.

Gee had positioned himself between everyone and the oncoming zombies. He wasn't even looking at the container, keeping his efforts entirely on stopping anything that got close to our group. He looked like he was slicing whole heads off with his huge knife. He was doing a fucking amazing job of protecting everyone, as usual.

I was so distracted by Gee's heroics that I wasn't paying attention to what I was doing. My foot caught on something, sending me stumbling to the floor. I managed to roll and was back up on my feet almost straight away, although I ended up running in the wrong direction. Before I had time to adjust my angle, a shape moved in front of me. I swung my bat upwards. It connected with, and obliterated a zombie's head. As I was bringing the Smasher back up, another blurred shape lurched towards me. I swiped at it, making contact with one of its knee caps. The leg snapped backwards in a very unnatural and sickening way, the zombie collapsing to the floor.

I quickly scanned the field for the easiest route through the scattering of monsters, lit up in reds, oranges, yellows and blues. Some of our group were already climbing up onto the roof of the container. I ran straight towards them, keeping the Smasher by my side. I shoulder barged a zombie out of the way, then another, and another, before body slamming one into the side of the container. It slowly and disgustingly slid down to the ground. Their lightweight and long dead bodies made it easy to push them out of the way.

Killing them is definitely getting easier.

Gee and Jack had their backs to the container, holding off the ever increasing threat of dead creatures. I spun around and slammed my bat overarm into the top of a zombies head.

Jack's face looked like he was in pain from swinging his big axe, but he seemed to be dealing with it. He didn't have much choice.

'Where did you go?' he asked me.

'Got a bit lost.'

He shot me the briefest of glances between swings of his axe. 'What?' he asked.

I swung my bat, very luckily hitting three zombies' heads with one blow. 'It's not really that important is it?' I yelled.

The space between us and the bus was almost full of zombies. If we'd waited just a couple of seconds we wouldn't have made it. I could see the bus actually rocking from side to side from the force of the zombies hitting it. We needed to move before we were overrun.

A scream echoed out from above me. I swung my bat into a zombie's face, before turning to see Sandra staring wild eyed at the bus.

'Steve! Max!' Ali shouted.

Who the fuck is Max?

I spun around. Looking over the zombies running for us, I could see a human shape carrying something. It was crawling up the front of the bus. A few seconds later, the shape made it onto the roof. The unmistakable figure of Steve, carrying the blond kid, slowly turned around to face us.

Oh, that's Max.

Sandra screamed out the word, 'No,' drawing it out for four or five painful seconds.

Jack grabbed my shoulder and pulled me back towards the container. 'We can't get back to them now! There are too many!' he shouted.

I dropped my bat and put my back against the container. I interlocked my fingers together and crouched down slightly. Jack placed his foot in my hands and I heaved him up so he could catch the edge of the container.

I stepped away and punched an oncoming zombie in the face, and then elbowed another in the side of the head. Immediately after picking up my bat, Gee wrenched it out of my hands, using it to decapitate a zombie, splattering us both with its innards. 'Go up now Chris!' he ordered.

I turned back around to face the container, narrowly avoiding a charging zombie, but only because Gee stepped between us and took it out with my bat. I ran and jumped at the container, placing the sole of my right foot on its blue metal wall and trying to launch myself as high as possible. It wasn't going to be enough.

Ali and Shannon caught my outstretched hands and started pulling me up. I glanced to my left to make sure Jack was okay, he was almost on the roof, being dragged up by Michael and Pete. Sandra and Theo were staring at the bus, screaming at Steve.

Once I was up, I spun around on my belly, shouting, 'Hurry the fuck up Gee!'

Gee's crossbow was on the floor by his feet. He was swinging my bat from side to side, taking out four or five creatures with each swing. Most of them seemed to be obsessed with the fireworks, but there were still plenty coming for him.

There's no fucking way he's gonna have time to make it up here before they take chunks out of him.

I was desperately trying to think of a solution, when he suddenly spun around, threw my bat at us, and hurled himself towards me.

Fucking hell. This is going to hurt.

Gee's right hand somehow found mine, and I held on. At the same time there was a loud thud next to me, as Jack slammed into the container, grabbing Gee's other hand. I couldn't move at all, let alone try and pull him up.

'Help us pull him up,' Jack pleaded.

I felt at least two pairs of hands on my arms, and as one, we all heaved Gee up onto the roof. Michael and Ali stamped on, and then kicked the three zombies that were clinging onto Gee's legs, eventually forcing them back into the gathering swarm below us.

I clambered to my feet as the Daphne and Celeste song was replaced by the Spice Girls, singing Wannabe. It was blaring out through the hidden loud speakers.

'Why the fuck is that playing?' I whispered.

'Don't move! Just stay there!' Pete called out.

'I can't!' Steve shouted back.

'Don't move!' Pete repeated.

The bus wasn't level. Because I'd crashed us into a ditch, the front end was lower than the back, and it was angled to the left. It was being jostled around whenever more zombies joined the crowds around the right side of the bus. It seemed to be leaning more by the second.

Steve looked like he was struggling to keep his feet. Max was clinging onto him, his face pressing into Steve's neck. Steve's mouth was moving, probably trying to reassure the boy.

The field below us was now filled with the dead, and more were coming, all still illuminated by the seemingly endless fireworks.

'What should I do?' Steve shrieked.

I looked at Jack, and then at Shannon and Michael. They stared back at me, desperation in their eyes. We had nothing.

'Stay real still!' Ali shouted. 'Don't move and keep quiet. They'll move on eventually.'

There was a loud scraping noise from under the bus. Steve momentarily fell to one knee, before regaining his balance and standing back up. A few seconds later the bus violently shifted beneath him, the back end rising slightly. He immediately fell back down to land on both knees. He lifted his face to stare back at us, mouthing the words, 'Help me.'

'Keep low!' Pete shouted. 'Lie down.'

There were several sharp intakes of air as the bus started to dramatically lean to the left. Steve placed his right hand down on the roof to steady himself. A few moments later, the bus leaned back to the right and stopped moving.

'What can we do?' Shannon pleaded. 'Anybody? We need ideas.'

Steve very slowly got back to his feet. He gently prised the boy's arms from around his neck, and lifted him high above his head.

What the fuck is he doing?

Even over the hissing, the Spice Girls and the fireworks, we could hear both Max and Steve, sobbing loudly.

'What is he doing?' Pete asked.

'No fucking idea,' I replied.

'I'm coming!' Steve shouted, and stepped towards the front of the bus.

'You fucking what?' I said.

'No!' Sandra screamed, followed by the rest of her family all echoing the 'No.'

Steve moved closer to the edge, and the clawing hands of the dead. More and more zombies were making their way up the front of the bus. Because it was in the ditch, the roof was easier to get to from that end. Steve stepped forward and kicked one in the head. It toppled back into the crowds.

My hand fell to the holster at my hip, resting on my gun.

'Guns. Who has a gun,' I asked, pulling mine out of the holster.

Sandra, Michael, Jack and Shannon all pulled out hand guns, the rifles all left on the bus.

'Who is a better shot than me?' I quickly asked. Gee took the gun out of my hand. Ali leaned over and took Jack's, he didn't protest.

'Aim for the ones on the front of the bus,' Ali said. 'And please be careful.'

Before the guns started firing, I just managed to shout, 'Wait two seconds Steve.' He can't have heard me, as he just carried on.

The gunfire started, dropping the zombies closest to the front of the bus, and the ones climbing up. Some of the bullets pinged off the snow plough.

'Careful!' Sandra shouted.

Steve, with the boy still held aloft, stepped down onto the bonnet, using the fallen dead bodies almost as a staircase. He paused and looked to us, tears filled his eyes. He'd reached the point where he would have to jump down to the ground. It was only a couple of feet, but he was jumping into a swarm of zombies. There was a mass of hands banging and clawing at the bus in front of him.

I could only imagine how he was feeling.

There was one more barrage of gunfire, all aimed at the area directly in front of Steve. It hardly made a difference. The newly formed spaces were immediately filled with more zombies.

Shannon dropped to her knees and started banging her gun on the container. We all followed suit, banging whatever we could to make as much noise as possible. It did draw the zombies' attention towards us, but only the ones between us and the bus, and they were already occupied by the fireworks. It wasn't making any difference to the ones trying to get to Steve.

Along with several very audible gasps from the roof of the container, he did it, he did the unimaginable. Steve stepped off the edge, and into the dead.

He fell into zombies, his weight moving them out of his way. When he hit the ground he must have bent his knees slightly, or not landed on level ground, because the boy came precariously close to the zombies reaching hands. Like animals, they pounced on Steve, their hands clawing at him, and mouths biting into his torso. He immediately started screaming. Almost as loud were Max's cries of terror. The sound was almost unbearable.

On the container, there were cries that sounded almost as full of pain as Steve's. I didn't look to see who it was. I just kept my eyes on Steve, and willed him on.

He was slowly moving through them, too fucking slowly. Steve was a tall guy, almost as tall as Gee, so at least they weren't biting his neck and head. Ten agonisingly long seconds later, and he'd only travelled a quarter of the distance.

'Close your eyes Max,' Sandra called out between gasping sobs.

Steve's screams were horrific, like nothing I'd ever heard before.

'Come on Steve!' I half heartedly shouted. I couldn't see him making it much further.

I'm definitely turning away when they get the young boy.

The rest of the group joined in with my shouts, trying to encourage him as best as we could.

His arms didn't looked they'd weakened at all. The kid was still high above him and the zombies' hands. Steve's face was contorted in pain, and tears coursed down his cheeks. He was now silent though. I had no idea if that was good or bad, but I guessed it was bad. His silence meant they at least weren't all crowding around him. Some were staring upwards, watching the fireworks.

Hopefully that meant he wasn't hitting as much resistance.

Theo was also sobbing, his breathing sounding erratic.

When Steve was about ten feet away, Gee said to me, 'Chris, get on back.'

'You what?' I asked, shaking my head and looking around. 'Get on my back? Why?'

'Get on floor. Lay on back. Hang on edge. We hold you,' he rapidly replied.

Lay on back and hang on edge. What the fuck does that mean? Hang on the edge?

Oh right, I think I know what he means.

Fucking brilliant.

I quickly glanced around at everyone. Jack, Gee, Michael and Shannon all stared back at me.

What am I gonna do? I can't say no can I? Just look at what Steve is doing for that kid. Fucking Steve.

I got down on the floor and crawled to the edge, as close to where Steve would hopefully be, when and if he could ever reach us. I turned over and stretched out on my back. Gee and Jack put all of their combined weight down on my shins.

I fucking hate the zombie apocalypse.

'Stiffen up Chris!' Jack shouted.

I lifted my head to look back at him, really wanting to make an erection joke. 'What the fuck are we doing?' I asked.

Gee just stared back at me. Jack nodded, fear in his wide eyes.

'Ready?' Gee called out.

No, I'm really fucking not ready.

'Yeah go on then,' I muttered.

They started to slowly push me. I was soon edging out and over the fucking zombies.

Fucking hell. I should have done a lot more core strength exercises.

Only my legs below my knees were resting on the container, held down by Gee and Jack. The rest of me was hanging above the dead. My knees gave way slightly, only for a split second, but enough so my head lowered to brush against the reaching dead hands. I quickly straightened up as much as I could. My stomach and thigh muscles felt like they were trying to tear their way out through my skin.

Fuck, fuck, fuck, fucketty fuck. Hurry the fuck up Steve. I can't hold out for much longer.

I arched my neck and looked back towards Steve. Our eyes met, and I immediately knew he wasn't going to make it. From what I could see of his body through the zombies tearing and biting him, he was a mess, a terrible bloody mess. Large sections of him were missing and there was blood everywhere, splattered up onto his neck and face. I had to swallow back the impulse to be sick, my eyes were glistening at the horrific sight.

How the actual fuck is he still conscious?

He mouthed the words, 'I'm sorry.'

'No Steve!' I shouted, stretching my arms out towards him. 'Just one more push and that's it.'

He was only a couple of feet away. He could probably fall forwards and pass me the boy.

'Come on mate,' I shouted. 'You can do it. You need to pass me Max.'

I saw the fight reappear in Steve's eyes. With a roar I never imagined could come out of someone so close to death, he reached forwards and placed the kid in my hands.

As easy as fucking that.

However, the extra weight of the boy was a bit of a shock. I wasn't expecting it.

Because I'm a fucking idiot.

I dropped down into the swarm. The moment I felt the dead beneath me, I was dragged over the top of them, repeatedly banging the back of my head on the hard skulls of the zombies. My arse and back were slammed into the edge of the container before I was heaved up onto the roof. I had at least managed to keep Max away from the grasping hands and biting teeth.

'Steven!' Pete was shouting. 'Get up. Get back up. Please Steve!'

'Please Steve!' Theo cried out.

I turned around after Sandra had taken Max from my hands. Steve was being dragged under by the swarm. His arms were still raised, and his eyes stared upwards, like he was watching the fireworks. I couldn't hear if he was making any noise over the shouts and screams coming from the people around me. After climbing to my feet, Gee patted me on the back and handed me my baseball bat. I looked down at the blood splattered Smasher in my hands, and then gazed at the scene around us. The Rodriguez family were all crouched down at the edge of the container, their hands outstretched towards the place Steve had once been standing.

The loudest so far of the fireworks exploded very close to us, showering the container with multi-coloured sparks, causing everyone to flinch and duck down.

Scary Spice and Mel B were belting out their part of Wannabe.

Jack was suddenly forced to take two steps to his left, as a square hatch in the roof of the container was pushed upwards. When it was opened about six inches a metal chain was pulled taught, meaning the hatch couldn't be opened any further. The top half of a person's head filled the space below. Two eyes darted around, trying to look at us all.

'Place your guns down on the roof,' the container dweller ordered. 'If you keep your guns, you're not coming in. If you threaten me with the guns, you're not coming in. If you shoot me, you're definitely not coming in.'

Three metallic clangs rang out amongst the sound of fireworks as Gee, Michael and Shannon dropped their guns onto the roof.

Wannabe finished and Barbie Girl, by Aqua started playing.

I looked to Jack and said, 'We need to get in this container. It might be soundproofed.'

The Rodriguez family were still staring into the zombie swarm, maybe willing Steve to stand back up.

'No guns!' the container man shouted.

Looking around at Jack, Michael, Shannon and Gee, I hoped one of them would tell the Rodriguez's we had to go. It looked like nobody was willing to say anything, so I stepped forward and opened my mouth to speak. Thankfully, Ali stopped me by standing up. She dropped her gun to the roof, and said, 'Come on, we need to go.'

None of her family members responded.

'Sandra, Pete, Theo,' she said. 'Steve is gone. We need to get the kids to safety.'

The mention of the kids seemed to get through to Sandra. She stood up and angrily threw her gun into the zombies below us.

'Pete, you look after Seth,' she said, wiping her face and gently guiding her son towards Pete. 'Theo, you've got Jonah. I've got Max. Alison is right. We need to take care of the children.'

With that, Pete and Theo slowly stood up and turned to face Sandra.

'Right,' Shannon said to the roof hatch. 'That's all of our guns.'

'If you're concealing we'll find it,' the voice from under the hatch called out. 'Count to ten before opening the hatch, then climb down.'

The head dropped out of sight, and the hatch was closed.

One of the boys started to count, beginning at one.

'Good boy Jonah,' Sandra said, smiling down at her son, tears staining her face.

'What do you think?' Shannon asked Michael.

'Not much choice,' he replied, gesturing to the masses of zombies surrounding us.

'Seven...eight...nine...ten,' Jonah finished.

'Well,' Jack whispered to me. 'Age before beauty. Down you go.'

I bent over and managed to prise the hatch up using my fingertips. The guy inside must have unhooked the chain, because it opened all the way and came to rest on the roof. I peered into the dimly lit container. I could hear some kind of engine rattling away from inside. Flickering lights came from within, like candle light.

Anything's better than staying out here and listening to Barbie Girl.

I placed my hands on either side of the hatch, and lowered my legs in, eventually finding the metal rungs of a ladder. After grabbing my baseball bat, I climbed down into the container. Half way down I noticed a large rectangular hole in the floor. Inside the hole were wooden boards lying on the bottom. My feet reached the floor and I turned around.

Chapter 7: Zombies Don't Hide

Orange flickering lights illuminated two men sat on plastic chairs. The one on the left was pointing a rifle at me. The guy on the right shone a torch towards the ground at my feet. A small wooden coffee table sat in front of them, three large candles burned brightly in the middle of the table. A chess board sat on the edge of the table closest to the two men, the positions of the pieces showing we had disturbed their game. The music from outside was at least muffled by the generator in the back corner, a pipe ran from the back of it into a hole high up on the wall of the container.

'Step over to your right so Martin here can do a quick body search,' the guy with the rifle said.

Martin stood up and gestured for me to step towards him. I moved closer and the small, bizarrely well groomed man gave me a very brisk, but thorough frisking.

'Stand over there fella,' Martin said to me, pointing to the wall closest to us.

'I'm okay with the axe and the baseball bat then?' I asked him.

'Just looking for guns.' He looked over my shoulder. 'You, you're next.'

I turned to see Jack had joined me. He then stood in front of Martin and was searched.

One by one, everyone climbed down and stepped in front of Martin. All the while the other guy sat on his little plastic chair, instructing the newcomers, and keeping his rifle aimed at us all.

Once everyone was in and searched, we were told to line up against the wall, facing Martin and his rifle wielding friend.

The guy with the rifle spoke up, 'I'm Elliot. This is Martin.' He pointed his thumb at Martin, now sat next to him again.

'Hi Elliot,' Shannon said angrily. 'Care to explain what the fuck all this is?'

Jack and I both stared at her. I'd never seen Shannon talk like that before. Her tone caught me by surprise.

'This,' Elliot said, ignoring Shannon's aggression, and gesturing with an open hand to our surroundings, 'Is the entrance to one of the refugee camps.'

'The what camps?' Jack asked.

'Refugee camps,' Elliot replied. 'Where us, the refugees presently live.'

'Nine adults and three kids,' Martin remarked. 'We ain't had this many come in for a while. We thought that was it.'

'What the fuck are you on about?' I asked.

Michael stepped forward, his hands in front of him in a calming gesture. 'Please, could you explain everything to us? What is happening at the border?'

'The border is now a wall,' Elliot said, with a look of resignation on his face. 'Then there is a couple hundred feet of no man's land. Then we've got a fence, with the camp, or Blaine as it was once called, on the other side of that. Then you've got two more fences keeping the dead out.'

'So the Canadians aren't letting us in?' Shannon asked.

'Yeah they are,' Elliot replied. 'But only a few hundred a week, at least that many from our camp.'

'How many camps are there?' Jack asked.

Elliot tilted his head slightly. 'Don't know.'

'And there is a wall along the entire border?' Michael asked.

Elliot paused and looked up to the ceiling. 'Don't know for sure, but I think probably not.'

'How many people are in the camp?' Shannon asked. 'How do you decide who crosses into Canada? Why are we in a shipping container in the middle of a field?'

Before Elliot could answer, I added, 'And why are you setting off fireworks? Who is actually setting them off, and why are you playing shit nineties music?'

Again, Elliot paused for a few moments. 'First question, don't know. Second question, I don't decide. You get a number when you enter the camp. Third question, like I said before, this is the entrance to our camp. There are too many of the dead at the outer fence. And what were your questions?' he asked, looking at me. 'Ah yes,' he said, remembering. 'Martin usually sets the fireworks off. We have those big display packs, and stagger them so they go off at different times. The fireworks, and in my opinion, the very enjoyable nineties music, are distractions for the Fencers and Zombie Patrol. Gives them time to shore up the outer fence and kill the zombies that made it through to the inner fence.'

I raised my hand up into the air. 'I forgot what Shannon's questions were.'

'Not to worry,' Elliot said, rising to his feet. 'That hole over there,' he said, pointing to the hole with the wooden floor I'd noticed earlier, 'Is the tunnel that leads to the camp. Well actually, it leads to Blaine High School, where you'll spend twenty four hours. Just to make sure you're not one of the running dead.'

I looked into the dark hole. 'You fucking what?' I muttered.

'After twenty four hours,' Elliot continued, ignoring me. 'If you're still breathing and talking like a normal human being, you'll enter the camp and get your number and job.'

'Number and job? Gee asked. 'What is this shit?'

'Don't worry big guy,' Elliot said. 'The sheriff will explain it better than me. We just play the music, set off the fireworks, and shepherd refugees through the tunnel.' He stepped towards the tunnel entrance before turning back to us. 'So, who wants to go first? It's two at a time.' He looked down at the kids and grinned. 'Maybe two and a half,' he added.

'Why aren't you two wearing masks if you need a quarantine period?' Shannon asked them.

'Me and my good friend Martin here,' Elliot said, slapping Martin on the back. His good friend didn't look too happy with the physical contact. 'We don't think the virus is around anymore. But it's not up to us if we have a quarantine policy or not.'

Our group all exchanged glances in silence. The Rodriguez family definitely looked in shock. Their glassy eyes seemed to look right through me.

'I'll go last,' I said. 'Had a bad experience in a hole. Just need to psyche myself up.'

'Okay. Chris and I go last,' Jack said.

Michael and Shannon volunteered to go first. Nobody else seemed ready to make any decisions.

'Lay on your backs, side by side,' Martin said. 'Then one of you pulls on this rope.' He leaned into the hole and grabbed a rope lying on the wooden boards.

'It's a straight line all the way,' Elliot added. 'The trolley is on tracks so it's real easy.'

'Is it safe?' Shannon asked, bending down on her hands and knees at the edge of the hole, trying to look into the tunnel.

'No accidents yet,' Elliot replied. 'It's a former sewage pipe so it does stink.'

'Great,' I said. 'Fucking Shawshank Redemption.'

'There ain't no shit to crawl through,' Martin said. 'All been cleared out.'

Elliot shook his head. 'Can't get rid of the stink though.'

'Excellent,' Michael said, as he stepped down onto the trolley. 'How long does it take?'

'It's about two miles, so if–,' Martin started.

'Two fucking miles?' I exclaimed.

'Don't worry. You can pick up a fair bit of speed down there. Me and Elliot can do it in twenty minutes.'

'Holy fucking shit,' I said, before turning to pace up and down.

Fucking hell. What if I have a panic attack down there? There will be nowhere to escape to.

Martin produced a radio from his hip and brought it up to his mouth. 'Martin to base,' he said.

Shannon stepped down and laid next to her husband on the wooden trolley. 'Wish us luck,' she said. 'See you on the other side.'

'Good luck,' Jack said.

'Yeah,' I almost squealed. 'Good fucking luck.'

Martin's radio crackled into life. 'Go ahead Martin.'

'Two coming through,' Martin replied. 'Ten more to follow.'

'Okay. Thanks Martin,' the voice over the radio said.

'Don't worry Chris,' Shannon said. 'You'll be fine.'

Michael pulled on the rope, rolling them into the tunnel and out of sight.

'Fuck's sake,' I whispered.

Their feet disappearing into the darkness sent a shiver of fear through me. I hadn't realised the night in the hole under the sofa would have had such an effect on me.

I heard Jack speaking. 'Have you had many British people come through here?'

I turned to see him facing Elliot and Martin.

'Erm…yeah, we've had people of all nationalities,' Elliot replied.

'I'm looking for my wife,' Jack said, suddenly sounding anxious, his eyes darting between Elliot and Martin. 'She's called Beth Tillman, white, about five foot seven, blue eyes, light brown hair down to about here.' He placed his hand just below his chin.

Elliot raised his hands. 'Whoa there fella. For a start, me and Martin don't do every shift out here, and also, do you know how many people have entered the camp in the last two weeks?'

'Well…no,' Jack answered.

Elliot hesitated. 'Well, neither do I, but it's a lot. I met a fella the other day and his number was thirty seven thousand and something.'

'Fuck,' Jack whispered.

'Once you get through to the other side, there are lists and lists of everyone that has come in,' Elliot said, obviously trying to placate Jack. 'If you ask the sheriff once you're over there, he might be able to help you.'

Jack turned to look at me. 'I can't stay here and wait,' he said. 'Do you mind if I go next?'

Bollocks. I'm not ready for this.

'I stay with Chris to end,' Gee offered.

Fucking hell. Gee might get stuck down there. I'd be well and truly fucked then.

'Thanks Gee,' I said. 'Probably best I get it over and done with. Face my fears and all that shit. That's as long as nobody else minds?' I directed this final bit to the group.

A few waves of hands meant we were going next.

Bollocks.

Thirty minutes later and I was lying on the trolley in the hole, my baseball bat and Jack's axe separating us. Bringing the empty trolley back had taken less than ten minutes. I'd been expecting, and hoping, for a bit more time.

Out of the corner of my eye I saw Jack turn his head to face me.

'Do you want to pull or shall I?' he asked.

'Erm...you, if you want.'

'Okay. See you all soon,' Jack said, as he pulled on the rope. The wheels squeaked as the trolley started to roll, and our heads entered the tunnel.

'It will be okay Chris,' Gee called out.

'Yep, cheers,' I just about managed to say.

It only took a few seconds until we were far enough away from the candle light in the container to make it pitch black. I'd been worried about being in a small space again. I hadn't taken into consideration the lack of light.

'I hadn't thought about it being this dark,' I said.

'What were you expecting? For the whole tunnel to be lit up?'

'Nope, just hadn't thought about it. Talk to me about something though please. Otherwise the smell of shit is gonna get a lot stronger.'

'I really don't think that is possible,' Jack said.

Fuck's sake. We're going really fucking slowly.

'Actually Jacqueline, on second thoughts, I'll pull the rope if you want?'

'I'm doing it now. I'm just getting into a rhythm.'

'A really fucking slow rhythm,' I muttered.

'Fuck off. I'll get quicker. We've only just set off.'

'I honestly don't mind doing it,' I offered.

'I'm doing the fucking rope pulling!' he shouted, his voice echoing back to us.

'Okay, okay. You can fucking do it.'

At least that argument had momentarily taken my mind off feeling like the tunnel was closing in around us. I didn't dare move my hands in case they would touch the ceiling. If the space was indeed that small, my head would probably explode. My thoughts were getting too loud again, making it impossible to think of anything rational. I could almost feel my nose scraping against the roof.

Calm down Chris.

I tried to take in slow, deep breaths.

I wanted to talk but I couldn't swallow all of a sudden. With a very painful gulp, I managed to get down whatever was making me mute. 'I'm starting to freak out Jack. Talk to me.'

'Really?'

'Yes. Talk about something, anything.'

'Erm...I don't know. What about Steve dying like that? That was very dramatic wasn't it?'

I couldn't stop myself from laughing. 'Yeah, I suppose you could say that.'

'Do you think he thought he was going to make it?' Jack asked. 'Or did he know he was sacrificing himself for Max.'

'Jesus. Dunno. No, I don't think he thought he was gonna survive that. He wasn't the brightest spark but he must have known.'

'Well, either way, that was the bravest thing I've ever seen,' Jack said.

'Yep, I honestly can't believe he did that. It was fucking mental. Horrible and mental.'

'What else could we have done though?' Jack asked. 'It was only a matter of time before the zombies got to him, or he fell off the bus.'

'Yeah I know. Not sure what I would have done if I was in his place. What actually happened after he left the bus? He got off before me.'

'Don't know,' Jack said. 'I think he had Max the whole time, so I don't know if the kid ran off or something.'

'How are your arms?' I asked. 'Do you want me to take over yet?'

'They're fine, and no I don't. You don't think Steve thought he would survive all the bites because we told him about Shannon surviving her bite?' Jack asked.

'Nah, he didn't do it because of what we told him. He must have known he'd be eaten alive.'

Fucking hell. That was a horrible to say about somebody I kind of knew.

A shiver ran down my spine. I wasn't sure if it was because of the cold down here, or from talking about Steve's death. Probably a bit of both. My heart was still working overtime, but at least my head was starting to clear slightly.

'In the last couple of weeks, Pete and Theo have lost their mother, father and brother,' I said. 'Not good is it?'

'Slight understatement, but yes, not good at all.'

'All in very horrific circumstances as well.'

'Did their mother die from the virus?' Jack asked.

'Nope, eaten by zombies.'

'They did well to all survive the initial outbreak,' Jack said. 'I'm still amazed we did.'

'I think we survived it because we were on holiday, so we weren't interacting with lots of other people. If you'd have been at home you would probably have died.'

Fuck. It had already left my mouth by the time I knew what I was saying. Fuck, fuck, fuck. Chris, you absolute twat.

A few moments of silence passed. All I could hear was the sound of Jack's hands moving up and down the rope.

'Sorry mate. I didn't realise what I was saying. I meant if you'd have been at work, with lots of other people. I'm sure she'll be fine.'

Jack took in a deep breath and slowly released it. 'Don't worry about it. Beth doesn't really work does she? And she doesn't have many friends over here. She made it to Sarah and Roy's, and they left

Mountain View to get up here, so those three definitely didn't catch the initial virus. She's going to be in this camp, and after a quick look through the list to confirm, I can go and find her.'

'Yep, she will be.'

I really fucking hope she is.

'When did Gilberto die?' Jack asked. 'It feels like it was a week ago.'

Sleeping during the day and being awake all night was messing with my internal clock, and Jack's by the sound of it.

'I think it was today?' I replied. 'No, it was yesterday.'

After a few moments of silence, I asked, 'Am I becoming a bit blasé about people dying, because it's happening all over the place? Or am I just a horrible twat?'

'Do you seriously want me to answer?'

'Okay, maybe you weren't the best person to ask that.'

The sound of hands pulling on rope continued to faintly echo in the darkness.

'Hopefully we're in shock,' Jack eventually said. 'Otherwise we are just horrible twats.'

'Ali and her family are gonna be devastated,' I said. 'How do you get over seeing a family member die like that?'

'They have to carry on. What else can they do?'

'We've only just met these people,' I said. 'I'm sure we'd be more upset if they were our friends or family.'

'Or if your girlfriend died. You know? Ali.'

'Yeah well done, I get it. Don't start that shit again. You'd be upset if your new parents died.'

'Michael and Shannon? I think they're younger than me.'

'Fuck off.'

'Yeah, I think they're both the same age as each other, thirty one, maybe thirty two.'

'Fucking hell,' I said. 'I better not be the oldest one in the group. Gee must be older than me?'

'He's only twenty nine.'

I snapped around my head to look in his direction. In the darkness, I could only see a slightly darker shape next to me. 'No he fucking isn't.'

He laughed. 'Nah, I don't know really. He must be in his forties. Even if you are the oldest, I wouldn't worry, nobody will expect you to take charge.'

'Take charge,' I scoffed. 'What is this? The army? I'm more than happy for Shannon to take the lead. It's not that anyway. Just don't want to be the oldest, makes me feel old.'

The darkness was impenetrable. I honestly thought my eyes would have grown accustomed, but I might as well have had my eyes closed.

'Jack?'

'Yes Chris.'

'If Beth isn't in this camp, it doesn't mean she isn't already in Canada, or in another camp. There must be other camps.'

'They'd have headed for here. The most direct route to Canada would take them through here.'

'Yeah I know, but look at the Rodriguez's. Their path was blocked loads of times.'

'We came the same way as Beth. She would have followed the same route we've just travelled from Mountain View.'

'Over a week ago though, things might have changed in that time. Anyway, it doesn't matter. I'm just telling you not to give up if she's not in this camp.'

'Yes I know,' Jack said.

It turned out we'd been going faster than I'd thought. When we reached the end, Michael leaned in to take my hand, saying, 'That was quick, think you may have beaten Elliot and Martin's time.'

'Don't care,' I spluttered. 'Just get me away from this tunnel.'

Michael pulled me out. I threw my baseball bat to the ground and jogged around them in circles. The cold air on my skin, and in my mouth was the best sensation I'd ever felt.

'Base to Martin. Ready to go back,' a voice from behind me said.

I stopped jogging around and stood still. With my eyes closed I lifted my face up to the sky and took in a deep breath. That was when I realised I could still hear the fireworks going off, just two miles away.

I slowly released the breath. 'Oh my fucking god. That was horrible.'

'It wasn't too bad,' Shannon said.

'Nope, fucking horrible,' I replied.

'Are you the sheriff?' Jack was asking.

'Yes I am. Sheriff McCallany,' the voice that had crackled out of Martin's radio said.

Jack was standing at a chain link fence topped with barbed wire. Softly glowing light bulbs, I guessed solar powered, hung from the top of the fence. On the other side, standing a few feet away was a man who looked a lot like a sheriff. He had the gold badge to go with his uniform of varying shades of brown. Tired looking would be the best words to describe him. His eyes looked like they were trying to bury themselves into his stubble covered face.

I was disappointed he wasn't wearing a cowboy hat.

'Is there any chance I could have a look at the list of everyone that's entered the camp?' Jack asked.

The sheriff let out a short bark of a laugh. 'When you get out of quarantine.'

'Can I please look at it now?' Jack pleaded.

'The list has over forty thousand names in it. You don't have time to look through it now.'

'Okay,' Jack said. 'But I'm looking for my wife. She's British, she's–.'

'Let me stop you there,' the sheriff interrupted. 'In twenty four hours you can sit in my office over here.' He pointed to another shipping container behind him. 'Then you can look through the list. I'm more than happy to let you look through it.'

Jack's whole body slumped, making him look almost a foot smaller.

'At six o'clock tomorrow morning I'll let you out of the school.' Sheriff McCallany pointed over to the building to our left. 'You don't have to wait for the rest of your group to arrive, just make your way over there. You'll have beds and a bit of food. Don't worry, this is just a precaution. Better to be safe than sorry. I'm sure you understand.'

It was only then, as I looked over to the school, that I got a good look at my surroundings. Behind the fence and the sheriff, was a football pitch, which probably belonged to the school. Bigger and brighter lights illuminated the far side of the pitch. They looked like small floodlights, all shining in our direction. We were on one of six tennis courts, all surrounded by a high chain link fence. A corridor of fencing led from the tennis courts to the school.

I remembered Elliot saying there were two fences on this side of Blaine. 'Hey Sheriff,' I said. 'Where are we in relation to all the zombies that have been distracted by the fireworks?'

'We are currently between the inner and outer fences. The outer fence is about seven hundred and fifty feet that way.' He pointed behind me. 'We're kind of in the middle.'

'So we've got to spend the twenty four hours in no man's land?' I asked, not trying to hide my disbelief.

'Don't worry. The outer fence got fixed up this evening, and the school buildings are secure. You'll be safe. And what we call no man's land is actually between the border wall and our north fence.'

I looked around at the row of trees, the running track behind me, and the shitload of other dark shapes surrounding us. 'This isn't a big open space that can easily be cleared. It's a big open space with lots of places that zombies can hide.'

'Son,' the sheriff said. 'Zombies don't hide, but even if they did, these are the rules. If you don't do the quarantine, you can't come in.'

I raised my hands in surrender. 'Okay, fair enough. Just pointing out that I don't feel safe in your designated quarantine building.'

'Okay, thank you for your observations. Now, like I've already said to your two friends here,' he said, gesturing to Michael and Shannon. 'I'll try and answer any questions you have tomorrow. Right now I'm going to go and sit in my office, and watch out for the rest of your group from there. Just head for that door over there.' He pointed to a blue door in one of the school buildings, before turning and starting to walk away. 'There are beds and a little bit of food waiting for you.'

DAY SEVENTEEN

Chapter 8: One Step At A Time

Someone was making shushing noises, and then Sandra was telling someone to be quiet in case they woke everyone up.

Thanks Sandra. You woke me up.

On entering the school in the early hours of this morning, we'd found what looked like a former classroom. Two rows of bunkbeds now ran down two of the walls, opposite each other. In the middle of the room were four long tables, and more than enough chairs for us all. I'd counted fifty bunks. One hundred people sharing this space would have been a nightmare. Six portable toilets, much like the ones I'd used at festivals, sat outside in a row.

After the sheriff had retired to his office, we'd tried waiting for everyone else to arrive, but we were too tired. We knew that Ali, Sandra and Gee would take care of everyone, so we shuffled ourselves off to bed.

'Morning Chris,' Shannon said brightly. 'We have coffee, milk and bread.'

'The luxury,' I mumbled. 'Is it still morning?'

'Only just,' Shannon replied, glancing down at her watch.

Sleeping on a mattress had actually felt quite luxurious. Up until I was very rudely awoken by Sandra, I'd had a great sleep.

Still fully dressed, I got out of bed. I'd been too tired to do anything other than collapse onto a bottom bunk. I stumbled over to where Shannon, Michael and Gee sat around one of the tables.

Shannon stood up and stepped towards me. She leaned in so she was just a couple of inches from my face. The peak of her cap was almost touching my nose.

I was suddenly very aware that my breath would probably stink. 'Morning Shannon. What ya doing?'

'The band aids have fallen off your face,' she said. 'Just looking at my handiwork.'

'How does it look? Do I still look like I was splattered with someone's insides?'

She briefly screwed up her face, before reverting back to normal. 'No, it looks good. I'm very impressed with myself.'

'Good, so am I. Just glad you were there. If it had just been me and Jack, I'd have probably ended up leaving the bits in my face. I wouldn't have trusted Jack to do it.'

Shannon sat herself back down and picked up her coffee. 'When you get the chance, you should definitely get checked for Hepatitis and the rest.'

Gee leaned in once I'd sat down. 'Earlier I go for walk,' he whispered. 'I think we can escape.'

I looked at the walls and to the corners, expecting to see security cameras or some other kind of monitoring equipment.

'Why are you whispering?' I whispered back.

'They probably watch us,' Gee replied, a deadly serious expression on his face.

Michael sat back on his chair, a big grin on his face. 'Gee thinks we've been imprisoned and they're spying on us, in case we have some kind of valuable information.'

Gee sat up straight. 'I do not think that,' he said, his voice returning to its normal volume.

'I don't think we need to...' I paused and leaned in to whisper, 'Escape,' before sitting back up and speaking normally. 'We just have to sit tight and wait until the quarantine period is up.'

'I walk around here for hours,' Gee said. 'There is no sound of people. Where are thousands of people they talk of? Only sound is hissing of dead.'

'We're not in the camp,' I said. 'We're between the–.'

'In daylight you can see inner and outer fences from outside,' Gee interrupted. 'I only see two, maybe three people guarding inner fence. Not thousands of people.'

'Oh right,' I said, not really sure how to respond.

'Gee has got his conspiracy head on today, that's all,' Shannon said, placing a hand on Gee's arm. 'He's not going to do anything stupid until after the twenty four hours is up. After that, and if they're still keeping us locked up, I've given him permission to go crazy and smash the place up.'

'How are the Rodriguez's doing?' I asked.

'They're very quiet,' Michael replied.

A cup of coffee was suddenly slammed onto the table, startling everyone, apart from Gee I noticed, who sat there like a statue.

'Oops sorry,' Ali said, a grimace on her face. 'Didn't mean to bang it down that hard.' She sat down on one of the chairs. 'This place is weird. Apart from the hissing, it's really quiet out there.'

'Don't you start,' Michael said. 'You and Gee would make the perfect couple.'

Gee and Ali shared confused glances.

Standing up, I said, 'I'm gonna get a coffee. Then you can take me outside for some fresh air. I can see what you're all talking about then.' I quickly scanned the room, looking for Jack. He wasn't in there. 'Anyone seen Jack?'

'Yeah he's outside,' Ali said. 'He's been staring at that container in the soccer field for ages.'

'Football pitch,' I corrected.

With a wave of her hand, Ali replied, 'Whatever.'

I made myself a coffee, with two little pots of milk, the kind you find in a hotel room. There was also a large bowl full of plastic wrapped pastries. I moved the cheese ones aside, and grabbed a cinnamon Danish.

Ali and I made our way outside. At the end of the chain link corridor, I could see Jack in the fenced off tennis courts.

As we approached him, I said, 'Morning Jack, or afternoon.'

As he turned, I noticed the hissing sound coming from the south, still sounding like crickets.

'Hi,' Jack said. 'I'm just trying to get the sheriff's attention, to see if he'll let me look at the list.'

I peered through the fence. 'Have you seen him? Is he definitely in there?'

Jack turned again to gaze at the container. 'Nope, not seen anyone, apart from those few guys at the far fence,' he said, pointing towards the other end of the football pitch.

There was another fence similar to the one around the tennis courts, although it looked a lot sturdier. There were large concrete posts situated along the area that was visible to us, and the chain link fence seemed to be attached to the posts. I could see two men standing on what may have been platforms or small stages.

Ali placed a hand on my shoulder and spun me around. 'The zombies are just on the other side of that,' she said, pointing to the south.

Beyond the tennis courts was a running track, on the other side of that was some kind of playing field, and on the other side of that there was a wall of shit. That was the best way to describe it. It must have been about fifteen feet high, made up of corrugated metal mostly, but really anything the people could get their hands on by the look of it. There were large wooden sections, parts had been bricked up, and some of it looked like concrete breeze blocks.

'So that's the outer fence then?' I asked.

'Yep, doesn't look too secure, does it?' Jack said.

'Nope, looks like a bag of shite.'

The sun was shining but it was still a bit cold, Jack was even shivering.

'Come on then, let's get back inside,' I suggested. 'Just be patient Jack. Sheriff Hopper, or whatever he was called–.'

'McCallany,' Ali said.

'Yeah that's the one. He said he was more than happy for you to look at the list once we're out.'

With a small groan, Jack spun around and started towards the school. Ali and I exchanged a glance before I nodded towards Jack.

'Why can't we hear the people in the camp though?' Ali asked. 'It's literally just there.' She was pointing towards the camp.

'They'll be staying as quiet as possible,' Jack said, without turning back. 'So not to draw the attention of the zombies. They don't like noise around here.'

'It's not working,' Ali said.

Jack made an exaggerated shrug. 'I don't know. Maybe there'd be a lot more trying to get in if there was more noise.'

'See, what I tell you?' Gee said, as we walked inside. 'We are being held against our willies.'

'Nobody is holding my willy,' Michael said, laughing.

The kids found this especially funny, they were almost in hysterics.

'Held against our wills Gee,' Shannon said. 'And you're right. We are, but only until tomorrow.'

'That is what I said, willies,' Gee said, this time drawing out the word willies even more so, eliciting more high pitched laughter from the three young boys.

'Nope, you're saying willies Gee,' I said.

Seth, Jonah and even the very quiet Max started repeating the word willies, a couple of times actually doing very good impressions of Gee's thick Lithuanian accent.

'Boys,' Sandra scolded, albeit through a smile. 'Stop saying willies please.'

Sat on one of the bottom bunks near the kids, Theo actually let out a chuckle, before glancing at his older brother and stopping himself. Pete looked back at him, giving him a small smile and a nod.

Steve's blood splattered face suddenly flashed through my mind, the expression he was making as he handed me Max. He'd looked like he'd been resigned to his fate, almost relieved it was all over after saving the boy.

A shiver ran through my entire body.

Michael was pointing towards the only window in the room. 'Erm…everyone. I just saw two people walking around out there.'

Jack was first up onto his feet, his chair skidding away from him. I followed him up and looked out through the wire mesh fixed to the outside of the window. Two women were disappearing into the hole we'd all clambered out of in the early hours of the morning.

Shannon shrugged her shoulders. 'Shift change?'

About an hour later, Elliot and Martin pulled themselves out of the hole.

Not long after we'd seen the two women disappear, I wandered outside to wait. Jack, Shannon, Michael and Ali soon joined me.

Upon seeing us, Elliot waved and told us to stay near to the school, and not to enter the tennis courts. They both walked over to us and stopped a few feet away.

Elliot hooked a thumb towards the sheriff's shipping container. 'Don't want him seeing us get too close while you're in quarantine. Otherwise he'll make us join you. So let's just keep it at this distance. Okay?'

Ali pointed at Martin. 'But you frisked us this morning.'

Elliot smiled and held his hands up. 'True, but the sheriff doesn't know we weren't wearing the full protective clothing, the gloves and the masks. Does he?' He gave the container a furtive glance. 'Let's keep that between us yeah?' he said, tapping the side of his nose with his finger.

'So is that your shift over then?' Michael asked.

'Yeah. We're heading to the pub for a few,' Martin replied. 'It's over by the water. You should pay it a visit once you're settled into the camp. It's called Pea's Place, can't miss it.'

'How does all this work?' Shannon asked. 'I'm assuming money is no good?'

'Canadian dollars are still good for trading,' Elliot said, 'If you have any. The ATMs aren't working. We have to work for credits now.' He put his hand in his pocket and came out with a playing card between his thumb and forefinger. 'This is a credit now, believe it or not. This is how you get fed. Very hard to forge one of these.'

'What if I just found a pack of cards?' I asked.

'Then you've won the jackpot, and I'm your new best friend,' Martin said.

'What? Seriously?' I said. 'That's fucking ridiculous.'

Shit, my cards are in my bag, the bag I left on the bus.

Elliot showed me the queen of diamonds in his hand. 'It's gotta be signed by one of twelve people, who kind of run the camp.' He leaned in and winked. 'Hard to make a playing card, but quite easy to forge the signatures.'

'How do you buy beers then?' I asked. 'With the playing card system?'

Elliot screwed up his face. 'That's a bit more complicated. Trade, favours, information, Canadian dollars, if you have any.'

What the fuck does that mean? That's very helpful.

'Who are these twelve people?' Ali asked. 'Is it all policed by the sheriff?'

Elliot laughed. 'It's not policed at all, well, I suppose it's kind of self-policed. The sheriff is just in charge of people coming into the camp. He did have a lot more people working for him, when there were more refugees coming in.'

'The twelve people?' Ali reminded him.

'Yes. There are twelve work groups with twelve bosses. But like I said, the sheriff isn't the boss of anyone no more.' He put the playing card back into his pocket, and then lifted his hands up with his fingers and thumbs spread out. 'We've got the Fencers. Medical. Zombie Patrol. Erm...Caterers.' He was counting them off with his fingers as he said each one. 'Shepherding,' he said, pointing at himself, and then at Martin. 'Fishing. Plumbers, which is one of the most important jobs in here. Then there's Retail, Border Control, that's the sheriff, and then...there...is...Martin, what are the last two?' The thumb and forefinger on his right hand sprung back up.

'Scavengers and Cleaners,' Martin replied.

The thumb and finger curled back into Elliot's fist. 'And that's it,' he said.

'Why does the sheriff do it?' Jack asked. 'Surely he should be in the camp doing sheriff stuff? Where is he from?'

'He's from here, Blaine,' Elliot said. 'I think he only had a couple of deputies working for him before the fall. They probably got into Canada straight away, before the wall went up. He wouldn't be able to cope with the amount of people in there now. I think he's got some kind of deal with the Canadians. When you get out of here,' he said, pointing to the school behind us. 'He'll take all your details. Name, age, etc. He's not doing that for his own weird personal records. They asked him to do it, in exchange for something. Just what I think anyway.'

'And that's what Pea told you,' Martin said.

Elliot looked to his partner. 'He didn't tell me all of that, just some of it.'

'Why didn't he follow his deputies into Canada?' Shannon asked.

Elliot turned to gaze at the container. 'Waiting for somebody, wife, kid, parents, I don't know. He's the quiet type, doesn't like to divulge too much information about himself.'

Martin very loudly cleared his throat, causing Elliot to flinch and turn back to look at him.

'Beer,' Martin said under his breath.

Elliot smiled at us. 'Yes, so...we'll see you on the other side.'

Martin gave us a brief wave, before they both turned and headed towards the padlocked gate in the corner of the tennis courts. Martin murmured something into his radio as they walked. Just as they reached the gate, the door on the container swung open, and the sheriff emerged from inside.

'Hey, Sheriff McCallany,' Jack called out.

The sheriff quickly raised his finger to his lips, and mouthed the word, 'Quiet.' He then lowered his hand and tapped his watch with the same finger. 'As soon as you get out,' he softly said.

Jack looked at his watch and said, 'Shite,' before setting off towards the school.

Michael sighed and looked to his wife. 'Sounds like it might be like the wild west in there.'

'At least they've got different work groups organised,' she replied. 'It won't be complete chaos.'

We followed Jack and headed back inside.

'I hope there's more than one pub. One pub!' I exclaimed. 'Can't be one pub for all those people. It's gonna be fucking heaving.'

Ali laughed. 'That's your biggest worry at the moment?'

'Well, one of them.'

I suppose the right thing would be to ask her how she's doing.

'Hey Ali,' I called out to her back. She turned to look at me, stopping halfway to the door. I waited until Jack, Michael and Shannon had gone back inside. 'How are you all doing? The last couple of days have been fucking terrible.'

She raised her hands, saying, 'No. Stop right there please. Thanks for asking Chris, but just no. I'm not going to talk about it until me and my family are definitely safe. If I went over it all now, I think I would just crumble.'

'Okay, that's fair enough.'

Thank fuck for that.

'Thank you for asking though.'

'No problem.'

'You looking forward to going to the pub?' she asked. 'Even if it is going to be, what did you say, heaving?'

'Yeah, I wouldn't say no to a pint. How much will a beer cost? How many credits do you get per hour, at whatever job I might get? What if I don't get a job? Do I just starve to death?'

'All reasonable questions,' Ali replied, smiling. 'I have no idea.'

'They were rhetorical. I didn't actually expect you to know the answers.'

'We'll soon find out everything,' she said.

We had been sat in our room for what felt like days, when there was a knock on the door in the corner. I think we all must have tried the handle of that door in the time we'd been there. It must have been locked from the other side.

After a few seconds of just staring at each other, Michael walked over to the corner. 'Hello?' he timidly called out.

'It's McCallany. Please step away from the door. I'm just going to roll in your food and then leave you to it.'

Michael took three or four steps backwards. 'Okay, go ahead Sheriff.'

The sound of keys jangling and being inserted into the keyhole made everyone sit up in anticipation. The door slowly creaked open. An old fashioned dessert trolley rolled into the room on squeaky wheels. The sheriff appeared behind it, pushing the trolley through.

Once it had cleared the door, he stopped. 'Dinner is served ladies and gentlemen.' He suddenly pointed at Jack. 'No,' he said. 'Don't ask.'

I followed the sheriff's gaze to see Jack, his mouth open, as if he was about to speak.

'Bon appetit,' the sheriff said, before grabbing the door handle and pulling it closed. The keys jangled again as he locked it.

'What have you done to him?' I asked Jack.

Jack raised his palms to the ceiling. 'Nothing.'

'You must have done something,' Sandra said.

'I think it might be something to do with you shouting at his container this morning,' Ali said. 'Do you not think Jack?'

'I was just calling his name,' Jack replied. 'Just trying to get his attention. And there was more waving than shouting.'

'Fuck's sake Jack,' I said. 'He has to sleep as well. Best be careful. We don't know him. He might make it difficult for you to check the list if you piss him off.'

'Yeah, yeah, alright. They should have told us they don't like shouting around here at the very beginning,' Jack said, as he made his way to the food trolley.

'We've got fish and potatoes,' Michael said, as he leaned over the food. He took in a deep breath through his nose. 'Looks like tuna steaks. We'll have to slice the portions in half, but they smell delicious.'

It also tasted delicious. We all sat at one of the long tables in the middle of the room. Nobody was talking, all far too busy eating. I looked around at the paper plates in front of everyone, hoping that someone might be a vegetarian or a vegan, but there was very little fish left.

No chance of an extra portion.

'They wouldn't feed us this if we were their prisoners Gee,' Michael said.

Gee responded by turning the corners of mouth down and shrugging his shoulders, before placing a butter soaked potato into his mouth.

'What job do you think they'll give you Chris?' Ali asked.

'No idea. I've never been fishing. I reckon I could throw some scraps of metal at the outer fence. I'll probably be in the Zombie Patrol.'

Jack laughed. 'Why, because you're such a badass?'

'A badass? You're from Norwich Jack. You're not allowed to say that out loud. And no, not because I think I'm a badass. I can't do anything else. I doubt there's much call for a graphic designer around here.'

'You could make them some new signs,' Shannon suggested. 'Replace the ones leading to Blaine.'

'That's true,' I said.

'What did you do Jack?' Sandra asked.

'Tax law,' he quickly responded. 'Very boring. Honestly, too boring to talk about.'

Sandra actually perked up a bit. 'I was in law school before the kids came along. I was always planning to go back and finish at some point. Where did you work?'

Jack sipped on his glass of water. 'Google.'

Sandra's eyes lit up. 'Wow, Google. That must have been exciting?'

'Nope. It doesn't matter where you work when it comes to tax. I'm sure it was exciting for the creative people, but tax is tax.'

Michael laughed. 'You enjoyed it then?'

Jack shrugged. 'The money was very good, and I got to travel a bit. It obviously allowed me to move to America…for a while.'

Sandra turned her attention to Michael and Shannon. 'How about you two?'

A grin spread across my face, waiting to see everyone's reaction to Shannon explaining what she did for a living.

'High school math teacher,' Michael said, pointing at himself. He beamed at Shannon. 'And my wife is a much respected doctor of–.'

Shannon placed a hand on her husbands arm, interrupting him. 'When we get into the camp, maybe not mention I'm a doctor. People always immediately think medical and expect things from me, especially at the moment.'

Michael smiled back at his wife. 'Okay darling.'

Shannon looked to Sandra. 'I mostly did research, taught a little as well.'

'It's a lot more complicated than that,' I added.

'Gee, what job do you think they'll give you?' Jack asked him.

'Do not know,' he shrugged. 'I was janitor in building we live in here. Before, in Lithuania, I was in army.'

'Really?' I asked, but then thought about it for a couple of seconds. 'Actually that doesn't surprise me at all. How long were you in the army?'

'Twelve years. I go in when eighteen. It was how you say? Erm...when have to go in?'

'National service?' Jack offered.

Gee furrowed his brow. 'No, that is not it. When, at eighteen the government make you join army, just for one year, but I stay for twelve.'

'Yeah I think that is called national service,' I said.

Gee thought about it for a few moments, before saying, 'No, do not think so.'

'Whatever,' I said. 'What did you do in the army?'

'At the end I train new soldiers. I build my own house from being in army.'

'They taught you how to build a house?' Jack asked.

'No, army was shit. I steal all building supplies from army stores, and build house for my wife and...' He trailed off and lifted his drink to his mouth.

Again, I noticed Michael and Shannon exchange glances.

Maybe they know what happened to Gee's wife?

'Theo was going to graduate from high school this year,' Sandra said. 'How about you Pete? What do you do?'

Pete shot his cousin an annoyed glare. 'I'm taking some time out thank you Sandra. Just trying to work out my options. I guess most of those options have been taken away from me now.'

'What about you Ali?' I asked. 'Bounty hunter? Cop? Ninja?'

She smiled. 'Yes, I'm a ninja. Been doing that professionally for the last five years.' She performed a pretend karate chop on Max. He gave her a very adult looking, polite smile, and continued eating his food. 'I decided if people qualified for loans. More boring stuff, and completely uncalled for in the zombie apocalypse.'

'I'm sure people will still want loans,' Shannon said.

'I don't want to go back to it,' Ali sighed. 'Time for my new life I think.'

After we'd eaten, we loaded the trolley back up with our dirty dishes and left it by the locked door. It wasn't long before Sandra and Pete put the kids to bed. After being very politely shushed by Sandra for the third time, we decided to get an early night. The temperature outside had dropped, so nobody wanted to sit outside and talk anyway.

I was genuinely excited as I lay on my bottom bunk, staring up at the underside of a mattress. Combining the excitement with the fact I hadn't been sleeping at night for a while, meant I was awake in the darkness for hours.

When I woke up it would be time to go into the camp. One step closer to Canada, and then…

What am I thinking? How the fuck am I gonna get back to Joanne?

For a long time, that one thought seemed to constantly go around and around in my head.

She must think I'm dead. Nope, can't worry about that now. One step at a time, one step at an annoyingly slow fucking time.

DAY EIGHTEEN

Chapter 9: Gayter

An alarm was going off. In my sleep induced confusion, I leaned out of bed and fumbled around, first looking for my phone on my bedside cabinet, and then searching the floor. The alarm suddenly stopped.

Pete saying, 'Sorry,' brought me back to my senses, reminding me where I was.

I tried to open my eyes, just about managing to get my left one open. My right eye was not cooperating. People around me were beginning to stir.

'What time is it?' I asked, trying to aim it in the direction I thought Pete had been sleeping.

'Five thirty,' he whispered.

I must have only been asleep for a couple of hours.

Half an hour until we're in the camp. Might as well get up then.

I hope Beth is in there.

We shared out, and ate what were left of the pastries. We took turns using the toilets, and then crowded around the locked gate we'd seen Elliot and Martin use the day before. We had nothing to gather up apart from a few weapons, so it didn't take us long to get ready.

'What time is it Pete?' Jack asked.

Pete moaned and looked at his watch. 'It's three minutes after the last time you asked me, so it's seven minutes to six.'

'Where's your watch?' I asked Jack.

He rolled up his sleeve, showing me his watch.

'Why are you asking me all the time?' Pete asked him.

'Just making sure my watch is correct.'

One of the doors to the container swung open, and out staggered the sheriff, tripping over the lip of the doorway and stumbling forwards a few paces.

I leaned in towards Jack. 'He looks shitfaced.'

'Morning campers,' the sheriff said, unhooking a bunch of keys from his belt.

Jack and I exchanged bemused glances.

'Was that from Hi-de-Hi?' Jack asked.

I shrugged. 'Was it on TV over here?' I asked him.

Jack shrugged, saying, 'Don't know.'

Sheriff McCallany reached the gate, and after the fourth attempt, managed to unlock it. 'Make your way over to my office. Once inside, don't just crowd around the doorway. Keep moving forward.'

Jack and I were at the back, so we waited until everyone had filtered through the opening before following them.

'Ah, it's Shouty McShouterson,' the sheriff said as Jack passed him. 'You'll be glad your brief stay in the Overlook Hotel is over.'

'Yep, just anxious to look at the list,' Jack replied.

'Well, I just need to get all your details first, and then you can see it. Don't worry, it won't take long.'

The sheriff locked the gate as we walked to his office.

'So he's a Hi-de-Hi, and a Stephen King fan,' I quietly said.

'And a whiskey fan by the smell of him,' Jack replied.

At the far end of the container was an ornate desk, inset with green leather. It did not suit its surroundings. Behind it was a large, well used leather office chair. Behind them were bookshelves, stacked with pads of paper, presumably containing the names of the incoming refugees. An eighties style boombox sat on the floor in front of the shelves. As I'd walked in I noticed an old looking sofa, tucked into the corner by the big double doors. It looked like the sheriff had spent many a night sleeping on it.

'Coming through, make space,' the sheriff said as he manoeuvred his way through us. 'Oh yeah, forgot to ask, are any of you zombies?'

He was answered with blank stares.

'Zombies don't speak,' he said. 'So it's probably best you answer me with actual words.'

One by one, we all said no. I looked down and smiled after seeing the three kids vigorously shaking their heads.

'That's good then.' He opened up a pad of paper and placed it on his desk. 'Oh hey,' he exclaimed, looking up at us and smiling. 'A new pad. Just need to write the date on.' He closed it and started writing on the front. 'Okay then.' The sheriff looked up at us, scanning our faces. 'You,' he said, pointing at Theo. 'Come here,' he requested, leaning down to open a draw and pulling out what looked like an iPad. 'My hands weren't built for modern technology, so I need you to input everything I write down onto this.' He held it out towards Theo.

Theo's eyes darted between Sandra and Pete for a few seconds, before shrugging his shoulders and walking around to stand by the sheriff. He took the iPad. 'Where do I? Oh right.' Theo showed the screen to the sheriff. 'This one?' he asked.

'Yep, that's the one. They tell me it's real easy but I always struggle.'

'Have you got electricity here?' Shannon asked, staring at the iPad.

'Oh no, the Canadians charge it up when I give it back to them.'

The sheriff finished writing on the front of the pad, and then opened it up again. 'Okay, iPad Boy, you first. Name and age?'

Theo continued staring down for a couple of seconds, before realising it was him that was being questioned. 'Theodore Rodriguez. I'm seventeen.'

'Mexican American?' the sheriff asked.

'He's American,' Sandra stated.

'Don't worry,' the sheriff said. 'Nothing sinister going on here. They just want to know for...I don't know, to see if anything adds up, you know? To explain why whoever survived, survived.' He threw his hands up into the air. 'I'm not a scientist.'

'Our family is originally from Mexico, yes,' Theo said, glancing at his surviving family members.

'Okay let's stick with the...' He paused to read his own writing. 'The Rodriguez's.' He pointed at Sandra. 'You can go next.'

'Sandra Walker, thirty one. These three are mine. Seth is six, Jonah is four, and Max is four.' Sandra closed her eyes when she realised her mistake. 'I mean three, Max is three.'

The sheriff looked up. 'It's okay. I don't care.' He leaned forward slightly and whispered, 'Father?'

Sandra gave her head a brief shake. 'I would also like to look through your list when we're done please.'

The sheriff sat back and smiled kindly. 'Of course you can. Next, how about you,' he said, pointing at Pete.

'Peter Rodriguez, I'm twenty two.'

'Next,' the sheriff said.

'Alison Rodriguez, twenty eight.'

'Right, I'm guessing you two aren't Rodriguez's?' the sheriff asked, looking at Michael and Shannon.

'You are correct. I'm Michael Presley, thirty one, African American.'

'Shannon Presley, thirty two, also African American.'

Jack elbowed me in the ribs. 'Told you,' he whispered.

'Hey, like the actor?' the sheriff exclaimed.

Michael and Shannon glanced at each other, shaking their heads.

'Michael Shannon, the actor,' the sheriff repeated.

'Don't waste your breath Sheriff,' I said. 'They don't even know who Tom Hanks is. I doubt they'll have heard of Michael Shannon.'

'Surely somebody has said this to you before though?' the sheriff asked.

'No, sorry,' Shannon replied.

'Okay, don't worry about it. How about you big guy?'

'Gintaras Adomaitis, I am thirty nine years old, Lithuanian, but resident of United States of America for ten year.'

Thank fuck for that, I thought he was gonna say thirty five for a second.

'Okay, now onto the Brits, you first,' the sheriff said, pointing at me.

'Christopher Taylor, thirty six, and yeah, British.'

'Living here or on vacation?' he asked.

'Vacation.'

'How's that going?'

'Pretty shit.'

The sheriff let out a little chuckle before glancing up at Jack. 'Shouty?' he said.

'Jack Tillman, thirty four, British but I live here, I've got an L-1 visa.'

Shaking my head and laughing, I looked to Jack. 'What the fuck?' I asked him.

'What? I do have a visa.'

Theo placed the iPad down on the desk, saying, 'I'm done.'

'Thank you very much,' the sheriff said. 'I've taken the liberty of already stamping out your numbers. I'm assuming you're all friends and aren't going to fight over these.' He opened a draw and pulled out small strips of paper, laying them out on the desk. 'I think there are twelve there.'

When everyone moved to the desk, I stayed back to let them all decide amongst themselves. This meant I got the last number.

I looked down at the piece of paper in my hand. Stamped onto a thin strip was the number, *41 789*.

'There's forty one thousand, seven hundred and eighty nine people in the camp?' I asked.

'Not anymore,' the sheriff said. 'Some have gone across into Canada, and people die. The population of Blaine was about five thousand. Half of Blaine's houses are on the other side of the fence, so it's a tight squeeze.'

I shook my head in amazement. 'And they let five hundred people in a week?'

'Yep.'

I couldn't figure out the maths. 'Jack?'

'About eighty weeks, so...about eighteen months,' Jack said solemnly.

I felt a bit light headed and had to lean against a wall. 'Fucking hell,' I slowly whispered. It felt like my stomach weighed a tonne, and was trying to pull me to the floor.

'Hey, look on the bright side,' the sheriff beamed. 'Nobody is going to kill you for your number.'

'Do people get killed for their number?' Shannon asked.

The sheriff seemed to think about it for a few seconds, before saying, 'Yeah, no point in sugar coating it for you. It happens. But you're safe.'

'Sheriff?' Jack asked, nodding towards the bookshelves.

'Yes, just one more thing, job assignments. You,' he said, pointing towards Sandra and looking down at his pad of paper. 'That's it. Sandra. You are a single parent, so no work for you.' He opened another draw in his desk, this time pulling out a playing card. He reached out towards Sandra. 'Don't lose this please, if you do, it means you have to come back and see me. Never hand this to anyone, just show it to them when you're in the food tent.'

Sandra hesitantly took the ace of spades from him. 'Okay, thank you.' She held the card up. 'Will people try and kill me for this?'

'No. Don't worry about that.'

Sandra didn't look convinced. We all shared a few anxious glances.

'Everyone else,' he continued. 'I expect you'll be with either the Fencers or the Zombie Patrol. There seems to be more and more of the dead getting in every day.' He pulled out a map of Blaine and placed it on the desk. 'Okay, everyone crowd in.'

We all moved forward to stand around his desk. He pointed out where the south and east inner fences were situated, then moved his finger over to where we would be assigned accommodation, and finally where we needed to go to speak to Frank or Amber, our new bosses.

'Go to the Blaine Senior Centre first to sort out where you'll be sleeping,' the sheriff instructed. 'Make sure you sort out these two somewhere as well,' he said, pointing at Jack and Sandra.

'And me,' I said. 'I'll help Jack look through the list. There's no point in you staying here Sandra. We'll look for Dale and Sophia's names. You take care of the kids. It's Walker, right?'

Sandra looked torn. 'And you'll look through every single one of these?' she asked, pointing at the bookshelves.

'Yes, of course,' I replied.

She looked down at the kids, and then back at me. 'Okay,' she sighed. 'Yes okay. Dale Walker, thirty three, and Sophia Walker, she's eight. I have no idea if Dale would have mentioned anything about her having a Mexican family.' She shot a glance at the sheriff, but he seemed more concerned with the contents of one of the desk drawers.

'If their names are here, we'll find them,' I assured her.

As they started to leave the container, a thought jumped into my head. 'How do we find you when we're done here?'

'After you've got your accommodation sorted,' the sheriff said. 'Just leave the Brits names with the guys at the Senior Centre.' He turned to look at me. 'Then when you've finished here, just go there, and they'll tell you where you're sleeping.' He gave us a toothy grin. 'Problem solved.'

'Okay, see you soon yeah,' Ali said.

Sheriff McCallany stopped as he was leaving, turning back to face us. 'I need to let them into the camp. I'll only be five minutes. Please wait until I get back before you start. I don't want you messing my system up.' He spun around and exited the container.

Jack and I stood in the open doorway, and watched them walk towards the inner fence.

'Eighteen months? A year and a fucking half?' I said. 'I can't stay here for that long. Nobody could live here for eighteen months. Eighteen fucking months.'

'We won't be here for that long,' Jack said.

'Why?'

'Because things always change. Don't worry about it yet. Let's find Beth first.'

I started to pace up and down in the container. 'Fuck's sake. Eighteen fucking shitty fucking months. No fucking chance. I need to get back home.'

'Find Beth. Find a way to cross into Canada,' Jack said.

I stopped pacing and tried to calm myself down. 'Okay. Fine. The names are on the iPad,' I said, turning back to face him. 'Surely we can search for them on that?'

'I hope so.'

When the sheriff returned, carrying two chairs he'd picked up from the school, he delivered us the bad news.

'It's wiped every time I hand it over to the Canadians. I don't even think it's the same iPad I started with.'

'Fuck's sake,' I said.

'You can check it for the last few days. That's when I last handed it over. Only had a few people enter the camp in that time though.'

A quick search on the iPad gave us nothing. Not for Beth, or Dale and Sophia.

'Do you speak to the Canadians?' I asked him. 'Do you know what's happening in the rest of the world?'

'We exchange the odd word here and there. They don't really tell me anything. I would always ask them something at the beginning, but I soon gave up when they wouldn't answer my questions.'

Jack was looking anxious to get on with searching through the lists.

'No idea at all then?' I asked.

'Oh there are rumours. The Russians, the Chinese, the rest of the world embroiled in a new Cold War. Who knows?'

'Okay,' I said flatly.

He placed the two plastic chairs in front of his desk, and pointed at the shelves. 'From the beginning?' he asked.

Jack slumped down onto one of them. 'They set off from California ten days ago, so we don't need to start at the very beginning.'

'I think we probably should start at the beginning Jack. What about Sandra?'

Jack's head rocked back and he let out a long sigh. 'Yeah okay, we don't know when they'll have got here. Beginning please.'

'Okay, this here is the very first one,' he said, pointing to the left side of the top shelf of one of the bookcases. He then pulled out two pads, placing them in front of us. 'Please put them back in the same order you found them.' He walked over to the sofa and sat down. 'Had over one hundred people working for me just a week ago.'

Jack looked to me and sighed again, shaking his head.

'I thought the first few days were like hell on earth,' the sheriff continued. 'It only got worse though. Everyone in Blaine and Whatcom County got out of Dodge, escaped into Canada.'

Jack was trying to ignore the story, and concentrate on the list of names.

'The Canadians soon stopped letting people across, put up a fence, on U.S. land as well. Then the wall started going up.' He reached his hand down the side of the sofa, coming back out holding a bottle of something, probably whiskey. He unscrewed the cap and took a long swig. 'More and more people started turning up, talking about the dead rising and eating people. It was the people that turned up with the horror stories that got all these defences built up around us. I didn't believe a word they were saying. Fucking zombies. What a crock of shit eh?' He looked to me, holding up the bottle, and gave it a little shake.

I waved my hand and shook my head. 'No thanks.'

'Hey Shouty, want a drink?' the sheriff asked.

Jack kept his eyes on the list.

I answered for him, 'No he's fine thanks.'

'Please yourself,' he said, and swigged back another mouthful.

'Did the virus not get into Canada?' I asked.

The sheriff shrugged. 'Must have done, but they had more time to isolate the sick, and to prepare, evacuate, just make sure everyone knew what to do.'

Jack was already a few pages into his pad.

The sheriff leaned back and closed his eyes. 'For days on end, that room you slept in last night, and many others like it, were full of people, sometimes thousands at a time. I'll tell you something, they didn't eat as well as you did,' he said, pointing at the empty metal wall next to me. 'Been on my own, just me outside the fence for five, six, seven days now. Just waiting…just waiting.' With a start, he opened his eyes, then twisted around and lifted his legs up onto the arm of the sofa. 'Going to catch up on some sleep. Wake me up before you go go.'

Jack looked at me wearily.

'Fan of Wham, Sheriff?' I asked.

'Never heard of them. Sleepy time now. Don't mess up my system.'

I think the sheriff may have gone a bit stir crazy.

Shaking my head, I started searching down the page. 'Beth is thirty one yeah?' I asked.

Jack was drawing his finger down the page in front of him. 'Yeah she is, and I'm sure Roy is actually called Royston, and their surname is Gayter.'

'Royston?' I laughed. 'How old is he?'

'I think they're both thirty one, and both English as well, British.'

'Thirty one? He must be the youngest Royston in the world.'

'Yep, they're from Norwich as well.'

'What?' I said, looking up from the list. 'You never told me they were from there.'

Jack looked up and shrugged. 'They're Beth's friends.'

'I'm just surprised you never mentioned it. I'd have probably told you if Joanne became friends with someone from Middlesbrough, and that we lived near them on the other side of the world.'

'Well, I'd have found that news completely irrelevant and boring. That's why I didn't tell you.'

No wonder there were so many pads on the shelves. The sheriff had double, and sometimes triple spaced the names on the list. He'd also only used one side of each page.

'This is gonna take fucking ages,' I said, leaning over to look at the pages in front of Jack. The names on his were also similarly spaced.

'We'll soon get through it,' he said. 'Just keep going.'

I was on the twentieth pad when my eyes fell on a Royston.

'Jack, Jack, Jack, I've found a Royston and...' I tracked across and saw the surname. 'Yep, Gayter, thirty one, British, Caucasian. Looks like it could be him. Is he white?'

Jack stood up and took two quick steps to stand over me. 'Yeah he is.'

There was no Sarah, but underneath was a Beth.

'Where is it?' Jack asked impatiently.

'There's a Beth underneath him,' I said, quickly glancing at the rest of the information. 'Oh...that's weird.'

Jack leaned in. 'What is? Where are the names?'

'Look.' My finger rested on the page under Beth's name.

It read, *Beth Gayter. 31. British. Caucasian.*

'No sign of a Sarah Gayter,' I said.

Jack leaned over the desk, his hands planted on either side of the pad. He stared at the page for a good twenty seconds.

'What you thinking Jack? Can't be them. Can it?'

Jack continued his silent stare.

'Hello Jack, have you fallen asleep standing up?'

'The ages are right,' he slowly said. 'There can't be another Royston Gayter in the world. And it's Beth, not Elizabeth, or Bethany, or whatever. Beth was christened Beth. It's not short for anything.' He brushed his fingers through his hair. 'What the fuck? What does this mean?'

'No idea?' I replied.

Jack started to trace his hand over the page. 'And definitely no Sarah?'

'I've not seen a Sarah Gayter, no.'

Jack stood up straight and stared at the ceiling. He let out an exasperated groan, before saying, 'Let's carry on.'

'Is that them or not?' I asked. 'It'd be a bit of a coincidence if not. Maybe the sheriff just wrote the name down wrong. He could have been drunk.' I stood up and turned to the sleeping sheriff. 'I'm gonna ask him.'

It took longer than expected, but I eventually managed to wake up the very disgruntled sheriff, and asked him if he remembered. He did not. He did tell us it was entirely possible he could have written the wrong information down.

So, with the sheriff already back in a deep slumber, we sat ourselves back down at the desk, and carried on reading. We still had to look for Dale and Sophia's names anyway.

Chapter 10: Maps

I had no idea how long we'd been there by the time we finished. The sheriff was still asleep. We hadn't found any Dale and Sophia Walkers, a Beth Tillman, a Sarah Gayter, or any more people called Royston Gayter.

'Okay,' Jack said, putting the last pad back on the shelf. 'If it is her, why did she put Gayter? And where is Sarah?' And if it is Beth, how do I find her?'

'Speak to the bosses. They probably keep a record of everyone that works for them.'

Hang on, forty odd thousand people. Bollocks.

'Maybe,' I added.

'Fuck,' Jack muttered.

'Right, let's wake him up again.' I pointed to the unconscious McCallany on the sofa. 'We get out of here, find out where we'll be living for the foreseeable future, and then search the camp for Beth and her new husband.'

'Fuck you Chris.' Jack hesitated while walking over to the sofa. 'What if she thought I'd died, and married Roy?'

I laughed. 'Don't be so fucking ridiculous. It's been two weeks. Sheriff Hopper here will have been shitfaced and written it down wrong.'

I stood over the sleeping McCallany. 'Wake up Sheriff, the...' I looked to Jack. 'What are those creatures called from Stranger Things?'

'Demogorgons,' Jack replied.

I prodded the sheriff on the shoulder. 'Wake up. Eleven needs your help, the Demogorgons are chasing her.'

'What the fuck you talking about?' the sheriff said, his eyes still shut.

'We're finished,' I replied. 'Can we go into the camp please?'

'Wait outside,' he barked.

A few minutes later, Sheriff McCallany walked out of his container. He waved the iPad at us, saying, 'Two birds with one stone.'

'So Sheriff,' I said, as we followed behind him.

'Yes.'

'This credit playing card money system thingy. How does it work?'

'Just imagine this place is like a big cooperative. The cards don't equate to anything really, not anything of value anyway. They just prove you've done something for the cooperative. And as long as you continue to do something to help your cooperative, you won't be shown the door.'

'Do people get thrown out?' Jack asked. 'How strict are you?'

'I personally haven't thrown anyone out. But some of the other bosses have. This place ain't my Blaine anymore, it's Refugee Camp 33.'

'As in, there's thirty two other camps?' I asked.

'I guess so.'

'You don't know for definite?' Jack asked.

'No'

'Well, who gave Blaine its new name?' I asked.

The sheriff spun around and walked backwards. He lifted the iPad up and flipped it over, showing us the underside of it. *Ref. Camp 33* was written on a bit masking tape, stuck to the bottom.

I nodded. 'Okay, so the iPad named it.'

Sheriff McCallany grinned back at me, and then spun around.

'What if the number of a boss gets called and they get to go over to Canada?' Jack asked.

'Ain't happened yet. But I'm sure someone will move up and take their place. They each have fifty or so people working directly under them. It's not just one person taking care of four thousand people.' He stopped when we were about ten feet from the fence, and turned to face us. 'I said this to your friends earlier, and now I'm telling you. This ain't America anymore. I'm the only thing that resembles the law around here, and there ain't no fucking way I'm gonna try and control that lot in there. Keep your heads down, and stay away from people that look like they might want to hurt you. That might be hard to do in such a small space, with forty thousand people crammed in, but it's the only way you'll survive.'

I forced a smile. 'You're really painting a pretty picture of Refugee Camp 33 Sheriff. Thanks very much.'

He returned my smile. 'Well you've been warned. Come on then, welcome to Thunderdome.'

Jack and I exchanged amused glances.

While the sheriff was unlocking a gate in the chain link fence, a short and stocky woman started to walk in our direction.

She waited until she was a couple of feet away before speaking. 'Hey Sheriff. These the last two?'

'Yep, the last two, for now. I'll leave them in your capable hands. I'm going to speak to our Canadian friends.' He turned to us. 'Gents, this is Tina Turner.'

The woman gave the sheriff a sardonic smile. 'Thank you Sheriff, always a pleasure.'

The sheriff closed the gate behind us and locked it. 'Good luck fellas, see you around.'

Jack and I said our goodbyes as he stumbled past the woman, who looked nothing like Tina Turner, and crossed the empty road behind her.

'My name is Naomi,' she said. 'As you may have noticed, the sheriff is an asshole. Probably got a bit of PTSD. If he just left that office of his more often, it would do him the world of good. Drinking two bottles of whiskey a day doesn't help.'

Jack and I just smiled and politely nodded.

Slightly unhinged maybe, but I wouldn't say an arsehole.

Jack pointed at me and said, 'Chris,' before telling her his name.

'Follow me,' Naomi said. 'I'll take you to see Tim's guys, so you can find out where you're staying.'

We followed her down an empty road. The inner fence looked like it ran all the way along this straight road, at least as far as I could see. The map the sheriff had shown us had the fence running all the way down H Street to the water. So I guessed this was H Street. It was still deathly quiet. Apart from the odd person stood along the fence, staring at the buildings and spaces beyond, there was no sign of all these people.

'Hey Naomi,' I called out.

She stopped and spun around to face me. 'Keep the volume down guys. We can talk normally, at this kind of level, but no shouting, not anywhere in the camp.'

'Does it make that much difference?' I asked. 'The dead are at the outer fence.'

'Why find out?' She had a stern look on her face. 'There are thousands upon thousands of people in here. If we all just thought fuck it and starting shouting and hollering, I think it would make a difference. But why find out?'

'Very true,' I said, raising my hands. 'Sorry.'

She swiftly spun around and starting walking again. 'What were you going to ask me Chris?'

'I was going to ask you where everyone is. The part of Blaine that had been sectioned off for the camp didn't look that big on the map.'

She pointed to a road coming up on our right. 'Look down there in a few seconds.'

I looked down the road as we continued by it, still walking along H Street. About one hundred feet up the road, it turned from a normal, if empty looking street, into a bustling and chaotic looking market street. The front gardens of people's homes on both sides were now filled with stalls and tents, and the space in between, formally the roadway, was filled with masses of people. The most remarkable thing was the people were going about their business in almost silence. There was just the slightest murmur of conversations going on, like a swarm of bees quietly buzzing in excitement.

'Come on guys,' Naomi said. 'You'll see the same again on the next street, and the street after that, and the street after that.'

'Fucking hell,' Jack whispered. 'People, lots of fucking people.'

We picked up our pace and followed her. She was right. The next street was the same, as was the one after. We turned right onto that street, and headed towards the mass of people.

'Keep close to me. Try not to get lost,' Naomi warned, just before she slipped effortlessly into the crowd.

Just a couple of seconds later, I was also in amongst them. For a split second I thought I wouldn't be able to get in, they would all turn on me and start taking bites out of my flesh, and clawing at my face with their bony, dying fingers. But they just parted, or changed direction to walk around me. Some glanced at my face, or the baseball bat in my hand, but most didn't pay me any attention at all. Beards seemed to be very fashionable at the moment, making me think they didn't have any hot water.

I realised I'd been holding my breath, and had to fight to force some air into my lungs.

I turned my head to check on Jack behind me. 'Alright?' I mouthed.

He must have been thinking something similar to me. He gave me a very brisk nod. His mouth was tightly closed and his eyes were trying to look everywhere, almost bulging out of his face.

Up ahead, Naomi took a left turn and walked between two canvas covered tents. One looked like it was selling clothes, second hand by the look and smell of them. The other had tables displaying pillows and blankets. A large man was leaning over one of the tables. He was holding three or four leather belts in his hand, reaching out towards a woman. She looked like the vendor, her arms were crossed and she was slowly shaking her head.

Everyone smelt of body odour, some much more than others. I was pretty sure I also smelt terrible.

Deodorant must be hard to come by around here. I bet the tent selling that must be making a killing.

'Repent, you must repent,' a woman was repeating, much louder than everybody surrounding her. I found her in the crowd, and our eyes met almost immediately. 'Only Jesus can save you now,' she called out to me. Everyone in the vicinity of the woman spun around to face her. Some told her to be quiet, others shushed her. 'You are all fighting the hand of God,' she cried.

I slipped between the two stalls, and tried to catch up with Jack and Naomi.

Naomi had stopped in front of a building. 'This is the Senior Centre, where Tim and his team organise where everyone sleeps. Just go on through that door,' she said, gesturing behind her. 'I'll see you around, okay?'

'Okay, thanks Naomi,' I said.

Jack was staring at something behind him, only just stopping himself before he walked into Naomi.

'Shit, sorry,' Jack said. 'It's not been that long since almost everyone died. Why am I freaking out?'

'What, with the crowds?' Naomi asked.

'Yeah,' Jack replied.

'Don't worry, you'll soon acclimate. It takes some folk a while to get used to it again.' She gave us a smile and a nod, before disappearing into the throng of people.

'Let's get inside,' I said. 'I think it's the fact that there's so many people, all on one little street. Is this what it's gonna be like everywhere?'

'I fucking hope not,' Jack said, as he pulled open the door into the Senior Centre.

Thankfully, relatively speaking, it was almost empty of people. We walked into a large room. Rows and rows of desks filled the space, maybe forty or fifty desks. Only half of them had someone sat behind them.

As we approached the closest occupied desk, the man sat behind it looked up from the book he was reading, and said, 'Complaints? Speak to Melvin.' He turned his head slightly to his left, and still keeping his voice down, called out, 'Melvin, these are yours.'

'No we're–,' I started.

'Melvin,' the man said again. 'Melvin? Oh hang on, Melvin didn't show today. You need to see...' He trailed off and spun his seat around so he was facing the other way.

'We're not here to complain,' Jack said.

'Speak to Aisha,' the obnoxious man said, swivelling back around and continuing to read his book.

'Hello.' I waved at him until he looked up at me. I spoke as slowly and as clearly as I could. 'We are not here to complain. We are new.

Our friends should have already been here and found us somewhere to stay.'

The obnoxious man seemed to take offence. 'No need to be so condescending,' he said.

What the fuck?

'Over here,' a woman, a few rows back, called out to us. Her hand was up above her head.

'I'm gonna go and make a complaint about you,' I said, pointing at the idiot sat in front of us.

Jack shoved me towards the woman with her arm raised. 'Come on Chris.'

We walked through the gaps between the desks until we reached hers.

'You Jack and Chris?' she asked.

'Yes, that's us,' Jack said.

She handed Jack two sheets of paper. 'I've circled in red where your accommodation is situated on these maps.'

Jack handed one of them to me and I looked down at an approximation of Refugee Camp 33. It looked like it had been drawn with a biro pen, and the street names were almost illegible.

'Before you say anything,' the woman said. 'My daughter drew those maps, so don't say anything insulting. We ran out of actual maps two weeks ago.'

I compared mine with Jack's. They looked like two completely different places. 'I'm gonna have to say something, and you might find it insulting,' I said.

The woman rolled her eyes. 'Yeah, go on.'

I took Jack's map and showed both of them to the woman. 'Which one of these would you say was the most accurate?'

She leaned forward slightly, taking in both sheets of paper. A few seconds passed while she inspected them, before prodding the one in my right hand with her pen. 'Probably this one,' she told us.

I placed the least accurate of the maps back down on her desk. 'Okay, thanks very much.'

She forced a smile onto her face, a split second later it was gone.

As we left, I noticed most of the people sat at the desks seemed to be asleep, or well on their way.

Jack stopped by the door. 'Before we go back out,' he said. 'Let's figure out where we need to go. I don't want to get lost in the crowds.'

A building was circled on the right hand side of the map, quite close to the east inner fence. The child's drawing made it impossible to see which road it was on.

'Is that on F Street?' Jack asked. 'Or 12th Street?'

'Fuck knows. I'm not going back over to ask the shit artist's mother. We'll just have to go and knock on doors.'

'Brilliant,' Jack said. 'Go back the way we came, and then turn left onto 12th Street? We can't get lost that way. Where do we need to go to speak to the Fencer's and Zombie Patrol bosses?'

'Can't remember. I doubt this map looks like the one in the sheriff's container anyway. Let's find everyone else first.'

As we left the building, Jack said, 'I'm gonna complain about you,' mimicking me. He was swirling his finger around in front of him.

'I didn't say it like that, and I wasn't doing that with my finger.'

Jack then wagged his finger at me. 'I'm gonna complain about you too.'

'Yeah, fuck off.'

Chapter 11: Lost Souls

With a little bit more ease, we entered the crowds again. I kept my eyes on Jack's ginger hair as we forced our way through thousands of silent or quietly muttering refugees.

Word of a fight on the other side of the street quickly made its way to us. What followed was almost a stampede, as people tried to escape getting caught up in the brawl. All I could see over the bodies scurrying past were occasional fists swinging through the air. No words were spoken. I just heard grunts of pain.

Jack grabbed my arm and said, 'Let's get out of here, before we get crushed.'

We let the crowds take us to the end of the street, both of us releasing a sigh of relief after reaching the outer road and leaving the crowds behind us.

We were soon turning left onto 12th Street, and walking with the east inner fence on our right. Every twenty feet someone stood watch, staring out through the line of trees on the other side. Jack spotted Gee first, pointing him out to me. He was stood on the corner of 12th and F Street. He noticed us and waved.

When we were closer, he shouted, 'Hey fuckers,' with a big smile filling his face.

One of the guards by the fence turned to him, saying, 'Shut up.'

Gee raised his hands to the angry man, not looking apologetic in the slightest. He turned back to us with a sheepish grin.

'What's up with Gee, why is he so happy?' I asked Jack.

'No idea.'

When we were a few feet away from him, Jack asked, 'Why are you so happy Gee?'

'Not happy, just not fucked off as much as before.'

'Why?' I asked. 'Have we been given a nice place to stay?'

'No. It shit. Follow me,' Gee replied, turning and starting to walk down F Street.

'So why do you look happy all of a sudden?' Jack asked again as we followed.

'I don't,' he snapped.

Jack looked at me and shrugged, saying, 'Okay, fair enough Big Gee.'

Gee took us to the end of F Street, and then turned right onto what must have been 11th Street.

Jack pulled the map out of his pocket. 'This is a shit map.'

We walked past a house on our right before Gee made a right turn. 'This is house,' he said, and headed towards it.

A single story, white wood panelled house stood before us. It looked like it might be a bit of a squeeze for all of us to fit in.

We entered into the hallway and Gee opened the first door on the right. 'This is where you two sleep,' he said, gesturing for us to enter.

Our bedroom looked like a room in a hostel. Ten bunkbeds had been crammed into the space, with just a two foot wide gap separating the beds. It was going to be very cosy.

'What the actual fuck?' I muttered.

'You two look like I look, when I see room,' Gee said, the big smile returning.

'Are you in here as well?' I asked him.

He nodded.

'Fucking hell,' I whispered.

Gee spun around and walked further down the corridor. 'Come with me, others in the yard.'

He pointed to the door of the only bathroom as we passed it. *Maximum visiting time – FIVE MINUTES*, had been written on a sheet of paper and taped to the door. We walked past the kitchen, before following him out through another door, and into the back garden. Our group sat on the grass, quietly chatting to each other, the kids ran around the garden playing some kind of chasing game.

'Hey guys,' Shannon said.

Everyone else welcomed us with a smile or a glance in our direction. Sandra quickly stood and stepped towards us. I shook my head and apologised.

Her face dropped, and she glanced at the kids still running around, oblivious to our arrival. She looked to me, and then Jack. 'Don't say anything,' she whispered. Ali stepped behind her and placed her hands on Sandra's shoulders, while Jack and I both nodded in agreement. Ali guided her sister back over to the kids.

'Beth?' Michael asked.

Jack screwed up his face, saying, 'I think so.'

Michael and Shannon shot each other confused glances, before looking back to Jack. 'What do you mean?' Shannon asked.

Jack and I both sat down on the grass, and Jack told everyone what we had found in the list of refugees.

After a few moments of silence, Michael spoke up. 'Maybe they pretended to be married, in order to get into the camp.'

'Why?' Jack said. 'Nothing like that happened with us. The sheriff doesn't give a shit about that.'

Shannon placed a hand on Jack's arm. 'Calm down Jack. If this is your Beth, I'm sure there will be a perfectly reasonable explanation.'

'Maybe they just fucking,' Gee said.

Jack shot him a look of utter disdain.

'What the fuck Gee?' I said, trying to hold back a laugh.

'Gee,' Shannon said. 'That isn't helping anybody.'

'And it doesn't make any sense,' I said. 'Why would she take Roy's name just so she could shag him?'

'Shag him,' Gee laughed. 'Yes, they just shagging.'

'Has he taken something?' I asked everyone, gesturing towards Gee.

'He found some other Lithuanians in the camp,' Michael replied. 'I think they shared a few bottles of vodka.'

'Probably not just the vodka,' Shannon said under her breath.

'What time is it?' I asked.

Michael glanced down at his watch. 'Nearly two.'

'A few bottles,' I said. 'That's impressive.'

'We need to speak to the bosses,' Jack said. 'Then I'm going to look for Beth.' He shot an angry glance at Gee, who just beamed back at him.

Michael scrambled to get to his feet. 'I'll take you to see them,' he quickly said. 'I expect you'll be with us on Zee Pee, that's the Zombie Patrol. Amber, she's the boss, told us we'd probably have the night off. They usually have two or three nights off in a row.'

'Sounds good,' I said.

'Not when you have to live here,' Shannon interjected. 'The house is nearly full, almost every bed is taken.'

'Shite. How many people?' I asked.

'Thirty eight, thirty nine, forty, maybe,' Michael said. 'Come on, let's go.'

'Enjoy yourself Michael. Don't stay too long,' Shannon said, waving him off.

Michael smiled at his wife, and then led us around the house and back onto the street.

'Thirty eight people in that little house?' I muttered. 'How is that going to work exactly?'

'Not sure to be honest with you Chris,' Michael replied. 'I'm guessing it's going to be done with a lot of discomfort. Shannon and I are only sharing a room with Alison and her family, so we've got a slightly better deal than the two of you and Gee.'

'Twenty of us in one room,' I said. 'I might find a tent.'

Jack was very quiet for the walk, probably desperate to get his search for Beth underway.

Michael explained that our breakfasts and evening meals were served in a large tent or marquee, set up on D Street. It was one of many situated around the camp.

'Before you turned back up, we were talking to one of your new roommates. She said that the food was very basic, porridge and water in the morning, mostly rice and potatoes in the evening. Two or three nights a week there might be fish on the menu. She reckons this place doesn't have long left. A lot of the fishing boats they started with have vanished, and–.'

'What do you mean? Vanished?' I asked.

'Sailed away and never came back, probably trying to get north like everyone else. So they don't have many boats left, or fishermen that know what they're doing. And the scavengers are coming back with less and less each time apparently, if they come back at all. She said she can't imagine it'll be long before people start revolting.'

'So everyone goes to one of these food tents twice a day?' Jack asked. 'What time do they serve? How many are there?'

'Not sure how many, but breakfast is from seven until ten in the morning,' Michael replied. 'Dinner is six until nine in the evening.'

'What about running water?' I asked. 'Do the toilets flush?'

'Looks like they have water, cold obviously, but it's running,' Michael replied. 'The toilets flush, but there is a sign up in the bathroom saying to use it sparingly. I'm guessing you know what that means?'

'The bathroom is gonna stink of piss?' I guessed.

'Yes, but better than a hole in the ground,' Michael replied.

He stopped at the corner of 12th and H Street, just near the gate we had used to first enter the camp.

'This is it,' he said, pointing to the house on the corner. 'I'll show you where to go.'

We followed him up to the front door. After two knocks, Michael opened the door and a cloud of smoke drifted out towards us. The smell of marijuana hit me immediately. Without hesitation, Michael stepped through the smoke and into the house. Jack and I looked at each other, smiled and then both shrugged. Jack followed him in first.

'Tonight Matthew, I'm going to be...' I paused for dramatic effect. 'Off my fucking face,' I said, stepping through the doorway and into the corridor. The thick smoke enveloped me, drawing me into the house.

'What was that?' Michael asked me. 'Who is Matthew?'

'Ah it's nothing. Just a TV programme in England.'

'Fucking hell,' Jack coughed. 'No wonder you wanted to come with us Michael, you fucking stoner.'

Michael turned to him and nodded, a huge smile filling his face.

Jack looked back at me. 'It's always the so called respectable ones, like the teachers.'

We followed Michael into the living room. It reminded me of a student house, the curtains were drawn and it was very sparsely decorated. People seemed to be everywhere, sprawled across the few pieces of furniture, just an armchair, a sofa and a couple of bean bags. Over in the far corner, five people were lying together on the carpeted floor. A notice board was on the wall opposite us, different coloured squares adorned the the top of the board, with hundreds of names listed under each colour. Candles flickered away, some dangerously close to the curtains, and people. The scene before us felt weird with no music playing. All I could hear were the grunts of acknowledgements as joints were passed around.

The three of us stood in the open doorway, waiting for one of the obviously stoned people to speak. They were either unconscious or stared back at us with untrusting eyes, like we'd just invaded their private drug den, which I suppose we had.

Michael leaned in closer to the guy nearest us. He was wearing incredibly short denim shorts and a t-shirt. He'd positioned himself sideways on the large comfy looking armchair, his head hanging upside down off the edge of it, and his legs dangling off the other side.

'Hey, have you seen Amber?' Michael asked.

The guy slowly opened his eyes, and after a few seconds of trying to focus, centred in on Michael's face. 'She ain't here. Whaddya need?' he eventually said, drawing out every word.

Michael gestured to Jack and I. 'These two are new. They need to be assigned to a team.'

The stoned guy attempted to look at us, but after a few attempts, just closed his eyes again. 'Blue Team,' he mumbled.

'We came here earlier and were placed in Green Team,' Michael said.

'There is no Green Bream fucker. Blue Team, fucking Blue Team.' He lifted his right hand off the floor and took a long drag from the joint he was holding between two fingers. 'Blue lost some peeps, need new pee-opps,' he croaked, before blowing a long smoke trail out of his mouth. 'Tell them to come here and speak to Crab tomorrow evening at six. No worky work tonighty night.'

'Okay,' Michael said, turning to us and shrugging his shoulders. 'Crab it is then.'

'Hey man,' Stoned Guy said. 'Not Crabab, I never said Cra...' He trailed off and seemed to pass out, before coming back with a jolt. 'It's Caleb, fucking Ca...leb,' he said. 'You fucking deaf or what? It's Caleb.' The hand holding the joint shot out above him, and he drew the letters with his finger, while spelling it out, 'C. A. L. E. B.'

'I think you'll find you actually said Crab, and then you said Crabab,' Michael insisted.

'Caleb man,' Stoned Guy slowly replied, drawing the two words out. His head lolled back even further, a big grin slowly appearing on his face.

'What?' a voice called out from the other side of the room.

Peering through the haze I could see a man now sitting upright on the sofa opposite us. The people on either side of him moaned and shifted slightly, complaining about him moving.

'What Rory?' the man on the sofa said. 'What do you want?'

Stoned Guy, or Rory, lifted his head slightly. 'Hey Caleb, you're here man, what's up?'

'Nothing, what's up with you?' Caleb replied, his eyes barely open and squinting in our direction.

Rory dropped his head back so it was upside down again. 'Just chilling,' he slowly said.

'Sweet,' Caleb answered, slumping back into his seat.

We watched the surreal exchange like a tennis rally, our heads going back and forth.

What the fuck? These guys are high as fucking kites.

'Do you need their names?' Michael asked.

Rory's head moved slightly so we waited for a response, seconds passed and nothing came.

'Caleb,' Michael said to the sofa.

Caleb was now indistinguishable in the four or five people crammed onto the sofa.

'You want their names Caleb?' Michael asked him.

Caleb's right arm shot up, making him visible, his fist clenched. 'Yo,' he croaked, puffing out smoke.

'Names? Do you want their names?' Michael repeated.

'Sweet,' Caleb said, his clenched fist still held high above his head.

Fuck's sake, this is a waste of time.

Michael turned to us, his eyelids also starting to droop. 'Does that mean he wants your names, or what?'

'Okay, thank you fucked people,' Jack said to the room, grabbing Michael's arm and pulling him backwards. 'Let's get out of here. We're going to be the same as this lot if we stay here any longer.'

'Yeah probably a good idea,' Michael said, allowing Jack to pull him into the corridor. 'I don't think they wrote our names down this morning anyway. Don't forget to pick up a card on the way out.' Michael was pointing to a tray on a small table, just inside the front door.

Inside was what looked like hundreds of playing cards. As far as I could tell, they were all the four of clubs. I picked up two, both had a five pointed star scribbled onto the bottom corner in biro. I handed one to Jack.

'Is that it?' Jack asked. 'Just pick up a card and get fed?'

'I think we have to turn up for work,' Michael said, a spaced out expression on his face. 'Otherwise they take the card off us, somehow, maybe. I don't know. I'm very confused.'

I grabbed Michael by the elbow, guiding him towards the clean and fresh air outside. 'Come on Mikey Boy. I think you're just topping up from the last time you were here.'

We left the house, pulling out a large cloud of smoke into the front garden with us.

'What the fuck was that? Was that just weed? Or something else?' I asked Michael.

'Probably whatever they can get their hands on,' he replied, his eyes looking more and more glazed over by the second, but sounding relatively coherent. 'And, that's the base for the Fencers and Zombie Patrol. I think they were all the bosses.' Michael still had enough of his senses to notice the look of disbelief on mine and Jack's faces. 'It's their night off,' he casually explained.

'The scavengers aren't struggling to find drugs then?' I asked.

'Not yet anyway,' Michael replied.

'So are we in the Zombie Patrol or the Fencers?' Jack asked him.

'Colours are Zee Pee, so I think that means you are Zee pee. Zee pee. Zee Pee? Yeah, Zee Pee.' Michael started giggling to himself.

'Okay, we're in Zee Pee,' I said. 'Stop saying Zee Pee. Fucking hell, you've got me doing it now.' I couldn't stop a giggle escape my mouth.

'I think the Fencers use football teams for their names,' Michael added, still giggling slightly. 'I'm not into sports. I'm not really a sporty guy.'

'I think we just found out what you are into Mikey,' I laughed.

'I may have dibble dabbled a bit in college,' he replied. 'Just a little bit mind you. I wasn't a waster.'

Jack and I smiled at each other and moved a bit closer to Michael.

We started walking back to our new house, occasionally having to redirect Michael. My legs were feeling a little lethargic, and my head was definitely lighter than usual.

'An alcoholic sheriff,' Jack mused. 'Half the people in the accommodation place didn't turn up for work, and the half that did were either asleep, or arseholes.'

'Probably both,' I interrupted.

'And the Zombie Patrol and Fencer bosses are all smashed on a concoction of drugs,' Jack continued.

'Yep, Refugee Camp 33 looks a bit of a mess,' I replied. 'I agree with the woman Mikey Boy spoke to earlier, can't see it lasting much longer. I reckon we get out of here. What do you think?'

Jack looked uncomfortable. 'First things first Chris. Get back to the house, and then we search for Beth. I could do with some help. Is that okay?'

Michael and I both agreed. I had to nudge Michael to get him to respond, but he eventually did.

Two men appeared from around a corner, upon seeing us, they headed in our direction.

'What do they want?' Jack asked.

They were both incredibly thin. Their gaunt faces seemed to be all cheekbones.

'Jesus is our saviour,' the man on the left said as they neared us. 'Join us at 1, 986 D Street. All that accept Jesus into their lives are welcome.'

His friend had a ragged cut running down the whole length of his face. It looked like it had only recently been given to him. The bright red and painful looking cut was suddenly split by a huge grin, making his cheekbones even more pronounced. 'Please join us,' he said. 'Only Jesus can save our souls now. Every one of us can be saved, just by allowing Jesus in. Please accept him into your lives.'

I gripped Michael's arm tightly, and swerved around the wild eyed men. 'Okay thank you,' I said, with a polite smile.

'There is always somebody there. Please stop by,' one of them said to us as we briskly walked away.

'I suppose the apocalypse is enough to make anyone turn to religion,' Michael said.

'Well, not quite anyone,' I said.

Chapter 12: Pub

Back at the house, everyone was still in the back garden, albeit now with wet hair, and smelling a whole lot better than us.

'You three,' Shannon said as we walked, or in Michael's case, staggered towards them. 'Go take a shower. We managed to trade in some stuff for toothbrushes, toothpaste, soap and towels.'

'Who, what and when?' I asked, surprised.

'We took a walk over to some of the stalls in the middle of the camp,' Shannon answered. 'Traded my watch for our stuff.' She handed Jack two towels, two toothbrushes and one bar of soap. 'You and Chris are sharing this soap. Make it last.' She nodded over to the three young boys. 'Sandra traded a few pieces of jewellery for their things. Got some clean clothes and a few bits for the kids.' She handed a towel and another bar of soap to Michael, looking into his face with concern. 'How long were you guys in that house?'

'Too long,' I replied.

'Not long enough,' Michael quickly said, a smile spreading across his face.

'I need to start looking for Beth,' Jack said.

'Half an hour won't make any difference. She'll still be here,' Shannon said to him. 'If you're quick, you'll be out there even sooner. You don't want to find your wife when you smell like that. Do you?'

Jack shook his head in resignation. 'Okay Mum.'

'I am not the mother figure,' Shannon exclaimed. 'Now, don't forget to wash behind your ears.' She shoved Jack towards the house, a smile on her face.

Jack was in and out of the bathroom within the allotted time of five minutes. Michael followed him.

I stood outside waiting for my turn, thinking about what I could use to trade for some clean clothes. All I had was my wedding ring, my phone, a fitness watch, with no means to charge either, my axe and my baseball bat. I'd need the Smasher and the axe for my new job. I didn't fancy killing zombies with my bare hands.

A new person walked by me, a woman in her twenties maybe. We both said hello, before she carried on towards the kitchen. I thought she might have been English from the way she spoke. I couldn't stop myself from glancing down at her bum as she walked away from me.

I didn't really try too hard to stop myself though.

Fucking hell I miss Joanne. Would she forgive me if I had to give up my ring? Not for clothes I suppose, but I'm sure she'd understand if it was for something to help me stay alive.

Who am I fucking kidding anyway? How would she even find out if I traded it? It's not like I'm going to get back to England anytime soon. Not now that I have to wait eighteen months before getting out of here. I really can't stay in this shithole for eighteen months.

Eighteen fucking months! I'd almost forgotten about that. This camp isn't gonna last that long anyway. Not a chance. I need to convince Jack that we have to leave here.

The bathroom door opened, and the still clean shaven Michael exited. 'You're next Chris.'

'Are you somehow shaving everyday Mikey Boy?' I asked, running my hand through my three week old beard.

'I only get a few hairs coming through on my chin and upper lip, so yes, I just shave it every day. That way it doesn't hurt too much.'

'Lucky you,' I said.

'I used to wish I could grow a beard,' he said. 'Not anymore.'

After an incredibly cold shower, I got dressed in my dirty clothes and headed back outside to the garden. Sandra, Pete and Theo were sat with the kids while Shannon, Michael, Jack, Gee and Ali were stood on the other side of the garden. I noticed a few more people were now out there, although separated from our group. The woman with the nice bum wasn't amongst them. I nodded in their direction as I passed. They were sat in two groups of three. They responded with nods of their own, a couple of people saying, 'Hi.'

Jack looked at me as I approached. 'Chris. You, Gee and Ali are going to walk counter clockwise around the camp, working your way inwards.' He gestured to Shannon and Michael. 'We're going to go clockwise. We've kind of figured out where the food tents are by comparing everyone's maps, but it's anyone's guess really, they're all as bad as each other. We hit the food tents when we see them. Try and spend twenty minutes in each one you find. Dinner starts at six.' He looked to Michael, who nodded in agreement, looking a lot more sober after a shower.

'Have you got a photo of Beth?' I asked Jack.

'Yeah on my phone.'

'Has your phone got any battery left?' I asked.

'No.'

I laughed. 'So you don't have a photo then.'

'No I don't, come on let's go.'

Shannon handed out bottles of water, informing us she'd filled them up from the tap in the kitchen.

I hesitated before taking one. 'Is it okay to drink?'

'Spoke to the other residents.' She nodded to the other people sat on the grass. 'They said they haven't got dysentery yet.'

I took the plastic bottle. 'Okay, suppose we don't have much choice anyway.'

The six of us made our way back to the road that ran around the edge of the camp, just inside the inner fence. Gee, Ali and I turned left, the other three turned right.

'Good luck Jack,' Ali said as we parted.

'Thanks,' Jack replied. 'If we don't see you at our food tent, meet back at the house at midnight.'

We got our first look at the border wall as we headed towards the north fence along 12th Street. It wasn't as big as I was expecting. It looked like it was made up of large concrete sections.

'How tall do you think it is?' I asked.

'Don't know,' Ali replied. 'Hard to tell from here. Must be about two hundred feet away. It looks smaller than I thought.'

'Wall is about six or seven metres high,' Gee said. 'Can tell by people on top.' He pointed to a few different spots along the wall.

'Not that small then,' I noted.

Human shapes could just be seen walking along the top, their heads and shoulders visible. Large unlit floodlights were spread out along the wall.

Unlike the south inner fence, which ran in a straight line, following H Street all the way to the Harbour and the water, the north fence didn't have a straight road to follow. Rather than cut through gardens and woodland, the fence followed the easiest path. It ran alongside the route the roads took. Vast amounts of the woodland had recently been felled in a large section of no man's land, presumably to allow the Canadians to spot any illegal border crossing attempts.

The sound of building work could be faintly heard on the other side of the wall. Other than that, it was still eerily quiet. I'd assumed there would be more noise coming from the Canadian side. They must be under strict instructions to stay quiet also. The outer edges were still clear of people. Unlike the south and the east fence, nobody stood guard on this side of the north fence.

The amount of people dramatically changed when we reached the end of the north fence. To carry on would have meant walking into the water, so we turned left. The harbour was a hive of activity, still silent, but people were everywhere. Hundreds crossed the road in front of us, going back and forth. They seemed to be carrying crates of all sizes.

Considering fish is only on the menu two or three nights a week, I think we may have been quite fortuitous the first night we arrived, in order to get tuna steaks.

The harbour jutted out at a right angle from the mainland, going in almost a straight line into the water. At the end of the harbour I could see a small stretch of water, and then some more land with buildings on it. I really wished my phone was working so I could check Google Maps.

More people meant I was saying, 'No, it's not her,' a lot. Gee and Ali had a very vague description of Beth that Jack had given them. So any female they spotted with shoulder length brown hair would mean them frantically pointing at her, and asking me if it was Beth.

I had to keep reminding Gee that Beth was white, and not literally every female he saw. I was pretty sure he was still drunk.

We spotted a few of the food tents as we made our way around, marking them on the best of our maps so we could pay them a visit when it was time. To my relief, I spotted a couple of pubs. I was glad the entire population wouldn't have to cram into Pea's Place. I marked them all on my map also.

After doing a full circle, we started to move further in, towards the middle of the camp. This meant having to walk through more and more people. My eyes constantly scanned the crowds as we made our way through. Behind me, Ali stopped people as we passed by, asking them if they knew a Beth Tillman or Gayter. Every thirty seconds Gee would point at a woman, literally any woman, asking me if it was Beth.

We passed a lot more fights. They all seemed to finish as quickly as they'd started. More than once, it began because somebody took it upon themselves to try and shut another person up. Usually because that person suddenly cried out something religious, such as, 'God is punishing us for our sins' or, 'Only Jesus can save us now.' We made sure we stayed as far away from them as possible.

As we passed one of the food tents, placed in a former Blaine residents back garden, Ali pointed out it was six o'clock, and she was starving. So we went in and joined the queue.

'Do you think we have to go to our designated food tents?' Ali asked, after we'd been slowly shuffling along for a few minutes. 'I'm pretty sure it's supposed to depend on where we live. Our house isn't near here.'

'The catering staff won't give a shit,' I said. 'They'll probably be drunk or stoned, or both.'

Twenty minutes of queuing later, we were stood in the corner of the large tent, holding our bowls of rice and vegetables, watching the crowds come and go. The amount of people stuffed in here at any one time was incredible. Luckily it didn't take long for people to spoon rice into their mouths, so it was a quick turnover.

I'd flashed my four of clubs to the guy behind the counter, but he didn't even glance in my direction. Like an automated machine, he just handed me my bowl of beige food, before scooping some more into another bowl, and handing it to Gee behind me.

'I think we're gonna lose a bit of weight in here,' I said. 'You might have to change your name to Little Gee.'

Gee grunted an acknowledgement before spooning more rice into his mouth.

Ali looked down at her bowl. 'I might see about joining the scavengers. The only issue is going through quarantine every time you come back.'

'So you wouldn't be able to bring stuff back for personal use? They'd take everything off you?' I asked her.

'Yeah I suppose. Okay, I'm not going to see about joining them.'

'Where do they do the quarantine? The same place as we did it?'

'No,' she answered me. 'They do it on Semiahmoo, and then get a boat over to the harbour.'

'What the fuck is Semiahmoo?' I asked.

'It's a bit of land that curves around to almost meet Blaine harbour. You probably saw it when we were walking around that side. The guy that ran one of the market stalls was telling us about it, that's where everything comes in to the camp, not just the fishing boats.'

I managed to squeeze between people so I could place my empty bowl down on the closest table. 'Could we have come across on a boat? Rather than through that tunnel?'

Ali shrugged. 'Probably, I didn't ask him. Come on, we've been here long enough. Time to move on.'

We started to weave our way through the mass of people and long tables, towards one of the exits.

'Fucking Elliot and Martin,' I said to Ali. 'They never mentioned the boat option. Did they?'

Ali spoke over her shoulder as she walked, 'We were surrounded by zombies. What were you going to do? Fight your way to the coast?'

'No, but I could have waited until the zombies had fucked off back to the outer fence. Then I could have strolled over to the coast.'

'The tunnel wasn't that bad,' Ali said.

'Tunnel fine,' Gee added.

We finally made it outside. There was marginally more space to move around, now that a lot of people were crammed into the food tents.

'The tunnel wasn't fine,' I said. 'It was incredibly shite.'

Ali walked away, her head down and looking at the map in her hands. 'Come on guys, let's find another food tent.' She stopped and had a glance around her, before starting again down another road. Unfortunately, the route she'd chosen meant we had to fight through a mass of people all walking towards the food tent, and us.

This is gonna get really fucking annoying. No, it is really fucking annoying.

Beth wasn't in the next food tent we found, or the one after that, or the one after that.

'Does she like drink?' Gee asked me.

'What?'

'Beth, does she drink beer?' he asked.

'Not really, she's drunk and falling asleep after one glass of wine. Why?'

'Just thinking,' he said, tapping the side of his head.

Nine o'clock came and went, so we gave up on the food tents and continued with our concentric circles. The inner fence and parts of the harbour had solar lights, so it was reasonably well illuminated around those areas. Closer to the centre of the camp, where people seemed to congregate and just walk around for no reason, it was much harder to see what I was stepping on. Old steel barrels had been positioned on street corners and set alight. The market stalls had candles laid out, and some people even walked around with flaming torches. Even with all that, it was still difficult to see.

If they're not careful this place is definitely gonna burn down.

Gee was leading as we walked around the west side of the camp, close to the harbour again. He stopped and pointed towards a building. Above the door hung a white banner. Pea's Place had been stencilled onto it. 'Pub?' he asked.

'Love to Gee, but how are we gonna pay for drinks?' I asked.

He smiled down at me. 'Do not worry about that.' He turned and strode confidently across the traffic free road, towards the pub.

'What the fuck does that mean?' I asked him.

He just carried on walking, so Ali and I followed him.

I turned to Ali as we walked. 'Seriously, what does that mean?'

'I don't care. If he can get me a drink, I'll take it. We aren't going to find Beth in the dark.'

We caught up with Gee just as he opened the door. Two very surly looking guys stood on the other side, both of them bigger than Gee. They stepped closer together, blocking our path.

Well, that's the end of that idea then.

Chapter 13: Vegas

The expressions on the two huge bouncers' faces changed. The difference was instantaneous. They were suddenly all smiles. Gee shook both their hands in turn. There was a lot of shoulder grabbing and back slapping, all the while they spoke in what I'm assuming was Lithuanian. I heard the two big guys say Gintaras a lot, and at one point Gee turned to Ali and me, still speaking in Lithuanian. Both of our names were mentioned a couple of times. Ali and I both smiled. The two bouncers held out their hands to us and we shook them.

'This is Andrius and Matis,' Gee said, a huge smile on his face. 'They are from Lithuania, like me.'

'Yeah we guessed that Gee,' Ali said, a big smile spreading across her face as well. 'Hi guys.'

'Hey, any friend of Gintaras is a friend of ours,' Andruis said. He leaned around Gee and almost scooped Ali and me up with his right arm, guiding us into the pub. 'Welcome to Pea's Place. You can call me Andy. It's easier for non-Lithuanian speakers to say.'

Andruis's, or Andy's English was a lot better than Gee's. There was also a bit more American in his accent.

As Andruis opened an inner door, Matis quietly said, 'Have a good night guys.'

The inner door opened up onto a very nice looking, but bizarrely quiet pub. Each table had three of four people sat around it, but all carrying on with the low volume rule of the camp. They all seemed to be in full conversation but speaking very softly.

I'm definitely gonna forget this rule after a few drinks.

The slate fronted, wooden topped bar stretched along the entire length of one wall. Two barmaids busied themselves serving people who were sat at the bar. Two waiters stood at the right hand side of the bar, waiting for their drinks orders. Behind the two barmaids, the wall was entirely mirrored. Bottles filled the many shelves that sat in front of the massive mirrors. All of the bar stools were occupied. I had a quick glance around and there weren't any free seats in the house.

'Come with me,' Andruis said to us.

It was weird to be in a pub this full of people and be able to hear someone so easily.

We followed Andruis.

I'm sticking with his real name, it's really not that hard to pronounce.

He took us towards the far left of the bar, where one man was sat on a bar stool. He was slightly separated from the others at the bar, resting his back against the wall behind him. He looked like he was all arms and legs.

Andruis guided us into the space between the leggy man and the next person along. 'One minute,' he said.

Ali and I exchanged bemused looks. I raised my right hand in front of my face, rubbing my thumb and forefinger together. I mouthed the word 'Money,' and shrugged my shoulders. Ali just smiled and returned my shrug.

Fuck's sake, this is gonna be awkward after all this fuss has been made.

Gee seemed like he was in his element, just looking around at his surroundings, the smile on his face getting bigger.

Only seconds later, Andruis appeared as if from nowhere, carrying two tall bar stools. He placed them onto the wooden floor behind us. 'Just need one more,' he said.

'Andruis,' a voice said, making the Lithuanian bouncer spin around. It was the leggy man calling him over.

I saw the man's mouth moving, but couldn't quite discern what he was saying. Andruis listened and nodded his head. The man picked up his wine glass, slid off his stool and walked past us to lean against the bar. I think he may have been even taller than Andruis, and he wasn't just all arms and legs, he also carried a bit of extra weight around his middle. Andruis then moved our two stools closer to the one the leggy man had just vacated.

Andruis turned to us smiling. 'Here you go.'

I looked to the man who had given up his stool. 'Are you sure?'

He just smiled, giving us a quick and exaggerated wave of his hand. Up close it was hard to tell his age. He had a big face, with large full lips, and he looked very young. Below his eyebrows, there wasn't a single hair on his face.

'Thanks very much, that's very kind of you,' I said, climbing up onto the stool closest to him. The little axe tucked into my belt was digging into my hip, so I quickly slid it around so it was more comfortable.

'I've been sat down long enough,' he replied, briefly glancing down to my axe. He sounded like he was English.

Ali sat between Gee and me, so I leaned around her and whispered, 'Gee, how are we going to pay for the drinks?'

Gee continued to smile that annoyingly smug grin. 'Do not worry,' he told me.

'What the fuck?' I whispered.

'Excuse me,' Andruis said to a barmaid. He was leaning across the bar between me and the leggy man. She hadn't heard him so he clicked his fingers. She noticed and rushed over to him. He muttered something into her ear, before turning back to us. 'Okay. Drinks are on me tonight guys. Enjoy.'

'Eh?' I replied, before realising what he'd just said. 'Okay, thank you,' I said to his back, as walked towards the exit.

'What can I get you?' the woman behind the bar asked.

'Erm...any IPA's? I asked.

She smiled back at me.

Probably forced, but nice all the same.

'Just the one darling. It's Goose Island.'

'Yeah perfect,' I said.

'Make that two,' Ali said.

'Three,' Gee added.

The smiley barmaid returned with three opened bottles. 'You okay with no glasses? Running a bit short.'

'That's absolutely fine,' I replied. 'Thanks very much.'

Her smile looked more sincere this time.

'What just happened Gee?' Ali asked him, once the barmaid had left to serve another customer.

'I meet them earlier today. They from same part of Lithuania as me. I think one of them fuck my cousin.'

'Nice,' I said, shaking my head. 'What about this Pea fella? Is he happy his bouncers are giving away free drinks all night?'

Gee shrugged. 'I do not know. You ask him. He stand behind you.'

I stared straight at Gee, and asked, 'Really?'

He nodded, bringing his bottle up to his mouth.

I looked to Ali and whispered, 'Do you think he heard all that?'

'Probably,' she replied, and leaned closer to me. 'But you didn't say anything bad.' She took a swig of her drink, and then raised the bottle up to me. 'Nice.'

I took a mouthful from my bottle, and swivelled around to face the bar. I glanced to my right and the man was angled towards me. I swivelled a little bit further and reached my hand out to him. 'Hi, are you Mr Pea? I'm Chris.'

'Pleased to meet you Chris,' he said, shaking my hand. 'Call me Charles.' He was definitely English, from somewhere down south.

'This is Ali and Gintaras,' I said, leaning back on my stool.

Charles reached around me, took Ali's hand and kissed the back of it. 'Pleased to meet you also Ali.'

Ali just smiled. After she retrieved her hand she surreptitiously wiped it on her jeans. I didn't think Charles had spotted the move.

Gee just leaned forward and raised his bottle, saying, 'Thank you for drinks.'

'You're very welcome Gintaras,' Charles replied.

'What are you doing over here then?' I asked him.

'In America? Or in the camp?'

'Both,' I said.

'I've been in the States for a few years. Most recently I was a yacht broker in Santa Barbara. Here in the camp, I run this bar.'

'How do you end up running a bar in an apocalyptic refugee camp?' Ali asked.

'Short story? This place was available when we got here.'

'What is the slightly longer story?' I asked him.

'Well, back in Santa Barbara, I borrowed one of my client's yachts. He didn't need it anymore on account of being dead. I then sailed Andruis, Matis, and their families up here from California. We were trying to get to Canada but their navy wouldn't let us pass. Do you know the geography around here?'

I shook my head. 'Nope.'

'Not really,' Ali said.

Gee stared at the bottle in his hand.

'Well,' Charles continued. 'We were trying to get to Vancouver Island, and dock somewhere around there, but their coastal vessels appeared from nowhere. We entered the Salish Sea hoping they would leave us alone, but they just followed us until we came upon another one of their vessels, and then another one, and another. You get the picture. Then we ran out of American water and had to dock here, in Blaine's harbour. Like I said, this place, the pub, was just available,' he said, using both of his overly long arms to dramatically gesture to our surroundings. 'Not many takers you see, and I had Andruis and Matis to help me get started. I figured we were going to be here a while, so we just did it. Twelve days later and here we are. Things can move quickly, but also incredibly slowly in the apocalypse.'

'How old are you Charles?' Ali asked, her Goose Island almost empty.

I took a long swig of mine, trying to catch up.

Charles smiled back at her. 'I'm thirty four, Alison.'

'How did you know the big Lithuanians?' I asked.

The smiling barmaid appeared with three new bottles. I had to snatch my old bottle out of her reach. 'Not finished yet,' I said. 'Thank you.'

'Come on slow coach,' Ali said.

Charles waited for us to finish talking before answering. 'I only met Andruis and Matis for the first time when trying to get out of Santa Barbara. I figured we could help each other out, and so we did.' He raised his glass of white wine and took a sip.

'How do you make any money from this place?' I asked.

'I don't. Nobody makes any money here. But this affords me a relatively easy and comfortable life. I don't want to go scavenging and fishing, or venture into the wastelands killing zombies. Far too dangerous.'

'Where does all the booze come from?' Ali asked.

I looked up at the shelves and noticed a lot of the bottles were actually empty, probably just there for show.

'I have my own scavengers,' Charles replied. 'They're separate from the so-called official scavengers. May I ask how long you three have been here?'

'We got here yesterday,' Ali answered. 'This is our first day in the camp.'

'I imagine in the brief time you have been guests here, you will have noticed that this place is not run like a well-oiled machine? Corruption and laziness is rife.'

'Yep, we've noticed,' I said.

'Well there you go then, you should be able to surmise from what you've witnessed, that it is quite easy to smuggle certain items into the camp. Getting items, or people, into Canada is another thing altogether.'

'Are you from Suffolk?' I asked. 'I'm getting a slight farmer accent from you.' I realised too late that the farmer comment was probably quiet offensive. The beers were going straight to my head.

Luckily Charles just let out a high pitched giggle. 'Yes, I'm from Stowmarket. An Ipswich fan for my sins.'

'I've got a friend in the camp from Norwich,' I said. 'I'll bring him in here sometime. He'll probably hate you.'

'Chris,' Ali said. 'Try not to insult our host too much.'

Charles laughed again. 'It's okay Ali. Just a joke, it's an English football rivalry.'

I glanced up and three new bottles had appeared. 'Fucking hell,' I exclaimed. 'Gee, are you ordering these?'

Gee turned to me and smiled.

I finished off my first bottle and quickly downed half of the second.

'I have discovered over the last few weeks, that Lithuanians drink like fish,' Charles said.

'Hey Pea my old buddy.' A hand slapped down on Charles's shoulder.

Charles turned to face the new arrival and smiled. 'Evening Elliot, how has your day been?'

I twisted around to see Elliot's smiling face. I recognised him as one of the container guys.

'Awful, like every day before it. And I've been moved off night shifts.' He glanced at me, and then at Ali and Gee. 'Hey new guys.' He looked back to Charles. 'Me and Martin shepherded this lot in early yesterday morning.'

'Hello again,' I said.

Andruis the bouncer stepped between Ali and me, and spoke to the same smiley barmaid. 'Elliot is okay for tonight,' he said.

I've got no fucking idea how all this works.

'Usual please Amy,' Elliot said to the smiley barmaid. 'How has your first day been?' he asked, diverting his attention back to us.

'It's been an eye opener,' Ali said.

I remembered my drink and finished off the second bottle.

'New rumours today, direct from across the border,' Elliot said.

Charles laughed. 'From your very reliable, but secret source once again Elliot?'

Elliot frowned. 'Yes Pea, the same.'

'Okay, go ahead,' Charles said. 'Please divulge to us this accurate and truthful information, gleamed from God knows where.'

Elliot stared at Charles, shaking his head, before continuing. 'It was definitely the Russians and the Chinese, working in cahoots.'

'Cahoots,' Charles said. 'Is that the term the international press are using?'

Elliot ignored him. 'Apparently they're both denying it, but of course they would. The rest of the world is readying their defences. The United Nations is imposing all kinds of sanctions on the Russians and the Chinese. It's definitely a cold war out there. The biggest news is that Canada is sending half its naval force over to Europe real soon.' Elliot's beer arrived and he took a sip, leaving foam on his moustache. He wiped it away with the back of his hand.

'Apart from the Canadians setting sail,' Charles said. 'None of that is new, and it was only a matter of time before Canada's navy was mobilised.'

'Just letting you know the latest,' Elliot said.

I turned to Ali. 'So you were right, maybe.'

'Yeah,' she said glumly.

'Hey,' Charles said. 'It's just rumours. The virus might have been caused by parents refusing to vaccinate their kids for all we know.'

'Everything I said is true,' Elliot retorted.

'Any idea how to get out of the camp?' I asked Elliot.

'What are you thinking?' Ali asked me.

I shrugged. 'How to get across the border in less than eighteen months.'

'Across the border? Not easy,' Elliot replied. 'Out of the camp? Now that is easy. The same way you came in.'

'Oh yeah,' I remembered. 'Why didn't you tell us there was another option of going in by boat?'

Elliot looked confused. 'Because you were in our container, and the tunnel was just there.'

I shook my head. 'Okay, doesn't matter. What about getting into Canada?'

'You do know the wall isn't finished?' Charles said.

'Nope,' I replied. 'Well, Elliot briefly mentioned something about it yesterday.'

Ali shifted in her seat slightly to move closer to the conversation.

'This is a big country, and the border stretches across the whole entire lot of it,' Elliot said. 'They can't have had time to finish the wall. We think they concentrated on the heavily populated areas first. They're bound to have weak spots, where it's just a fence, or only guarded by soldiers.'

'Fifty miles,' Charles said. 'One hundred perhaps. If you go far enough you'll definitely find one of Elliot's weak spots.'

'Why don't people try it then?' Ali asked.

'I'm sure they do,' Elliot said. 'People leave here all the time. They probably die trying, or they make it. And there are the other camps. They might just go to one of them if they can't get across.'

'Why are you thinking of leaving us so soon?' Charles asked me. 'You've only just arrived, so you must know how bad it is out there?'

'Because I can't stay here for eighteen months. I need to get home.'

'Back to England?' Charles asked, looking surprised.

'Yes, back home. By the sounds of it there won't be an England if I wait much longer.'

I heard bottles clinking together as Amy the smiley barmaid placed three more bottles on the bar.

I quickly picked up my third. 'Gee, for fuck's sake.'

'I've got two words for you–,' Charles started to say.

'If those words are Atlantic and ocean, then I don't want to hear them,' I said.

'Okay,' Charles said, smiling and raising his glass to me. 'Then I won't say them.'

'Yes I know. I'm taking it one step at a time. I'm really trying not to think about the distance, and the huge ocean.'

'You guys aren't like...' Elliot paused and glanced around the pub. 'You aren't one of those fundamentalist types are you?'

I laughed. 'No, obviously not.'

'What were you looking for Elliot?' Charles asked him. 'That lot don't frequent my pub.'

'Can't be too careful,' he said. 'They give me the heebie-jeebies. I bet they get us before the zombies do. Anyway, I just wanted to warn these three to keep an eye out for them.' He turned back to us. 'You stay clear of them, they're trouble.'

'Elliot,' Ali said. 'Where do you guys go to use the restroom? When you're in the container.'

Elliot shifted his weight from one leg to the other. 'Well...' He paused to take a long drink of his beer. 'Let's just say it's a good thing you came to the container from the side you did. You would probably have slipped off if you tried climbing the other side.'

'What a delightful image,' Charles said. 'Thank you Elliot.'

'What do you do if someone does come from that side,' Ali asked, laughing.

'We don't usually let people in through the roof. We do have a door you know.'

'Why did you go in through the roof?' Charles asked us.

Before one of us could answer him, Elliot explained to Charles the circumstances that led to us gaining access to Elliot and Martin's container.

'That was bad timing,' Charles said.

'Yeah,' Elliot said. 'Only the second time we've had to set the fireworks off, so very bad timing.'

Ali sat back slightly, moving away from the conversation. She was probably thinking about Steve meeting his gruesome end during those very circumstances. Elliot and Charles had also stepped away slightly, and seemed to be discussing something. I took the opportunity to try and catch Gee up on his drinking.

'You okay?' I asked Ali.

She smiled up at me. 'Yeah fine, think I might go back to the house after this one, update Jack on our failure to find Beth. Hopefully he's found her.'

Ali was on her fourth bottle, I was still halfway through my third. 'Let me finish mine and I'll walk you back.'

'No you don't have to do that,' Ali replied. 'I'm a big girl.'

'It's got nothing to do with you being a moderately sized woman.' That received a quizzical look from Ali. 'I don't think anyone should walk anywhere alone around here,' I added. 'Especially at night.'

Out of the corner of my eye I noticed Charles stepping towards us. 'Chris is right, but let him stay here and enjoy himself. I'll get Matis to walk you back. Don't worry, he's happily married with four kids, I would trust him with my life, and my friends' lives.'

Ali finished the last of her drink in one go. Standing up, she said, 'Okay, I'll take you up on that kind offer.' She had a slight wobble, reaching her hand out to grab her bar stool. 'Whoa, feel a little bit tipsy.'

'You did just down four bottles in an hour,' I said.

'It's only weak,' Ali said, picking up her empty bottle and struggling to read the label. 'Shit. Five point nine percent, it's not weak.' She laughed and placed the bottle back down on the bar. 'Goodnight gentlemen. I'll see you in the morning. Charles, is my escort available?'

Charles stepped to Ali's side, taking her arm and walking her to the exit. 'Walk this way my dear.'

'Goodnight Ali,' I said.

Without turning, she lifted her hand into the air and waved, before exiting through the inner door.

I spun around on my seat to find two new bottles. 'Gee, when are you ordering these?'

'When I finish last one.'

'Well yeah, I guessed that.' I downed the last of my third bottle and picked up the fourth.

Charles sidled up next to us and sat on Ali's vacated stool. 'Don't worry about your friend. Matis will take good care of her.'

'She could probably handle herself anyway,' I said.

'Are you two a couple?' he asked me.

'Me and Gee, or me and Ali?'

Gee let out a loud roar of a laugh, before raising his hands in the air. 'Sorry, no loud noise.'

'It's okay Gintaras,' Charles said, before looking back to me. 'Yes, I meant you and Ali.'

'Nope, I'm married. Need to get back to England to my wife.'

'Do you think I'd be in with a chance?' he asked.

'With Ali?' I laughed. 'I honestly don't know her well enough to give you an answer, but I reckon you should go for it if you want. Life is even shorter these days.'

'Why not ask me?' Gee asked Charles.

I turned and shot Gee a confused look.

'I'm sorry Gintaras, you're not really my type,' Charles said, a smirk on his face.

'No fucker,' Gee said. 'Why not ask if me and Ali are couple?'

'My apologies again, I just thought there was a bit of an age gap.'

Gee finished another bottle. 'Okay.'

Seems it's very easy to resolve things with Gee.

Just as I finished my fourth bottle, Charles stood up and wished us a goodnight, telling us to enjoy the rest of the evening. I looked around for Elliot, finding him sat with another group on the other side of the pub. There was no sign of his partner Martin.

Without asking me, Gee ordered two more bottles from Amy, the barmaid.

Jesus fucking Christ, I'm feeling shitfaced already.

Suppose I better converse with the giant Lithuanian to try and slow him down.

'I went to watch England versus Lithuania, a few years ago now.'

'What sport?' Gee asked.

'Football, what else?'

'I am not fan of football. In Lithuania basketball is popular sport. I play when younger.'

'For a team?'

Gee shrugged. 'No.'

Okay, exhausted that line of conversation then.

'Where were you living before you got to Austin?' I asked.

'I live in Las Vegas.'

'I've been there a few times, can't imagine living there.'

'We not live in centre, with all lights and craziness,' he said, waving his arms around in the air, almost flamboyantly. 'More to Las Vegas than casinos.'

'Oh right, what did you do again? Was it a janitor or something?'

'I only do it first time in Las Vegas.'

'What do you mean?' I asked.

'You ask if I do again. I never do janitor job before. First time was in Las Vegas, at three apartment complexes I work.'

What the fuck is he talking about?

'Sorry Gee, I've got no idea what you're on about.'

Gee just laughed and drank more of his sixth bottle, I continued with my fifth.

'Okay, doesn't matter,' I said. 'Wife, family?'

He downed his bottle and ordered another two.

He obviously doesn't want to talk about it.

'What's your plan when you reach Canada?' I asked. 'If we ever make it up there.'

'I had wife and two children,' he said. 'Boy seven. Girl ten.'

Shite.

'They were visiting family of my wife when disease start to spread. I try to find them, drive half way to California. I must miss them when they go back home. I come home to find wife come back sick. Told me children died on journey back. She would not let me near her because she was sick.' He drank half his beer in one go. 'Next day she die.'

Fucking hell. Why did I ask? I could have easily known Gee the rest of my life without finding that out.

'Gee, I'm truly sorry. That is horrible.'

'Yes it is,' he stated. He leaned over and knocked his bottle against mine. 'Let's get shitassed.'

'Shitassed?' I laughed. 'It's shitfaced Gee. You mean shitfaced. But yeah, I'm well on the way already.'

'I have no plans for after, when in Canada,' he said. 'I do not know what I will do. How will you get back to England?'

'No fucking idea mate.'

The drinking continued, me playing catch up with Gee. I lost count of the beers we consumed, and had no idea what the time was.

DAY NINETEEN

Chapter 14: Eavesdrop

My bed was moving.

This must be a dream. Was I dreaming I was back in our old truck, Blue? Are the zombies pushing us over again?

I don't think that's it. Hang on a second...this is more of a rocking motion. An earthquake maybe?

Where am I again?

I remember. We're trying to get into Canada. So we're at the border. Do they get earthquakes in Washington State? Probably.

A woman moaned. It sounded like it was coming from directly underneath me.

Bollocks. I forgot I was on the top bunk. Who the fuck is having sex in the bed below me?

I opened my eyes and looked around, trying to look for Jack and Gee, but I couldn't remember which beds they were in.

Do I even know which beds they're in? Did we go to bed at the same time last night? What did we actually do last night? I really can't remember.

The bed was still being rhythmically rocked. I could now hear heavy breathing beneath me, and then another stifled moan.

Fuck's sake.

I turned over, making sure I made as much noise as possible. Beneath me a few giggles mixed in with the heavy breathing. The bed continued to rock.

They know I'm awake. Fuck's sake. Just make it quick please.

I pulled my elbows up, trying to sit myself up, but a wave of nausea washed over me, making me quickly rest my head back down.

Oh fuck, I remember now, we went to the pub last night. What time did we get back? I can't even remember leaving. What pub were we in?

A memory flashed through my mind. Me and Gee sitting at the bar, an Ipswich fan, and one of the guys from the container. Had Jack been there? I don't think so. No, he definitely wasn't there. Ali was there. Yes, Ali was there, I remember that.

The rocking was increasing in speed, the moaning becoming more frequent and louder.

Hopefully that just means it's gonna be over soon. What the fuck? Is nobody else hearing this?

I rolled over onto my side so I was facing the room. Nobody else's eyes were looking back in my direction.

Fucking hell. It better not be Gee down there. I do not want to listen to Big Gee having sex.

The whole bed was now squeaking.

Surely everyone else in here must know what's going on?

With a loud of expulsion of breath from one of the people beneath me, the rocking and squeaking came to an abrupt end. Only a few seconds later, I heard sheets being thrown back, and the springs in their mattress shifting.

'No don't go,' a female voice whispered. 'Anyone that can make me fanny fart five times can stay the night.'

What the actual fuck? Did she just say that? Fuck off.

The mattress below shifted again, the fanny fart comment obviously drawing her sexual partner back into her bed.

She's gonna be English if she's saying fanny fart. Fucking hell. Probably the woman I saw yesterday with the nice bum. Fucking Brits abroad. Nice of her to continue the reputation, even in the apocalypse.

Someone was saying my name.

I dragged the pillow around so it covered my face and both my ears. 'Nope. Need more sleep,' I muttered into the pillow.

'Come on Chris,' Michael said. 'You need to go for breakfast. You can't skip the meagre excuses for a meal in this place. Gee is up. He's in the bathroom.'

I suppose he's fucking right.

'Okay. I'm getting up.' I forced myself to sit up, the pillow falling to land on my lap. I wasn't feeling sick anymore, not like last night, but my head was killing me.

Oh yeah, I woke up in the middle of the night, and felt like I was gonna be sick.

Fuck. The fucking fanny fart sex as well.

'Give me five minutes Mikey Boy,' I croaked. 'I'll meet you outside. Just need to go to the toilet.'

Michael agreed to wait for me outside, but told me I should hurry up.

I joined the queue to the bathroom. There were three people ahead of me. The man in front of me turned and smiled when I stopped behind him. He was a short man, maybe in his forties. He was balding slightly, and in keeping with the majority of the guys in the camp, was sporting a beard.

'Morning,' I said to him.

The other two people in the queue glanced behind them when I spoke, but then quickly turned back around to face forward.

'New to the house?' he asked.

'Yeah, only my second day in the camp.'

He looked surprised. 'Where have you come from?'

'When the virus shit started? My friend and I were in Colorado.'

'How did you end up here?' he asked.

I smiled. 'Long story.'

'You from Great Britain?'

'Yep, I'm here on vacation. At least I was here on vacation.'

'I visited London a few years back. Do you live near there?'

'Well,' I said. 'About two hundred miles away.'

'Not far then,' the man stated.

I shot him a puzzled look. He turned around when the bathroom door opened. A woman left and the man at the front took her place in the bathroom. We all shuffled forwards, filling the space.

The man in front of me seemed to use the interruption as an excuse to end the conversation.

Thank fuck.

'She didn't say that?' Shannon exclaimed.

I swallowed a mouthful of porridge. 'She did. Five time fanny fart sex. Sounded quite proud of it.'

Sandra, the kids, and her two cousins, Pete and Theo, were sat on the end of one of the long tables in the food tent. They all had bowls of porridge and water. The kids had been very reluctant to eat theirs, until a very nice old lady offered Sandra some sachets of sugar. A sachet each had changed the kid's minds. I'd hoped to be offered some sugar, but no such luck. It was almost as tasteless as the rice and vegetables we'd eaten the previous night.

Shannon, Michael, Gee, Ali and I were stood a few feet away, huddled together next the edge of the cramped tent. Jack had apparently decided to wake up early to check all the food tents during breakfast hours. I felt guilty he'd gone on his own, but Shannon assured me he'd turned down their offers of help.

'Is it even a good thing?' I asked. 'To elicit five fanny farts, or any at all?'

'I do not understand,' Gee said. 'Why would fart during sex be good thing?'

'Chris means a British fanny,' Ali told him. 'Not a real fanny.' She pointed at her own behind, but then looked uncomfortable. 'I mean an American fanny.' She let out an exasperated groan. 'You know what I'm saying,' she muttered, shaking her head. 'I drank too much last night.'

I laughed. 'You drank too much? Fuck knows how much we drank,' I said, pointing at Gee and then myself.

'What time did you get back to the house?' Michael asked.

'Fuck knows?' I looked to Gee. 'Any idea?'

Gee shrugged. 'So you mean fart out of vagina?'

'Yes exactly that,' I replied. 'I didn't even hear one fanny fart, let alone five. And I heard everything. Did you not hear them Gee?'

Gee shook his head. 'I heard no farts. I maybe fart in sleep.'

'Not just the farts. I meant the whole thing. Did you hear them having sex?'

He just shook his head again.

'Fanny farts as you call them Chris, can be a good thing,' Shannon said, leaning forwards slightly, as if to impart some valuable information. 'It can mean it's aggressive sex. Not violent aggressive. You know? Nicely aggressive.'

We all grinned at Michael.

His eyebrows arched as he returned our glares. 'What?' he asked.

185

With my grin broadening, I said, 'Aggressive with a crossbow, and in the bedroom Mikey Boy?'

Michael just shrugged and chewed on his lumpy porridge, a slight smile at the corners of his mouth.

'Well either way,' I said. 'I think it's a weird thing to say to somebody.'

'No, I'll definitely agree with you on that one,' Shannon said. 'I've never said it to anyone.'

'Oh, by the way Ali,' I said. 'Charles likes you. He asked if you were single.'

'Charles? The guy who runs Pea's Place?' she asked.

'Yep, did you meet many other people called Charles last night?'

'Interested?' Shannon asked, smiling.

Ali screwed up her face. 'I don't know, can't really remember what he looked like.'

Michael grinned. 'Made a big impression then?'

'Big lips and long arms,' Ali mused, before looking at me. 'Did his hair look like it had been stuck on his head? Like Lego hair?'

Laughing, I said, 'Yep, that pretty much sums him up.'

Shrugging, Ali placed her empty bowl inside mine. 'Yeah, why not? I'd give him a go. Come on. Let's go back.'

When we got back to the house, the English woman with the nice bum was leaving through the front door, just as I was walking in. She looked me in the eyes, smiled and said 'Good morning,' before continuing onto the street.

It either wasn't her last night, or she doesn't care that I heard her, or she doesn't know I'm on the bed above her.

I'd gone in to use the toilet, while everyone else walked around the side of the house to get into the back garden. After I'd finished, I opened the bathroom door to find Jack stood in the corridor, smiling back at me.

'Morning Jacqueline. Any luck?'

'Yes Christopher. Beth is in the garden with everyone else.'

'What? That's fucking brilliant.' I stepped forwards and hugged him.

He patted me on the back. 'Yes I know, but get off me. I came here to have a piss, not just to tell you the good news.'

I quickly released him and he grabbed his crotch, before shuffling into the bathroom. 'Nearly pissed myself then,' he said, closing the door behind him with his arse.

I walked to the back door and stepped out into the garden. It was still cold out. A little shiver ran through me as I walked. The sun was out but my breath was visible.

It must start getting warmer soon.

Beth was talking to Shannon and Michael. I thought she might have had a bit of a baby bump, but she wasn't showing at all. I'd forgotten that she wasn't actually that far along. A few feet behind her stood a tall man, about six foot three or four. He was slim, with only a little bit of stubble on his face. His hair was short and scruffy. He looked awkward.

Beth's attention was on Shannon, but then she noticed me walking towards her. 'Chris,' she said, tears filling her eyes. She walked towards me, her arms outstretched.

We met half way and embraced. 'Thank you,' she said. 'Jack told me everything.'

I released her and took a step back. 'Thanks? For what? What did he tell you?'

'Thank you for getting Jack here. What else?'

'Nah, I didn't do anything. Shannon, Michael and Gee did more for him than I did.'

'You saved his life,' she said.

'He threw me in a fucking bin and left me,' Jack said, as he walked towards us from the house, a smile on his face.

I stuck two fingers up in his direction.

'Jack,' Beth scolded him. 'Chris carried you to safety while you were unconscious. I bet you haven't even thanked him, have you?'

'It's okay,' I said. 'I don't want him to thank me. It'd be weird.'

'No it's not okay.' She looked Jack straight in the eyes. 'You should thank Chris.'

Jack rolled his eyes and groaned.

'Seriously, it's fine,' I said. 'This is already weird and uncomfortable.'

'See, he doesn't want me to thank him,' Jack said.

'Jack,' Beth said, giving him her most disappointed look.

'Oh for fu…' Jack started, and then turned to me. 'Thank you for carrying me away from the zombies and leaving me in a bin.'

'No problem at all,' I replied. 'I'd happily dump you in a bin anytime.'

Jack turned back to his wife, his arms out and palms up.

'It'll do for now I suppose,' she said. 'Chris, come and meet Roy.' She turned and beckoned the tall bespectacled man over.

Jack took the opportunity to lean in closer to me, whispering in my ear, 'Sarah is dead.'

Fuck me. He left that until the last second. Would have been pretty bad if I'd opened with, how's the wife? Speaking of which, has Jack figured out why Beth put Roy's surname on the list yet?

'Roy, this is Chris,' Beth said.

I shook his hand. 'Hi Roy, really good to finally meet you.'

'You too. Beth told me all about you. I'm really glad you and Jack made it up here.'

Do I mention his wife? Better not. Let him start that topic of conversation.

'Where have you been staying?' I asked, gesturing behind me with my thumb. 'I hope it's nicer than our place?'

Roy let out a little chuckle. 'It's on the other side of the camp. It's not much better than this house.'

'How long have you two been here?' Shannon asked.

'Seven days, or is it six? It's easy to lose track of the days.'

Jack and Beth slipped away and headed towards the house.

'What jobs were you both given?' Michael asked him.

'Beth works in the food tent near our house,' Roy hesitated, suddenly looking uncomfortable. He scratched his head and shifted his weight from his left to his right foot. 'The house we live in I mean. That we share with other people. It's over by the harbour. I work on the docks, unloading the fishing boats. Not exactly where I imagined myself working.'

Michael nodded, before excusing himself and wandering off towards the house.

Ask about the name thing or not? Fuck it.

'Why did Beth put your–?'

'What was your job before all this Roy?' Ali quickly asked, cutting me off mid question.

What the fuck?

Roy's eyes nervously darted between me and Ali. 'Erm…I was a Data Science Manager.'

'Oh, okay,' Ali replied.

Roy's eyes settled on Ali. 'It was looking at data and finding interesting patterns and shit. I was in the Sea Cadets until I was sixteen, so I wouldn't have minded working on the fishing boats.'

Ali just smiled politely and nodded her head.

'When we were looking through the list of names…' I paused to glance at Ali rolling her eyes. 'Beth had your second name,' I continued.

'Yes.' Roy put his clenched fist in front of his mouth and cleared his throat. 'We travelled up here with another group. They were very…let's just say friendly with Beth. She was worried they might try something, so we pretended to be married. They were still with us when we gave the sheriff our names.'

I looked to Ali. 'There you go. A simple explanation. That wasn't hard was it?'

She scowled back at me.

Roy leaned in closer and lowered his voice. 'Jack seems a bit off with me. He should know that nothing untoward happened between Beth and me. It was all just for show. What with Sarah…and everything, we just helped each other through all of this.'

'He'll be fine,' I said. 'He's just been worried about everything. Emotions running high and all that.'

Michael reappeared and handed Roy a cup of something, steam rising up and out of the cup. 'So Roy, what happened in California?' Michael asked. 'We were there at your house after you'd left.'

I shot a glance towards the kitchen window.

Do we have tea and coffee in this shithole?

'I don't suppose the house was still standing was it?' Roy asked.

'No sorry,' Michael said. 'It was a pile of rubble.'

'Thought it would be,' he sighed. 'When we realised it was going to be bad, Sarah, my wife, called Beth and told her to come to our place. She knew that Jack was away, and that Beth was alone. We bunkered down for the first few days in our house. We started smelling the smoke on day five or six. It just got thicker and thicker, eventually it was so black we could barely see anything outside. It was so dark it was like night all the time. We didn't want the house to burn down around us, so we decided to get out and try and come here. Or to Canada anyway. We went via Beth and Jack's apartment so she could leave him a note. It was a good job we left when we did.

When we got out of the city we could see the fires taking over everything. It wasn't long after we got outside the city, that Sarah...' He broke off and stared at the ground for a long moment.

The moment carried on for a while longer. Ali and I exchanged glances. I shrugged and nodded in Roy's direction.

'What?' she mouthed to me.

'I don't know?' I mouthed back.

'Sorry everyone,' Roy finally said. 'It's just so hard. You know?'

'Don't worry,' Michael said. 'You don't have to talk about it.'

I need a way out of this conversation.

'I'm gonna go and make a drink. Does anyone else want one?' I asked.

'That was the last one,' Michael said, pointing at the cup in Roy's hand.

'I'm gonna get some water then, does anyone want one?'

Nobody wanted anything, so I headed to my shared bedroom. I remembered sitting on a bottle of water that morning when trying to climb off my bunk.

After a brief search through my bedding, and pushing aside my Brooklyn Smasher, I managed to retrieve the bottle.

Maybe I shouldn't sleep with a blood covered baseball bat.

I turned to head back to the corridor, stopping when I heard angry whispering from just outside the bedroom door. I crept a bit closer to listen in.

'Stop shouting at me,' Beth hissed.

'I'm not fucking shouting,' Jack replied. 'I'm obviously not shouting because I'm whispering.'

'Well, stop using a shouting tone.'

'What the fuck does that mean?' Jack whispered, sounding exasperated.

'It means you're being very aggressive Jack.'

'What do you expect when you've been shacked up with another man for the last three weeks?'

'I haven't been shacked up with anyone Jack. Roy's wife and my friend died. She died in front of us.'

What the fuck do I do here? I can't walk out now. They'll know I've been listening to them. Please don't come into the bedroom.

'I'm obviously very sorry about that,' Jack said. 'But that doesn't mean you had to start sleeping with him. I wasn't dead. Was I?'

'I wasn't sleeping with him. We shared a bedroom, but he slept on the floor. His wife has literally just died.'

'Sleeping on the floor, a likely story–.' Jack suddenly broke off for some reason.

'Jack,' Gee said. 'This is Beth?'

Where had Gee been? Probably off drinking vodka with Andruis and Matis.

Shite. Don't come in here Gee.

'Yes, this is my wife. Beth, this is Gee.'

'Very nice to meet you,' Beth said. 'Jack has told me how much you've helped him. Thanks for getting him here.'

Shit, what do I do? Hide under a bed? Get in my bed?

'No problem,' Gee said, and then walked into the bedroom.

My finger was pressed against my lips, but it didn't make any difference. As soon as Gee saw me, he said, 'Chris, what you doing here? Hiding?'

Gee, you fucking twat.

I waived the bottle of water in my hand. 'Just getting this,' I said brightly.

I walked out into the corridor. Jack and Beth both shot me identical glowering looks.

I gave them both a big smile. 'Morning, see you outside.' I stepped between them and quickstepped down the corridor, towards the back door.

Back outside, Roy was back to talking about how he and Beth had bumped into a group of five guys, also heading north. He said they were hesitant at first, but both agreed it would be safer to join them.

'They never did, or really said anything, but we were both a bit wary, Beth especially. I said we should maybe pretend to be married. Just to put Beth's mind at ease.'

Fuck. Definitely don't tell Jack it was Roy's idea.

The back door swung open and Beth and Jack stepped into the garden.

'Right okay,' Beth said to us all. 'I'm going back to our place to get my stuff.' She looked at Jack. 'My husband is going to stay here and wait for me.'

'Why not just keep your own bedroom,' I asked. 'We could squeeze Roy in here.'

'That might be an issue,' Roy said. 'We share the house with the guys we came in with. They think me and Beth are married.'

'Roy, you're moving here as well,' Beth told him.

Roy looked awkwardly to Beth, and then to Jack, and back to Beth again. 'Oh, erm, okay.'

Jack just stood there, a look of glum resignation on his face.

Beth pointed at Roy, saying, 'Come on then. We'll be back soon. We don't have much stuff.' She kissed Jack on the cheek, and then walked towards the side gate, Roy following behind her.

Once they were out of sight, I said, 'Fairy tale reunion then?'

Jack was still looking at the gate. 'No, not exactly.'

'I think you should be grateful to Roy,' Michael said. 'He did help Beth get up here. Although by the looks of it, Beth probably helped him more than he helped her.'

'Yes, you might be being a bit hard on him,' Shannon added.

'Alright,' Jack said. 'Let's not turn this into a group discussion. I'll handle it thank you.'

'Okay, let's change the subject,' Shannon said. 'Michael and I have been talking.' She exchanged glances with her husband. 'We're thinking about moving on from here.'

Ali looked at me and raised her eyebrows.

'What does that mean?' Jack asked.

Michael grasped his wife's hand. 'Shannon and I have been talking to a few people, and after giving this place the once over, we don't think it's going to be safe for much longer.'

Sandra must have overheard the conversation. She stepped into the circle that had been formed. 'And go where exactly?' she asked.

'A couple of guys that live here in our house, Robert and Bob,' Shannon said. 'They've been told the wall isn't complete. You only have to go a few hundred miles, and it's still under construction.'

'I've heard the same thing,' I agreed, before looking at Ali. 'Well, we did, last night. Elliot from the container told us about it.' I directed my attention back to Michael and Shannon. 'He told us the same thing the two Bobs told you. Although Pea told us it'd only be between fifty and one hundred miles. Whatever the distance though, I've been thinking exactly the same thing as you. I can't wait here for eighteen months.'

'Who is Pea?' Jack asked me.

'The guy from Pea's Place. I'll tell you about it later. He's an Ipswich fan.'

Sandra stepped forward slightly and lowered her voice. 'I can't leave here with the children. This place might not be ideal, but I can't risk their lives out there again. I wish you the best of luck, but count us out.'

Ali looked disappointed. 'Okay. I'm staying with my sister.' She forced a smile, looking to Sandra. 'Whatever you decide Sis.'

'Pete, Theo,' Sandra said. 'Come over here. What do you want to do?'

The brothers left the three kids to play amongst themselves, and wandered over.

'Did you hear all that?' Sandra asked them.

'Yeah we heard,' Pete replied. 'We'll obviously stay with you and the kids Sand.'

Sandra smiled. 'Thanks Pete. Theo, that okay with you?'

'Whatever Pete says.'

'You're old enough to make your own mind up now Theo,' Sandra said to him.

Theo looked at his remaining family members. 'I'm not going to leave you all here am I?'

'Chris, could I have a word with you in the house please?' Jack asked me.

'Yeah, if you want.'

'Excuse us for just a moment please,' Jack said to everyone.

As we walked towards the house, Shannon said, 'Where is Gee? He keeps disappearing.'

'He'll be drinking with his Lithuanian friends,' Michael replied.

Once inside the house, Jack stopped and turned to me. 'I can't take Beth out of here. Like Sandra says, it's too risky.'

'I understand, but maybe ask Beth what she wants. Do you really want your baby born in this camp? We don't even know what medical facilities they have.'

'I want the baby to be born, simple as that. If we have to go back out there and fight through the zombies, even before trying to illegally cross a border, there is an extremely high chance the baby, along with all of us, will die.'

'You do understand I have to go, don't you? The rest of the world is in the middle of a new cold war. Russia and China are just about to attack everyone else.'

'Yes I know. Beth and Roy told me about some of the rumours going around the camp.'

'Rumours or not, I have to go.'

Jack sighed, 'Yes I know.'

'So you're not telling anyone about the pregnancy? Does Beth know I know?'

'No and no. She doesn't want anyone to know. She thinks people will treat her differently.'

'Fair enough. Let's get back outside and find out when Shannon and Mikey Boy are planning on leaving.'

Fuck. I wanted Jack and Beth to come with me. Is it bad that I'm relieved Sandra and the kids are staying?

Probably.

She's right though. It's too risky to take them outside the fences. Also, they'd really slow us down. Just me, Michael and Shannon then. I've no idea what Gee will do. Not now he's found some of his fellow countrymen to hang around with. I suppose a smaller group will have more chance of sneaking into Canada.

'In a few days I think,' Shannon said. 'We could do with getting some supplies together. If we leave the same way, we could pick up our stuff from the bus. Unless it hasn't already been ransacked by the Container Brothers, or by the actual Scavengers.'

Shite. I hoped we could avoid going in the tunnel again. That being said, my passport is in the bus.

The side gate swung open, crashing into the fence with a loud bang. Gee strode into the garden, holding a large cardboard box in front of him.

'Gee,' Shannon hissed. 'You have to be careful. No noise.'

'Yes, sorry. I have things,' he said, placing the box down on the floor in front of us.

The box was full of clothes. Sandra, Michael and Ali almost dived in to it.

'Where did you get this Gee?' Shannon questioned him.

Gee smiled and waved his hand. 'You do not need to worry about it.'

Shannon leaned over to look in the box. 'Did you trade something for it?'

'Hmmm...no, not exactly,' he replied.

'Did you steal it?' I asked him.

He looked at me and continued to grin. 'You do not need to worry about it.'

'Yep, he stole it,' I said.

We all got a new set of clean clothes out of Gee's thieving, so none of us really cared how he'd acquired the box. Nothing quite fitted right, but new socks, pants, combat trousers and a t-shirt were exactly what I needed.

Using the soap, and our bare hands to scrub, we took turns in washing our dirty clothes in the bathroom and kitchen. Michael offered to do my washing, but I had to turn him down. There was no way I was gonna make anybody go near my underwear.

Chapter 15: I Am Batman

I was hanging up my wet clothes on the fence at the back of the garden when the noise started.

I froze with my hand in mid-air, just as I was placing a sock on the fence.

It began as a quick burst of what sounded like automatic gunfire, soon followed by screaming. Not too close to us, but close enough. Then there was another quick burst, and another. Within seconds the gunfire had become almost non-stop. The terrified screams and shouting were getting closer and closer.

The back door of the house burst open. I spun around in a panic, dropping the clothes in my hands. Jack led, as everyone spilled into the back garden.

Jack looked terrified. 'What the fuck?' he shouted. The rules about volume control now seemingly pointless.

'Fuck knows?' I said. 'Have the zombies got in?'

The shouts and screams from outside our garden got even louder, as people ran past our house.

'Sandra,' Ali shouted over the noise. 'Get the kids in the house, barricade yourselves in the bedroom. Pete, Theo. You guard the room. Don't let anything in.'

I ran into the house after them. After grabbing my baseball bat from my bed, I exited the house through the front door. People were sprinting down the street, all in the direction of the fences. Jack, Ali, Michael, Shannon and Gee were outside on the front lawn, trying to stop people that were running by.

Jack ran back to me. 'It's not zombies,' he quickly said. 'There are people shooting people. It's not fucking zombies.'

'It's not zombies,' Shannon said, as the rest of our group made their way back to Jack and me.

'Yes we know,' I said.

Jack looked around at the people running towards the outer edges of the camp. 'I'm going to get Beth.'

'I'll come with you,' I said. 'Everyone else, lock yourselves in the house.'

'Do you know where her house is?' Michael asked.

'No...' Jack said, hesitating. 'But I have to go. I know it's over by the harbour. She might have been walking back. It's been over an hour since they left.'

'Everyone in house,' Gee said. 'Lock doors. Me, Chris and Jack will get Beth.'

Jack didn't wait for a response, immediately turning and running down towards the south inner fence. Gee and I sprinted to catch him up, slowing only to weave through the mass of panicked people. I could feel my heart pounding in my chest, and it was nothing to do with running.

'If they were on their way back,' Jack said, still staring ahead. 'They would have been walking around the outside. Nobody would walk through the middle.'

Hundreds of people were running past us, trying to get away from the shooting, which continued to rage on. It sounded like it was coming from two or three different places, all in the middle of the camp, where the majority of the residents congregated.

As we ran alongside the fence, I looked up 8th Street on my right, where the Senior Centre was situated. I slowed and tried looking over the heads of the people desperately trying to escape the gunfire. Bodies were lying in the street, too many to count. A bit further up, a small group of people were attacking someone, or something. They were swinging sticks over their heads, bringing them down on something on the floor. I didn't want to slow down any more to get a proper look, and continued to follow Jack down H Street. We stuck as close to the fence as possible, trying to keep our heads down.

As we neared Pea's Place, the gunfire didn't seem to be as continuous. It was much slower now, and sounded like there was only one shooter. The other shooters must have either ran out of ammunition, or been clubbed to death.

Hopefully the latter.

I almost tripped over a group of people, all on their knees in the middle of the street. They were bent over, all mumbling something and making life even harder for everyone trying to escape. Jack and Gee moved around them. I was already pretty much in the middle of them, so I decided to try and carefully step through the group. One of them reached out a hand as I passed, grabbing my leg. He looked a little bit like the two religious guys from the other day. I looked down at the rest of them. They all seemed to share that same gaunt look.

'God has spoken,' the leg grabber said to me. 'Why should we have the right to take just one of God's angels? Tell me why?'

I yanked my leg out of his grasp, and aimed for Gee's obvious frame running away from me.

'Why?' the leg grabber screamed after me.

We were now moving in the same direction as the escaping crowds, making progress a bit quicker. Although peoples' faces still looked panicked, the screaming had at least quietened down.

We stopped at the end of the road, terrified looking people rushing around, but mostly barging into us. They must have been heading towards the boats.

The sporadic gunfire in the distance abruptly stopped.

'What now?' I asked. 'It's mostly shops and stuff around here. I don't know if there are any homes.'

'I don't know,' Jack said. He spun around on the spot, desperately searching the crowds.

'She will have gone inside when shooting begin,' Gee said. 'We are better off going back to our house. That is where she will go.'

Jack stopped spinning around and looked at Gee. 'Why did you come with me if you think that?'

Gee shrugged his shoulders. 'Because you want to look for her.'

And Gee came to look after Jack.

'Gee's right. Let's make our way back to the house Jack,' I suggested. 'We'll pick her up on the way, or find her back at the house.'

'They might start shooting again,' Jack said.

'Well either way,' I said. 'We don't know where her house is.'

'This was a really fucking stupid idea,' Jack said, as people still filed past us, but at least no longer running. 'We can't find her like this. Fucking hell. I only just found her.'

We started walking back, having to push through the crowds.

'They're dead. They killed them,' a man whispered as I passed him.

'They got them all. I bet it was them,' I heard another man say.

'I hope they killed them all,' a woman said.

Naomi, the woman who'd shown us to the Senior Centre, was walking along the fence, talking to people as she passed them. As we neared her, I heard her repeating the words, 'The shooters have been taken out. Everyone just needs to calm down and go to your homes. It's over. Please go back to your homes.'

A bit further along the road, Sheriff McCallany was making his way through the crowds gathering by the inner fence. He was repeating what Naomi had been saying.

'Hey Sheriff,' I said when we got close to him. 'I thought there were no guns in the camp.'

He raised his palms to the air. 'This may not be America anymore, but it's still full of Americans.' He shot me an insane looking grin, before continuing to instruct the crowds.

He's definitely crazy.

Naomi's and Sheriff McCallany's assurances didn't seem to be making any difference. The normally quiet H Street that ran alongside the south fence was still packed full of people, all heading in the direction of the water.

There was a sudden cry of, 'Oh Jesus, why have you forsaken me?'

The sheriff said, 'Somebody shut that man up,' before wading through the crowd towards the crying man.

Jack constantly swept his eyes from left to right as we walked against the tide of people. When we got to the end of our street, he broke into a run, so Gee and I jogged to catch him up. We found him banging on the front door of our house.

'It's us, we're back,' he was saying.

The door swung open, Michael stood inside. 'Are you all okay? Did you find them? What is happening?'

Jack's head rocked back and he looked to the sky. 'Fuck,' he said. 'I'm going back out.'

'Just give it twenty minutes,' I said. 'Give her time to get through all the people.'

Michael had been joined by Shannon, Ali and the Rodriguez brothers. They all looked at us with questioning eyes.

'Sheriff McCallany said all the shooters have been killed, or stopped,' I told them. 'He said it's all over.'

Relief seemed to wash over their faces. Ali turned and headed back down the corridor, towards their bedroom.

'What happened?' Shannon asked.

'Don't know,' I replied. 'Some people with guns.'

'But why?' Pete asked.

I shrugged. 'No idea mate.'

'Jack,' Gee said. 'Turn around.'

We all turned to Gee. His back was to us. I peered around him and saw Beth and Roy walking side by side towards us, both carrying bags over their shoulders.

Jack dropped his axe and was off, running down the street towards them.

'Thank fuck for that,' I said.

Panicked yells from behind us made me spin around. In front of the house next door, three people were sprawled across the road. One of them was apologising and attempting to separate himself from the other two, trying to get back to his feet. Once he was up, he ran in our direction.

'What is it now?' Ali fearfully asked as she walked out of the house. Sandra and the kids followed closely behind her.

He slowed down as he neared us. I took a step back, worried he was going to run straight into us as well.

'Any Zombie Patrol and Fencers,' he spluttered, breathing heavily. 'Go to your base now.'

Before anyone could ask him anything, he sped up and continued on towards Jack, Beth and Roy.

Bollocks. My heart rate had picked up its pace again.

I picked up Jack's axe. 'Fuck. Must have been all the noise.'

'We better get down there,' Shannon said.

'I'm coming too,' Theo called out.

Sandra gripped tightly onto Theo's arm. 'No you're not. That's not your job. You'll be needed elsewhere, and if you're not, I need you here.'

Theo looked disappointed, but stayed alongside his cousin.

I'd happily exchange jobs with him. I didn't know Theo had been given a different job.

Pete and Ali said goodbye to their family, as the rest of us walked down the street. I waited for Jack to finish hugging Beth, and then handed him his axe.

'Any idea what's happening?' Beth asked.

'Nope, just what that running guy said,' I replied.

'They have been warning us about making too much noise,' Michael said. 'I guess they were right.'

'Are you two okay?' Shannon asked, looking at Beth and Roy. 'You didn't get caught up in any of the shooting did you?'

Roy shifted his bag to his other shoulder. 'No, we were coming back when it started, but went back inside when we heard the shots.'

Ali and Pete walked up behind us. 'I think we better go guys,' Ali said.

'Good luck,' Beth said to us all.

'Thanks. See you in a bit,' I replied, trying to sound calmer than I actually felt.

People were rushing around us as we made our way down to where the east inner fence met the south inner fence. Some carried steel joists on their shoulders. Others pulled wheeled carts behind them, full of scaffolding boards and poles. It was chaotic.

A woman ran up to us, saying, 'Zombie Patrol and Fencers go to work,' and then ran past us, repeating the words to everyone she came across.

A man stepped in front of us, lifting his hand up to stop us. 'Only Zee Pee and Fencers please.'

'We're Blue and Green,' Michael said.

The man stepped aside. 'Okay, be careful out there guys.'

The first group we saw had yellow bits of material wrapped around each of their arms. Next to them was a neatly stacked pile of chain link fence panels.

'Look for blue on their arms Chris,' Jack said.

'Coming through, watch your backs,' a voice called out from behind us.

We parted to let another cart through. Two people were pulling it, while a third person was pushing from the back. They each had a white strip around their upper arm. The cart was full of wooden planks.

I spotted another group. There were maybe one hundred people, slightly bigger than the yellow group. They were tightly packed in together, all trying to listen to a woman stood on a chair in front of them. They all had something green wrapped around an arm.

'You're over there guys,' I said, nodding to the group.

Shannon walked over to us and hugged Jack, and then me. 'Be careful and look after each other. We'll see you both soon.'

'Yeah of course we will,' I said. I first shook Michael's hand, then Gee's, and finally Pete's, wishing them good luck.

Ali stepped forward and wrapped her arms around me. 'Take care of yourself,' she whispered into my ear. She let go of me, and then hugged Jack.

We watched them walk towards their group.

'Right,' I said. 'Where the fuck is Blue?'

A man slowed as he walked past in front of us. He was carrying a large wire mesh panel. 'Blue is at H and 11th. Next street along,' he said, before continuing.

'Thanks,' Jack said.

I turned around and was almost taken out by a man pushing a wheelbarrow. It was full to brim with electric power drills. He rushed by us, heading towards the fence. Large sections of the inner fence were being covered with sheets of corrugated metal. Massive wooden and metal joists were being placed up against the fence at an angle.

We walked along to the next street, having to weave our way around the Red Team and White Team, before spotting arms wrapped in blue. Caleb, the incredibly stoned guy we'd kind of met, was stood on something, so his upper half was above the group of people between him and us. He was looking down to his left, talking to somebody. We joined the back of the group.

I could hear hissing, it was only faint, but it was definitely there in the distance.

They're getting closer.

'Can you hear that?' I asked Jack.

Jack looked at me and nodded, before tapping the person in front of him on the shoulder. The English woman from the bed below me turned to look at him. 'What's happening?' he asked her.

'Nothing yet,' she replied. 'Caleb is waiting for more people to get here.'

'Okay, thanks,' Jack said.

She smiled and turned back around.

I nudged Jack, and whispered, 'Fanny Fart Girl.'

'What?'

'Fanny Fart Girl,' I repeated, although slightly louder, and nodded towards her.

'You what?'

'Fucking Fanny Fart Girl.'

Her head turned towards me ever so slightly.

Fuck, I think she heard me.

'What the fuck are you talking about?' Jack asked.

Shit, I haven't told him about that yet.

'Doesn't matter. I'll tell you later.'

He shot me a very confused look, then turned back to face the front.

A man in front of me passed back two strips of blue material. They looked like they'd been torn from a t-shirt. I handed one to Jack, before trying to tie mine around my arm. We soon realised it was a lot easier to do each other's, so I tied Jack's, before he returned the favour.

'Our fencing team today are the Mariners,' Caleb said, his voice just about travelling to us at the back. 'They'll be wearing the blue as well. We protect them at all cost.'

'Baseball teams, not football,' Jack said to me.

'What?'

'Michael said the Fencers were named after football teams. The Mariners are a baseball team, from Seattle.'

Caleb spoke up again. 'If you get a bad injury, and you're capable of getting back here on your own two feet, then do so. If you see someone who's injured and not able to get themselves back, help them. The med tents are being set up all along H Street. You won't be able to miss them. If you do bring someone back, immediately turn back around and get back out there. Now, all of you that went out on the last firework mission, this one isn't going to be the same. Large sections of the outer fence have been destroyed. A lot of those things are inside the perimeter, a lot more than last time. It's going to take the Mariners a lot longer to do their job, so we need to be patient with them. This isn't going to be another half hour job.'

I looked to Jack and raised my eyebrows, whispering, 'We're fucked.'

'Make two groups,' Caleb called out, pointing to someone at the front. 'I need you all to split the group in half. Make a gap behind this woman here.'

I raised myself up onto the tips of my toes to see where the woman was, but then a space opened up in front of me. I could now see Caleb standing on step ladders. Jack and I were pretty much in the middle, so we shifted to our right slightly.

The hissing was getting louder.

Caleb looked over to the fence behind us, seeming to hesitate slightly, before returning his attention to us. 'Everyone on my right,' he said, pointing to the other half of the group. 'You will be sweeping. You go in first and clear a path to the fence. All of you on my left.' He pointed at our group. 'You surround the Mariners and guard them as they follow the sweepers.' He paused to look over the two groups for a few seconds, before seeming to settle his eyes on me. 'You five there,' he said, pointing in mine and Jack's general direction. 'Little Axe Woman, Machete Woman, Bat Man, Big Axe Man and Man with No Weapon. Sorry, but move to the other group, it's more even that way. And Man with No Weapon, quickly find a weapon please.'

As we stepped to our left, Man with No Weapon ran off into the crowds of people behind us.

'Hey Jack,' I said.

'What?'

'I am Batman.'

Jack couldn't hide his smirk. 'Twat.'

Laughing, I said, 'Big Axeman, who the fuck is that? Never heard of him.'

'Remember I gave you that bat? I could take it back.'

'You'll have to prise it from my cold, dead hands,' I replied, immediately regretting using that quote, considering the predicament we found ourselves in.

I leaned in closer to him and whispered, 'Sweeping sounds like the shittest of the two options.'

'Yep,' he simply said.

'Talking of weapons,' Caleb said. 'If possible, make sure you have a secondary one. If it's not possible, don't lose your primary weapon.'

I reached behind me and my finger tips brushed the little axe I always kept tucked into my belt. I turned to look at Jack. He was holding a huge knife.

'Have you stolen that from Rambo?' I asked him. 'Where did that come from?'

He returned it to the sheaf attached to his belt. 'This is Gee's back up knife. If you think this is big, you should see his main one.'

I remembered Gee using his main knife to kill that guy in Costco.

'Shame on you!' a woman cried out from behind us. 'Shame on you!'

I spun around to see a young woman staring at us. She looked young enough to have been a teenager. She slowly scanned her hate filled eyes across our group.

'Get her out of here,' Caleb ordered.

'Shame on you,' she spat. 'How dare you take the lives of God's children? We are all God's children on this Earth.'

A hand was wrapped around her mouth as two men grabbed her, lifting her off the ground. They carried her away until they were out of sight, becoming a part of the crowds.

'What the fuck?' I whispered.

The hissing sounded like it was all around us now.

'We wait until the fireworks,' Caleb continued, almost having to shout over the hissing. 'Until then, stay together. Do not wander off. Once the fireworks are set off, sweepers, you wait for my signal to go in.'

'What is the signal?' someone at the front asked.

'I'll tell you it's time to go,' Caleb replied, shrugging. He pointed to a section of the fence behind us. 'We'll be using that gate if possible. I'll let you know if we have to change gates.'

I couldn't see a gate, just a load of people organising piles of scaffolding boards. The fence had been entirely covered now, at least the part of it I could see. Supporting joists were spread out along it, about every five feet. Two ladders were leaning against the fence. A woman was atop one of them, she seemed to passing on information to people on the ground.

Loud rattling noises erupted from the other side of the fence. It must have been the zombies slamming into the chain link fence. The sound seemed to move along it from left to right, like a wave crashing onto a beach. Everyone stopped what they were doing, hundreds of people all turning to stare at the fence.

The hissing was now all encompassing.

I noticed the woman on top of the ladder was completely still, so not being jostled around at all by the zombie horde hitting the fence.

Hopefully that means the fence is strong enough to hold them back.

My heart was now trying to beat itself out of my chest, and my legs had an uncontrollable jiggle.

Looking at Jack, I very quietly said, 'Shitting myself.'

Another runner rushed past, speaking softly as he ran. 'Zombies are at the fence. Zombies are at the inner fence. Keep the volume down.'

'Yeah thanks. No shit,' I muttered.

Jack was staring at the runner. 'Chris, you watch my back, and I'll watch yours. Okay?'

'Yeah, obviously,' I agreed.

A woman from Blue Team started to make her way through the people going back and forth, she was coming from the direction of the fence. She ran up to Caleb and spoke something close to his ear.

Caleb listened intently and nodded. 'Okay everyone!' he shouted over the hissing, ignoring the runner's instructions to keep the volume down. 'The fireworks will be going off any minute now. Sweepers take your position in front of the gate. The gate has not changed.'

Chapter 16: Holiday

Our half of the group started walking towards the fence. When we were most of the way across the road I spotted the gate. A large sheet of corrugated metal sat in front of the pieces that had been permanently attached to the fence behind. Two huge wooden beams held the temporary sheet in place. Behind that must have been the original chain link gate. We all grouped together by the fence.

Caleb stepped in front of us. 'I'll be coming with you,' he told us. 'I'll guide us to the collapsed section we've been assigned to fix. Once we're there, we clear the area, making it safe for the Mariners to join us. Everyone understand?'

He received a few murmured responses, but mostly nods.

Caleb looked like a different person from the stoned guy on the sofa. I could tell he was nervous, his eyes didn't quite have the same conviction his words did, but he looked much more capable than I would have imagined.

'The fireworks will draw some of them away,' he told us. 'But it's like a wasp trap out there. Most of them won't be able to find their way back outside, so they'll be stuck between the two fences.'

There was a sudden loud whistling noise in the distance, followed by an almighty boom. It echoed around us. Even the zombies stopped hissing momentarily. More fireworks whooshed and whistled into the air, before exploding and crackling.

I looked to Caleb. He was staring up at the woman on top of the ladder, his chest heaving up and down. I looked down at my own chest, only then noticing I was also breathing heavily.

The hissing wasn't as loud now. The fireworks must be doing their job in drawing the zombies away.

The woman atop the ladder glanced down to Caleb and held up one finger. Caleb nodded to a man standing on the other side of the wooden beams. They got into position and heaved one of the heavy looking beams out of its supports, laying it on the ground out of the way. They walked back and repeated it with the second higher beam. A third person stepped between them and helped them lift it up and out of the way.

In absolute silence, the forty or so Sweepers waited. The woman on the ladder still had one finger raised.

A sudden clarity washed over me. I looked around at the nervous faces around me, and then at the many people rushing up and down the street behind us. A former town, now turned into a refugee camp, was on the other side of the busy street. An unknown number of those refugees were recently murdered, needlessly mowed down in the streets by fucking crazy people with guns. As if we didn't have enough problems. And now we're just standing here, waiting for a guy in his mid-twenties, who very recently was as high as a kite, to tell us to run into a load of flesh eating zombies. What the actual fuck is going on?

'What the fuck are we doing here Jack?' I whispered.

Jack hesitated, before saying, 'What? We're going to go and clear out the zombies.'

'No, I mean, how the fuck have we found ourselves here? We were supposed to be on holiday.'

Jack opened his mouth to speak, but Caleb and his assistant stepped towards the temporary corrugated sheet. They picked it up and moved it out of the way. I looked up to see the woman was now holding up two fingers. Once the metal sheet was out of the way, the double chain link gates were visible. On the other side was an empty car park, with Blaine High School on the other side of that.

A loud clanging noise made me look to my left. The Sweepers of Green Team were positioned in front of another section of the fence, doing the same as us I suppose. I tried to spot our friends, but couldn't see anyone I recognised. I thought I might have seen Gee's head and shoulders popping up above everyone else.

Hopefully that means they're in the second group, protecting their Fencers.

The woman on the ladder raised a third finger and nodded her head at Caleb. His assistant stepped forward and unbolted the double gates. There were six bolts in total, three on each gate.

Caleb opened the two gates, turned back to us, and said, 'On the other side of the school, we'll find the football field. Once we're there, spread out in a line, not too far apart, but not within swinging distance. Now follow me.' He faced forwards and ran into the car park.

My heartbeat now racing, and adrenaline threatening to overpower my senses, I followed my fellow Sweepers as we funnelled through the open double gates. Caleb had taken a right and ran diagonally across the car park. He then cut through a gap between the school buildings. Presumably to avoid having to travel around the fenced off tennis courts, and also, so we didn't get in Green Team's way.

Luckily the school didn't have any tall buildings. Otherwise running down the alleyway would have been even more nerve-wracking. Buildings looming over us would have made it feel claustrophobic. We were all still tightly grouped together, nobody wanting to be in the lead, or left behind. Only Caleb was apart from the group slightly, as he ran ahead of us.

When we reached the end of the alley, Caleb was waiting for us. As we filed past him, he said, 'The football field is just there. Form a line and remember to spread out, but make sure you're only a few paces from the person next you. If you're on the end, try to hook up with the other teams. Green on our left, and Red on our right.'

We had a clear view to the outer fence. Caleb hadn't been lying. Huge sections of it had collapsed. The gunfire and screaming must have sent the zombies into a frenzy for them to cause that much damage. Behind the layers of metal and wood that were now lying on the ground, parts of the scaffolding that held up the structure were loose and swaying in the wind. At the bottom of the fence, at least the parts that were still standing, thousands of zombies scraped and banged their hands on the metal. They were desperately trying to get through and get to the noises being created by the fireworks.

Fucking idiots, just go through the fucking gaps and make all of our lives easier.

So, there's about forty to fifty in each team, and I remembered only seeing ten, maybe twelve colours on that notice board in the drug den, or the Zombie Patrol base. So that's somewhere between four and six hundred of us, against thousands of pissed off mindless cannibals.

Yep, we're well and truly fucked.

I looked to the sky. The wind looked like it was bringing in some dark and rainy looking clouds.

Don't fucking rain. I really don't want to be cold and wet on top of all this.

'Chris,' Jack said, pointing over to our left. 'Look.'

I followed his gaze to see Shannon, Michael and Ali in the distance, walking along with the rest of the Green Sweepers.

'Fuck,' I said. 'Fuck's sake.'

I wouldn't have been half as scared for them if Gee had been alongside them. He must have kicked up a fuss when they told him he couldn't be with them.

I bet Ali told him to stay behind and look after Pete. They'll be fine. You can't afford to be worrying about them at the moment.

On the other side of Green Team, I could see another group, all strung out in a line. On the other side of them, much further away, another team were heading towards the east outer fence.

We reached the far side of the football field and crossed the running track that surrounded it. Caleb suddenly started shouting, 'Hold the line here. Let them come to us. They're too packed in by the fence.'

I could hear a woman's voice shouting something similar to the Green Team.

'Can't we just sneak up on them and bash their brains in from behind?' I asked Jack.

He just stared ahead, looking as scared as I felt.

'We tried that before,' the man on my left said. 'There weren't anywhere near as many as there are now, and we were quickly overrun.'

'Fucking zombie cunts!' Caleb shouted. 'Here we are, come and get us.'

I turned to Jack. 'Well, I don't think that language is necessary.'

Jack stared at the zombies, many of them peeling away from the frenzied horde and running towards us. 'Shut up Chris,' he said.

I joined him in staring at the masses heading our way. 'It's a Ricky Gervais joke,' I muttered.

The leader of the Green Team also started shouting.

'Do we shout as well?' I asked Jack.

'No. I think there are enough of them coming for us as it is.'

Only a car park was between us and hundreds of hissing creatures. It would only take seconds for them to reach us. Hundreds will soon become thousands.

This is gonna be fucking horrible.

'There are too many, far too many,' the man next to me said, sounding as scared as I felt.

'Wait until they're closer,' Caleb shouted, his voice still keeping its authority. 'Then we're going to run at them. Otherwise they'll take us all down. We are stronger than them. Wait for my signal.'

The few cars parked up in front of us weren't slowing them down. The car park was quickly filling with hissing creatures. I couldn't look away to see if they were everywhere, and not just in front of us. I guessed they were coming for all the teams. We stood and waited. I was desperate to hear Caleb's signal, and also dreading it. Jack was bouncing on the balls of his feet. I raised my bat over my shoulder.

What the fuck am I doing here? This could be the stupidest thing anybody has ever done.

The man next to me cried out, 'Too fucking many.'

'Jack?' I shouted over the hissing.

'I don't know mate,' he shakily answered.

This is fucking crazy. I honestly cannot believe this is happening.

According to the white lines on the tarmac, they were about two parking spaces away from us when Caleb shouted, 'Now!' He left the line, running towards the horde.

Jack and I both set off at the same time, only half a second behind Caleb. I still wanted to look to my left to check on my friends, but I couldn't afford the distraction.

Decaying faces stared back at me as I ran towards what looked like certain death. All of my senses were telling me to do the complete opposite. The repulsive things' mouths were wide open, and their dead flesh literally hung from their bones, swaying from side to side.

And that fucking hissing.

I swung my bat at the last second, connecting with two or three of them. My body twisted with the swing, my shoulder connecting into multiple bodies. Grunts and cries of pain mixed in with the zombies' hissing. Zombies seemed to fly in all directions as we made contact with the first row of them. I wasn't stopping anytime soon, I continued barging into them, their weak bodies not slowing me. I felt teeth and hands scraping against me as I passed through the horde.

All of a sudden, I found myself on my knees, painfully skidding to a stop along the tarmac. I must have tripped over something. It was utterly terrifying to look up and see I was surrounded by rotting zombie faces, all staring down at me. I swung my bat at them, trying to hit everything and anything. I didn't care what part of them I hit.

I stood up and screamed in agony when a sharp pain shot up my left leg. I kicked my leg out, feeling the mouth of a zombie let go of my calf.

Mother fucker.

I stamped down on the biter's head and carried on swinging. There was more pain as another tried to bite my back, up by my shoulder blade. I felt the thing's teeth scrape against bone. I spun around, still swinging my bat. The biter's hands still had hold of my jacket, so it swung around behind me as I spun, its legs knocking other zombies to the ground. I stopped spinning and reached back, grabbing the back of its head. I pulled and a large clump of skin and hair came away in my hand. I reached back further and dug my hand into its skull, until I got a firm hold of something. I pulled it up and over my shoulder, and threw it away. The long dead body weighed next to nothing. I spun around again, swinging my bat at whatever was closest to me, also trying to see where Jack was. More of the dead were coming towards us from the damaged fence.

I spotted him. He was still up and fighting, although not in amongst the horde like me. He must have backed away somehow to gain a bit of space, or not been stupid enough to carry on running into them.

I needed to get out of there, and try and get over to Jack, so there was nothing attacking me from behind. I wasn't gonna last long if they were coming at me from everywhere.

'Mother fucking fuckers!' I roared in pain as one of them sunk its teeth into the back of my left arm, just below my armpit.

I had to keep on swinging my bat one handed at more attackers, just to keep them a bay. I tried to reach its head with my left hand but couldn't quite get the right angle. The thing's hands were clawing at my chest and back. I lifted my left arm up, feeling the weight of it as it left the ground, and smashed my bat into its skull. The loud shattering sound filled my ears. The now unmoving hands fell away as it dropped to the ground.

I'd lost sight of Jack again, so I spun around, looking over the zombies' heads. I was indiscriminately swinging my bat, hitting heads, shoulders, just anything. I stopped spinning when I saw Jack's axe arching through the air.

Fuck it.

I moved towards him, punching with my left fist, and the handle of the baseball bat in my right.

Being dead for a few weeks can't be good for muscle tone and strength. The zombies were putting up a fight, but I could easily move them out of the way, their skulls collapsing, sometimes when I hit them with my fist. It felt like hundreds of disgusting skeletal hands were scratching and grabbing at me as I barged through them.

There was space in front of me, I'd made it through. A bony hand clawed at my face from behind. I reached up and wrenched it away from me, the hand and lower part of its arm tearing away. The rest of it was still attached to my back somehow. I ran at a car, spinning around at the last second and slamming my back into the driver's door. The zombie on my back was crushed in the impact.

Winded slightly, I stood up and raised my bat, only having to wait a second before some of them were on top of me again. I swung mercilessly at them, overhead, side swing, uppercuts. It was never ending.

Over the sound of hissing and fireworks, I could now hear a song playing. It sounded like Head Over Heels, by Tears for Fears.

Has there been music playing all this time?

'Chris!' Jack called out.

I looked for him in a panic, thinking he must be calling for help. He was stood on the bonnet of one of the parked cars. It was a big black SUV.

'Over here. Get on this car you fucking prick,' he screamed.

Fuck's sake Jack, that's a bit harsh. I'll put that one down to the adrenaline.

I pushed away a zombie that was only inches away from chewing on my elbow, and then brought the bat down on its head. I kicked another in the groin, almost flipping the thing over. Its face slammed into the ground. I ran towards Jack, barging three more zombies out of my way before I reached the SUV. Jack swung his axe down into the shoulder of a zombie blocking my path to him. It literally flew through the air, hitting tarmac at the back of the SUV. He swiftly moved his axe to his left hand and reached out to me with his right. I grabbed his outstretched hand, placed my right foot on top of one of the front tyres. He pulled me up onto the bonnet.

'This really isn't working,' I shouted. 'There's too many of them, and there's more still to come from the fence. How are we supposed to clear this for the Fencers?'

'Don't know,' Jack said, breathing heavily. 'Keep going.'

I put my back to Jack, and started clubbing the zombies on the top of their heads. They were making it easy for us, just queuing up to get their heads caved in.

I swung and swung, and swung some more, not caring about the hands grabbing for my legs. They were too weak to pull my feet out from under me.

'Although it's a lot easier up here,' I said. 'Fucking brilliant idea. Have you noticed the zombies are getting weaker and slower?'

'Yep, I've noticed,' Jack said between deep breaths. 'Can you hear that music?'

'Yeah. It's Tears for Fears.'

'Good, didn't know if I was going crazy. It sounds like it's coming from the school.' Jack took a second to point over to far side of the school, where we'd spent the night in quarantine.

The majority of the zombies seemed to be bypassing us, and heading to wherever that music was being played.

I took the opportunity to try and find the Green Team. They were just in an open field, so didn't have anything like we had to gain an advantage. I couldn't tell who was who in the chaos. All I could see were various types of weapons swinging and connecting with the dead. Dark coloured liquid flew in every direction.

I slammed my bat into more heads and looked down at myself. I was also covered in dark splatters.

The vehicle beneath us shifted. I quickly moved my feet further apart to regain my balance. Squeaks from the back of the SUV made me twist around. Caleb was on his hands and knees on the roof.

'Hey dudes. What's up?' Caleb said. He withdrew his knife from a zombie's eye socket, before bending forwards to stab another.

'This isn't going well,' Jack said, swinging his axe down again and again. 'What's the plan Caleb?'

Caleb continued stabbing. He was either blatantly ignoring Jack's question, or he'd sustained some kind of injury to his ears.

I looked past Caleb to see some of the rest of Blue Team had also climbed on top of cars. Two were on the roof of a car, and six or seven people were in the back of a truck, so they had a bit more protection than us. The rest of the team members that were still alive were on the flat roof of a single story building, over in the corner of the car park. They weren't doing anything to help the situation from up there. They couldn't reach down to kill anything.

'We need everyone out here Caleb,' I shouted. 'The Fencers can fucking wait.'

Caleb just continued stabbing.

The fucking twat is ignoring us.

A sudden shock of pain rushed through me again. I instinctively kicked my leg out, connecting with a zombie's face. I felt bones and teeth disintegrate when I made contact. The face that was biting me was still attached to my leg though. Teeth were trying to gnaw their way through my shin bone. Its arms were wrapped around my thigh, trying to drag itself up to a meatier part of my leg. I repeatedly brought the handle of the Smasher down onto the top of its head, eventually turning it into a mushy mess. It released its grip on me and I kicked my boot into what was left of its face.

'Mother fucking fuckers,' I shouted, lifting my freshly bitten leg up off the bonnet. I could feel blood running down both my legs.

Maybe I should be worrying about them grabbing my legs.

Why didn't Gee steal me some jeans? Instead of these paper fucking thin combats.

All of a sudden, the rain came, and not just a light smattering. It was heavy, torrential rain, like standing under a waterfall. The hissing, combined with the fireworks, and the rain bouncing off the SUV, was incredibly loud.

'Fuck off rain!' I shouted, quickly smashing in four more heads that had come too close to me.

'Caleb!' Jack shouted.' If we stay out here we're all going to die.'

'Keep fighting,' Caleb ordered him.

'Look at the fence,' Jack said. 'There's still a lot more to come. We need to retreat back to the camp.'

'We need to make it safe for the Fencers!' Caleb screamed, still thrusting his knife into faces.

'Caleb,' I shouted. 'Jack's right. This is fucking stupid.'

'I need to go and find Isaac,' Caleb called out. 'Keep going.'

He jumped off the back, barrelling into three zombies when he landed. He faltered slightly, but quickly regained his balance and ran across the car park.

Jack paused for a moment, watching Caleb run away. 'Who's he going to find?'

'Isaac, whoever the fuck he is.'

Jack slammed the top part of his axe down into a head, destroying it easily. 'I think he's probably still stoned,' he shouted.

The piles of bodies lying around the SUV were getting higher and higher with every zombie we killed. This meant the zombies' faces were getting a lot closer to us now, once they'd climbed on top of the fallen ones.

'Jack,' I said. 'Roof?'

He looked at me, and then down at the piles of dead surrounding us. 'Roof,' he agreed.

We both stepped up, being careful not to slip on, or break, the soaking wet windscreen. This gave us a slight reprieve, as the zombies were struggling to get a grip on the wet vehicle, and we were also a lot higher than them.

I dropped to one knee. 'I'm gonna try and catch my breath.'

Jack lowered himself down to join me. 'Yep, good idea.'

We were both desperately out of breath.

I pointed to the area Green Team had been fighting, asking, 'Have you seen any of the others recently?'

'Nope.'

Two things then happened, almost exactly at the same time. The fireworks stopped, and I spotted Ali.

'Shit, that can't be good,' Jack said. 'Bet it's the fucking rain.'

Chapter 17: Wrecking Balls

I tried to shield my eyes from the pouring rain. 'I can see Ali.'

Jack started scanning the horizon. 'Where?' he asked.

I pointed her out. She and three other Green Team members were surrounded by a group that must have been twenty zombies deep, and more were coming. The four remaining humans had their backs to each other in the middle. Ali was constantly stabbing with two knives. I couldn't see Michael and Shannon anywhere.

One of her fellow team members suddenly became a lot more animated. Her head snapped back, her face contorted with pain. She started to frantically swing her arms around, trying to reach something behind her. I couldn't tell what was happening. And then all of a sudden, she was gone, dragged off into the horde, disappearing almost immediately.

I quickly glanced around us. The car park in front of us was full of hungry skeletal creatures, some rushing towards us, but mostly towards the source of the music. It was almost clear at the back of the SUV. Caleb hadn't had too many issues when he went that way.

I looked at Jack.

He was already pointing at the mass of zombies between us and Ali. 'These ones would just follow us over there.'

I think he actually read my mind.

'I'll go,' I said. 'You stay here and keep these ones distracted.'

'What are you going to do when you get over there?'

'No fucking idea. But I can't just stand here and watch her get eaten.'

Jack let out a long breath. 'Okay, try not to die.'

'Will do. Don't stay here too long. As soon as they look like they can get up onto the bonnet, make a move.'

'Yes I know. Good luck mate.' He reached his fist out towards me. I bumped mine against his.

I tried to smile, saying, 'See you in a bit.'

Jack started to bang his axe against the window in the door. After the third hit, the window shattered. I took the opportunity to jump down, swinging my bat into a distracted zombie's face after hitting the ground.

I kept my head down and ran towards the running track, avoiding numerous zombies as they reached out for me. I just had to make sure I kept moving.

They're definitely slower now.

There were still a lot of zombies over by the edge of the American football field, but they were much more spread out. Most of them still heading towards the camp, attracted by the music, or the noise everyone must have been making on the other side of the inner fence. I just continued trying to avoid them, clubbing the ones I couldn't.

What the fuck am I actually going to do here? Die trying to get to Ali, or just die once I'm next to her?

The tennis courts where we'd spent some of our quarantine were surrounded by zombies.

That must be where the music is coming from.

Fuck me this has been a disaster. Who thought this was gonna work?

I crept towards the horde I thought I'd seen Ali surrounded by. It was hard to tell now I was on ground level, and there were fucking zombies everywhere. The dead all looked the same.

Head Over Heels ended, and People Are Strange, by The Doors started playing.

A weird soundtrack for my suicidal rescue attempt. It'll have to do I suppose. I've got no choice, just kill as many as I can.

The first head exploded under my bat. I raised it up again and smashed in another, and then another, and another. Their backs were still towards me, only a few breaking away to come for me. A vast amount of them still ran around the horde in front of me, heading for the source of the music.

A car horn blared out. I glanced to my right and a black SUV was speeding across the field towards me. Zombies were hanging off almost every part of it.

There was another flash of pain, this time coming from my arm. I brought the handle of my bat down on the zombie biting into my left forearm. Again and again, I smashed the thing in the skull, until it eventually fell away.

The SUV hit the edge of the horde in front of me, and carried on going. I was covered in a wave of blood and guts. I heard Jack whooping from inside as it hurtled past me. Zombies were sent flying, clearing a path and leaving a bloody trail of destruction behind it.

A lot of the zombies chased the SUV, but I still had to take out two of them as they ran towards me. The first fell after a swing of the Smasher to the head. The second, I took out at the knees first, then quickly brought the bat down on its head as it fell to the ground. I headed towards where I thought Ali would be.

The horn blared out again, making me hesitate. The SUV drove through the other side of the horde. I shielded my face with my hand as I was splattered with more zombie innards, even though I was a good twenty feet away.

Thanks to Jack, the horde was much smaller now. I reached the edge of it and started bashing in the back of more heads. I could hear screaming coming from the middle, making me swing harder and faster. I knew I wasn't going to be quick enough, so I stepped back a few paces and ran at them. I got my elbows up in front of my face, and forced my way through the four or five thick zombie wall, stumbling and falling to my knees once I was in the middle. It was lucky I fell, because a sword flashed close above my head as I skidded to a halt.

Only one of the Green Team was still standing. It wasn't Ali. I frantically looked around for her. A zombie clamped its teeth into my shoulder from behind me. I ignored the zombie, and the pain, because I'd seen Ali. She was screaming and shouting, lying on her back on the floor. Her arms and legs were wildly punching and kicking out, trying to stop the three zombies desperate to get to her. There were slashes on her face but I couldn't tell if she was badly injured. We all looked as filthy as the things we were trying to kill.

The last remaining man in the middle was covering a lot of ground, basically fighting off the zombies on his own. He was swinging a massive broad sword, a fucking four foot long broad sword.

I gave him a wide berth, avoiding the swing of his sword. I barged into two zombies, whilst moving my bat to my left hand. I pulled out my axe and stepped behind the zombies on top of Ali. I used the blunt end of my axe blade to quickly cave in the backs of their skulls.

I felt another bite on my right arm, but managed to knock the biter off, smashing its head into another's skull. I tried to put my axe back in my belt, but accidentally dropped it to the muddy and blood soaked grass. I didn't have time to pick it up. I pulled the bodies off Ali and dragged her to her feet. She swung her knife at me, narrowly missing my shoulder. I felt a weight drop away from my back.

'You had a zombie on you,' she weakly said.

Holding Ali up with my left arm, I tried swinging my bat into another head. I missed and hit its shoulder, but it still fell to the ground. I kicked another in the chest, forcing it back into the crowd.

'Come on, we're leaving,' I said to Ali. 'Hey Braveheart,' I called out to the man. 'We're fucking leaving.'

The man swung his sword, decapitating heads and slicing into the bodies of numerous zombies. He twisted around to look back at me. I took the opportunity, running towards him and putting my right arm around his back as we passed, dragging him along with us.

The three of us crashed into the zombies. We forced our way through, bones crunched and ligaments snapped as they tried to stop us. I desperately clung on to Ali's back, kicking out with my legs as we ran, my knees crashing into soft, decomposing bodies. I was conscious of the fact her arms weren't up to protect her face. Although neither were mine, my left holding up Ali, and my right dragging along Braveheart. Zombie faces slammed into my chest as we ran. I could feel their mouths trying to take chunks out of me, scraping across me as they fell away, unable to gain purchase.

We finally made it through. Once clear, Ali must have lost her balance, dragging me down to the grass with her.

Braveheart immediately spun around, his broad sword going to work, body parts instantly falling to the ground. 'Get her back to medical,' he called out, slicing three or four zombies up at a time.

I got back to my feet, dragging Ali up alongside me.

'So tired,' she managed to say.

Yep, so am I.

I tried walking with her but she wasn't going to be able to walk. Her feet were starting to drag. I turned around and kicked the legs out from under a zombie, crushing its head with the heel of my walking boot once it was on the ground. I then smashed the handle of my bat into another's face. It toppled over backwards to the grass.

I quickly looked around for some help, trying to find the black SUV. Without the fireworks, thousands more zombies were spilling in through the gaps in the fence. They must have been following the hissing.

Fuck's sake. We need to get out of here. This has somehow become even more ridiculous.

I heard him before I saw him. Jack was doing his very best to stop the oncoming swarms. The black SUV's engine was loudly revving as it tore through the zombies. He was driving close to the gaps in the fence, obliterating the dead in their hundreds as they entered through the missing sections.

'Nobody to help us Ali,' I said, pressing my baseball bat against her. 'Carry this for me.'

'Okay Chris,' she weakly replied, struggling to keep her eyes open.

Leaving my left arm around her back, I bent forwards and placed my right arm behind her knees, and picked her up. She laid my bat across her chest.

'Go!' Braveheart shouted.

'Yeah yeah. We're going,' I muttered, and started running towards the tennis courts, the most direct route back from there. I'd been intending to run around the horde surrounding them. When I got closer, I spotted one of the other Zombie Patrol teams fighting in the tree line, not far from the edge of the fences surrounding the courts.

Fuck it. I'm going the long way back, the way we came in.

I crossed the running track and entered the American football field, stopping when I heard a vehicle skidding across the car park. I looked to my left to see the zombie covered SUV crashing into another car. With the loud squeaking of bending metal, the driver's door opened and out stepped Jack. He leaned back into the SUV, coming back out with his axe. Hissing close behind me made me spin around. Ali murmured something unintelligible. Too many zombies to count were running in our direction.

We're not making any noise. Go towards the music and leave us the fuck alone.

I started running for the alleyway between the school buildings. Wind of Change, by Scorpions played out as I cut a path diagonally across the field. I had to stop myself from whistling along to the tune.

I'll come back and help Jack after dropping Ali off. He'll be okay.

Ali began to stir. 'There is music playing Chris.'

'Yep, I know,' I said, between breaths.

There was nothing between us and the alleyway. Just a shitload of zombies chasing us. I was beginning to feel really tired. The exertion of fighting for so long had really taken its toll. Then I remembered all of the bites. I hadn't thought they'd been that bad. It wasn't like they'd been biting chunks out of me.

Hopefully.

Blood loss would probably make me feel tired though.

I reached the alley and glanced behind me. They were still chasing us, but were far enough away to make me think we could make it.

They're definitely slower. Two weeks ago they'd have easily caught me. We can fucking make it. We are gonna make it.

The alleyway was clear, so I just ran, forcing myself to only look ahead.

We were soon nearing the end. I could see the inner fence. It felt like Ali was getting heavier with every step. I started shouting for the people at the gates to unlock them, my panic starting to increase. The hissing was getting louder behind us.

Shapes appeared at the end of the alleyway as the hissing surrounded us. The shapes were zombies. They were running towards us, more and more following them into the alley.

Give us a fucking chance. I can't run through that many, not while I'm carrying Ali.

Resigned to the fact that we were trapped, I stopped and gently lowered Ali down to the ground. I grabbed my trusty Smasher. Jack's gift had been an excellent replacement for the bat I had lost. When I stood up straight, I felt lightheaded and had a bit of a wobble, having to concentrate on not collapsing.

I glanced over my shoulder to see which group was closer, trying to blink away the fuzziness that had suddenly fallen over my eyes.

I've no fucking idea how far away they are.

I placed a foot on each side of Ali, who was much too still for my liking, and waited for them to reach us.

I've just fought my way out from the middle of them a few times. I can do it again.

'Hey fuckers,' a Lithuanian accented voice shouted out.

Behind the zombies running towards us from the inner fence, three huge figures appeared, more than head and shoulders above them. Bodies started to fly in all directions, slamming into the walls surrounding us. The three figures were now roaring as they ran. It echoed down the alleyway towards us.

Filled with hope and immense gratitude, I placed my bat down on Ali and picked her back up. She let out a faint moan.

The zombies behind me were closing in. The zombies in front had turned at the sound of the roaring. I ran towards Gee, Andruis, and Matis. They were crashing through the zombies like three wrecking balls, shoving them into walls and crushing their frail dead bodies.

Gee's expression quickly changed to a look of concern as we neared him. All three Lithuanians ran around us, moving towards the zombies at my back. They each carried a long scaffolding pole in their hands.

Without turning, Gee shouted, 'Run Chris. It is clear to fence now.'

The sound of steel slamming into dead flesh, and then dead flesh thwacking into brick walls, rang out behind us.

We made it to the car park, turning right when I remembered where the gate was. I looked up to see two people now peering over the top of the fence. Upon seeing us, they both quickly looked down to the ground behind them. By the time we made it to the gates, they were already being opened for us. All my energy left me once we were safely inside, and I fell to my knees once again.

Chapter 18: Smile

Two people appeared from nowhere and took Ali from my arms, my blood encrusted baseball bat rolling to the ground in front of me. They carried her off somewhere, quickly disappearing into the crowds. I tried to see where they went, but there were too many people.

I felt hands under my arms.

'Come on, we need to get you to a medical tent.'

I was lifted to my feet.

'No,' I said, shrugging off the hands and reaching back down to pick up the Smasher. 'I need to go back out. I just need to rest a minute.'

I turned to see white teeth surrounded by a huge ginger beard.

'You look like shit. You ain't going back out there.'

'I am. My friends are out there.' I walked around him, heading towards the gates.

A hand gripped my shoulder, sending a wave of pain down my left arm. 'Wait, just wait,' Ginger Beard said. 'Let's get you bandaged up and get some fluids in you at least.'

I didn't have the energy to pull away from his grip.

'Come on, the medical tent is just over there.' I turned to see him pointing down H Street. He handed me a plastic bottle of something orange coloured.

I struggled to remove the cap, before downing it in just a few thirsty gulps. 'Okay, but just a few minutes,' I said. 'Then I have to go back.'

We passed by a group of people, just standing there in the rain. They all had blue strips wrapped around their arms. I spotted Fanny Fart Girl amongst them.

I stopped alongside them. 'What's going on?' I asked the few closest to me. 'Has Caleb come back? Has anyone told you what they're planning to do?'

They exchanged glances, before Fanny spoke up. 'We were told to wait here. Nobody has told us anything. We haven't seen Caleb since you left.'

A short man stepped towards me. 'What is it like out there? Are we clearing the dead out?'

'No, there's fucking shitloads of them, far too many. It's been a fucking disaster from start to finish.'

'What should we do?' one of the group shouted.

Ginger Beard stepped to my side, grabbing my arm. 'We need to keep extra quiet now,' he told them. 'They're just on the other side of that fence.' He tried pulling me away, but I resisted.

'Do not go outside the fence,' I said. 'Whatever any so called boss says to you, do not go outside.' I went to walk away, but paused. 'That being said, I am gonna go back out to help my friends. So if anyone wants to join me in about ten minutes, it would be very much appreciated.'

'Come on now,' Ginger Beard said, gently pulling me away.

I twisted around to look back at Blue Team as we walked away. They continued to stand there, looking lost and just staring at each other.

The medical tent was full. Every bed was occupied. People rushed back and forth, none of them wore scrubs, or anything else that made them look like medical staff.

I looked around for Ali, but she wasn't in there.

'They're full,' I said. 'I'll go.'

'No, just wait,' Ginger Beard said, quickly glancing around. He sat me down on a chair just inside the entrance. My back was to the side of the tent.

He handed me another drink. 'Wait here. I'll go and get someone to help you.' He spun around and walked away, stopping people and talking to them, before moving on to another.

There was a clock hanging from one of the supporting posts inside the tent. Ten minutes had passed since Ginger Beard had sat me down. I was just about to get up and walk out, when he reappeared, having to fight to get around the walking wounded. He had a woman in tow.

She very briefly hesitated when Ginger Beard pointed me out, but then took the last few steps to stand before me.

She ordered me to strip down to my underpants.

'All of these need to be sutured,' she said, seeming to point at my whole body. 'You probably need a blood transfusion. Jordan here says you only want to be patched up, so you can get back out there.'

'That's right,' I replied.

'Okay, just making sure that's what you want.' She handed me some pills in a little plastic cup. 'Here, take these. They're painkillers.'

I threw them into my mouth, and swallowed them with my drink. 'Not gonna try and stop me from leaving?' I asked.

She shook her head, inspecting the multiple bites and scratches on my arms. 'No I'm not. But if you don't mind, I'd like to put a few stitches in these ones.' She gestured to my arms. She could have been pointing at any of the many cuts and bites. 'Won't take long,' she continued. 'Your face though, I think I...' She paused as her eyes roamed across my face. 'Doesn't matter, they're only superficial. It will be fine.'

'Okay, thank you.'

Just get on with it.

I stared at the clock on the wall, willing the medic to speed up. The minute hand seemed to be flying around much faster than normal. Thirty minutes later she was finished. A few incredibly painful stitches, and a lot of bandages, meant I felt I was ready to leave. I was desperate to get back, but also terrified to go back out there. I'd loved to have collapsed somewhere and fallen sleep. It would have been so very easy.

The medic handed me a Snickers and an energy drink. I started to pick up my dirty, blood splattered clothes to get dressed, but she placed a hand on my arm.

'I'll get you something else,' she said. 'Two minutes.'

She returned, carrying a neat little stack of folded clothes in her hands.

Jeans, t-shirt and a thick denim jacket. Perfect.

'The stitches might, or probably will fall out if you start running around anytime soon. But I've at least done my job for now.' She turned and walked away.

'Thank you again,' I called after her.

I've been gone far too long. Jack is gonna fucking hate me. If he's still alive.

I quickly got dressed, picked up my baseball bat and started to walk back to the gate. I considered checking on Ali, but I didn't know which tent she was in, and I couldn't leave them out there any longer.

I ate the Snickers, and quickly knocked back the energy drink as I walked.

I was definitely not feeling one hundred percent.

The sun was starting to set on this terrible rainy day. Grey and angry clouds still rolled across the sky above me. The rain wasn't as heavy now, but not looking like it was stopping anytime soon.

I again passed by the half of Blue Team that had been left behind. There was a lot more activity surrounding them now. They were handing out torches. I spotted Caleb, standing apart from them. He looked like he was involved in a heated discussion with another member of Blue Team.

My spirits lifted, I jogged over to him. 'Caleb, what's happening?' I asked. 'Is everyone back?'

He shot me a glance before looking up to my face, his eyes briefly widening. He then glared at me, annoyed that I'd interrupted him.

Prick.

'I was just out there,' I said. 'Where is everyone Caleb?'

'I don't know for sure. We're waiting until nightfall. Then I'm taking the rest of Blue Team out. We'll kill the fuckers when they're asleep.'

I stared at him, waiting for him to tell me he was joking. 'You've left them all out there?'

The guy he'd been talking to stared at the ground, looking ashamed.

'Yes, I've...erm...' Caleb stuttered. 'They're fine, some of them are fine. They're on top of a building.'

'On top of a fucking...' I took a deep breath to try and calm down. 'The zombies aren't gonna go to sleep you fucking moron. What are the bosses of the other teams doing? Where are they?'

The deep breath didn't help.

He shoved me in the chest, forcing me to take two steps back.

'Fuck off and wait with the others.' He turned away from me and continued his conversation with the other guy.

What the fuck is going on here? This stoner dude is a fucking idiot. Fuck him.

I looked to the rest of Blue Team and pointed at Caleb. 'Do not follow this fucking idiot anywhere. Ignore everything he says.' I turned and walked to the gate. Looking up to the people on the ladder, I said, 'Hey. Is it safe to go out?'

They both looked downwards, their eyes lingering on me for a moment, and then looked back outside the fence. The woman on the left ladder turned back to me and said, 'Not safe in the slightest. But we'll let you out.'

'Who was playing the music?' I asked her.

'It's the sheriff. He's still going strong. What is that he's playing now Tanner?' She looked to the guy on the other ladder. 'Sounds like Live and Let Die. McCartney or Guns N' Roses?'

'Is that a serious question?' Tanner scoffed. 'It's obviously McCartney.'

Thirty seconds later, I was out and running across the thankfully, empty car park again.

Bolts slotting back into place sounded behind me. Then someone was shouting my name. I stopped and spun around. Royston Gayter was jogging towards me, a machete in each hand.

Where the fuck has he found them?

'Alright Roy?'

He hesitated slightly, staring at my face. 'Hi Chris, thought I'd come down and lend a hand. Who knows what's going on back there?' He gestured behind him with one of the machetes. 'They've been sitting around, doing nothing at all. I just spotted you when they were letting you out.'

'Have you seen anyone?' I asked, stepping towards him. 'Jack, Michael, Shannon, Gee or Pete?'

'I think I saw Pete. He's related to Sandra isn't he?'

'Yeah, where was he?'

'He was back there, hanging around with a load of other people.'

'Good. Hopefully he stays there.'

'Am I going to regret coming out here Chris?'

'Maybe. Come on, follow me.' I turned and headed towards the alleyway.

Roy chased after me. 'Chris, you look terrible. Are you sure you're okay.'

'Yep. I'm fine,' I lied.

'I've got water bottles in my bag. Do you want one?'

'No thanks. Hopefully we'll find some people still alive that'll need them.'

'They wouldn't tell me how bad it is,' Roy said.

'It's really fucking bad,' I said, stopping and turning back to face him. 'If you don't want to come with me, then I'll understand. But I could really do with the help.'

'I don't need the speech thanks Chris. Beth would never forgive me if I didn't come back with Jack.'

'Good. We're just gonna get him, and a few others, then get back inside the camp.'

Inside the alleyway, body parts were strewn across the path. Dark stains were splattered over the brick walls of the school buildings. Apart from the decimated zombies we were now running through, the alleyway was clear. I'd assumed the swarms would be right up to the inner fence by now. I could still hear Paul McCartney singing. That must be attracting a lot of the zombies still.

The hissing was getting louder as we got closer to the end of the alley. I remembered that having a height advantage had fared us well so far today.

I stopped and turned to Roy. I raised my left hand and placed my finger to my lips. Then I pointed with the Smasher to the roof next to us. He looked up to where I was pointing, and then glanced down the alleyway. He slowly nodded in agreement.

Roy walked up to the wall, placing his machetes into his belt. He spun around to face me, crouched down, and interlocked his fingers in front of him. I stepped into his hands and he stood up straight. I reached up and grabbed the edge of the roof. With Roy pushing, and me pulling, I just about managed to clamber up. There were a couple of seconds when I was sure I was gonna slip, and come crashing down to land on him. Once I was up, I spun around on my belly and stretched my hand down, taking the Smasher from him as he passed it up. He stepped backwards a few paces, and then ran at the wall. We missed each other the first, and the second time, but I managed to grab his hand on the third attempt. He scrambled with his feet while I pulled him up, so he could grip onto the roof's edge. Then I got up onto my knees and heaved him up onto the flat roof.

We were both out of breath at the end of all that.

We kept to the flat parts of the roof, not wanting to slip on the wet tiles on the steeper, more angled sections. From this vantage point, I could see the damaged fence. There didn't seem to be as many zombies streaming in through the gaps. When we reached the edge, and looked out over the American football field, and the car park beyond, we both stopped and stared at the sight in shock and awe.

The reason there weren't as many zombies trying to get through the fence, was because every fucking zombie in America was already through. It looked like a massive ant migration. They were all being funnelled in the direction of the quarantine area, and the sheriff's container.

'That's a lot of zombies,' Roy whispered.

I quickly scanned the area where the car park was situated, now completely covered with the shuffling dead. Before I'd left there was a lot of Blue Team on the building in the corner of the car park. That was now empty. Nobody was stood on any of the vehicles. I looked right, towards more of the schools buildings. There wasn't anyone in sight, not from any of the teams. That didn't mean people weren't in the buildings. Jack and everyone else would have been hard pressed to get all the way over there though. When I looked to the other side of the swarming zombies on my left, there was just some kind of lorry park, a field with what looked like a disused runway, and then the heavily damaged east outer fence.

I hope Michael and Shannon got out long before I carried Ali out of that field. There was no way anyone could have survived around there all this time.

The sheriff was now playing Whole Lotta love, by Led Zeppelin.

I pointed over to the building on the other side of the alleyway. 'Let's see if we can get closer to the sheriff. Hopefully everyone made it to him. If they're not with him, we'll have to get into the school somehow, and check in there.'

'Okay, good idea,' Roy said.

The edge of the swarm was definitely getting closer to us. There must have still been some zombies coming in through the outer fences, and forcing them closer to the camp. It would only be a matter of time before they were at the inner fence. The sheriff couldn't keep the music going forever.

We walked back to where we had climbed up. The distance between the two buildings wasn't as far there. I crept over to the edge of the roof.

'We can jump that,' Roy said. 'It's only eight or nine feet to the other side.'

Standing at the very edge and looking at the gap, it seemed too far to me. I wasn't sure if Roy's extra couple of inches in height made any difference to his perspective.

'Really?' I asked him. 'Why not just drop down and climb back up the other side?'

'Because that other side is a little bit higher than this side, and we only just managed to climb up here. Also, the zombies are just at the end of the passage. Now that I know that, I'm really hesitant about going back down there.'

'So you're happy to jump nine feet onto a higher roof?'

'Eight or nine feet,' Roy said. 'And yeah, easy.'

'Okay, after you.'

He turned and walked until the flat section of the roof ended. He spun back around, and momentarily placed his hands around the handles of his machetes, still tucked into his belt. He let go of them and started running. I couldn't help but smile at the expression on his face. It was a look of complete concentration. His eyes were fixed on the other roof.

Roy planted his right foot down close to the edge, and launched himself. He sailed through the air, his left leg stretching out before him. His left foot came down to land on the other side, but immediately slipped off. With a loud grunt of pain, his right shin collided with the side of the building. Luckily his momentum carried him through, slamming him face first onto the tiled roof.

He slowly got to his feet and forced a pained looking smile. He raised both his thumbs in my direction.

Fuck's sake.

He beckoned me over whilst rubbing his shin. 'Come on Chris.'

'Are you taking the fucking piss?' I hissed, staring down to the end of the alleyway. I was checking to see if any of the massive swarm had heard Roy nearly kill himself. 'Are you okay?' I asked, and pointed to his waist. 'You didn't stab yourself with your machetes did you?'

He quickly patted his hands over his hips and thighs. 'Yeah I'm fine. Just make sure you jump a bit closer to the edge. I probably jumped too early.'

'No you fucking didn't. You were right on the edge when you jumped.'

'Just jump further than I did.'

'Just jump further than I did,' I repeated, under my breath. 'Here, catch my bat.' I raised the Smasher and Roy stepped closer to the edge, I tossed it across and he caught it with ease.

I turned and walked to the spot Roy had started his run up. 'Get ready to fucking catch me,' I said to him.

I tried to get up as much speed as possible in the short run up. As soon as both of my feet were off the roof, I knew I wasn't going to make it.

This is gonna hurt.

I didn't even manage to plant one of my feet down. My left thigh crashed into the edge, swiftly followed by my right. My balls then seemed to take the brunt of the impact. I wasn't sure what happened after that, but I opened my eyes to find myself lying face down on the roof. My feet dangled over the edge, and my testicles felt like they were in my throat.

'I've crushed my bollocks,' I moaned into the roof, my lips squashed against the tiles.

I got halfway up onto my knees and tried to suck some air into my lungs. My mouth filled with blood so I spat it on to the tiles.

'See,' Roy said. 'We made it. Easy.'

The intense pain in my balls didn't seem to be leaving any time soon. 'Fuck you Royston,' I mumbled. Sticking out my tongue, I tried to say, 'I think I bit my tongue.'

He had a quick look, before screwing up his face. 'Yeah, I think you did.' He grabbed my arm at the elbow, and I let him lift me to my feet. He handed me back the Smasher.

'Let's try and get to the other side,' he said. 'See what the sheriff is up to.'

I nodded and gestured for Roy to take the lead. I hobbled along behind him. Welcome to the Jungle, by Guns N' Roses accompanied us as we precariously made our way across the rain soaked roof tiles.

The fences that had once been around the tennis courts were gone. They were still technically there, but were now lying flat on the ground, trampled over by thousands of zombies. The sheriff's container was still there, just with an incredible amount of the dead surrounding it.

Sheriff McCallany sat on top of the container. He must have thrown one of the plastic chairs up there. He was sat on the chair, leaning back on two legs, like he didn't have a care in the world. A large umbrella, maybe even a parasol, was propped up against him. He held a bottle of whiskey in his right hand. The big eighties boombox I'd noticed the other day sat on his lap.

We waved at him to get his attention, still trying to make as little noise as possible. We were directly in his eye-line so it didn't take him long to notice us.

'Hey guys!' he cheerfully shouted, making me flinch. 'Any requests?'

Roy and I exchanged concerned glances, before looking back to the sheriff.

It didn't feel right to shout with so many of the dead that close to us, but I shrugged my shoulders, and shouted, 'More Tears for Fears?'

The zombies closest to us all turned their attention to us.

He placed the whiskey bottle down on the roof, and rummaged his hand around in a plastic bag behind him. He pulled his hand out and shook a cassette tape above his head, before exchanging it for the tape in the boombox. Mad World started playing. The sheriff gave us a thumbs up.

Roy turned to me. 'Well, that was a bit surreal.'

'The sun will be down soon,' I said. 'Let's find a way into the school before it's too dark.'

'What about the sheriff?' Roy asked.

'We can't do anything. He's safe for now, and he seems to be happy enough.'

Roy pointed back the way we came. 'Back to the passage?'

'Yep, hopefully it's still clear.'

I took one final look at the sheriff and waved. He lifted his bottle to us, before taking a swig.

Turning to catch Roy up, I said, 'Yep, very fucking surreal.'

We reached the other side of the building where it overlooked the alleyway below, and turned right, planning to drop down further away from the eyes and ears of the zombie swarm.

Roy placed a hand on my shoulder, stopping me in my tracks. 'Can you hear that?' he asked.

I tried to listen for something new. 'Hear what?'

'Voices, I'm sure I just heard voices,' he said.

'I can't hear anything.'

'Jack, I think I just heard voices,' somebody whispered from below us.

'I heard that,' I said, clapping Roy on the shoulder.

I crept over to the edge and looked down. The faces of Jack, Pete, Gee, Andruis and Matis looked back up at me. Their hopeful expressions instantly turning to smiles.

Apart from Pete, who looked like he'd just stepped out of the shower, they were entirely covered in dark brown coloured streaks.

'Alright, what are you lot doing here?' I asked them.

'Looking for you,' Jack said, his eyes shifting when Roy stepped alongside me and leaned his head out. 'Roy, what are you doing here?'

I pointed down the alleyway. 'Meet you down there, further away from the swarm.'

We hurried along the edge of the building until we felt like we were far enough away, and dropped down to join our friends.

Pete looked anxious. 'Where's Ali?' he asked. 'Jack said you brought her back. Is she okay?'

'I think so. They took her to a medical tent. Don't know which one, sorry.'

'But she's okay?' he asked.

'I think so, but I don't know for definite.'

'I think we should go back,' Andruis said. 'Walk and talk guys.'

We set off at a brisk pace.

'Have you seen Michael and Shannon?' I asked the group.

'No,' Jack answered. 'We haven't seen them.'

'How did you know we were here?' I asked.

'We didn't know Roy was here at all,' Jack said. 'Caleb told me the annoying British arsehole had gone back out to look for his friends. So I safely assumed that was you.'

'Caleb is a fucking twat. Have you seen Sheriff McCallany sat on top of his container?' I asked. 'He's the one playing the music. It's drawing a lot of the zombies to him.'

'Yes we saw him from the fence,' Jack said. 'His batteries will only last so long though.'

It was at that exact moment that Pale Shelter, by Tears for Fears was cut off half way through the song. We all stared at each other with fearful eyes.

'Run,' Gee said.

'That was your fault Jack,' I called out as we sprinted down the alley.

We reached the car park at the end and turned right, aiming for the same gate I had repeatedly used that day. Zombies were now streaming towards us from around the bend, all coming from the sheriff's container. The front of the swarm crashed into the inner fence, ferociously attacking the chain links with their hands and teeth.

The two people on top of the fence were staring at the oncoming swarm. They hadn't seen us. We all shouted but the hissing was deafening.

An ear piercing whistle came from my right. I looked over to see Roy pulling two fingers out of his mouth. It had worked. The two people were now looking at us, and speaking to the guys below them.

It also meant every zombie was coming for us.

We weren't gonna make it to the gates before they got to us. I think we all knew that, but we carried on regardless.

I saw the metal panel being removed, and then two people starting fiddling with the bolts. They paused to look at the zombies heading straight for them. I was willing them to continue unlocking them. They slotted the bolts back into place and stepped out of sight. The metal panel slid back to cover the gates.

Mother fuckers.

We all started to slow down slightly from our desperate sprint.

'We need to get up on the roof again,' I called out.

The three Lithuanians changed direction and started running towards the swarm. They still carried their long scaffolding poles.

Fuck knows how they can swing those heavy things with any control, never mind run with them.

Out of the corner of my eye, I noticed something soaring over the fence to my left. The square shaped object was trailing something behind it. It hit the ground and shattered. A length of rope must have been tied to it. Three more bricks flew over the fence, all trailing rope behind them.

Whilst I'd been watching the ropes appear from over the fence, the Lithuanians had already met the swarm. They were cutting swathes of the front runners down with the scaffolding poles.

'Climb up the rope!' Jack screamed. He shoved Pete towards the fence and one of the dangling ropes.

'Gee!' I shouted. 'We have a way out.'

He glanced over his shoulder to look back at me. He was swinging the pole in wide arches across his body. Zombies were being smashed to pieces, hurtling away to land amongst the swarm. It was a truly awe inspiring sight.

'Lithuanians!' I shouted. 'We need to go.'

A couple of zombies slipped through their onslaught, running for the person making the most noise. That was me.

I slammed my bat into the first. I didn't have time to get the Smasher back up for the second, so I side stepped. It missed me and staggered past. I crushed its head after it made its slow turn to come back for me.

'Climb Chris!' Gee called out. 'We will follow.'

Pete was almost to the top, and Jack and Roy weren't far behind. I stuffed the Smasher into the back of my belt, and ran for one of the ropes. I started to pull myself up, using my feet to walk my way up the fence. I looked over to Gee, Andruis and Matis. They were close to the fence now, slowly backing up towards the ropes, constantly swinging the poles as they walked.

Three zombies managed to get around Matis's wide swing, and launched themselves at him. He had to stop swinging to fight them off, and that was all it took. The front of the swarm capitalised on the opportunity, and enveloped him.

I reached the top and straddled the fence, a leg on each side. More ladders were leaning against the corrugated metal panels. Jack, Pete and Roy were using them to climb down. All I could do was watch what was unfolding outside the fence.

Gee was closest to Matis. Upon seeing his friend in trouble, he threw his pole at the oncoming zombies, and turned to help him. He was soon surrounded, so he had to battle through the zombies with his bare hands, throwing them in all directions as he went. Three or four were biting into his back.

Andruis turned and launched himself at a rope, immediately pulling himself up. Zombies clung to him as he climbed. He stopped when he was half way up and ripped away the creature biting his thigh. I started climbing back down, pausing when he reached around and grabbed the final one clawing at his other leg. He threw it back down into the swarm. I stopped where I was.

Matis was completely covered in the dead, but still fighting. He was swinging his arms and kicking his legs. Gee was wading through a sea of death, pummelling skulls and ripping off heads. He finally made it to Matis, and started tearing away the zombies covering him. Within seconds Matis's top half was visible again. With a roar, Gee lifted him up and walked him over to the fence. A blood covered Matis weakly reached out for the rope and gripped it. Gee pulled away the last of creatures from Matis's legs.

He wasn't gonna be able to pull himself out of there.

I climbed back up to the top of the fence and leaned over. Looking down into the camp, I shouted, 'Pull the first rope!' I was desperately pointing, shouting to anyone who would listen. 'Pull the first fucking rope!'

Jack, Pete and Roy were the first to figure out why I was screaming down at them. They threw themselves at the rope. All three of them heaved it down to the ground, and then pulled on it hand over hand. Two more people grabbed a hold, and the five of them almost ran in the opposite direction of the fence, pulling the rope behind them. Matis's grip was strong as he rose up alongside the fence.

Gee was now covered in dead creatures. He staggered over to the fence, grabbed a rope and started hauling himself, and the six zombies attached to him, up the side of the chain link fence.

Andruis and I both started climbing back down, stopping when we were alongside Gee.

'Hold on Gee!' I shouted.

I gripped the rope with my left hand and steadied myself with my feet against the fence. I reached over to grab a zombie's back, my fingers dug into flesh and my fist closed around bone. I pulled and heard a repulsive ripping noise as it tore away from Gee's shoulder. I then punched my gore covered hand into the back of another's neck, my fist almost going all the way through. The zombie dropped away. A spurt of blood erupted from somewhere on Gee's neck. Andruis was kicking his heel into the head of one hanging from Gee's legs. I leaned over and grabbed the hair of a zombie biting into Gee's back. I yanked it backwards and it came away with a chunk of Gee's flesh and clothing in its mouth. Andruis removed the final one, and threw it down into the swarm.

Gee looked at me straight in the eyes and smiled. It was the biggest, most genuine smile I'd seen on Gee's face, then he let go of the rope and fell backwards.

Chapter 19: Weary

I screamed Gee's name as my hand shot out to catch a hold of him, but it closed around thin air. Andruis reached out for him, but also missed.

Gee's face looked peaceful as he fell. His eyes were closed as he slammed into the swarm below, crushing the ones directly under him. He was gone almost immediately, zombies diving on top of him.

I screamed something, I don't know what, and started lowering myself down the rope towards him.

I've got to get him out of there. I have to help him.

A huge hand tightly gripped around my wrist and the rope, stopping me from moving any further down.

I looked at Andruis through the tears filling my eyes. He stared back at me, slowly shaking his head.

Gee can't fucking die. It's Gee. It's fucking Gee.

'But...' I started to say.

'No. Come on,' Andruis said. 'Climb up with me. Yes?'

I looked down, still hoping Gee was gonna get up and fight them off. If anyone could have done it, it would have been him. I stared at the zombies fighting each other to get to him, like frenzied sharks.

Come on Gee.

'Chris,' Andruis very calmly said, releasing his hold on my wrist. 'Let's climb up. Let's go. Matis needs our help.'

I had to force myself to look away from the mass of zombies below us. I turned back around and focussed on the top of the fence. I started hauling myself up the rope.

Jack must have climbed back up one of the ladders, and was trying to drag a barely conscious Matis over the top to get him onto a ladder. 'Chris, I need some help,' he said.

Andruis got to him first and straddled the top of the fence. He very quickly tied his rope around Matis's chest, and under his arms. He then lowered him down to the ground. I climbed down one of the ladders. By the time I'd stepped off at the bottom, three people were already rushing Matis off towards one of the medical tents.

Jack was looking up, his eyes skimming across the top of the fence. He looked at me, and then at Andruis. 'Where's Gee?' he asked us.

He knew what had happened to him as soon as he noticed my glistening eyes.

'I'm sorry, but he's gone,' Andruis said. 'He died saving Matis's life. I really am sorry, for all of us.'

Jack looked back to the fence. 'What?' he asked.

Andruis patted a huge hand on Jack's shoulder, and nodded to me. 'I need to check on Matis.' He walked off in the direction they'd taken his friend.

Jack continued to stare at the top of the fence.

Roy walked over and handed me a bottle of water. I thanked him, and he stepped over to Jack, offering him one as well. Jack glanced to his left and saw Roy standing there. He looked down at the bottle, before violently slapping it out of Roy's hand.

I stepped towards them as Roy backed away, his head bowed. 'Thank you Roy,' I said, and bent down to pick up the fallen bottle. I forced it into Jack's hand. 'We need to find Michael and Shannon.' I patted Jack on his arm. The palm of my hand came away bright red. 'Jack, is this your blood? There's a lot of it.'

He glanced down at his upper arm. There was a large tear in the sleeve of his jacket. 'Yeah I think so. I got bitten. I got bitten a lot.'

'Pete.' I looked around, trying to find him. 'Pete, where have you gone?'

'Yeah I'm here,' he said from behind me.

'Are you gonna go and find Ali?'

'Yes, of course I am,' he quickly replied.

'Good, can you take Jack and leave him at the first medical tent you go to?'

'Yeah sure.'

'No I'm alright,' Jack said.

'You can search for Michael and Shannon while you're there,' I said to him. 'And once you're sorted, you can search the rest of the tents.'

'Okay. I can do that,' he said, slowly nodding his head.

'Good. You've got quite a big cut on the bridge of your nose as well.'

Jack reached up and carefully ran his finger up and down his nose.

'Meet back here in an hour?' I suggested. 'You too Pete. If that's okay? I'd like to know how Ali is doing.'

'Yeah that's fine,' Pete said.

Jack checked his watch. 'Yes okay, one hour from now.'

'What time is it?' I asked him.

'Twenty past eight. Where are you going?'

'I'm gonna try and find the rest of the Green Team. See if they know anything.'

'One hour,' Jack said, turning around.

Pete watched Jack take a few steps away, before turning back to me. He grabbed and then shook my hand. 'Thank you Chris.'

I forced a tight smile. 'Okay Pete. See ya soon yeah?'

He turned and jogged after Jack.

'I'll help you Chris,' Roy said after stepping by my side. 'If you don't mind?'

'Yeah cheers. Could do with the company.'

We walked towards the area I'd seen the Green Team. The first person I noticed was the guy with the massive broad sword. He was talking to the woman who had led the Green Team out. They were both keeping their voices low, so I couldn't hear what they were saying until we were stood a few feet away from them.

Braveheart pointed to the fence behind him. 'This needs to be the outer fence. Look at all the fencing materials around us. Build another fence on the other side of the road. That can be the new inner fence.'

'That will only give us forty feet between the two fences,' the woman said.

Braveheart looked incensed. 'We have no fucking choice. You saw what it's like out there. What do you want us to do? Ask them if they want to go back out there,' he said, pointing to the very small group of his fellow Green Team members. They all looked exhausted, bloody, and dishevelled.

Michael and Shannon weren't amongst them.

'Him, ask him. He was out there,' Braveheart said. I looked back to see them staring at me, Braveheart pointing directly at me.

'Erm...yeah,' I said. 'Every single thing he said is correct.'

The woman continued to stare at me.

'We're looking for our friends,' I told them. 'They're in Green Team. Michael and Shannon Presley. Both black, early thirties. She was wearing a baseball cap, or maybe she wasn't. Fuck, I can't remember. She's got curly black hair, about five foot two or three. He's about five ten, short black hair, and clean shaven. No beard.'

'Sorry friend,' Braveheart replied, sounding genuinely apologetic. 'I don't really know many names here. Hey, how is the girl you got out with?'

'Don't know yet, her cousin has gone to look for her.' I looked to the woman. 'How about you? Have you seen them? Michael and Shannon.'

She shook her head. 'Sorry, don't recognise the names.'

'We only got here yesterday,' I muttered. 'You won't know the names.'

'Hey,' a man said as he walked towards us. 'I think I remember your friends. I noticed the guy didn't have a beard,' he said, stroking his own facial hair. 'Don't see many guys without some kind of beard nowadays.'

He must have been one of the members of the Green Team Sweepers. His clothes were splattered in zombie blood.

'Do you know where they are?' I asked.

'They were there at the beginning, when we were lined up and waiting. I'd been speaking to them as we walked over towards the fence. Nice folks. I've not seen them since.' He looked back to the other members of his group. 'I'll ask everyone else.' He paused to look back at us. 'Come on, you can talk to them.'

One of the other Green Team members also remembered them. She was sat on the ground, nursing an injured arm.

'I think they both got brought back here quite early on,' she informed us. 'Jerry and Mark carried them back.'

'Were they badly injured?' I asked. 'Do you know where they took them? Where's Jerry and Mark?'

'Jerry and Mark died getting some of the injured back here,' the first man said. 'Absolute fucking waste of life.' He glanced over to the woman still arguing with Braveheart. 'The asshole bosses knew how many of the dead were out there. It was so fucking stupid.'

'So my friends will be in a medical tent?' I asked them both.

Another member of the dishevelled group stepped forward, a tall muscular woman, her bare arms were covered in cuts. 'Or over there,' she said, pointing to the front lawn of a house, over on the other side of the road. 'That's where we laid out the ones in our team who didn't make it.'

I stared at the line of bodies.

'Hey dude,' the muscle bound woman said. 'Your face is pretty fucked up. You had it checked out?'

'Yeah,' I simply said, still staring at the bodies. Sheets covered each one, but the shape of a human underneath was unmistakable.

I took a very slow walk across the road, dreading what I was about to do.

'I'm right behind you Chris,' Roy said.

There were twenty, maybe twenty five bodies in a line across the lawn, all lying on their backs. I dropped my bat and crouched down by the first. I tried to pull back the sheet, but it was tucked under the head, so I had to yank it out before revealing the face. It was a white woman. She looked young, far too young. I made sure to tuck the sheet back under her.

I slowly moved along the line, trying to be as respectful as possible.

Please don't be here. Just please. Not Gee and them.

As I reached the tenth body, and stood looking down at the white, blood stained bed sheet, I think I'd known it was her.

I pulled the sheet back to reveal Shannon's beautiful face. I couldn't stop the strained low moan escape my mouth. An excruciatingly painful tightness seemed to grip my insides.

She'd been wearing her baseball cap backwards. It wasn't sat on her head properly because its peak was caught under the back of her hair. As hard as I tried, I couldn't get it to stay on. It just kept popping off to fall back onto the grass. My tears were now heavily flowing.

'Chris,' Roy softly said from behind me. 'Just take it off. She looks better without it.'

I looked down at her for a long moment, and then gently pulled the cap out from under her hair. I folded it and put it my jeans pocket. After pulling the sheet back over her, being careful not to pull it too tight, I stood and moved onto the next body.

It wasn't Michael.

Please let Mikey Boy be okay. He's in one of the medical tents getting fixed up. Jack will have found him by now.

I wiped away the new flow of tears from my face and bent down to pull back the next sheet. Michael's eyes stared up to the sky.

I fell backwards to sit on the grass, bringing my hands up to cover my face.

After a few seconds, I said, 'No,' and stood back up. I walked over to the body next to Shannon and bent down to grab it by the shoulders, stopping myself when I realised I was about to start dragging somebody. Looking over to Roy, I said, 'I need a hand, could you help me please?'

'What do you need? What are you trying to do?' he asked.

I loudly sniffed and wiped my face. 'They need to be together. I'm just gonna swap this person with Michael.'

If Roy was hesitant about touching a dead body, he didn't show it. He immediately stepped to the other end of the person, and helped me carry it out of the way.

We walked over to Michael. 'Be careful with him please,' I said.

'Yes, don't worry about that,' he replied. 'Let's put him next to his wife.'

We very gently laid him down next to Shannon, so their arms were touching. Then we placed the other body in the space Michael had occupied. I walked back over to sit by my friends' bodies.

Roy sat next to me.

'Fuck's sake,' I said, wiping my face with my sleeve. 'I've only known them for a few days.'

Roy patted me on the shoulder, before placing his hand back onto his knee. 'They say traumatic situations can bring people closer together, and the last few weeks have been kind of traumatic. You shouldn't be ashamed of your emotions.'

We sat in silence for a long time, the night drawing in around us. The solar lights on the fence came on at some point. Hundreds of people still busied themselves in front of us, rushing up and down the road alongside the fence. The noisy hissing of the dead could still be heard from the other side.

'Chris,' Roy said. 'It's nine fifteen. We should go back and meet Jack and Pete.'

'Yeah okay. I really don't want to tell Jack.'

'I don't think he'll like it, but I can tell him if you want.'

'No it's fine Roy,' I sighed. 'Thank you, but I'll tell him.'

We stood up and started back, before I paused. 'Could you do me a favour Roy?'

'Sure.'

'Could you ask the guys from Green Team if they know what's happening with them?' I pointed towards the line of bodies. 'I don't trust myself not to cry. Don't want to embarrass myself any further.'

'Of course. I'll be back in two seconds.'

Roy walked across the road. I looked past the fallen bodies of Green Team, and noticed more bodies on another lawn further up the street. I spun around to look down H Street. More covered bodies filled another lawn.

I was so incredibly angry, I was fucking livid. Like the guy in Green Team had said, this whole thing had been so fucking stupid. A ridiculous waste of life. Like enough people hadn't died already.

Roy was coming back, trying to avoid the many people ferrying equipment.

'They said they aren't sure. But nothing will be happening tonight.'

We made our way back to the meeting place. I was worrying about what they were gonna tell me about Ali. Jack and Pete were already there, waiting for us. We walked past Caleb and some of my fellow Blue Team Sweepers. There were nine or ten of them remonstrating with him. There was a lot of aggressive pointing and arm swinging. Caleb cowered away from them, slowly stepping backwards.

I hope they beat the shit out of him.

'Ali is going to be okay,' Pete excitedly told us. 'She lost a lot of blood but she's going to be fine. I donated some of mine.' He held out his arm, showing me a cotton pad taped to the inside. 'I need to go and find Sandra and Theo, get them to donate as well. Okay?'

'Yeah. Which tent is she in?'

'Number four.' With a quick nod, he turned and ran off in the direction of our house.

'Did you find them?' Jack asked.

'Yes we did.' I took a breath to steady myself. 'Sorry Jack, but they both died.'

Jack's face dropped. He brought his hand up and dragged it roughly through his hair, scraping across his scalp. 'No,' he whispered. 'No, no, no.'

'They got injured quite early on I think,' I told him. 'They were brought back. Their bodies are back there,' I said, pointing behind us. 'Do you want to see them?'

He slowly shook his head, continuing to draw his hand through his hair. 'I need to get back to Beth.' He turned to walk away but stopped, his head bowed, avoiding eye contact. 'Erm...we saw Gee's friend, Matis. The medics think he is going to be alright.'

'Okay, that's good news. Roy will go back with you.'

'No, I'm fine.' With his head still down, he walked away.

'I'll make sure he gets back okay,' Roy said to me.

'Cheers Roy.'

I watched them walk around Caleb and the angry members of Blue Team. I made my way towards Caleb.

'Hey Caleb,' I called out to him, interrupting the argument. 'Where is your boss? Is it Amber? I'm assuming this fucking plan was her idea?'

Caleb looked back at me with disdain. 'She's dead.'

'Good, means I don't have to kill her.' I turned and started to walk away.

'Hey,' Caleb said. 'Hey Brit.'

I stopped and looked over my shoulder.

'Amber never meant for anyone to die,' he said. 'We didn't want anyone to get hurt.'

'Fuck off Caleb.' I carried on walking.

Sandra and Theo were stood around Ali's bed. I was at the back of the medical tent, stepping from right to left, trying to see through everyone rushing around inside. I eventually caught a glimpse of Ali's face. She was smiling, and looked like she was joking around with her big sister. I left them to it.

It took me longer than it should have done to get back to the house. I was completely drained of all energy. I felt empty, and not just because I'd hardly eaten anything all day.

DAY TWENTY

Chapter 20: Weak

A loud bang woke me up with a jolt. I thought it sounded like a gunshot. I wiped at my eyes and tried to blink away the sleep. Nothing stirred in the room. There were still people asleep in the beds around me, so it must have been early. I got up anyway, spotting Jack and Beth crammed into one of the bottom bunks as I climbed down. I passed Roy as I left, in a bed by the door.

When I'd made it back to the very quiet house the previous night, I headed straight for the bathroom. My face in the mirror had been a series of bright red slashes and scratches. Some of my shrapnel wounds had been made torn and stretched open. I spent a long time in the shower, the freezing water not bothering me in the slightest. I could have stood there all night.

That morning however, I had a very quick, freezing cold shower. I hadn't been in the mood for a repeat of the previous night.

The scratches on my face looked even worse in the morning, trying to scrub it clean in the shower must have opened them up again.

Fuck it. I'm used to having a messed up face now.

I dressed in the clothes the medic had given me, and went outside using the front door. I sat myself down on the front step and breathed in the cold air. It tasted of blood. I wasn't sure if that was actually in the air, or just in my mouth. I closed my eyes and put my fingers in my ears, trying to block out the hissing.

A tap on my shoulder startled me. I opened my eyes to see Sandra smiling down at me. I quickly dropped my hands down to my knees.

'Sorry,' she said. 'The hissing?'

'Yeah. Annoying isn't it? Is Ali okay?'

Her smile stretched even further across her face. 'She's fine. Stand up for a second please Chris.'

'Okay.' I painfully rose to my feet, my legs feeling every bit of the running around from the day before.

Sandra stepped closer, kissed me on the cheek, and wrapped her arms around me. 'Thank you, thank you, thank you. From the bottom of my heart, thank you.'

'That's okay, don't worry about it.'

She stepped back. 'Chris, it's not just okay. I will forever be in your debt. You saved my little sister's life. But right now I have to sleep. The chair by Ali's bed wasn't very comfortable.' She stopped on the way to the front door, and turned back to me. 'Pete told me about Gee. I'm really sorry. Did you find Michael and Shannon?'

I had to look away from her hopeful eyes. 'Yeah, but they died. We found their bodies.'

'Oh Chris, that's awful.' She hugged me again. I didn't want the embrace to end.

'It's okay,' I said, gently patting her on the back. 'You must be tired. Go and see your kids and try and get some sleep.'

She looked at me with tear filled eyes. 'Those two things don't really go hand in hand, but I'll try. Why don't you go and see Ali. She'd love to see you. She's in medical tent number four.'

I decided to check on Michael and Shannon on my way to visiting Ali. As I got closer to H Street, it sounded like there was a lot going on down there.

Aren't we supposed to be keeping extra quiet now the dead are so close?

At the end of 11th Street it looked like something was being constructed. Somebody must have listened to Braveheart's idea.

I made it to the end of the street and stood on one of the front lawns. A new fence was indeed being hastily built. It seemed H Street would soon be within the new no man's land, and no longer be walkable.

The Fencers must have been up all night.

A huge framework of scaffolding had been erected, and hundreds of people were still busy with its construction. Metal panelling and wooden planks were piled up on H Street. I walked back down to the lawn where I'd found Michael and Shannon. The bodies were still there. A large wooden cart sat on the grass next to them. A man sat on the edge of the cart, smoking a cigarette.

I walked up to him, surprised to find he wasn't smoking weed. 'Any idea what's happening with the people that died yet?' I asked.

'Yeah, I'm just waiting for someone. Then we're taking them over to the harbour for the cremation. It'll be for everyone that died, including the people who were killed by the psychopaths in town. Going to be at midday I believe. They'll be sending out runners to spread the word.'

'How many people were shot by the gunmen?'

'I don't know, not doing them. I'm only working around here this morning. Heard it was hundreds though.'

'Anybody know why they did it?' I asked him.

He shrugged and exhaled smoke. 'Nobody that's talking. Someone will know.' He took a quick glance around us. 'I think it was some of those religious zealots. The ones who thought killing zombies was against God's will and all that.'

'That's a bit hypocritical,' I suggested. 'Isn't it?'

He shrugged, saying, 'Crazy is as crazy does.'

Staring at the shapes I thought were Michael and Shannon, I asked, 'Could you take care of these bodies please? My friends are among them.'

He looked offended. 'Don't worry. We know how to respect the dead.'

'Yeah sorry, I'm sure you do.' I walked over to where Michael and Shannon were laid out and crouched down behind them. 'I realise this may be difficult, but if you could try your hardest to keep these two together, I'd be very grateful.'

He nodded. 'Yeah sure, we'll try our best.'

I thanked the man and left him to his waiting. I walked along the partly constructed fence, trying to stop my mind from wandering. I kept imagining the guys haphazardly throwing the bodies into the cart, like the body collectors during the bubonic plague times.

I'm sure they won't do that.

I walked past medical tents one, two and three. The Fencers would have to wait for the temporary hospitals to be dismantled before making the new inner fence one solid piece.

I stood outside tent number four, nervous about going in for some reason. I entered and headed towards Ali's bed. She was fast asleep. I'd forgotten it was still early, so I sat in the seat by her bed, and waited for her to wake up.

'Chris. Hi Christopher. Hey, Chris.'

I opened my eyes, taking a moment to remember where I was. People were hurrying past me, carrying medical equipment. I looked to my right to see Ali's scratch covered face. She was sat up in bed, smiling down at me.

'Hi Chris. Good sleep?' she asked.

I stood up and stepped closer to the side of her bed. 'Morning. Sorry, must have nodded off. How long have you been awake?'

'Only a few seconds. How you doing?'

'I'm fine. More importantly, how are you?'

'I'm okay. They said I have to be out in a few hours. They're packing up,' she said, gesturing to the mayhem going on around us. 'Sandra is coming back to get me.'

'How's the face?' I asked. 'Looks a bit sore. Sorry, but I had to drag you through a load of zombies.'

'I'm trying to beat you and Jack in the fucked up face awards.'

I laughed, saying, 'Nah, you've got a while to go before you catch us two up.' I pointed at my own face. 'Especially now.'

'Yeah, your face also looks like it's painful. I imagine that happened getting me out?'

'No, not all of it,' I replied.

'I'm sorry you got hurt helping me.'

'I did most of this on my own. The only people who should be getting any blame are Amber and the rest of the bosses. Fucking idiots. Oh, Amber died by the way.'

I maybe said that last bit with a bit too much satisfaction.

My hands were resting on the bed. She placed one of hers on top of mine. 'Pete told me about Gee, I'm really sorry.' She gave my hand a brief squeeze. 'Last night he also said you were still looking for Michael and Shannon. They were right next to me as we walked up to the outer fence, but when the zombies came at us, I got all turned around. I didn't know where anyone or anything was.'

'They're both dead.'

She gasped and brought both her hands to her mouth.

'We were told they were injured quite early on, and brought back into the camp,' I told her. 'We found their bodies with the rest of the Green Team's dead. The guys that brought them back are also dead, so we don't really know what happened.'

'They were right next to me,' she said through her fingers.

'There's gonna be a cremation for everyone that died, the shooting victims as well. It's today at twelve.'

'I have to be there,' she said, her hands dropping back to the bed. 'Sandra is picking me up at eleven. I'll be there.' She suddenly had a determined look on her face.

'Okay,' I said.

'They were so nice, a lovely couple. You could tell they loved each other just from looking at them.' A single tear ran down her face.

I stayed silent, not really knowing what to say, and worried I might cry.

'Chris?'

I'd been watching the large canvas tent being dismantled around us. 'Yep,' I answered.

'When are we getting out of this place?'

I looked back to see her looking even more determined. 'As soon as you're well enough,' I answered.

'Tomorrow, I'll be ready tomorrow.'

'What about Sandra and the kids?' I asked.

'She said they can't stay here. It's not safe. Pete and Theo are coming too.'

I nodded. 'Okay. Whenever you're ready.'

'Thank you for coming for me yesterday Chris. It really does mean a lot, it means everything.'

I shrugged my shoulders. 'What are mates for? You rescued me from the gun shop basement.'

She smiled back at me. 'Go and get some breakfast. You must be starving after yesterday. They've been force feeding me in here. Make sure Sandra is on time, earlier if possible.'

'Will do,' I said. 'See you soon.'

The two guys were loading the bodies into the cart when I passed by them again. Thankfully, they were being very careful and gentle.

I honestly didn't know what I would have done if they hadn't been.

Back at the house, everyone was up and just about to head out for breakfast. Beth hugged me, saying how sorry she was. Pete shook my hand again, saying thank you, again. I also got an awkward hug from Theo, while thanking me for helping Ali.

I told all of them about the cremation as we walked to breakfast.

'Will it be a big funeral pyre?' Roy asked me. 'Like a Viking funeral?'

'No idea, didn't ask,' I replied. 'We'll find out when we get there.'

'I suppose there's nowhere inside the camp to bury that many people,' Sandra pondered.

'Who is organising it all?' Beth asked. 'Is there an overall boss that runs everything? Or has someone just taken it upon themselves to do it?'

'I thought you and Roy might have known the answer to that,' Sandra said. 'You've been here longer.'

'No, we don't know,' Roy said.

'I don't think anyone knows the answers to those questions,' Jack said. 'This place is a mess.'

I nudged Jack and nodded behind me. I slowed and he got the idea, falling into step alongside me. 'Ali and Sandra have said they want to leave here, as soon as possible.'

'Good,' Jack said. 'Because so does Beth.'

I smiled as relief flowed through me. I'd desperately not wanted to leave them behind.

'That's fucking brilliant news,' I said. 'Ali said she'll be ready to go tomorrow.'

'I want to get out of here now Chris, two days ago if it were possible, but is that not a bit soon for her?'

'She said she'll be ready, and I believe her.'

'Okay,' he said. 'It's really hard to imagine doing anything without Gee, Shannon and Michael. If it hadn't been for them, I definitely wouldn't be here.'

'Yeah I know.' I put my hands in my pockets. There was something in one of them. I pulled out Shannon's blood stained baseball cap. I'd forgotten all about it. I think I'd been in a bit of a daze as I walked along the line of bodies.

Jack was looking at the cap in my hand.

'I couldn't get it to stay on Shannon's head,' I explained. 'It kept falling off, so Roy suggested I take it off her. I forgot I put it in my pocket.' I offered it to him. 'Here, you keep it.'

He took it from me. 'Won't fit my big head,' he very quietly said.

'Keep it anyway, something to remember her by.'

He gently folded it in half, and put it in his pocket.

'Yesterday,' I said. 'Roy really helped me out. He came with me to find you lot, outside the fence. And then after, he helped me find Michael and Shannon.'

'Yeah I know,' he said. 'We talked last night. It's fine.'

'What did you talk about?'

'Just shit. Don't worry. It's fine.'

'I'm assuming Roy will come with us?' I asked him.

Jack shrugged. 'Guess so.'

The porridge was terrible, again.

'I'm gonna go to Pea's Place after breakfast,' I mentioned to Jack. 'I want to speak to Charles about getting out of here.'

'Why him?' Jack asked.

'He can sail boats.'

'Are you hoping he's going to travel all the way across Canada, and then sail you to England?'

'Maybe.'

'Good luck with that,' Beth said, stepping closer to us. 'By the way, we've discussed it with Roy. He's coming with us.'

'Yes,' Roy agreed, appearing at her shoulder. 'I'm in, to get out.'

'Good,' I said. 'Anybody fancy coming with me to the pub? It's on the way to the harbour.'

Jack looked at Beth, she nodded.

'We might as well,' Jack said. 'There is nothing better to do.'

'Yes I'll come with you,' Roy said. 'As of now, I've quit my job, since we're leaving.'

Pete and Theo started packing up the three boys' things, as Sandra stepped towards us. 'We're going to pick Ali up and take her back to the house for a while,' she said. 'Then Pete and Theo will take Ali to meet you down by the harbour.'

'Okay,' I said. 'Meet outside Pea's Place? Ali knows where it is.'

Sandra agreed, and the Rodriguez's slowly left the busy food tent.

'Are you working this evening?' Jack asked Beth.

She swallowed her last mouthful of porridge and nodded.

'Why not quit?' he asked her. 'Like Roy.'

'Because we're still eating their food,' she said, shaking her spoon in front of his face. 'I'm still going to do my bit.'

We left the food tent and walked around the edge of the camp, so the other three could take a look at the fence being built. Medical tents one and two were gone, and the scaffolding frame of the fence was almost complete in the spaces that had been left. Number three was almost down. I expected Ali's bed to be outside by the time we walked past the fourth medical tent. Luckily for her, the roof had still been up.

We had a quick look for her inside, but she must have already been picked up by Sandra.

There was a very sombre mood inside the pub. I thought it'd been quiet on my first visit. Nobody had been on the door, so we walked straight in. Charles and Andruis were sat at the bar, in the same place Gee, Ali and I had sat. Charles spun around after hearing the door close behind us, and waved us over.

'How's Matis doing?' I asked Andruis.

'He's back with his family. Doing well thank you.'

I introduced everyone, forgetting that Jack had already met Andruis the night before.

'I must tell you all I was very sorry to hear about Gintaras,' Charles said. 'Andruis told me all about it. I owe him my gratitude for what he did for Matis. Can I get you a drink?' He called one of the bar staff over. It was a guy this morning.

'I'll have a gin and tonic please,' Beth said.

Jack and I stared at her. I quickly looked away when I remembered I wasn't supposed to know about the pregnancy.

'What?' she exclaimed. 'It's been a stressful few days.'

Jack leaned in and whispered something in her ear. Beth's eyes widened briefly.

She smiled to the barman apologetically, and said, 'Just a water please.'

'What time is it?' I asked.

Jack checked his watch. 'Half ten.'

'Fuck it then, it's not that early. And I'm going to a funeral today,' I said. 'Whiskey and coke please. Not bothered what the whiskey is.'

Jack and Roy both ordered a beer.

'I take it you heard about the sheriff?' Charles asked us. 'Dreadful news.'

The four of us exchanged confused glances.

'Nope, what happened?' I asked him.

'Shot himself in the early hours of this morning. Seems he woke up on top of his office, and blew his brains out.'

'Fuck,' I whispered.

'Didn't anybody try to rescue him?' Jack asked.

'I believe there was talk of it,' Charles said. 'But he didn't give them the chance. Let's hope whoever he was waiting for doesn't turn up now.'

Our drinks were placed on the bar in front of us.

I raised my glass towards Charles and Andruis. 'Thanks for the drink, and I hope Matis makes a full recovery.'

Charles raised his glass. 'Yes cheers. Let's hope we don't have too many days like yesterday.'

I took a sip of my drink. 'Speaking of yesterday. It confirmed it for all of us. We're getting out of here. What are you doing?'

Charles looked to Andruis, and gave him a knowing smile, before turning his attention back to me. 'What do you mean?'

'Do you want to leave the camp?' I asked him.

'No.'

'No?' I repeated.

'That is correct. No. The answer is no. I do not want to leave the camp.'

'Surely you know this place isn't going to last much longer?' Jack reasoned.

'Certainly. But while it's still here, I'm going to stay. I'll leave when the time is right. I don't want to go outside and live with the things that want to eat me. I'm old fashioned like that.'

'Shite,' I muttered. 'I was really hoping you'd want to leave after what happened yesterday. Maybe even pop over to England.'

Charles laughed. 'Because I can sail a yacht?'

I pointed towards him, saying, 'Bingo,' and then took a large mouthful of my drink.

'I would be more than happy to take you further down the coast, and drop you off somewhere safe. But no, I'm not going to try and permanently get out of the camp just yet, and certainly not try and sail across the Atlantic. I would kill us both if I tried. Anyway, I hear Canada is lovely, lots of open spaces.'

I looked to the others and shrugged, before turning back to Charles. 'We'll definitely take you up on that offer.'

'It would be my way of saying thank you to Gintaras. Talking of which.' He looked to his large Lithuanian friend. 'Andruis?'

Andruis had been staring at the shelves behind the bar, he turned back to us. 'Yes, we are having a few drinks this evening, a kind of a wake. You are all more than welcome. The drinks are on Pea.' He clapped a heavy hand on Charles's shoulder, nearly knocking him off his seat.

Charles quickly readjusted himself on his bar stool. 'Yes, more than welcome,' he said with a smile.

We finished our drinks and waited outside for Ali, Pete and Theo to turn up. A few minutes later they appeared from around the bend. Ali walked slowly, with the aid of Pete on her left, and a walking stick in her right hand. Theo was a couple of paces behind.

Jack shot me a worried glance on seeing the state Ali was in. 'That doesn't look good Chris. Maybe we should get Gee to carry...' He trailed off, realising his mistake. 'Fucking hell.'

'She'll be fine. We won't be leaving until tomorrow evening.'

She does look in a bad way. I really hope she's a lot more mobile by tomorrow.

'I'm fine, just feeling a bit weak at the moment,' she said through gritted teeth. 'I'll be good, no need to worry about me.'

She must have noticed our concerned looks.

Chapter 21: Not A Night

Roy had been correct. They had indeed built a funeral pyre, or four of them to be exact. They were close to the waters edge. A lot of people were in attendance, thousands maybe, so we were quite far from the front. I was more than happy to stay as far away as possible from the soon to be burning bodies.

Roy patted me on the shoulder. 'You alright,' he asked.

I told him I was fine. I'd been thinking about the fact that Gee's body wasn't there, with all the others, and if that would have really mattered to him. I had no idea if he'd been religious, or if he'd believed in an afterlife of some sort. And not the afterlife that was trying to get to us from the other side of the fence.

Through the crowds, I could see four people leave the edge of the spectators. They each walked up to a pyre, carrying flaming torches. The one closest to us slowly walked around his, occasionally placing the torch on the scraps of wood used to construct it.

There was a very ceremonial feeling to the whole thing.

The flames spread quickly, and all four pyres were soon ablaze. The torch carriers then stepped back into the crowds. Nobody spoke, there were no prayers, nothing at all.

It was actually very peaceful.

'The Lord has forsaken these fallen few,' a man's voice called out, shattering the peace.

'Somebody shut that fucker up,' another voice shouted.

A murmur started to ripple through the many spectators.

'You had no right to do this,' a man screamed. 'You had no–.'

There was a loud thud, the sound of a fist connecting with a face.

'Kill the fucker,' a woman's voice said.

The murmuring amongst the crowd increased, and people started to turn and move towards us.

Jack quickly spun around to face us. 'Right, let's get out of here.'

We started to move with the crowds, but Ali was slow. Pete and Theo stood on either side of her. The rest of us formed a line behind, and tried to hold back the crowds.

It wasn't working.

'Pete, Theo,' I said. 'Grab Ali under the arms. You're carrying her out of here.'

They lifted her off the ground and we immediately doubled our speed.

'Pub?' Jack asked me.

'Pub,' I agreed.

Once we were safely back in Pea's Place, all sat around two tables pushed together, I turned to Jack. 'If you forget about the religious freaks, and almost getting crushed, I'd say that was a perfect funeral.'

The bouncers on the door had been two American guys that I hadn't seen before. Once we explained who we were, and after one of them had gone inside to check, we were allowed to go in. Charles had very kindly reserved a few tables for us. He told us Matis had been very insistent on him making sure the friends of Gintaras were well taken care of.

Michael, Shannon and Gee were very noticeably missing from the group.

'No long winded speeches,' I added. 'From someone who wouldn't have even known the deceased.'

Jack nodded and drank his beer.

Charles was trying to charm Ali by the looks of it. She glanced over to me, rolling her eyes.

Beth leaned in closer to me. 'I think you should be careful with Ali.'

'Why, what do you mean?' I asked.

'I think she likes you.'

'Nah, we're just friends. She knows I'm married.'

'I've seen the way she looks at you.'

'Yep,' Jack agreed. 'I've seen it.'

'Bollocks. Have you seen me lately?' I pointed to my face. 'I look like I got my head trapped in a bag of cats.'

'Every now and then…' Beth started, but then laughed. 'Well yes, you do a bit.' She covered her mouth with her hand. 'I'm sorry Chris. That's an awful thing to say.'

'What are you on about?' I laughed. 'It was me that said it.'

'There was no reason for me to agree with you,' she said.

'Apart from all the scratches on his face,' Jack said, instantly receiving a punch from Beth on his arm. Jack immediately grabbed where she'd hit him. 'Ow Beth. You know I was bitten there.'

She rubbed his arm, apologising. He playfully slapped away her hand.

Jack looked back to me. 'I don't understand what she sees in you,' he said. 'But I think Beth might be right.'

I finished my drink and caught the eye of the waiter. 'Well, I haven't noticed anything, so I'm gonna carry on not noticing.'

'Just be careful, that's all I'm saying,' Beth said.

The waiter arrived and took our order.

'I thought she might have been a lesbian,' Jack said.

'Yeah, I briefly thought about that,' I agreed.

Jack laughed. 'I bet you did.'

I had to laugh with him.

'She might be bi-sexual,' Beth suggested. 'And so what if she is?'

'In that case,' I said. 'Can I take her home to meet Joanne?'

Beth placed her bottle of water down on the table. 'No, I don't think Joanne would be too impressed.'

'Okay I won't bother then.'

'It'd backfire anyway,' Jack said. 'They'd soon kick you out of the house.'

'Yep, probably.'

Beth started talking to Pete and Roy, so I took the opportunity to speak to Jack. 'Are you gonna tell me what happened yesterday after I left?'

'Yep,' he said nonchalantly. 'I wasn't not going to tell you. Just hasn't been a right time. You can also tell me what the fuck you were talking about yesterday. Something about fanny farts.'

'Oh shit yeah, forgot about that. I hope she didn't hear me.'

'Hear you do what?' he asked.

'You first. What happened after you crashed the SUV? In fact, how did you get in and drive the SUV?'

'I broke one of the windows, and just thought to myself, I wonder if the keys are still in there? I had a look, and there they were. They did bite me a few times when I was climbing in.' He touched the plaster on the bridge of his nose, saying, 'I think I smashed my nose into the steering wheel when I crashed it. I couldn't see a thing. The car was covered in them.'

'Yeah I heard the crash, and then saw you getting out.'

'I couldn't climb back on top of the crashed car, so I ran off looking for something else to climb on. I saw some of the other Blue Team in the back of a truck, and ran for them. I helped them for a while, but then someone noticed Red Team looked like they were really struggling, so we grabbed whatever Blue people were left, and went to help them. Gee and his two friends turned up as we were fighting our way over. You should have seen them three. They went out in front, and we just mopped up the few that made it around them, or came at us from behind. We made it to Red Team, rescued them so to speak, and then got back in the camp using some other gates. Then we came and found you.' Jack's once animated face had suddenly taken on a much more dour expression.

'We tried to save Gee, me and Andruis, but he fell. He just let go and...' I trailed off at the end, not wanting to relive the entire thing.

'It's okay Chris. Tell me about the fanny farts.'

Smiling, I said, 'That's the first time anybody has ever said that to me.'

I told him the full story about being woken up by the fanny fart sex, trying to remember every detail.

'And it was definitely that woman we were stood behind? Because I think she did hear you.'

'No it's not definitely her. It's just a guess because she's English. There seems to be a lot of us knocking about in the camp, so there could be another English woman that also lives in our house.'

'I thought you got up early this morning to visit your girlfriend? Was this woman not sleeping in the bunk under you?'

'There was somebody there, but I don't go around inspecting people's faces while they're asleep. How fucking weird would that be if they woke up, and I'm staring back at them?'

Jack glared at me. 'Especially with your Freddy Krueger face.'

'And probably best to keep the hilarious girlfriend jokes down while Ali is sat just on the other side of the table.'

'She can't hear me,' Jack said. 'Did you say Charles is an Ipswich fan?'

'Yep, so he reckons. Said he's from Stowmarket.'

'Do you think we can trust him to drop us off somewhere safe?'

I glanced over to Charles. 'I don't see why not.'

Theo seemed to have stolen Ali's attention away from him, so Charles was staring forlornly at his drink.

'Chaz,' I called out.

He looked up from his beer, a smile spreading across his face. 'Yes Christopher.'

I had a quick look behind me, found what I was looking for, and dragged over another stool. I nodded to it, saying, 'Fancy a chat about our great escape?'

With one last glance at Ali, he stood and walked over to us, sitting on the offered stool. 'When are you planning on leaving?' he asked us.

'All being well, tomorrow evening,' Jack replied. 'Would that be okay with you?'

Charles shifted on his stool. 'Well, that was sooner than I was expecting, but I think it should be fine.'

'How big is your yacht?' I asked him. 'Because there's eleven of us.'

Charles leaned in. 'Does that include Alison?'

I laughed. 'I'm afraid so. You should come with us. You could spend a lot more time with her.'

Charles grinned. 'No thanks. As delightful as she is, I'm still saying no to that offer.'

With hindsight, that sounded a little bit like I was trying to pimp Ali out. I bet Jack fucking tells her I said that. Note to self. Make sure Jack doesn't tell her.

'It's more than big enough to fit eleven,' Charles said. 'And we're not going far anyway. I hope you don't mind, but I took the liberty of picking you a possible place to dock. If it's clear, I was thinking of dropping you off in Birch Bay. It's in the next cove, just south of us. There should be plenty of vehicles there, and it's far enough away from the camp to avoid the dead things that are piling up outside.'

'Do you know how far Birch Bay is from Elliot and Martin's container?' I asked.

'Four, maybe five miles,' Charles replied. 'Don't worry, far enough away.'

'No, I was thinking we could go back and pick up our stuff,' I said. 'We've still got food and guns in our vehicle there.'

Charles placed his empty beer bottle on the bar. 'Well that's up to you. Once I drop you off, you can go in whichever direction you please. But if it's guns you need, just search enough homes in Birch Bay, you'll soon find some. Remember which country you're in.'

'Also,' I added. 'My passport is in the bus.'

'You don't need a passport to illegally enter another country,' Jack said. 'It's best to avoid the authorities in those kinds of circumstances.'

'What about getting back to England?' I asked.

Jack and Charles shared a quick glance. I furrowed my brow, looking at them both in turn.

What the fuck was that?

'Don't worry about the passport,' Jack said. 'But if it is possible, we can try and get to the bus.'

I'm not sure what they're thinking, but I'm going home to Joanne.

Charles dramatically waved a hand in front of him. 'Anyway, that's enough talk about that. We can arrange a time of departure in the morning. Now should be a time of remembrance, and drinking. Gintaras wouldn't have wanted it any other way.' He raised his hand and glanced over to one of the waiting staff. The guy rushed over. 'Thank you Jacob. Another round for everyone.'

'Sure Pea,' Jacob said. He hesitated, before bending down so he was closer to Charles. 'Everyone in the whole place? Or just this table?'

Charles lowered his voice. 'Sorry Jacob, just this table.'

'Hey Charles,' I said, after Jacob had left. 'Do you know if Elliot and Martin were working yesterday?'

'Yes, but don't worry about them. It was their shift yesterday, but they managed to get over to Semiahmoo. Spent a few hours in quarantine.' He checked his watch. 'Should be getting the boat over any minute now.'

I nodded over to Andruis, sat at the bar. 'How's the big Lithuanian doing?'

He'd greeted us on arrival, but then immediately went to sit on his own.

Charles glanced over at his friend. 'He's fine. I think he's just upset about Matis. Maybe the death of Gintaras as well. He told me he knew of him back in Lithuania.'

By the time Jacob returned with our drinks, Jack and Charles were deep into a conversation about Norwich City players. Jack was now talking about how he'd gone to school with a former Norwich goalkeeper. I'd heard the story many times, so I moved to sit next to Ali, Pete and Theo, to tell them the latest news on our departure.

'Hey Chris,' Pete said. 'I'm going to take Ali back to the house.'

Ali groaned and shook her head.

'Could you keep an eye on Theo for me?' Pete asked.

Theo shot his brother an annoyed look. 'Peter, I don't need anyone to keep an eye on me.'

Pete smiled back at him.

'Yeah okay,' I said. 'Before you go, Charles has agreed to sail us all down to Birch Bay. It's not far from here apparently. Can you be ready for tomorrow evening?' I directed this last question more towards Ali.

'Erm, I don't know if–.' Pete started to say.

'Yes we'll be ready,' Ali quickly said. She shot her cousin that same determined look I'd seen earlier.

Pete sighed, before saying, 'I'm sure Sandra will have something to say about it. We'll talk about it tomorrow morning.'

'Are you happy to go with Charles?' I asked them.

'Yeah sure,' Ali said. 'We can't use the tunnel anymore.'

'Thank god,' I muttered.

Pete tried to help Ali get to her feet, but she pushed him away.

'I can do it,' she said. 'I'm feeling stronger after that drink.'

'I very much doubt that,' Pete said. 'You shouldn't have even had one.'

Ali managed to get out of the pub with just the help of her walking stick. Pete followed closely behind, poised to catch her if she fell.

'I hope she is getting stronger,' I said to Theo, after the door had closed behind them.

'What if she isn't ready by tomorrow?' he asked.

I shrugged. 'We'll have to postpone I suppose. But you know your cousin. She'll be ready no matter what. Especially as it was her idea to leave tomorrow.'

Theo had a concerned look on his face, but nodded in agreement.

The drinking carried on throughout the rest of the afternoon. Jack and Beth both left at some point, Jack returning an hour or so later, after dropping his wife off at work.

'We should think about getting some food,' Jack suggested.

'Yep, I suppose so,' I reluctantly said.

I didn't really want to leave, but we needed to eat.

'Hey,' Charles said. 'Let's move this into the back room. We have a bit of food stored back there.'

'Brilliant,' I said. 'Charles, you are the perfect host. I've no idea how you manage to make any of this work, but I like it.'

Andruis joined me, Jack, Roy, and Theo as we followed Charles around the bar and through an open door marked private.

The room beyond was like a snug in an Irish bar, only bigger. Charles told us all to sit at the round table in the middle of the room.

He then opened up a hatch in the wall. The bar area was just on the other side.

Charles leaned his head through the opening. 'Zoey, same again please.' He turned around to face us. 'All happy with the same again?' We all agreed, and he spun back around to talk with Zoey.

The change in location had managed to break up the once flowing conversations. Most of us sat there staring at our drinks. I looked to Jack, smiled and raised my eyebrows. He blew air out of his mouth, flapping his lips slightly.

Charles was handed a tray through the open hatch, containing our drinks. 'Come on guys. I know there was a funeral today, but cheer up,' he said, placing the drinks on the table. 'Your friends wouldn't want you to be miserable.'

I thanked Charles for my beer, before turning to Roy. 'Are you a Norwich fan? Did you know Charles supports Ipswich?'

'Yes he told me earlier. But no, I'm a Rochdale fan. Sarah got me into them.' His face dropped when he mentioned his wife's name.

Bollocks, that's not gonna help the mood.

A door opened and one of the women who had been serving behind the bar walked in, carrying a tray. She placed it on the table in front us. The tray contained two loaves of home baked bread, and a selection of tinned tuna, salmon, and crab.

Saved by the food.

We ate it in no time at all, only bread crumbs were left by the end. I think I must have had five sandwiches. We were obviously sick of the rice and vegetables we'd been eating.

The various conversations started flowing again, and we continued pouring alcohol down our throats.

'You know what Jack?' I said.

Jack placed his drink down on the table. 'What Chris?'

'I was really looking forward to having a night out with Michael and Shannon. I think they'd have been a good laugh.'

'They were a good laugh.'

'No, you know what I mean, a good laugh on a night out.'

'Yes I know what you mean.' He picked up his bottle and raised it in the air. 'To Michael and Shannon. The breast of us.'

I lifted my drink and knocked it against Jack's. 'Yep, they were the breast of us.'

'And to Gintaras,' Andruis said. 'He sacrificed himself to help others.'

We all raised our drinks, and called out, 'Gintaras.'

'Yep,' I said. 'Gee always looked after everybody else. Always put himself in harm's way to protect us.'

Jack suddenly stood up, saying, 'Shite.' His chair toppled over to land on its back. 'I'm supposed to pick Beth up from work.'

'You are a terrible husband Jack,' I said.

'I'm just going to stop her off at the house.' He paused, frowning. 'Drop her stop. Drop her off.'

'Drop it like it's hot?' Theo offered, with a broad smile on his face.

'Yes that,' Jack said, pointing at Theo. He opened his mouth to speak, but hesitated, before letting out a long and loud burp.

'Thanks for that Jack,' I said.

'And then I'm coming bright sack here.' He looked around with a confused expression on his face. 'Where are we again?'

'I'll come with you,' Roy said. 'I know where we are.' He placed his hands on the table and tried to stand up. His hands slipped off the edge and his forehead smacked into the table. He fell back onto his seat, holding his head in his hands. 'Ow,' he cried out.

There were a few seconds of stunned silence when everyone thought he might have actually hurt himself, then we all started laughing. Even Roy joined in, eventually.

Theo stood up and patted Roy on the back. He looked relatively steady on his feet. 'I'll come with you Jack. I'm going to call it a night.' He looked at his watch. 'Nine o'clock. Shit, that's not a night.'

'Okay, come on Theo,' Jack said, walking towards the wrong door. Theo took him by the arm and guided him towards the correct door.

After they'd left, Andruis asked me, 'Will he be okay finding his way back here on his own?'

I waved my hand. 'I bet you we won't see Jack again tonight.'

About an hour later, while Andruis was telling me the same joke for the fourth time, something about a teacher and some eggs, there was a knock on the door leading to the bar.

Charles stood up and staggered over to it. He turned the key in the lock, and opened it a few inches. 'Good evening, nice of you to join us,' he said to the newcomers. He opened the door all the way. Jack and Matis stood on the other side.

DAY TWENTY ONE

Chapter 22: Painful Death

I could hear somebody talking. It sounded like Beth's voice, but it was far away. She was berating someone, about something. All of a sudden her voice was right next to my head.

'Breakfast time Chris. You only have half an hour before they stop serving. Roy, come on, get up.' Her voice was further away from me again. 'You have a perfectly good bed there. Why sleep on the floor? Jack? What are you doing? Are you getting up?'

I turned over and half opened my eyes. Roy was lying on the floor, in the open doorway. The bedroom door was pressing against his head. His legs must have been out in the hallway. Jack was unmoving, but at least he was on his bed.

Fuck me I feel like shit. My head feels like it weighs a tonne.

I groaned and rolled back over to face the wall.

Beth let out an exasperated sounding squeal, before saying, 'Right, okay, I won't do this for you again.' I heard her step over Roy and walk out of the room.

'Chris,' Jack said. 'You need to get up. Beth brought us back some porridge. She'll kill me if we don't eat it.'

I thought I'd smelt the food, but assumed I was dreaming. I opened my eyes to see a very scruffy looking Jack. He was holding a porridge filled bowl in each hand. Roy was now sat on the edge of his bed, hunched over the bowl on his lap, looking very sorry for himself.

'Alright, alright. I'm getting up.' I sat up and took the bowl from Jack's outstretched hand. 'Ta very much.' My throat felt like sand paper. 'Anybody got any water?'

Roy grunted, and started rummaging through his bag. He pulled out a bottle of water.

'Thanks Roy,' I said, and raised my hand.

He threw the bottle under arm. It fell woefully short, landing on the fanny fart bed below me.

'What the fuck was that?' I asked him.

'Sorry,' he muttered.

Jack stood up from his bed and retrieved the bottle, before passing it up to me.

I thanked him and got back to the chore of eating my disgusting breakfast.

Ali walked into the room. 'Morning guys,' she said brightly, before screwing up her face. 'It absolutely stinks of beer in here.'

We all just grunted in reply.

'We need to go and speak to Charles and finalise our plans,' she said. 'I don't know if you've noticed, but I'm walking without a stick. So we're ready to go.' She spun around and started walking out. 'And make sure you all have a shower.'

Roy very slowly got to his feet, making a peculiar groaning noise as he rose. He ended the groan by saying, 'Shower,' and walked out of the room. He immediately returned and grabbed his towel off the end of his bed.

I closed my eyes and waited for my turn in the bathroom.

I had another freezing cold shower, which did nothing for my headache.

'Sore head Chris?' Sandra asked, as I walked out into the incredibly bright garden.

It was so bright I had to keep my eyes almost closed, so I couldn't actually see where anybody was. 'Keep talking so I can find you,' I said.

'Over here,' Sandra said. 'Yes, keep going, keep going.'

I walked towards her voice, trying to block out the sun with my hands. 'Why is it so bright? Has something happened to the sun?'

'Yes, you drank too much last night,' Beth said. 'That's what happened to it.'

'Oh right, that explains it then,' I said.

'Do you need some shades?' Pete asked me.

My eyes were slowly adjusting. 'No thanks. I'll be fine.'

We all made our way over to Pea's Place. Jack, Roy and me slowly trudged along at the back of the group. Sandra told us the boys didn't like it near the fence, so we were forced to walk through the middle of the camp. That meant having to weave our way through the crowds.

'Either of you remember what happened last night?' I asked them.

'Most of it, I think,' Roy replied.

'I remember you and Matis turning up Jack,' I said. 'Nothing after that.'

I bumped into a woman, apologising to her after she shot me a very disgruntled look.

'Not much happened after that, just more drinking, I think,' Jack said. His hand shot to his mouth as a horrible noise came from within him. 'Oh fuck, I was just sick in my mouth.'

'Lovely,' I muttered.

'For at least half an hour, you kept repeating the word Showaddywaddy,' Roy said.

'Who did?' I asked. 'Me?'

'Yes you,' he said.

I laughed. 'Why?'

Roy raised his hands. 'I don't know.'

'And you ran home,' Jack said. 'As soon we left the pub, you ran off, saying you had to run.'

I shook my head. 'No idea why I did that. Where did you find Matis?' I asked Jack.

'I was lost, couldn't remember where the pub was, and then I bumped into him. He said he was out taking a walk to get his strength up.'

'Did he stay for long in the pub?' I asked.

'Yeah he was there all night, until we left,' Roy said.

'What time was that?' I asked.

'About three,' Jack replied.

'Fuck's sake. And we were worried about Ali not being ready to go today.'

'I don't think we're going to try and get to the bus,' Jack said. 'We were talking about it in the garden. Sandra, Pete and Theo don't want to go anywhere near there. Because of Steve.'

'I doubt the British Embassy in Canada will have the time to issue me a temporary passport,' I muttered. 'Pretty sure they'll have more important things to worry about.'

'I think you should worry about it after we're in Canada,' Jack said.

'Have you got your passport?' I asked him.

Jack patted the back pocket of his jeans. 'Yep, right here.'

'Roy?' I asked.

'In my bag, back in the house.'

Well that's just fucking brilliant.

It was the same two American guys on the door, they'd been expecting us.

Charles was sat in his usual spot, at the end of the bar. He was wearing dark sunglasses and nursing a short glass containing a bright red drink.

'Morning Charles,' I said. 'I'm guessing the sunglasses and the Bloody Mary in your hand mean you're feeling as bad as me.'

Charles lifted a hand to his sunglasses, and with one finger, very slowly pulled them down to end of his nose. 'Morning everyone. You are correct Christopher, I'm not entirely on top form, but I sincerely hope I don't look as bad as you three.' His eyes slowly tracked across us, settling on Jack. 'If you don't mind Jack, please don't be sick in my pub.'

'I'm fine,' Jack said.

'Hi kids,' Charles said, looking down at the three boys. He looked back up to Sandra. 'You brought your kids.'

'Certainly did,' Sandra said, smiling.

Charles carefully slipped off his stool to stand on his feet. 'Okay, follow me through to the back room.' He walked towards the room we'd spent the previous night. We all filed in behind him.

Charles lazily gestured for us to take a seat around the table, and walked over to a small cupboard set into the wall. Sandra gave the boys some toy cars to play with. They took them to the corner of the room and sat on the floor.

'Quiet time please,' Sandra said to the kids.

'Sandra,' Charles whispered. She looked at him and he glanced down to his hand. He was holding three Hershey's chocolate bars. Once she'd seen what he was holding, he nodded to the kids. Sandra smiled and returned his nod.

'Kids,' Charles said. 'Would you like some chocolate?'

Like three meerkats, they suddenly stood to attention, still on their knees, but with straight backs and extended necks. All three of them looked to Sandra for approval.

'Yes go on,' she said as she sat down.

They quickly got to their feet and ran to Charles to receive their gifts.

'What do you say?' Sandra asked them after Charles had bent forward to hand the chocolate out.

In unison the three boys thanked Charles.

I wish I could get offered some chocolate.

Charles sat himself down on one of the chairs. 'Okay, let's get this over and done with please,' he said. 'The sooner I can get back to bed, the better. What time do you want to set off?'

I hadn't even thought about it.

Out of the corner of my eye, I spotted Roy's chin slip off his hand, nearly recreating his head slam from last night.

It was Ali that spoke up. 'How long will it take to sail down to Birch Bay?'

'One hour, maybe an hour and a half.'

'So if we set off at five,' Ali said, glancing at us all. 'We'll have enough daylight left to find somewhere else if Birch Bay isn't viable.'

'Five is fine with me,' Charles said.

'Are you okay to sit offshore for an hour if Birch Bay is clear?' Ali asked him. 'Just until it's dark enough? Will you be able to sail back here in the dark?'

I'm glad Ali has thought about all this.

'That's fine,' Charles said. 'But you're right to ask, if it's too dark, I'll come back in the morning.'

'That's settled then,' Sandra said. 'Five o'clock.'

'Meet me here at four thirty,' Charles said. 'I'll stock you up with some food and bottled water, to keep you going for a while.'

'That's very kind of you Charles,' Sandra said. 'On top of everything else you're doing.'

'Yeah, we can't pay you back for all of this,' I said to him.

'Don't worry about that. I've always liked helping people, but I never did it enough. I liked helping myself too much.' With a groan, he rose to his feet. 'Now, I don't wish to be rude, but could you please leave me alone so I can retire back to my bed. Don't worry, all arrangements have been made. We just need to turn up at the Mariette. Everything will be ready.'

'Mariette?' Ali asked him.

'The name of my yacht. Don't know the origins. She was already called that when I acquired her.'

We thanked Charles again, left the pub and started back to the house.

'Let's try and get as much sleep as we can,' Ali said. 'We're going to have to turn nocturnal again.'

'Sleeping today is not gonna be a problem,' I said.

Jack and Roy both grunted in agreement.

'I feel fine,' Theo said. 'I'm not sure what's wrong with you three?'

'Very funny Theo,' Jack said.

Roy suddenly ran off to our right, nearly knocking someone over and disappearing between two market stalls.

'Wait a minute everyone,' I said. 'I think Roy's gone to be sick.'

We all stopped to wait for him.

Thirty seconds later he reappeared, wiping his mouth with his sleeve and waving us on. 'I'm fine, carry on. I'm fine.'

With great difficulty, we forced our way through the crowds of people, eventually getting back to the house. I'd barely had the energy to heave myself up onto the top bunk.

The afternoon's sleep had been constantly disturbed by people coming and going. The bed rest had still helped me get rid of most of my hangover though, so by the time I was woken up by Jack at four o'clock, I felt much better.

We collected what little belongings we still had, and walked back through the crowds to Pea's Place.

Now that the day had actually arrived, the nerves were very much kicking in at the prospect of leaving. Even though I'd always wanted to get out of here, the short break away from dead creatures trying to eat me all the time had been very pleasant. Even with that break being interrupted by the needless fight with the zombies. We were now going back outside the camp, to live under the constant threat of dying in an excruciatingly painful way.

You don't have to think too hard to realise that is a fucking stupid thing to do, voluntarily. No choice though, I need to get back to my wife, and this refugee camp's days are definitely numbered.

Chapter 23: Flashing Lights

On arrival at the pub, Jack had gone in to get Charles. They walked back out a couple of minutes later, Andruis and Matis following them.

Charles looked at us with a big grin. 'Hello travellers. I hope you've all got your sea legs on today. I do not allow any vomiting on my yacht.'

'Are you feeling better?' I asked him.

'Yes, much better thank you. All ready then?'

'Ready as we'll ever be,' Sandra replied.

Charles looked directly at Jack. 'Seriously though, please don't be sick.'

Jack looked back at him wide eyed. 'What? Why me?' He pointed at Roy, saying, 'He's been sick. I haven't.'

Roy glared back at Jack and raised his hands. Shaking his head, he simply asked, 'Why?'

'Okay, follow me,' Charles said, and started walking in the direction of the harbour.

Considering Michael had been told a lot of the fishing boats had disappeared, the harbour looked full. All I could see were fishing boats.

The Mariette turned out to be very impressive and modern looking, to my eyes at least. I'd been expecting something with a sail, but this one looked more like the yachts people hired to go sport fishing. It was hidden away amongst the many fishing boats that hadn't yet been used to escape this dying country.

Matis stayed on the dock, shaking all our hands as we passed him. Andruis was going with us, apparently to help Charles on the way back.

'You can go down into the cabin, or stay up here on deck,' Charles said. 'It's up to you.'

I had a quick glance down into the cabin. Two large boxes sat on the floor down there. They were full of bottled water, different kinds of snacks, some packets of jerky, and what looked like sandwiches. The bread looked similar to the loaves we'd eaten the night before.

I turned to look at Charles. He was stood behind the very small wheel, looking at something on the dashboard in front of him.

I'd also envisioned a large pirate ship sized wheel to go with the sails.

'This is brilliant Charles,' I said to him. 'We won't have any issues getting out of here will we?'

'Yes, she's a beauty isn't she? And no, there's nobody to stop us. Not unless we venture too close to Canadian waters. Then I imagine we will be torpedoed by the Canadians.'

I assumed he was joking about the torpedoes. But we would probably be shot at until we turned around.

'Make sure you only go south then,' Jack said.

We all stayed up on the large deck area, which was situated behind the wheel.

The water was calm within Blaine's harbour. I hoped it would stay that way after we left the cove.

Charles pushed two levers into position, and switched on the ignition, the engine instantly roaring to life. 'Matis came down here earlier to check her out,' he called back to us. 'Just to make sure she was shipshape and Bristol fashion.'

Ali shot me a questioning look. I smiled back and shrugged.

He manoeuvred the boat out from between the two fishing boats alongside us, and then turned left. We sailed past rows and rows of boats. The smell of fresh fish had been strong on the dock, but had increased tenfold after getting underway.

I turned to Jack. 'Is it still called sailing if you don't have any sails?'

Jack continued to stare at all the different kinds of fishing trawlers as we passed them. He shook his head, saying, 'I don't know.'

As soon as we were clear, the yacht took a right turn, and the strong breeze hit us, making me wish I'd been wearing another layer.

My face was really starting to sting from the biting wind, so I spun around to watch our wake in the water. I noticed Jack and Ali also turn.

'The salt,' Ali called out.

'What?' I asked.

She pointed to her face. 'The salt in the air will be getting into the scratches.'

Charles shouted back to us, 'It'll be colder once we get out of this cove.'

I turned into the painful wind. Charles was pointing to the gap between the harbour and the bit of land known as Semiahmoo. I pulled my t-shirt up so the neckline was just under my eyes.

'You might want to get inside once we're out in the open,' he continued. 'Especially the children.'

Sandra hadn't wanted to wait, very sensibly taking the three boys down into the cabin straight away.

I'm pretty sure I'll be sick if I go down there. Best to be cold and be sick over the side.

As we left the cove, Charles pointed out two grey ships in the distance. 'That's two of Canada's coastal defence vessels. It was probably them that forced us to dock at Blaine.'

'Why didn't you just go around them?' Theo asked.

'Because they're faster than us, and they're armed with all kinds of deterrents,' Charles replied. 'Also, there are four more of them out here somewhere. They'd have blown us out of the water if we tried getting past them.'

'Has anybody ever tried to swim from the camp to Canada?' Pete asked him.

'I'm sure they have, but I wouldn't want to try it. I'd maybe consider it in the summer.'

Once out of the cove, Charles was forced to slow the yacht down. The choppy waters had made it feel like we were bouncing completely out of the water every time we hit a wave. Once we were travelling along at a more sedate pace, and he'd moved us closer to the shore slightly, we didn't rise out of the water half as much.

My stomach was very thankful to him. It had felt like it was being turned inside out at times.

Eventually, one by one, everyone went down into the cabin. I pulled my jacket up around my head, and stayed up top. I sat at the back, and watched Canada get further and further away from us.

The thought of travelling through zombie infested land again was terrifying, especially without Michael, Shannon and Gee.

The three boys were worrying me. When it was just me, or even when it was me and Jack, it was so much easier. Just jump in a car and drive. Granted, we fucked up a lot, and very nearly died every half an hour, but we didn't have three kids to worry about. There are a lot fewer people to protect those boys now, compared to when we first met up with them outside that Costco.

So when we finally made it the waters next to Birch Bay, and Charles had dropped the anchor, I would have been more than happy to stay on the yacht forever.

'It looks clear,' Andruis said, holding binoculars up to his eyes.

'Excellent,' Charles said. 'So we'll wait here until it gets darker. Then if it still looks okay, I'll kick you out over by the dock over there.' He was pointing to our left, where the water fed into the dock area.

The sun had been nearing the horizon when we started moving again. Birch Bay had been quiet the entire time we'd been waiting. We hadn't spotted any movement at all.

As we entered the mouth of the dock, Andruis offered me the binoculars. 'Here, may come in handy.'

'Thank you very much,' I said, gladly taking them from him.

I was starting to feel a bit overwhelmed with all this generosity.

'We have another on the yacht,' he told me. 'So no big deal.'

While Andruis was tying us up to the dock, Charles walked up to the deck from the cabin. He was carrying one of the boxes of water and food. Theo followed him, carrying the other.

I took the one Charles was holding. 'We really do appreciate this,' I said to him.

'Honestly, don't worry about it. We have more than enough. You'll have to find some bags to carry it all. You don't want to be walking around carrying boxes.'

'We have flashlights as well,' Andruis said, handing one to Ali, Jack, and then Sandra. 'Sorry, that's all we have.'

We said our farewells to Charles and Andruis, thanking them again for everything they'd given us, and for the vast amount of beer we'd drunk.

We briefly stopped to watch them sailing back out towards Birch Bay's cove.

'We need to get going before it gets too dark,' Ali said. 'Me, Jack, Chris and Beth try to find two vehicles. The rest stay here, and keep hidden.'

Beth raised her hand into the air. 'I can't drive.'

'Okay, you stay here,' Ali said. 'Roy can take your place.'

Ali and Roy went left, Jack and I went right.

There were a few vehicles in the car park adjacent to the dock. We checked every one. They were all locked. There were a lot of houses close by, so we rushed over to them to check for cars.

Jack stepped alongside me. 'We knocked up a little plan while we were in the cabin on the yacht. Do you want to hear it?'

'Yep, can do.'

'Get two vehicles. Drive to an outdoorsy shop. Pick up clothes and everything we'll need to break into another country. Drive along the border until we find a part we can cross, but stay far enough away from the border to avoid getting killed by zombies.'

I stopped outside a house with a car on the drive. 'Sounds like a good plan. Car?'

Jack paused to look at the sports car, and simply said, 'No.'

We continued down the street, looking for something more suitable, eventually stopping outside a large house with two identical looking Fords parked in front of it.

'Yep, these look perfect,' Jack said.

'What are they?' I asked him.

'Fords.'

'Yeah thanks twat,' I said.

Jack started walking up the drive towards them. 'I don't know what they are, they're cars.'

As expected, they were both locked. Now we just had to break into the house to find the keys. Jack walked up to the front door and lifted his axe. He was all set to swing it into one of the six glass panels that ran up the side of the door.

'Wait,' I quickly said. 'Try the door, it might not be locked. We don't want to set off an alarm.'

'They don't have electricity around here,' Jack said.

'Oh yeah. Try the door anyway.'

Jack grasped the handle and twisted, it didn't budge.

'Okay, smash the glass quietly,' I told him.

He used the handle of his axe, easily putting it through the glass. It shattered and some of it fell to the floor by his feet. It was much louder than I'd hoped it would be. We both stood still, listening for the sound of hissing. I held my breath and counted to thirty.

'Nope, nothing,' I said. 'Knock the rest of the glass out so you don't cut yourself.'

Jack managed to push the rest of the glass through into the house, so it made less noise. He then reached in and tried to unlock the door.

'Right, got it,' he said. He pulled his hand back out and tried the handle again. The bottom of the door moved inwards slightly, but the top wouldn't move.

'Fucking hell,' Jack said. 'There is a lock at the top. I can't reach that. I'll break another window.' He started to raise his axe above his head.

'Wait a minute,' I said, thinking I could use his axe as a battering ram. 'Can I borrow your axe for two seconds?'

'Why, what are you going to do?'

'Just give me it. We'd already be in there and have the keys in the time it'd take us to argue over it.'

'I'm definitely not going to give it to you now. Why would we have to argue over whatever you want to do?'

'Just give me the fucking axe.' I reached out for it, Jack instantly pulling it away. 'Oh for fuck's sake,' I said.

'Just tell me what you want to do, and I'll see if it's a good idea.'

I pointed to the two Fords behind us. 'We'd be sat in those two cars by now if you'd have just given me the axe.'

'I'd have broken the window and unlocked it by now it if you hadn't stopped me.'

The sound of engines made us both snap our heads around. We walked down to the end of the drive as two SUVs turned the corner, and started moving down the street towards us.

The first SUV, a maroon coloured Chevrolet, pulled up next to us. The driver's side window rolled down, revealing a smiling Roy.

'Hello,' he said.

Beth appeared from behind him, after she'd bent forwards in the passenger seat. 'You're in with us. Get in the back.'

Jack looked at the Chevrolet, and then down to the grey Honda behind. 'Ours would have been better,' he said to me. 'Ours matched.'

I opened the back door. Theo was sat in the middle. 'Hi Theo,' I said, climbing in to sit next to him. Jack sat on the other side.

'Where we headed?' I asked. 'The town centre?'

'Yep,' Roy replied. 'We think it's just down here.'

Birch Bay didn't have any of the kind of shops we required. It was more of a seaside tourist place.

Both of our vehicles were parked up on the main road, side by side, and with the windows down.

Ali was in the driver's seat of the other car, leaning out of her window. 'On the way to Blaine, we passed an outdoor mall. I can't remember what stores it had, but there might be something there.'

'There isn't anything around here so we might as well,' Beth said.

'What about guns?' I asked. 'Search through houses or wait until we see a gun shop?'

'Houses would be sensible I suppose,' Ali said. 'We might need guns before we drive by a store.'

Sandra popped her head out of the back window. 'It might take us a while to find guns. They'll be locked away in people's homes. There will be a gun store in or around the mall.'

'I think that's risking it,' Ali said.

'I don't like it around here,' Sandra said. 'It's too quiet with all these houses.'

'I'm easy,' I said.

'Yeah whatever, you decide,' Jack added.

'Beth,' Ali said. 'You have the deciding vote.'

Beth laughed. 'Oh thanks guys.'

'Wait for a shop, or search houses,' I said 'What's it to be Beth?'

'Shop,' Beth said.

'What a surprise,' Jack called out.

Beth twisted around in her seat to scowl at her husband. 'Why is that a surprise?'

'It's a joke isn't it? Women and shopping,' Jack said. 'I thought it was quite funny.' He leaned around Theo to look at me. 'Chris. That was funny, wasn't it?'

I smiled back at him. 'I think you're a disgusting, sexist pig.'

Beth had turned back to face forward. 'Thank you Chris.'

'Fuck off,' Jack exclaimed. 'He's taking the piss.'

'Stop showing off in front of your friends Jack,' Beth said.

'What? I'm not showing off. How am I showing off?'

'Show off,' I said.

'Hey,' Sandra called out. 'What are you doing? Shall we go?'

Jack opened his mouth to speak, but then thought better of it, sitting back in his seat.

'We'll follow you,' Roy said. 'Ali, do you remember where the mall is?'

She nodded. 'Kind of.'

'That will have to be good enough.' Roy pointed in front of him. 'Lead the way.'

'Wouldn't have had this problem if we'd have gone to the bus,' I said under my breath.

The windows in the grey Honda started to rise, as it moved ahead of us. Roy put the Chevrolet into drive, and followed them as they led us out of Birch Bay.

'It's very quiet,' Theo said, staring out of the window.

I followed his gaze to see the empty streets rolling past. 'Thank fuck,' I said to him.

'This is what it was like when we drove through this area on the way up,' Jack said. 'All the zombies must be outside the camp, or further along at the border wall.'

'Hopefully they stay there and leave us alone,' Beth said.

'Some parts of the border being free of the dead would be helpful,' I said.

We drove down a long straight road, the rear lights of the Honda guiding us.

'How much fuel do we have?' Jack asked.

I looked to my right and saw the petrol station that must have prompted Jack's question.

'Three quarters full,' Roy replied. 'The other car had about the same.'

Jack pointed at the petrol station up ahead. 'Should we get some more?'

'No electricity means no gas,' Theo said. 'Only way is to syphon it now.'

'They're indicating left,' Roy said. 'I think it's the mall.'

We followed closely behind the Honda, heading towards the back of some large buildings. There was a gap up ahead. Our lights picked up vehicles on the other side. We drove along the road that ran through the gap in the buildings. It opened up to a large car park beyond. Once through, we took a left turn and drove the entire length of the row of shops, before turning around and driving back. We eventually parked up alongside the other car. Roy started to lower his window, Jack did the same. Our combined headlights illuminated a sign on the building in front of us. It read, *W.A. CAMPING STORE LTD*, in large letters.

'This will do,' I said.

'The doors have been smashed in, people have already been here,' Beth said.

'It doesn't mean it's empty,' Jack said. 'It looks pretty big.'

'Guys,' Ali said from the other vehicle. 'Sandra and Pete are going to stay here with the kids. Who is coming with me from the Chevy?'

'How many torches do we have?' Roy asked.

'I've got a flashlight,' Ali said with a smile.

Sandra waved hers out of the back window of the Honda. 'Me too.'

'I've got one as well,' Jack replied.

I reached down to the floor and picked up my baseball bat. 'I'll take yours Sandra. If you want?'

Jack and I got out of our car, as Ali left the Honda. Sandra passed me her torch through the open window.

'If you see or hear anything,' Jack said. 'Just flash the lights.'

Chapter 24: Barricade

Jack, Ali and I slowly walked side by side over to the front of the camping shop. The glass that had once been in the doors was now shattered into tiny pieces. They covered the paving separating the shops and the car park, glinting in the light of the headlights. The light shone past us, illuminating our path, and casting our shadows across the glass fronted building. Jack's axe, my baseball bat, and Ali's large knife were five times their size as they stretched across the front of the shop.

The crunching under our feet was far too loud.

Beth's initial fears appeared to have been correct. It looked as though the shop had been ransacked. Empty clothes racks were broken and lying on the floor. Shelves just inside the doors were hanging askew on the wall. There wasn't any camping gear in sight.

Jack flicked his torch on and panned it side to side just inside the broken doorway.

He turned back to us. 'Looks empty. I'm just going to make some noise. Okay?'

Ali and I both nodded.

He slammed the head of his axe down into the ground three times in quick succession. We waited to see if anything stirred.

Nothing.

Jack looked back to us again. 'Nobody here.'

Ali nodded and I shrugged. We crept into the shop, slowly sweeping our torches in front of us.

The rest of the shop looked like a swarm had sprinted through and collided with everything, nothing was left standing upright.

'Well, this was a waste of time,' I whispered. 'I didn't see any gun shops either. Should have gone back to the bus.'

Ali was directing her torch light at the back wall of the shop. 'Stockroom,' she whispered.

Jack and I combined our torch light with Ali's, and a door became visible on the back wall.

We headed towards the door, being careful to step over, or walk around the fallen racking.

A loud clattering noise rang out around the empty shop. I immediately swept my torch to the right, following the noise. The light fell upon Jack, lying on the floor. He was tangled up in an overturned clothes rack, coat hangers scattered around him.

'Alright?' I asked him.

'Yeah I'm fine,' he said, trying to escape from the metal poles restraining him.

Again, we waited for any unwanted sounds.

Still nothing.

The door at the back marked *Employees only*, was locked.

'Break it open with your axe,' I said to Jack. 'It can't be any louder than you fighting with a clothes rack.'

Jack stared at the door for about ten seconds. I'd been very close to asking him if he was alright again, when he stepped forward and swung his axe from his hip. The axe head hit the door just to the left of the handle. Bits of wood splintered and the door swung open into the stockroom. We shone our lights into the pitch black room. I leaned in through the doorway, quickly looking left and then right. It was only about fifteen feet deep, but it ran along the entire length of the shop. It was filled with rows upon rows of metal racking.

I raised my bat and took one step back, waiting for whatever was trapped in there to emerge.

Luckily for us, nothing had been trapped.

We entered the room and started searching the many free standing racks. The first box I looked in was full of maps of Mount Baker and the surrounding area, so I grabbed a few of them. There were some plastic wrapped backpacks on one shelf. After unwrapping one, I stuffed three others into it and put it on my back.

'I've found clothes,' Ali said. 'And more flashlights.'

'I've got batteries,' Jack called out.

The sound of metal scraping across something made me stop. It lasted for less than a second. I tried to listen for it again, but all I could hear was Jack and Ali rummaging through shelves. A huge plastic bag, tied in a knot at the top, slid along the ground, stopping when it hit the wall by the door.

'Enough warm clothes for us all in there,' Ali said.

'Just be quiet for a bit,' I told them.

We waited in absolute silence. My breathing was all that broke it, until Jack asked, 'What's the matter?'

'Thought I heard something. Must have been us.'

I found a carton of energy bars and squeezed it into my new backpack.

Jack walked towards me, holding a large cardboard box in front of him. 'I've got some walking boots, in various sizes. I don't know what size everyone is.'

'Good idea,' I told him. 'Have you seen any wire cutters, or wire snips, or whatever the things you use to cut wire are called?'

'Not seen any,' he said. 'Not sure if they'll have them here.'

'There's a tool box down here Chris,' Ali said. 'I'll have a look for some.'

Thirty seconds later, Ali appeared from the darkness, also carrying a large cardboard box. 'Found some, they're pliers with the cutting bit, so they should cut through wire.' She put the box down and picked up a crowbar from within it. 'This is my new toy.' She swung it two handed across her body.

'Are you okay with that box Ali,' Jack asked.

She nodded and placed her crowbar back in it, before picking the box up.

'Chris, you get the bag of clothes,' Jack instructed.

I picked the bag up, surprised at how heavy it was, and awkwardly opened the door with my hand holding the Smasher. My torch was pointing up towards the ceiling as I walked back into the shop. I paused briefly when I noticed it was a much darker shop than when we had left it. The headlights from the cars seemed to be flickering, only occasionally shining into the shop, and the Chevy on the right looked like it was moving sideways, towards the Honda alongside it.

I carried on, and was only three or four steps in, when the hissing started. I quickly angled my torch down from the ceiling. The shop floor was full of dead eyes staring back me. Wide open, decaying mouths hissed that all too familiar noise.

I instinctively stepped backwards as they all seemed to move towards me at the same time. Some of them fell over the overturned clothes racks and tried to crawl along the floor. I felt a hand grab the back of my jacket and drag me backwards. My torch illuminated a flash of something, just a split second before a heavy weight slammed into the bag in front of me. It forced me into whoever was trying to drag me, and we tumbled backwards into the stockroom.

I was on my back, lying on something uncomfortable. The backpacks were digging into me. Hands were clawing at my face and my shoulders, trying to reach around the bag of clothes. I felt legs and hard boots being dragged out from under my back. Ali grunted, before I heard a loud cracking noise. The hands trying to get to me stopped moving. I raised my torch up to see Ali standing over me, her crowbar hanging at her side. A giant of a zombie was slowly forcing the compressed air out of the plastic bag full of clothes on my chest.

Jack ran past us, shouting, 'Door!'

He slammed his shoulder into the door, just as the zombies collided with the other side. He hadn't managed to get it fully closed. Hands, arms, heads and nearly whole bodies were trying to squeeze their way through the gap.

A second later Ali was next to Jack, putting her weight into keeping the door where it was. I rolled the dead weight off me and clambered to my feet.

I started swinging the Smasher at the many body parts trying to get in. If I hit a head, it slowly slid down, catching on the other zombies as it fell. Hitting arms didn't make any difference. Zombies don't feel pain, so they wouldn't withdraw their hands and arms if they were hit.

I bent down and dragged a zombie into the storeroom. It was almost in anyway. I crushed its head with the heel of my boot. I then rolled the giant zombie that had tried to crush me over to the door, leaving it wedged against the bottom.

'I'm going to push one of the shelving units over,' I shouted to Jack and Ali. 'Hopefully it'll force the door closed. Get out of the way when I shout for you to move.'

They both nodded, the soles of their footwear squeaking on the floor as they tried to hold their ground.

I rushed around to the other side of the closest set of shelves. I started to gently push it, just to see how easy it would be. It budged a little bit.

One big shove and it will topple over.

I took three steps backwards, so I was up against the shelves behind me. I angled myself so my shoulder would hit the shelves in front of me, and ran.

'Now!' I shouted, just as my shoulder connected.

Jack dived to his right, Ali went to her left. The shelves started falling away from me, and towards the now opening door.

There was a loud cracking noise as the shelves connected two thirds of the way up the door, cutting it in two, and slamming the top third shut. The bottom section was still open, wedged into the shelves. Zombies were managing to squeeze their way through the open gap.

Fuck's sake.

Jack was already up on his feet, with his axe in his hands. He was swinging it up and over his head, bringing it down on whatever parts of the zombies appeared first. They were crawling and dragging themselves out from under the side of the shelves.

More zombies were trying to force their way through the gaps in the empty shelving. I started clubbing at hands, arms, and heads with the Smasher. Ali ran over carrying two boxes. She forced them into gaps, and onto the heads trying to get through. She disappeared into the darkness to get more. I ran in the opposite direction, found a shelving unit full of tents, and starting throwing them towards Jack. Once I emptied the shelves in front of me, I ran back to the piles of tents I'd created, and starting stuffing them into every space I could see.

Jack was still wildly swinging. He'd almost blocked his side of the shelves with the amount of zombies he'd felled.

After Ali and I had filled all the openings, I dragged her to the shelving unit behind the one I'd knocked over.

'Let's push this one on top!' I shouted.

Ali nodded and got into position.

'Watch out Jack,' I shouted to him. 'This one is coming down.'

It wouldn't have hit him where he was standing, but I didn't want him to move at the last second.

We stepped back, and then put all of our combined weight into pushing it over. A couple of seconds later and a loud metallic clang rang out in the stockroom. I ran over to take a look.

Nothing else could have got in through there. We just needed to sort out the right hand side where Jack was fighting.

I stepped around so I was behind Jack, but out of the way of his swinging axe. Bodies were tightly packed into the gap, they seemed to wobble, almost vibrate, as more zombies tried to force their way through.

'Let's see if we can drag some more shelves over,' I said. 'Maybe rest it against all the bodies?'

All three of us managed to drag one of the empty shelving units into position. We pushed it up against the dam Jack had created, blocking the dead in. We dragged another over and slowly lowered it into place, so it rested against the upright shelves.

I lowered my head and rested my hands on my knees, the shock of what had happened only just seeming to hit me.

'Did you see them outside?' Ali asked. She was struggling to catch her breath. 'Were they okay?'

I was struggling myself. 'I thought it was too dark. I must have seen the headlights through all the zombies as they walked past. The Chevy was moving a bit, like it was being pushed.'

Jack stared at me, his eyes wide with alarm. 'Like we were pushed? What if they get pushed over?' He picked up his torch from the floor, and started to look all around the stockroom. 'We need to get back to the cars.'

'There must be a fire exit in here,' Ali said, turning and walking towards the back of the room.

Jack also left to scan the walls with his torch. I had one last look at our barricade. It looked surprisingly solid.

I had just turned to follow them, when Jack said, 'Found it.'

I looked for his torch light in the darkness. Ali soon joined me, and we found Jack at the far end of the room, standing in front of a door. Above it the words *FIRE EXIT* faintly glowed in the dark.

'Remember what happened last time you ran out of the back door of a shop,' I quickly said. 'Open it very slowly and only a little bit.'

He placed both his hands on the metal bar that stretched across the door's width. He very gently pushed, a grimace spreading across his face as he pressed the bar in towards the door. There was a high pitched squeak when the lock was disengaged. All three of us flinched when we heard it. Jack let the door swing outwards just a couple of inches, before he quickly shut it again.

He turned back to us, his face looked drawn. 'Nope. There are a lot of them out there.' He marched past us back towards the barricade, whispering, 'Fuck, fuck, fuck.'

I jogged to catch him up, thinking he was going to start dismantling the only thing stopping hundreds of zombies getting in and eating us. He walked up to the box he'd been carrying, and sat himself down on it.

With his head in his hands, he said, 'Fucking hell.'

Ali had caught us up and was now staring at the barricade.

'The cars will have just been pushed up against another shop,' I said. 'There aren't any hills around the mall.'

'You don't know that Chris,' Ali said, now pacing back and forth. 'Anything could have happened to them, and we're trapped in here.'

'Yeah we're trapped,' I agreed. 'But only temporarily. As soon as this swarm passes, we can go out and find whatever they've been pushed into.'

I sat on the floor and watched the barricade as it occasionally jostled and shook slightly. Eventually Ali stopped pacing and also sat on the floor. I removed the bag from my back and pulled out the carton of energy bars. We each ate one in silence.

Jack stood up and walked towards the back door, within thirty seconds he'd returned. 'Still out there,' he said glumly.

'How long has it been?' I asked him.

'About ten minutes.'

Jack had another look at the swarm passing by about five minutes later.

I went for a wander, shining my torch in every little nook and cranny, trying to find anything that could be of use. I came across a row of five lockers, two of which were unlocked. One was empty, the other contained a single can of deodorant, and a fur covered apple. I took the deodorant and sprayed a liberal amount under my arms.

Ali and Jack's torchlights suddenly appeared, moving towards me.

'What was that?' Jack asked.

I shook the can in front of me. 'Deodorant. Do you want some?' I tossed it at Jack. He caught it and shoved it under his t-shirt, spraying it on himself.

'Fucking hell Chris,' he said. 'It sounded like hissing.'

Ali shook her head, spun around, and started walking back.

'Nope,' I said. 'Just deodorant.'

We followed Ali and made ourselves comfortable again.

'Do you think that swarm is going to end up outside the camp?' Ali asked.

'Probably,' I replied.

'It looked like it was a big one,' she said. 'They might not be able to keep them out, if that many join the crowds at the fence.'

'If they're quiet they should be fine,' I said. 'They'll probably run out of food before they're overrun by the dead.'

Chapter 25: Distant Rotors

It had seemed like the barricade hadn't moved for quite a while, and we must have been sat there for thirty minutes.

Standing, I said, 'Just gonna have a quick look out the back.'

Jack looked at his watch, and then stood. 'Yep, let's have another look.'

I pressed the bar in on the exit door and peered out through the small gap. There was only a smattering of the dead creatures, as they slowly staggered past.

'There's not many,' I whispered, opening the door just a little bit more so I could squeeze my head through. I had a quick glance around the door.

There weren't many there, definitely the very back of the swarm.

I ducked back inside and very gently closed the door. 'Give it a few minutes, maybe five, and then we can go out.'

Jack looked at his watch and nodded. 'Okay, five minutes.'

Ali appeared at Jack's side, ready to go.

We stood in the same place for the next five minutes, Jack staring at his watch.

Eventually, he looked up and nodded.

'All ready?' I asked, my hand resting on the doors locking mechanism.

'What about all the stuff we found?' Ali asked.

'Leave it here,' I said. 'I'm gonna wedge the door open with my bag. We can drive around here and pick it all up.'

'Let's go,' Jack said impatiently.

I slowly opened the door and looked outside. The back of the swarm was still visible in the moonlight, but they were passing the far end of the mall's buildings. I shone my torch to the left. It looked like nothing was moving around out there.

We quietly made our way around the edge of the building, trying to keep as close to the wall as possible. We got to the end, and Jack peered around the corner, before waving us on. We could see the car park once we took the corner, it also looked clear.

The anticipation must have become too much for Jack, as he started to jog. Once we reached the next corner, we'd be able to see what had become of our friends and family. He got there ahead of us and stopped. He was quickly scanning the car park.

'The cars aren't there,' he said. 'They aren't fucking there.'

I walked past him, heading towards the front of the camping shop. 'Let's go and find them.'

Just as I reached the spot we'd left them, I noticed flashing lights coming from inside a small building, in the middle of the car park. In huge letters above the building, it read *BILL'S BURGERS*.

The flashing lights became much more rapid.

It must be them.

I turned to tell Jack and Ali, but they were already running towards the lights. I jogged in their direction before speeding up to keep pace with them.

The Chevy must have been forced through the plate glass windows, and was now inside the shop. I couldn't see the Honda anywhere.

'No,' Ali said. 'Where is the Honda? Where are they?'

The driver's side window rolled down, and Roy popped his head out. 'Hello. We fancied a burger.'

'Where's the Honda?' Ali asked him in a panic.

'Don't know. We didn't see where it went.'

The door behind Roy opened and Pete fell out of the car, Theo followed him, carrying Max.

Pete stretched his arms above his head. 'That was uncomfortable. Max wouldn't stay still,' he said, ruffling the boy's hair, before Theo put him back in the car.

'Boys, please let me out,' Sandra said, from inside the back of the Chevy.

Ali walked over to them, hugging Theo, and then Pete, before leaning in through the open back door. Jack was on the passenger side, talking to Beth.

'You all okay?' I asked

'Yeah we're all fine,' Pete replied. 'It was scary for a while back there, but they didn't seem to know we were in the car. We just got caught in the swarm.'

Roy climbed out and stood by the driver's door. 'When we saw them coming, everyone climbed in here, hoping the extra weight would stop them moving us.' He glanced around at the inside of the burger place. 'Didn't work.'

'Where were you?' Theo asked.

'Just trapped in the back of the camping shop,' I said. 'We had to wait until they'd left.'

'Have they all left?' Pete asked, staring out through the broken windows.

'Yeah they should have all cleared out by now,' Ali replied as she backed out of the car. 'We better find the Honda.'

I looked around at all the broken glass on the floor of Bill's Burgers, and then looked at Roy. 'We should sweep a path for the Chevy before we set off. We don't want a puncture.'

'Okay,' Ali said. 'Pete and Theo, you're with me. Let's go and find our car.'

They left the half destroyed Bill's Burgers, and disappeared into the night. Roy was using a chair he'd turned upside down to scrape away some of the glass. I picked up another and joined him.

It wasn't long before we heard the sound of a car approaching. We'd almost finished sweeping the glass out of the way when a banged up Honda pulled up outside.

'It still runs okay,' Ali said, leaning out of the window. 'The swarm has moved on. Let's get our stuff and get out of here.'

Pete and Theo got out of the car and walked over to the Chevy. The three boys climbed out of the back, swiftly followed by Sandra. She rushed them over to the Honda. Pete followed them, keeping an eye on his surroundings until they'd all entered the car.

'Meet you around the back,' Ali said, as the Honda slowly accelerated away from us.

The rest of us climbed into the Chevy, and Roy very carefully drove us out of the burger place, trying to avoid any glass we may have missed.

We stopped around the back of the building and recovered our salvaged items from the stockroom. After consulting the maps I'd found, we agreed on the best route to take, finding the roads that would take us to a place called Sumas.

The map was a bit shit. It was more of a Mount Baker visitor type of map.

The plan was to drive past Sumas, and head towards Mount Baker. Then we were going to miraculously find a stretch of the border with no wall, or fence, or guards.

As easy as that.

Driving along the long straight roads made me almost feel like I was on holiday again. Our headlights illuminated farm buildings and homes close to the side of the road. It could have easily been three or four weeks ago, before all the devastation had happened.

I rolled my window down, thinking I might be able to smell the countryside as we passed through it. A strong smell of human shit and blood soon filled the car.

I couldn't press my finger down any harder on the button to raise the window.

'Chris! What the fuck are you doing?' Jack shouted.

'Oh my god,' Roy called out. 'That stinks.'

Beth had covered her face with her hands. 'I feel sick,' she said.

Theo glared at me, shaking his head.

'Sorry,' I said, once the window was fully closed.

We were taking it slowly, just in case another swarm showed up in our path, as it was making its way to the border. By the time we were parked up just inside the city limits of Sumas, about an hour later, we hadn't hit any resistance at all.

For the last few miles however, we'd slowly been driving past very similar signs to the ones we'd seen as we neared Blaine. Our two vehicles were stationary, parked side by side in the middle of the road. *TWO MILES TO BORDER* was spray painted on a road sign on the side of the road.

'Turn around and go back to that road we passed earlier?' Ali suggested. 'We can drive around. Don't want a repeat of last time.'

During the journey, we'd told Roy and Beth about the bad timing of our arrival at Blaine. So everyone was very much in agreement, we would avoid going near the other camps.

I didn't want to mention it, but I was very surprised Sandra hadn't wanted to go and search for her husband and daughter in the camp. She must have had her reasons.

We spun the cars around and drove back the way we'd come, until we turned onto a much smaller road, almost a dirt track. As we drove along, almost off-road, we made sure to always head east, never north towards the camp at Sumas.

We eventually managed to find our way to the road that would lead us into the mountains. We were soon surrounded by woodland on both sides of the road.

It felt like the night was drawing in closer around us, all we could see was the road ahead. Only occasionally, when we turned a bend and glimpsed a path running through the trees, would the headlights illuminate something other than tarmac, and the surrounding blackness of the trees.

I was really hoping we weren't gonna hit any snow.

It was rapidly approaching daylight hours, so all of us in the Chevy agreed that we needed to stop. Roy flashed the headlights at the Honda in front. We pulled up alongside them as they were stopping. Roy rolled down his window and suggested we find somewhere to sleep for the day.

'This map is terrible,' Sandra said across the gap between the two vehicles.

'Whoa Sandra,' I said. 'Don't take the piss out of the map. I found them.'

She raised her eyebrows. 'Sorry Chris, but it's not a road map.'

'Let's just take the next left,' Roy suggested. 'Maybe we can find a farm a bit closer to the border.'

'Sounds good,' Sandra said. 'According to Chris's terrible map...' She paused to give me a quick glance. 'This road is going to take us further away from the border at some point, so we should find somewhere soon.'

'Okay,' Ali said, as she put the Honda back into drive. 'Next left turn.'

'You still leading the way Ali?' Roy asked.

Ali shrugged, and then the Honda accelerated away from us.

'Guess so,' Jack said.

The next left was just a few miles further along. We followed the Honda's rear lights down the road. A couple of miles later, after passing five or six more short lanes leading to homes, we came to a sharp right turning. The Honda sat in the middle of the road in front of us, the brake lights still on.

'I think this turn takes us away from the border,' Beth said, using the internal lights in the Chevy to look at the map. 'We'll be better off going back and trying one of those houses we passed.'

'Turn us around Roy,' Jack said. 'They'll soon figure out what we're doing and follow us.'

We headed back down the road, the Honda trailing behind us. Thirty seconds later, and we were parked in front of a house. Behind it a few farm buildings were visible, the headlights only just reaching them.

'Shall we all go in and check?' I asked.

'No,' Jack quickly said. 'Beth, you wait in the car.'

'I can take care of myself,' Beth said. 'You can't protect me every second of the day.'

'It makes sense to leave someone in the car,' Roy said.

'You stay here then,' Beth said to him.

'Okay,' Roy replied. 'I'll stay here.'

Two knocks on Beth's window got everyone's attention. Ali was stood outside, peering in and looking confused. Beth rolled her window down.

'What are you doing?' Ali asked. 'Are we going to go and check this place out?'

Jack opened his door. 'Yep, come on then. Don't forget your knife if you're coming with us Beth.'

Jack distributed torches out to Theo and Beth. Ali and I still carried the ones we had earlier in the night. Everyone else would stay with the cars.

The house was a two storey building, with the front door on the far left. The rest of the ground floor was mostly taken up by four large windows. Five windows filled the front of the first floor.

I walked up to the window closest to the door, and pointed my torch inside. The hallway inside looked like any normal, looked after home.

'It looks empty,' I whispered.

Jack, Ali and Theo were looking in through the other windows.

'All clear here,' Jack said.

'Yeah, here too,' Ali added.

'Clear,' Theo said.

'Going in then?' I asked, walking to the front door. I tried the handle and found it locked. 'Break a window?'

'Wait,' Ali said. 'Try around the back. Might not be locked.'

Jack looked back to the cars, and signalled that we were heading around the back of the house. Ali led the way, so she arrived at the back door first. With a twist of the handle, the door opened into the house.

Smiling, Ali glanced back to us, before walking into the house, her torch and new crowbar held out in front of her. 'We clear downstairs first,' she instructed, moving through the kitchen. 'Then we do upstairs.'

After searching the entire house we discovered it was empty of life, and death. Once everyone was inside, we barricaded the back door with the huge fridge freezer, and found somewhere to sleep. The three bedrooms upstairs were quickly taken, leaving me and Roy to sleep downstairs on the two sofas.

The agreed plan was to have four hours of sleep, and then we would walk over towards the border.

Hopefully we'll find some weaknesses that will allow us to very easily slip into Canada.

As well as the sun's early rising, the sound of distant helicopter rotors repeatedly woke me up.

DAY TWENTY TWO

Chapter 26: Idiot

There was a slight crack in the curtains, so the sun shone into the living room. I looked down at myself. A two inch wide strip of light ran all the way down my body.

I'm pretty sure that was the sound of helicopters I'd heard last night. The Canadians must have been flying around out there.

Roy was still fast asleep on the other sofa, and nobody else seemed to be awake.

I guessed the four hours of sleep we'd allowed ourselves hadn't elapsed yet. Just then the alarm on Roy's watch started sounding.

Bollocks. I was looking forward to some more sleep.

Jack, Ali and Pete soon appeared from upstairs, and were now sat with Roy and me in the living room. We ate some of the energy bars I'd found, and the jerky Charles had given us.

'We're going to have to be really careful in the daylight, and really quiet,' Ali said. 'It's only a few miles to the border. Hopefully we won't encounter another swarm.'

'So we're just going to walk over there, and take a look?' Roy asked.

'Yep,' Jack replied. 'And if there's no way to cross when we get there, we'll have to walk a few miles along the border as well.'

'But at a distance though yeah?' Pete asked.

'Of course,' Ali told him.

'Did anyone else hear helicopters last night?' I asked.

'Yeah I did,' Jack said.

'Me too,' Pete agreed.

'Keep an eye out for them as well,' Ali said. 'I doubt they'll fly into America though. Why would they do anything to us anyway? We're not going to try and cross the border today.'

Before we left, Jack and Ali quickly ran upstairs to tell everyone we would be back in a few hours.

We left the farmhouse and walked up the short lane to the road. On the other side of the road, thick woodland spread out in front of us, filling the horizon. We entered the woods, the thick underbrush making it hard going.

'It should only be a mile or so of this,' Ali said. 'Then it's open fields to the border.'

Roy slashed at branches with his machete, saying, 'At least there won't be any zombies in here. They'd just get stuck.'

'Open fields don't sound too good for sneaking across borders,' I said.

'Let's just have a look,' Ali said. 'I think if we go east, the border originally went through the woods. Although I'm guessing the Canadians felled a lot of the trees, like they did north of Blaine.'

As we battled through the low lying branches, Ali and I were a little behind the others.

'Hey Ali,' I said. 'If you don't want to talk about this, you don't have to.'

'Okay', she replied, sounding suspicious.

'How did Steve end up back on top of the bus?'

'Oh right,' she said. 'It's okay, I can talk about that. We've discussed it, my sister and my cousins and me, but nobody knows. None of us saw him run off or anything. You were there, it was a bit crazy. It was hard enough to take care of yourself. One second he was running alongside us, the next we were at the container, and he was back on the bus.'

'Okay, I was just wondering,' I told her.

'I think he panicked and ran in the wrong direction. And by the time he found his bearings, there were too many of the dead around him. I don't know. It's easily done. Jack said you got lost.'

'I didn't get lost. I fell over and ran in the wrong direction for a couple of seconds.'

'That's probably all it'd take to make someone panic.'

'Yep, probably,' I agreed.

It was hard and sweaty work, but we were soon seeing more blue sky at the edge of the trees. We could also hear a quiet hissing.

We stayed as low to the ground as possible, and crept to the edges. Large industrial looking farm buildings sat in the middle of overgrown grass fields.

I looked left and right, using the binoculars. On the other side of the field in front of us, as far as I could see, a mass of zombies pressed against a chain link fence. It didn't look far from the border wall, still being constructed behind it.

'We're not getting through there anytime soon,' Pete said.

There seemed to be a lot of movement on the Canadian side, but they were being incredibly quiet. Occasionally the sound of the concrete blocks being lowered into place, just about made its way over to us.

Surely it's not all being done by hand?

'There are a lot fewer zombies than I was expecting,' Roy said. 'I thought these fields would be full of them.'

'Yeah,' I agreed. 'There's a fair few by the fence, but maybe only twenty deep.'

'Hopefully there will be none further along,' Jack said. 'There can't be construction work going on everywhere.'

Ali started to step backwards into the trees. 'Come on then guys. Let's go east a couple of miles, see if it's any better.'

We followed the tree line for as long as we could. It was angled towards the border, so it wasn't long before we had to head back into the woods to avoid getting too close to the zombies. It did look like the dead were thinning slightly as we moved further east.

Ali was right. A huge amount of woodland had been felled close to the border.

After we must have been walking for an hour, the amount of zombies had been slowly decreasing, and was now at zero. There was no building work going on, and all that stood between us and Canada was a barbed wire topped fence, and heavily armed mask wearing soldiers, stood on the other side. They looked similar to the four soldiers we'd met a few weeks ago from Colorado. Silent jeeps constantly patrolled up and down behind the fence. Large guns were mounted on the back of them.

'We're not getting through there anytime soon,' Pete said, again.

'There must be shift changes and...other things?' I said desperately.

We were well within the woods still, hiding behind the trees and bushes. It looked like there was only thirty feet of tree stump filled ground from the edge of the trees to the fence. A soldier was positioned every twenty feet along the fence.

Another jeep silently zipped past.

'It doesn't look good,' Jack said.

'No you're right,' I grudgingly agreed.

'We need to head back,' Ali said. 'We told them we'd only be a couple of hours.'

'I'll wait here,' Pete said. 'Watch for any weaknesses.'

'You can't stay here by yourself,' Ali told him.

'I'll wait with you Pete,' Roy said. 'I've nothing better to do.'

'Okay,' Ali said. 'Just for a few hours.'

'How about I come back in four hours?' I suggested. 'I'll swap with one of you?'

Jack looked at his watch. 'It's taken an hour and a half to get here. But realistically it should take less than an hour, forty five minutes maybe. We did dither around for a bit.'

'Dither?' Pete asked.

'Not important Pete,' Jack told him. 'I'll come back with you Chris,' he offered, before turning back to Pete and Roy. 'Then both of you can head back and get some rest.'

'Deal,' Pete agreed.

'Keep an eye out for us,' I said, passing the binoculars to Pete. 'Because we'll probably not be able to find you.'

Jack looked into the trees behind us, and then to me and Ali. 'Can either of you guide us back to the house from here? Or do you think it'll be safer to go back to where we first saw the border?'

We all looked around at our surroundings.

There was no way I could get us back.

'Back the way we came?' Ali suggested.

Jack and I agreed, so we started walking along the tree line again.

When we reached the point we'd first stopped to look at the construction going on, there seemed to be a lot of commotion happening on the Canadian side. We could now hear loud machinery, and the hissing's intensity had definitely gone up a notch or two. The amount of zombies seemed to have increased where the majority of the construction was happening.

I could hear helicopters in the distance, rapidly getting closer.

We watched from the edges of the trees again, not far from where we'd been a few hours previously.

'Do you think they fly in and shoot the zombies?' Jack asked.

'They'll probably use the helicopters to draw the zombies away from the fence,' Ali replied.

'There they are,' Jack said, pointing to the horizon. 'Two of them.'

Two large military looking helicopters were flying close to the ground, heading straight for the fence, directly in front of us. They quickly reached the semi constructed wall, but then slowed as they got closer to the fence, hovering above the zombies. The dead creatures were mesmerised and stared upwards. Then the helicopters started flying out over the fields, towards us.

'Jack, remember that scene from Jurassic Park?' I asked him.

'Oh shit yeah,' he said. 'They're flocking this way.'

Ali started to back away. 'Yeah, let's go.'

We turned and started to run as fast as was possible in the thick underbrush.

'Pete and Roy will be okay. Won't they?' Ali asked as we ran.

'There's no zombies there,' I said. 'So no reason for helicopters to go there.'

We ran all the way back to the farmhouse, only stopping to walk when we reached the short lane.

'The helicopters won't bring them all the way out here will they?' Jack asked, sounding out of breath.

'Dunno,' I replied. 'Hopefully not. But it's not like it's a huge swarm. They won't carry the cars off or anything.'

Sandra let us in through the back door. After we'd explained where Pete and Roy were, and that they were hopefully safe, we told everyone to get upstairs. Just in case.

We needn't have worried. They never got as far as the house. I imagined the majority of them probably got caught up in the woodland. I mentioned this theory to Jack.

'We'll have to go back a different way,' he suggested. 'It won't be hard to find a way around them if they're still stuck in there.'

'We've just got to make sure we don't go too far east before cutting in,' I said. 'Otherwise we'll never find them two.'

We arranged with Ali and Theo to come and relieve us at ten o'clock, telling them of our plan to go back a different way.

Two hours later, with my bag stocked up with bottled water, energy bars and beef jerky, Jack and I headed back outside. We walked along the road until we reached the sharp bend, and then entered the woods.

It only took us forty minutes to reach the spot we both assumed we'd left Pete and Roy. We of course, couldn't find them.

'Pete, Roy,' Jack hissed.

'I'm pretty sure they were around here.' I pointed to a part of the border fence in the distance. 'We could definitely see that bit of barbed wire. Can you see where it hangs down slightly?'

'No Pete, you can't do that,' Roy's voice floated towards us from somewhere.

'Fuck's sake,' I said. 'I can hear them.' I spun around trying to listen for them again. 'Roy, Pete.'

'All we need are some guns,' Pete said.

'Fucking hell,' Jack said. 'Why can't they hear us, if we can hear them?'

'Jack?' Roy said. 'Is that you?'

'Yes,' Jack replied. 'Where the fuck are you?'

The sound of twigs breaking and leaves rustling made us both spin around. Roy's head and shoulders poked up from within a bush. We walked over to them.

I glanced around us when we reached them. 'Is this where we left you?' I asked.

Pete raised his head up. 'No, but there was more cover here. We've been watching for you coming from that way,' he said, pointing behind him.

'We had to come back a different way,' Jack said.

I passed them a bottle of water each and some beef jerky. Jack told them about the helicopters and us running back to the house.

Jack pointed the way we had just walked. 'If you walk straight that way, you'll reach open fields. Just turn right and you can't miss the road that the house is on.'

'Anything to report?' I asked.

'Nope,' Roy said, passing me the binoculars. 'Not a dickie bird.'

'Dickie bird?' Pete asked.

'Nothing,' Roy replied. 'It means nothing.'

'The soldiers haven't moved at all,' Pete said. 'And I've been to take a leak three times.'

'Not here I hope?' Jack asked him.

'No, I went down there,' he replied, waving his hand towards somewhere behind us.

'Is anyone going to come and swap with you?' Roy asked us.

'Ali and Theo are coming to do the night shift,' I replied.

Roy and Pete left to go back to the house. Jack and I tried to get comfortable.

'Why didn't we bring some blankets?' Jack asked.

'Fuck knows. Hopefully Ali and Theo will bring something to keep them warm tonight.'

'She's not stupid,' Jack said. 'She'll bring something.'

'So what's the plan?' I asked him. 'If we don't see any way to cross here by the end of the night, we move on to another spot tomorrow?'

'Sounds about right.'

'What if we have the virus?' I asked.

Jack pulled his gaze away from the fence. 'What do you mean? Where did that come from?'

'What if we're carriers, but can't die of it? And anyone that survived the initial virus is also a carrier? So, if and when we get into Canada, we infect everyone over there?'

He looked back at the fence. 'Nah, too much of a coincidence that me, you, Beth, and Roy all just happen to have the same something in our D.N.A. that only makes us carriers. And Sarah in fact. She survived the initial outbreak.'

'Yeah, suppose so,' I agreed.

Gunfire erupted from our left, making both of us flinch away from it.

'Jesus Christ,' I blurted.

The soldiers sprung into action, crouching down onto one knee, and firing their rifles into the woods. The fence started to wobble as the bullets flew through the links, occasionally hitting the metal.

Jack and I both laid as flat as we could manage.

With a loud bang, smoke and bits of earth suddenly exploded into the air, falling to the ground near to the fence. One of the soldiers closest to the explosion was holding his mask, and staggering around in circles. The soldiers on either side of their injured comrade continued firing into the trees to our left.

'What the fuck is happening?' Jack asked.

Two of those silent jeeps suddenly appeared, and stopped near to where the injured soldier was now on his knees. The rear guns were quickly aimed into the trees and started firing. More and more soldiers started appearing from right and left.

Out of the corner of my eye I could see more smoke, further to the right of us. I assumed it was from another explosion, but I didn't think I'd heard anything. The space between the edge of the trees and the fence was slowly filling with black smoke.

I quickly glanced around, trying to find who was doing all this. 'Can you see anyone Jack? I can't see a fucking thing.'

'There,' Jack said, pointing to people emerging from the trees.

They were running directly into the smoke. One, then two, three, four, and five people disappeared into the blackness.

I looked back to the soldiers. They were still concentrating on firing at whoever was to our left.

'It's a distraction,' Jack said. 'They're going over through the smoke.'

'Mother fuckers,' I muttered. 'This is our fucking spot.'

'Go with them,' Jack said.

'You what?'

'This is your best chance. You need to go now.' He placed his hand on my shoulder and pushed me away. 'Seriously, go.'

'No, I can't leave you here.'

'None of us are trying to get back to England. We're all going to stay in Canada, which isn't going anywhere. You need to get home.'

'Are you not gonna go home?' I asked him.

'That's not fucking important right now. You need to fucking go. This could be your only chance.'

I looked towards the smoke.

Fuck, fuck, fuck, fuck, fuck.

I climbed up onto my hands and knees, went to stand up, and then hesitated. I looked back at Jack. He vigorously nodded towards the smoke. I tried to stare into the smoke, to see if those people were succeeding in their mission.

Fuck. I can't leave Jack and Beth here. I can't leave any of them here, not knowing their fates.

I sighed, and keeping low behind the bushes, got up onto my feet. 'Come on Jack, we need to get back. We can't stay in this spot any longer.' I picked up my bag, turned and headed back into the woods.

Jack quickly caught me up. 'Chris, you are a fucking idiot.'

'Yeah I know.'

Looks like I'm trying to get back to England on my own then.

Once we were well within the safety of the woodland, with our heads still down, I said, 'So...Jack?'

'Yes, we're going to stay in Canada,' he instantly replied. 'Sorry, but it's the safest option for us. You know that.'

'Yeah I kind of guessed you'd stay. You haven't really been up for it whenever I've mentioned getting back to England somehow.'

'I've got to think about Beth and the baby.'

'Yeah I know that as well.'

'We'll help you get back though. If there's anything we can do, we'll do it.'

Chapter 27: Sacrilege

'There's no way we're killing innocent Canadian soldiers,' Sandra said.

'No of course we're not,' I said. 'We were just saying we need to do something similar, like create some sort of distraction.'

Roy and Pete shared a glance. Roy very briskly shook his head.

No idea what that was about.

The three kids were playing with something in the kitchen. All of the adults sat on the sofas, or on the floor in the living room. Roy had found a camping stove in the house, and had made us all coffee.

Whatever the kids were playing with, it was noisy. It sounded like they were destroying the place. Sandra didn't seem to pay it any attention, so I tried not to.

Does she know there are still zombies around here?

Sandra startled me by suddenly shouting, 'Boys! Quiet.'

We all sat there and listened, as silence descended.

Theo broke the silence, by saying, 'I'm surprised you didn't try and go with them.'

Beth very loudly cleared her throat.

'I didn't mean Jack,' Theo said to her. 'I was only talking to Chris really.'

Jack looked to me, his eyebrows raised.

I returned Jack's look with a sardonic smile, before turning back to Theo. 'I didn't go because I'm a fucking idiot.'

'Whatever we do,' Ali said. 'We can't do it in that same place. They'll be ultra vigilant now.'

'I don't know,' Jack said. 'I've been thinking about that. Surely the Canadians will be thinking that lightning doesn't strike in the same place twice?'

'There will probably be some zombies around there now,' Ali said. 'After all the noise.'

'That's true,' Jack agreed.

'Any ideas for the distraction then?' Sandra asked him. 'That doesn't include killing soldiers.'

Jack sat back in his seat. 'Not yet, no.'

Theo leant forward. 'What if we make lots of fires along the border? With lots of smoke, and then choose one to use as our cover? Snip snip at the fence. We all sneak through.'

'What's to stop them checking every part of the fence where there's a fire?' Pete asked him.

'That's why we create lots of fires,' Theo replied. 'So they don't have time to check every one.'

'What's to stop them only checking the fire we're going use as cover?' Pete asked. 'There's a lot of luck required.'

'We wait to see which fires they aren't checking,' Theo suggested.

'That's a bad idea,' Pete said.

Theo slumped back in his chair. 'Better than your idea. Oh yeah, you haven't had one.'

'Can we get one of the cars up there?' Beth asked. 'Set fire to it maybe, and roll it towards the fence? That would definitely divert their attention.'

'We can't really sneak a car up to the parts where there isn't a proper wall,' Ali said to her. 'Not anywhere around here anyway.'

'What if we make a huge fire?' Roy suggested. 'Burn down half the woodland if we have to. We'd have to get masks obviously, the soldiers already have them. And visibility would be terrible, so it'd be a struggle to see where to go, but it would be difficult for everyone, the soldiers included.'

'If we find some guns,' Pete quietly said. 'I don't mind being the diversion, so you can all get across. I was already thinking about it before Jack and Chris saw those people do it. It worked for them.'

Roy very dramatically looked to the ceiling.

Theo stared at his brother with wide eyes.

'You can forget that idea straight away,' Sandra said.

'Why?' Pete asked. 'Afterwards, I'll go back to that camp we drove by. The one at Sumas. I'll wait my turn and meet you all in Canada.'

'No, not happening,' Sandra told him.

'That's a very brave and selfless thing you're offering to do for us,' Ali said. 'But we're all going across. We're not leaving anyone behind.'

'Why don't we draw the zombies away from the fence,' I suggested. 'Near to where they're still constructing the wall. Like they did with the helicopters.'

'We don't have any helicopters,' Jack said.

'No,' Beth said. 'But we have two cars, with stereos.'

'Exactly,' I said. 'Then we do Roy's idea, and set fire to everything. That tall grass should burn easily enough. We'd just have to crawl through beforehand and cover the ground with petrol, or something else flammable.'

'There must have been some soldiers around the construction sites,' Ali pondered. 'But I can't actually remember seeing any.'

'I don't think I saw any,' Jack agreed.

'Nope,' I said. 'I didn't see any obvious ones with the binoculars.'

Roy sat forward in his seat. 'There must be some there, somewhere.'

'Maybe,' Ali said. 'But hopefully far enough away to give us some extra time.'

'That big industrial farm as well,' I said. 'If we could blow that up, or just set fire to it, that would definitely make a good diversion.'

'So we use music in the cars to draw the zombies away from the fences?' Sandra asked. 'After that we set fire to literally everything by the sounds of it. Then we just walk up to the fence, and a simple snip snip later, we waltz into Canada? With three small children by the way.'

'It's a plan,' I declared. 'We just need to iron out the details.'

Sandra rolled her eyes and slapped her hands down on the arms of the chair.

'When we set fire to everything,' Jack said. 'And especially if we blow up that farm, the zombies are going to come back pretty quickly.'

'So we're entertaining the destroy everything and burn ourselves to death plan?' Sandra asked.

'Even if we didn't blow up the farm,' Roy said. 'Burning the fields alone would hopefully create a lot of smoke.'

'Let's not blow up the farm though,' Jack said. 'Okay?'

'If we use music to draw the zombies away,' Beth said. 'The Canadian workers will soon figure out someone is trying to lure them away for a reason, and call the soldiers.'

'So we need to draw the zombies away some other way,' Ali said. 'With a naturally occurring sound.'

'Ca-caw, ca-caw!' I screamed.

Everyone flinched. There was a loud clattering from the kitchen as the three kids ran into the room.

'Like that?' I smiled.

Ali shook her head. 'Pretty sure I said naturally occurring.'

'That just sounded like an idiot screaming ca-caw,' Jack said.

'What was that?' Seth asked his mother.

'It's just Chris messing about,' Sandra replied. 'Now go back and play. Quietly though. And don't break anything,' she quickly added.

'Why not wait for the helicopters to do it?' Beth asked. 'Then there isn't any reason for the Canadians to become suspicious.'

'That would be easier,' I said. 'My throat is hurting just from those two ca-caws.'

'We could hide in the farm,' Pete said. 'And wait for the zombies to get dragged away.'

'That means you can't blow it up Chris,' Jack said.

I let out an exaggerated sigh. 'I suppose I don't have to blow the farm up.'

Roy placed his empty cup on the coffee table in the middle of the room. 'We'll need to be fast, and already have the petrol there, obviously.'

Sandra raised her hand into the air. 'One question. How do we all get to the fence, while everything is on fire?'

'The farm is quite close to the fence,' I told her. 'And I'm pretty sure there was a track that ran alongside the farm to the fence. We'd just have to take lots of water, maybe soak blankets and cover ourselves in them.'

Sandra frowned. 'Okay, another question, actually two questions. Does this tall grass cover the ground all the way up to the fence?'

'No it doesn't,' Jack replied. 'It must all be trampled flat by the zombies around there.'

'So why hasn't all of the grass been trampled flat?' Sandra asked.

'There aren't that many zombies,' I told her. 'It's not a huge swarm size. Some of it will be trampled, but not all of it.'

'Sorry, the grass question was an extra one,' she said. 'If the grass doesn't go all the way to the fence, what if the wind blows the smoke away from the fence? It'll be kind of obvious what we're doing when we just stroll up to the fence and start snip snipping.' She lifted her hand and imitated a pair of scissors with her fingers.

'If the wind isn't in our favour,' Roy said. 'We don't do anything. We just wait for another opportunity in one of the other farms. There are a few around here.'

'So you're all on board with this then?' Sandra asked, slowly looking around the room.

Ali nodded.

I shrugged, and said, 'Yep, why not?'

Jack said, 'Yeah.'

Beth raised her cup of coffee in front of her, saying, 'Yep.'

Roy also shrugged his shoulders, saying, 'I'm in.'

'Sure,' Pete said.

Theo looked to his brother, and said, 'Yes.'

Sandra slowly shook her head.

'I think we should go tonight,' Ali said. 'Oxygen masks are out of the equation. We won't be able to find enough, if any. We empty our cars of their gas, and do the same with all the surrounding vehicles. Then we pack up and leave.'

'We need to take as much water as we can carry,' Roy said.

'Swimming goggles, and snorkelling masks,' Beth said.

'What?' Jack asked her.

'To protect our eyes from the smoke,' she replied. 'Especially for the boys.'

Jack nodded. 'Good idea.'

'Fuck,' Sandra slowly whispered.

Ali stepped in front of Sandra, and crouched down. 'Don't worry. The kids come first. If it's not safe enough, we won't do it.'

'Safe enough,' Sandra replied. 'That sounds reassuring.'

'We're not going to drag them away from you and run away,' Ali told her. 'It will always be your final decision.'

Sandra nodded.

'Okay everyone,' Ali said, straightening up. 'Sandra and the kids, you look for goggles and masks. Anything to protect us from the smoke really.' She looked directly at Sandra. 'Probably best not leaving the house though.' She turned back to us. 'I'm on food scavenging. Chris and Roy, you get us blankets, and things to keep us warm. After you've done that, search the outbuildings for tools, stuff that will cut through fencing. I don't want to rely on the pliers I found. Jack and Beth, you fill up every possible thing you can find with water. Pete, and Theo, you know how to syphon gas. Get as much as you can carry and bring it back here, and then go and get some more. Two hours, that okay with everyone?'

Everyone agreed and rose to their feet.

Ali sidled up to me once we were in the kitchen, and away from Sandra. 'If it comes down to it, and the opportunity opens up, we might have to grab the kids and run. Sandra will follow us if we drag them away from her and run away. We're getting into Canada no matter what. I'm sick of this shit.'

Without another word, she marched off and climbed the stairs.

I hope it doesn't have to come to that. It's gonna be dramatic enough as it is.

Roy walked into the kitchen and stopped in front of me. 'Split up and save a bit of time?'

'Yeah can do,' I replied. 'Blankets or outbuildings?'

Roy pulled out a coin from his pocket. 'Heads, you do blankets? Tails, you do the outbuildings search?'

'Yep okay.'

He flipped the coin into the air, catching it with his right hand as it fell back down. He slapped it onto the back of his left hand, and pulled his right hand away.

'It's tails I'm afraid Chris,' he said. 'You're on outbuildings search.'

'What a fucking surprise,' I glumly said, walking towards the back door.

'We can swap,' Roy offered. 'I don't mind.'

I picked up my baseball bat and a torch before opening the door. 'No it's fine. Come and look for me if I don't come back.'

'I'll come and find you once I'm done in here,' he called out after me.

The sun was just setting as I made my way towards the first of the three outbuildings. It was made of red bricks, with a corrugated iron roof. The sky was a mixture of blues and oranges.

The big sliding door was unlocked. I knocked three times with the Smasher and waited a few seconds. I didn't hear anything, so I slid the door open a few feet and stepped in.

Small windows around the top of the walls allowed in what little outside light was left. The building was empty, just a few leaves lay on the floor.

I moved on to the next outbuilding, much smaller than the first. It looked like it was entirely made of wood, with no windows as far as I could tell. There was a padlock hooked through a rusty metal latch half way down the door. I rattled it with my hand, hoping it was unlocked, and was just there for show. It wasn't.

I tried to hit it with the Smasher, and missed. I had a quick glance around me, to make sure nobody had seen my embarrassing attempt. I couldn't see anyone. I did spot a large rock lying on the floor. It was about half the size of my head. I placed my torch down on the floor, and leaned the Smasher against the side of the building.

With the rock now in both hands, I raised it up above the padlock, and brought it down. It struck the padlock, tearing it away from the door, along with the metal latch. I dropped the rock to the ground and picked up my bat. All was quiet still. I pushed the door open and peered in. Boxes of screws and nails filled the many shelves.

One wall was filled with various tools, all hanging from hooks. Three tools immediately caught my attention, a large bolt cutter, and two smaller wire cutters. I grabbed the two smaller tools and put them in my pocket. I hefted the bolt cutter. It was about two foot long, and fairly heavy. I swung it two handed within the tool shed.

I'll take it. I could use it as a weapon if needs be.

I was just about to leave, when I noticed a box of builder's dust masks. I grabbed them as well, stuffing the box inside my jacket.

The third outbuilding looked like a garage. As I neared it, I could hear noise from within. It sounded like something was trapped. Whatever it was seemed to be thrashing about in there. The side door was slightly ajar, so I crept over to it. I put the large bolt cutter and my torch down on the ground. Holding the Smasher with both hands, I tapped on the door with the very end of it, and took three steps back.

The noise from within abruptly stopped.

'Hello,' I whispered. My heartbeat was now racing.

If this is another bear, I'm not gonna be very happy.

The door slowly creaked open. I peered into the darkness, there didn't seem to be anybody opening the door.

'Chris?' Pete called out.

Fuck's sake.

Pete stepped out through the door.

'What the fuck?' I said. 'You nearly scared the shit out of me. What are you doing in there?'

'Just getting the gas from this car.' He opened the door and shone his torch inside, illuminating the back of a beat up vehicle.

'What was all the noise? It sounded like a trapped animal.'

'Oh, that was just Theo. It was his turn to do the sucking.'

I screwed up my face. 'What?'

'He swallowed a bit of gas,' Pete said brightly, a smile on his face. 'Happens every now and then.'

I slowly nodded. 'Okay, anything else of any value in there?'

'Not really,' he replied, looking back into the garage. 'Just engine parts.'

'Right,' I said. 'See you back in the house. Enjoy your sucking.'

I picked up my belongings and headed back. I'd salvaged everything we needed from outside.

I bumped into Roy just as I entered through the back door.

'Hey,' he said. 'I was just coming out to find you.'

I leaned my bat against the wall and handed him the large bolt cutting tool. 'All done,' I said, pulling the two wire cutters out of my jeans pocket, and then the box of dust masks out from the inside of my jacket. 'Got these as well.'

Roy held the bolt cutter in both hands and swung them in front of him, almost exactly as I had done. 'The weight will make it a good weapon as well.'

'Yep. Did you find blankets and shit?'

Roy pointed to two piles of blankets and duvets on the kitchen table. 'Yeah, all sorted.'

We sat ourselves down in the living room and waited for everyone else to return.

Sandra and the kids had actually found some goggles and snorkelling masks. Only two pairs of each, but I was surprised they'd found them. Not enough for everyone, which of course meant I wouldn't be getting any to wear.

Ali returned with lots of tinned food.

Jack and Beth had filled every plastic bottle they could find with water, so seventeen bottles of various sizes sat on top of the coffee table in the living room.

Pete and Theo returned to the house last, carrying eight full jerry cans.

'You do realise we're gonna have to carry all this to the farm?' I asked them all. 'We can't drive up there.'

'We'll manage,' Ali said, looking at everything we'd collected. 'Somehow,' she added.

My back pack was now stuffed with blankets, and three new tools, one of which was very heavy. I was also carrying my baseball bat, and a plastic bag containing three petrol filled jerry cans. I wasn't alone, everyone else was also overloaded. Nobody more so than Jack, who had taken some of Beth's load as well as his own.

We left the farm in the dark. Sandra, the kids and Beth were the only ones with any free hands. We had to rely on them to light the way with their torches.

During the walk through the woods, I lost count of the amount of rest breaks we took. So by the time we reached the tall grass, we must have been walking for two hours or more.

Ali was down on her knees, leaning in close to the three young boys. 'We're going to go into the grass now,' she whispered to them. 'And no matter what, we can't make any noise. Okay?'

'Okay Aunt Alison,' Seth and Jonah replied in unison.

'Okay Max?' Ali repeated.

Max gave her three very quick nods of his head, saying, 'Okay Aunt Alison.'

'Good boys,' she said with a big smile. 'Nothing to worry about. We're all just going on a big adventure.'

'Stay close to me,' Sandra said to the boys.

Ali stood up and very briefly looked at us all. 'All the rest of you, don't group up. They might notice the movement in the grass if we all stay together.'

I over dramatically lifted the heavy plastic bag, nodding towards the farm in the middle of the field. She smiled and turned around. We followed her in, keeping our heads below the height of the grass.

We hadn't told the kids that there may be zombies in the fields, but we'd all decided beforehand, if we encountered any, we'd drop everything, pick up the kids, and run back to the woods.

Ten minutes later, we were stood outside the farmhouse. We hadn't met anything as we made our way through the tall grass. Where we were stood, we were hidden from the Canadians, but that also meant we couldn't see the border.

Behind the house were the large industrial looking buildings I'd seen earlier in the day.

I pointed behind the farmhouse towards them. 'We could do with being in them really. We need to be able to see what is happening at the border.'

'Stay here,' Ali quietly said. 'Pete, you come with me. We'll find the best way to get in.'

They both placed everything they were carrying onto the ground, and crept away into the night.

They returned a few nerve wracking minutes later.

'Okay,' Ali whispered. 'We've found a way in. It's easy. Follow us.'

They picked up their things, and led us down an alleyway between the house and a long shed. A tractor was parked on a thin lane behind the house. Ali passed the things she was carrying in her hands to Pete, and then started to climb up onto the tractor.

'Alison?' Sandra questioned her.

'There's no other way,' Pete said. The main doors are on the border side.' He pointed up to the flat roof adjacent to the tractor. 'There's an open window up there.'

Ali turned around on the bonnet of the tractor, and reached down for her stuff. 'It's safe,' she said. 'Don't worry. We both went in this way.' She turned around and placed her bags on top of the tractor's roof.

Passing the kids up and everything else we were carrying made it a much more complicated task than it should have been, but we were soon all inside the building. The window we had climbed through led us to a metal gantry walkway, which skirted all the way around the inside edge of the huge building. It was about twenty feet to the warehouse floor beneath us. Under the walkway were massive steel brewing tanks, maybe thirty of them. Three metal staircases led down to the warehouse floor.

Jack turned to me as we travelled along the walkway to the front of the warehouse. 'Blowing a brewery up would have been sacrilege.'

'I'm sure we'd have managed,' I said.

We unpacked the blankets and duvets, and set up camp on the cold, hard, metal gantry. Not the most ideal surface for sleeping on.

DAY TWENTY THREE

Chapter 28: Dancing

The night had been a cold one. My body wasn't adjusting well to the constantly changing sleeping patterns. I'd probably had about three or four hours at the very most.

Everyone looked as miserable as me as we sat on the walkway, eating cold food out of tins. I counted myself lucky at getting a chilli con carne. Jack's lucky dip looked like a gloopy macaroni and cheese, a repeat of the meals we'd shared in the Colorado Mountains three weeks ago.

Mine would have definitely tasted better heated up.

We'd left all of the fuel, matches, lighters, and a lot of the blankets and water, hidden away under the tractor. That way, when the helicopters arrived to lure the zombies into the woods, we wouldn't have to worry about climbing down whilst carrying everything.

The morning had consisted of us staring at the wall being constructed. We repeatedly went over our plan while we waited. It was approaching midday before anything of note began to happen.

We had opened the blinds covering the windows, just a tiny amount, so we could see through the thin gaps, and over to the border.

Theo had the binoculars in front of his face, his free hand pointing out towards the wall. 'There are things happening,' he excitedly said. 'They're rolling some kind of big machinery over to the edge of the wall. The zombies are moving around a lot more. They're crowding around that part over there. Look.'

We all peered out, listening for machinery, or for the helicopters.

'Can anybody hear anything,' Jack asked.

'Shush Jack,' Beth scolded him.

We stood in silence for at least a minute.

'Shite,' I whispered. 'Maybe they're not coming this time. They'll come eventually.'

'Wait,' Roy said. 'Listen.'

We all leant further over the barrier of the metal walkway, trying to get as close as possible to the windows. Eventually the sound of distant helicopter rotors reached my ears.

'Everyone get ready,' Ali said.

My chest suddenly felt tight, excitement, fear and nerves starting to rush through me.

'You all know what to do,' Ali continued. 'Theo, you stay here and watch the direction of the smoke. Pete, Beth, Sandra and the boys, you're by the open window, where we came in.' She locked eyes with Pete. 'Peter, do not take your eyes off Theo, and wait for his signal. The rest of us, let's go and make some fire.'

Ali, Jack, Roy and I stared out of the windows at the back of the warehouse. Firstly, we were waiting for the helicopters to fly over, and secondly, for a lot of zombies to walk past us.

The sound of the helicopters was getting louder and louder, increasing the levels of anticipation within our group. We heard them as they flew overhead, sounding like they were right on top of us. We couldn't see them at first, because they were actually way over to our left. They were so loud it just sounded like they were closer.

They flew away from us, the tall grass below them being blown in every direction.

'Come on zombies,' I said. 'Where the fuck are you?'

The first of them started to appear, some running, some walking, most looking like their time on this Earth was almost up. They were all staring up at the noisy machines in the sky. Their numbers gradually increased, until they were streaming around the farm house and surrounding buildings, moving further into the fields behind us. It only took a few minutes for the numbers to thin, and the incredibly slow stragglers to appear, crawling or staggering past us, still staring at the sky. They were truly fascinated by the helicopters.

We all looked back across the warehouse to Theo. Three flashes from his torch meant we were clear to go.

We climbed down as quickly as possible. Roy was the last to touch down on the lane, sending dust flying as his feet hit the ground.

As we all slipped on the dust masks, Ali said, 'Two gas containers each, and don't forget water, some matches, and a back up lighter just in case.'

We collected up everything we needed and headed out together into the grass.

After we'd gone about thirty feet, Ali said, 'Roy, this is you.'

Roy stopped and started unscrewing one of his jerry cans.

Another thirty feet, and we left Jack to do the same. Thirty more and Ali stopped. I carried on until I felt I'd ran far enough.

This is all fucking guesswork on my part.

I unscrewed both of the jerry cans. I then walked backwards in a wide zig zag pattern, emptying both cans as I went. When they were empty, I counted to thirty, just to make sure the other three had definitely finished. I stepped back from the petrol soaking into the dirt, lit a match, and threw it to the ground. The flame fizzled out before it hit the ground.

Fuck off.

I quickly lit another. This time I let it burn for just a little bit longer, before releasing it. It hit the ground and the fire was instantaneous. The flames started to travel away from me, through the grass and along the path I'd just taken. I was very briefly transfixed by the zig zagging flickering flames, until I remembered we were supposed to be sticking to a plan.

I turned away from the flames, and ran back towards the farm buildings. When I thought I was in Ali's general location, I started saying her name.

I heard her calling for me, but I couldn't see her anywhere. I eventually found her standing way over to my left.

She was very aggressively gesturing for me to come to her. 'Chris, get over here now,' she said.

Bollocks, I'm probably stood in her petrol. Maybe my zig zag pattern had been too wide?

I quickly ran over to her. Once I was behind her, she lit a match and dropped it to the ground, lighting the trail she'd left.

We ran together, looking for Jack. I spotted him in the distance almost straight away, peering through the grass towards us. Upon seeing us he lit the match he had ready in his hand, and dropped it. The orange flames danced away, seeking the path of the petrol. The three of us moved on, to search for Roy.

Roy was also ready and waiting. He had his trail alight before we made it to him. He stood and watched us running towards him, while the fire spread out behind him. We all sprinted back to the buildings together.

When we made it back to the tractor, everyone was already down on the ground and getting ready.

'It's working,' Theo said. 'There's already smoke everywhere. The workers are all leaving as well. They're not wearing masks. It's really working.'

'Okay,' Ali said. 'Don't get overexcited.'

Max and Jonah were wearing the swimming goggles. As Seth was the biggest of the three, he was wearing one of the snorkelling masks. Sandra was wearing the other.

With all the fire and smoke behind them, it was a peculiar sight.

Everyone had their dust masks on. Pete and Theo were soaking blankets with water and then placing them over the boy's backs.

'It's cold,' Seth complained.

'Sorry Seth,' Pete said. 'It soon won't be.'

Pete then picked Seth up. Theo picked Jonah up, and Sandra was carrying Max. I passed one of the wire cutters to Ali, and the other to Jack. So I could carry the Smasher, I'd strapped the large bolt cutter into my backpack.

'Now or never,' Ali said.

The sound of hissing made us all spin around. They were coming back.

'Now,' I said.

We ran around the buildings and down the dirt track that led to the fence. Black smoke filled our vision. We were coughing already, and we'd only been going for twenty seconds.

The smoke certainly was working. Although it also meant we couldn't see the fucking fence.

I could hear that flapping noise again, the same noise I'd heard outside Roy and Sarah's destroyed house in Mountain View, like wet towels being blown around on a washing line.

One of the kids started screaming. He must have been able to see the burning flames running towards us.

I glanced over my right shoulder. A flaming zombie was running straight for Pete and Seth. I changed direction to intercept it. I ran as quickly as I possibly could, trying to get to it before it could get anywhere near the kids.

Ali was slowing, moving off the track, also aiming to cut the flaming attacker off.

'Keep going!' I shouted to her. 'Get everyone to the fence.'

She spotted me running behind her, towards the burning zombie, and the fires behind it. She very briefly hesitated, before getting back onto the dirt track and running along with everyone else.

I tried to bend my approach, so its flaming body wouldn't just slam into me immediately after I hit it. The Smasher was poised over my shoulder already. I swung it and connected with its chest, or shoulder, or something. I closed my eyes as hot sparks flew everywhere, hitting my face and neck. The burning creature was thrown backwards, slamming the back of its head into the ground when it hit the ground. Flaming parts of its skull scattered behind it.

The denim jacket the medic had given me was alight in numerous places. I ripped it off and threw it away as I ran to catch the others. In a panic, I patted my hand all over my hair and beard, trying to extinguish any flames that I hadn't noticed.

I couldn't see anybody. With my painful eyes half on the dirt track beneath my feet, and half on trying to find them, I continued.

Through the smoke I ran, trying to blink away the stinging tears. I spotted Jack up ahead. He was waiting for three zombies to come to him. Parts of their clothing were ablaze. His axe crushed the head of the first one to reach him. It fell to the ground, only its legs were on fire. Then he turned and swung the axe, taking the other two zombies' heads clean off with that one swing. Their burning bodies slumped to the ground and skidded past him on the dirt track.

He patted himself down, before looking up to see me running towards him. He lifted his axe in my direction.

A fireball emerged from the smoke, only a few feet away from Jack. I pointed to it with the Smasher as I ran. He managed to turn and swing the axe. He hit the fiery thing right in its centre.

It was like a firework exploding. Tiny flickering fireballs went everywhere, hitting Jack like sparks. He immediately dropped his axe and started rubbing his head with his hands. There were little flames all over his clothing.

Without slowing, I let go of the Smasher and took my bag off my back, quickly pulling out the thick blanket I'd placed in there. The flames were rapidly spreading across Jack's entire body.

'Roll on the ground Jack!' I shouted. 'Get on the fucking ground!'

He must have heard me, because he immediately dropped to the floor and started rolling in the dirt. I made it to him and covered him with the blanket. Some of the flames wouldn't go out, so I basically had to whip him with the twisted up blanket. Once they were all extinguished, I pulled a bottle of water out of my bag, and emptied it over his head.

'Get the fuck up Jack,' I screamed close to his face.

I got to my feet, ready to fight off anything coming for us, with the bolt cutters if I needed to. All I could see was smoke. My eyes were feeling incredibly hot.

I offered Jack my hand, he took it and I pulled him up.

'Pick up your axe,' I told him, then ran back to get my baseball bat.

Ten seconds later, with the Smasher back in my hand, I was running alongside Jack, hopefully in the direction of the others.

'Are you okay?' I asked him.

'Yep, just a tad warm,' he replied. 'I might not have any skin left by tomorrow.'

We very nearly ran into the fence, just managing to stop before we ran face first into it.

'Check the fence,' Jack said, running his hands over the bottom of it, near the ground. 'They must have come through here.'

I could hear flapping again. I turned to see three more fiery zombies heading towards us. These three weren't entirely engulfed, and only one of them was moving quickly. The fires must have been destroying their already weakened states.

'Keep looking Jack,' I told him, and ran towards them.

I slowed as the faster one neared me, and then swung the Smasher into its knees. Both legs disintegrated and its top half flew past me. A burning arm stretched out for my face, making me lean back and almost fall over.

I quickly pulled out my other water bottle, and squirted it onto my left thigh, which seemed to have caught fire at some point. I stepped away from the burning arms trying to reach me on the ground. They were dragging a flaming head and torso closer to me. I headed towards the other two fiery creatures.

'Chris,' Jack shouted. 'Fuck those two, let's get out of here.'

I turned around to find him, but he wasn't where I'd left him. 'Where are you?' I shouted.

'Over here,' Ali shouted.

I followed her voice and waited for the smoke to shift. They were both standing together. Ali was in Canada. Jack was still on this side of the fence, holding a section of it up, and waiting for me to get through. I stepped around the burning creature still trying to drag its way to me along the ground, and ran towards them.

I ducked my head down to squeeze through, then reached back through the gap Ali must have made, to hold it open for Jack. He followed me in.

Into Canada.

'Is everyone okay?' I asked Ali.

'Yeah, they're all fine' she said, already turning around to move. 'Come on, we have to go, there are soldiers here.'

We ran through the construction site of the border wall, over concrete sections lying on the ground, and around wheel barrows, and stacks of plastic pipes. Everything appeared out of the smoke when we were almost right on top of it.

'You need to jump here,' Ali told us. She then launched herself over a three foot wide hole, and again over another similarly sized hole.

Jack and I followed her, jumping over what looked like the foundations for the wall, and then running through more of the swirling smoke, which seemed to be never ending.

'Wait,' she said to us, holding her hand out. 'Under here, now.' She got down onto her belly, and crawled under what looked like a huge mobile crane. We swiftly followed, not knowing what she'd seen or heard.

We stared out from underneath the massive machine, the black smoke swirling around us. Sunshine was trying force itself through, almost looking like it was dancing with the smoke. One of the silent jeeps zipped past in front of us, shining a floodlight towards the fence behind us. Only the bright white circle of the floodlight was visible once it had passed, it was still aimed in the direction of the fence. The sound of boots hitting the ground rang out.

'Keep low,' Ali whispered. 'Let's go.' She crawled out, and we dutifully followed her into the blackness.

I flinched and ducked my head down even lower when the gunfire started.

'Keep going,' Ali hissed. 'I don't think they're shooting at us.'

'Shite,' I called after her. 'Have we let burning zombies into Canada?'

Jack moved up so he was alongside me. 'They'll take care of it. We only made a small hole. Just keep running.'

The smoke had been thinning as we ran through open fields. I glanced behind me, nobody was following us. A thick wall of black smoke covered a large section of the border.

We really couldn't have done a better job.

Ali pointed ahead of us, towards woodland at the edge of the grass field. 'Everyone should be in those woods somewhere.'

'What do you mean? Somewhere?' Jack asked her.

'I had to tell them to keep going, soldiers started to arrive. I told them to wait for us as soon as they entered the woods. They'll be looking out for us.'

Chapter 29: Two Weeks Ago

Beth ran to Jack when she saw us, almost throwing herself at him when they met.

We'd found them hiding just within the tree line. They'd found us really, calling out our names as we neared the edge of the field.

When Beth finally let go of Jack, she ran her fingers through his hair.

'You've burnt some of your hair off,' she told him.

He stepped away from her slightly and looked down at himself. 'Burnt some of my clothes as well.'

'Come on everyone,' Ali said. 'We need to get further away from the border. I don't know if the soldiers know anyone alive made it across, but let's not risk hanging around.'

'Anyone alive? Did the dead manage to get through the fence?' Sandra asked.

'We don't know,' Ali replied. 'Come on. Let's get further into the woods before we take a break.'

As we walked, Roy passed around bottles of water to anyone that needed it. I certainly had. My throat felt like I'd been swallowing razor blades. I drank some, before pouring half the bottle over my face, desperately hoping to relieve some of the pain, in and around my eyes.

It worked for about twenty seconds, the pain soon returning after the water had drained away.

After an hour of trekking through the trees, we stopped to eat something and rest for five minutes. I threw on a fleece we'd found in the camping shop. The adrenaline, combined with slowly cooking in the fields, meant I'd still been quite warm after throwing away my frazzled jacket. I'd started to cool down after sitting down to eat something. Charles's beef jerky was still on the menu, so I was eating some of that.

Ali was eating something disgusting looking out of a tin. 'We haven't really discussed what we'd all do if we made it across.' She looked up and smiled. 'Well, we made it.' Her eyes were glistening as they slowly moved around our small group, taking us all in. She was probably thinking about the people that didn't make it. I certainly was.

'I'm going to try and get to the east coast,' I said. 'And then swim to England.'

'We're going to do whatever we can to help Chris get to the east coast,' Beth said, smiling at me. 'And then try and stop him from swimming across the Atlantic.'

I returned the smile.

'I'd like to come with you Chris,' Roy said to me. 'All the way back to England. Although preferably not by swimming.'

'You're honestly more than welcome Roy,' I replied, the smile stretching even further across my face.

Beth shot a grateful smile towards Roy.

'What about the Rodriguez's?' I asked. My mood was definitely lifted after Roy's offer to join me. 'What are your plans?'

'First of all,' Sandra said. 'There should be a town just south of Cultus Lake.' She looked down at the Mount Baker visitor's map. 'It's really not very far from here. It doesn't say what it's called though. This map really is terrible Chris.'

'We're in Canada now,' I told her. 'It's not going to have that much detail for another country.'

She flipped the map around to face me. 'It doesn't have much detail for the American side.'

'Yes okay,' I said. 'It's a rubbish map.'

'Anyway, after we've been to the nameless town, we need to go to Milk River. We have to meet up with two very special people. It's just on the other side of the border.' She looked down to the three boys, all munching away on strips of jerky, before looking back up to Ali. 'After that, not sure.'

Ali returned her gaze. 'Vancouver is nice, but too close to the States. Alaska maybe?'

'That's maybe a bit too far,' Pete said.

'We'll try and work our way north,' Sandra said. 'British Columbia is very nice, and a very big state. We'll stop when we find somewhere we like.' She smiled at both of her cousins.

'Michael and Shannon said they were planning on living in Alaska,' Jack said. 'In Anchorage I think.' He looked down at the energy bar in his hand, smiling to himself, thinking about happy memories maybe.

'Better get to this town with no name then,' I said, standing up.

We started moving again, soon coming across a road in the middle of the woods. We stood on the edge of the trees, looking down at the empty road.

'We should probably stay off the roads,' Jack said. 'Just in case any army vehicles drive by. We should avoid anyone official looking until we're much further away from our border crossing spot.'

'Yeah you're right,' Ali agreed.

'This road should lead to the nameless town,' Sandra said. 'So should we maybe try and follow it from a distance?'

We agreed and kept the road within eyeshot.

Ten minutes later, we saw a sign for Lindell Beach.

'Do you think it will have a beach?' Beth mused. 'On the lake maybe?'

'It's a bit cold for the beach,' I said.

'I hope there is a beach,' Beth said, more to herself than anyone else.

Not long after seeing the town's sign, there had been a residential street off to the right. We decided to risk it, and climbed down the steep embankment to walk on the road.

It was very quiet. We were all nervously glancing at our surroundings. Every little sound made our heads snap towards it.

The occasional bird calls were startling us. The wind was blowing litter across the road. A coke can skittered away from us along the road, making Sandra clutch Seth closer to her body.

'Sheriff McCallany and my wife did say parts of Canada might have been evacuated,' I told everyone. 'It would make sense to move everyone away from the border.'

We walked past more and more houses, nothing stirred in the windows or down on the streets. Some homes still had cars parked on the drive, or out the front. There were no people at all.

'I'm guessing the rules on car theft change when the car's owners are still alive?' Roy asked.

'I never finished law school,' Sandra said. 'But I think it's still illegal if the owners are dead.'

We were in no doubt the town of Lindell Beach had been evacuated. We carried on regardless, eventually finding ourselves near the lake.

Sandra, Roy, and the three kids were looking into Lindell Beach General Store's front window, trying to see if there was anything edible inside.

Something brushed against my shins. I looked down to see a black cat weaving in and out of my legs.

'Hello cat,' I said, crouching down to stroke him. He leaned into my hand as I scratched the side of his head. 'How come you haven't been evacuated?'

Beth crouched down alongside me. She stroked her hand down the full length of the cat's back. 'He doesn't look hungry. He's just after some attention. Aren't you? You beautiful little boy,' she said to the cat.

The sound of paper being blown around behind us was getting louder and louder. Just as I turned to look for what was creating the sound, a newspaper hit Beth on the back of the head. It stayed wrapped around her, flapping in the wind.

I laughed, and peeled the sheets away from her hair.

Beth was feeling the back of her head. 'It hasn't left anything disgusting in my hair has it?' she asked.

I glanced at her hair. 'Nah, I think you're alright.'

Despite the wind trying to rip the paper out of my hand, I managed to fold it back over and look at the front page.

In big red bold type, the headline read, *KILLER VIRUS CONFIRMED IN EUROPE.*

I quickly read the first few lines of the story below.

The number of victims has not yet been confirmed, but the south east of England and northern France today reported their first cases of the Florida Virus.

It hit me like a slap in the face. The words on the page began to blur, and I was suddenly unsteady on my feet.

'No, no, no,' I said. 'Fucking no!'

'What is it?' Jack asked me. 'What's the matter?'

Everyone started to crowd around me, trying to read the newspaper in my trembling hands.

'Oh no,' Roy exclaimed. 'What date was it published?'

I looked up to the top of the page, just about managing to read the date. 'It's from two weeks ago.'

THE END OF BOOK TWO: BORDER

Coming soon

BOOK THREE: FARM

Printed in Great Britain
by Amazon